QUEEN JEZEBEL

Due to illness, Jean Plaidy was unable to go to school regularly and so taught herself to read. Very early on, she developed a passion for the 'past'. After doing a shorthand and typing course, she spent a couple of years doing various things, including sorting gems in Hatton Garden and translating for foreigners in a City café. She began writing in earnest following marriage and now has a large number of historical novels to her name. Inspiration for her books is drawn from odd sources – a picture gallery, a line from a book, Shakespeare's inconsistencies. She lives in London and loves music, secondhand book shops and ancient buildings. Jean Plaidy also writes under the pseudonym of Victoria Holt.

D0037222

By the same author in Pan Books

The Medici Trilogy

QUEEN JEZEBEL

JEAN PLAIDY

UNABRIDGED

PAN BOOKS LTD : LONDON

First published 1953 by Robert Hale Ltd.
This edition published 1971 by Pan Books Ltd,
33 Tothill Street, London, S.W.1.

ISBN 0 330 02784 0

2nd Printing 1973

Printed and bound in England by
Hazell Watson & Viney Ltd,
Aylesbury, Bucks

To G.P.H.
whose practical help and advice
have been invaluable

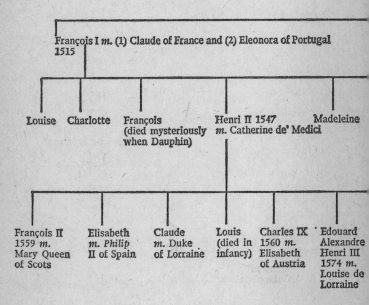

François I *m.* (1) Claude of France and (2) Eleonora of Portugal
1515

Louise   Charlotte   François   Henri II 1547   Madeleine
                     (died mysteriously *m.* Catherine de' Medici
                     when Dauphin)

François II   Elisabeth   Claude   Louis   Charles IX   Edouard
1559 *m.*   *m. Philip*   *m.* Duke   (died in   1560 *m.*   Alexandre
Mary Queen   II of Spain   of Lorraine   infancy)   Elisabeth   Henri III
of Scots   of Austria   1574 *m.*
                                                                         Louise de
                                                                         Lorraine

The dates indicate the years when the

Marguerite *m.* (1) Duke of Alençon and
(2) Henri D'Albret
(King of Navarre)

Charles   Marguerite

Jeanne D'Albret
m.
Antoine de Bourbon

Marguerite   Hercule   Victoire and
(Margot)   (François)   Jeanne
m. Henri of   Duke of   twins. Died
Navarre   Alençon   in infancy
(Henri IV)   Afterwards
1589   Duke of Anjou

Henri of Navarre   Catherine
(Henri IV) 1589
m. Margot

ings came to the throne of France.

One

Within the thick stone walls, Paris sweltered in the heat of the summer sun. For weeks now, from the far corners of the land of France, travellers had been passing through the city's gates. Noblemen came with their retinues, and following in their train were the beggars, rogues and thieves who had joined them on the road. It seemed that the whole population of France was determined to see France's Catholic Princess married to the Huguenot King of Navarre.

Now and then a glittering figure would ride by to a flourish of trumpets and with a band of followers to announce him as a nobleman. On his way to the Louvre, he passed through the streets of tall and slender houses, whose roofs crowned them like grey peaked caps, and if he were a Catholic gentleman he would be cheered by the Catholics, and if a Huguenot, by the Huguenots.

In the winding alleys, with their filth and flies, there was tension; it hung over the streets and squares, above which, like guardians, rose the Gothic towers of the Sainte Chapelle and Notre Dame, the gloomy bastions of the Bastille and the Conciergerie. The beggars sniffed the smell of cooking which seemed to be perpetually in the streets, for this was a city of restaurants, and *rôtisseurs* and *pâtissiers* flourished, patronized as they were by noblemen and even the King himself. Hungry these beggars were, but they also were alert.

Now and then a brawl would break out in the taverns. A man had been killed at the Ananas and his body quietly thrown into the Seine, it was said. He was a Huguenot, and it was not surprising that he found trouble in Catholic Paris. One Huguenot among Catholics was a dangerous challenge; but in Paris this summer there were thousands of Huguenots. They could be seen in the streets, outside the church of Saint-Germain l'Auxerrois, strolling through the congested streets, past the hovels and the mansions; many were lodged behind the yellow

9

walls of the Hôtel de Bourbon; others found their way to the house on the corner of the Rue de l'Arbre Sec and the Rue Béthisy which was the headquarters of the greatest of all the Protestant leaders, Admiral Gaspard de Coligny.

Away to the east in the Rue Saint Antoine was one of the largest mansions in Paris – the Hôtel de Guise – and on this summer's day there came riding into the city a man, the sight of whom sent most Parisians wild with joy; he was their hero, their idol, the handsomest man in France before whom all others, be they Kings or Princes, looked like men of the people. This was the golden-haired, golden-bearded, twenty-two-year-old Duke, Henry of Guise.

The Parisians shouted their devotion; they waved their caps for him; they clapped their hands and leaped into the air for him; and they wept for the murder of his father, who had been another such as he. He was a romantic figure, this young Duke of Guise, particularly now when the whole city was preparing to celebrate this wedding, for Guise had been the lover of the Princess who was to be given to the Huguenot; and Paris would have rejoiced to see the Catholic Duke married to their Princess. But it was said that the sly old serpent, the Queen Mother, had caught the lovers together, and as a result the handsome Duke had been married to Catherine of Clèves, the widow of the Prince of Porcien, and gay and giddy Princess Margot had been forced to give up Catholic Henry of Guise for Huguenot Henry of Navarre. It was unnatural, but no more than Paris expected of the Italian woman, Catherine de' Medici.

'Hurrah!' cried the Parisians. 'Hurrah for the Duke of Guise!'

Graciously he acknowledged their homage, and, followed by his attendants and all the beggars who had joined them on the road, Henry, Duke of Guise, rode into the Rue Saint Antoine.

*

The Princess Marguerite, in her apartments of the palace of the Louvre with her sister, the Duchess Claude of Lorraine, listened to the cheers in the street and smiled happily, knowing for whom the cheers were intended. Marguerite, known

10

throughout the country as Margot, was nineteen years old; plump already, vivacious and sensually attractive, she was reputed to be one of the most learned women in the country, and one of the most licentious. Her older and more serious sister, the wife of the Duke of Lorraine, made a striking contrast with the younger princess; Claude was a very quiet and sober young woman.

Margot's black hair fell loosely about her shoulders, for she had just discarded the red wig she had favoured that day; her black eyes sparkled, and even Claude knew that they sparkled for the handsome Duke of Guise. Margot and Guise were lovers, although they had ceased to be faithful lovers; there were too many separations, and Margot's nature was, Claude told herself, too affectionate for constancy. The mild and gentle Claude had a happy way of seeing everyone in the best possible light. Margot had often told her sister that her life had been ruined when permission to marry the man she loved – the only man she could ever love – had been denied her. As a wife of Henry of Guise, she declared, she would have been faithful; but, being his mistress and being unable to become his wife, she had been dishonoured; in desperation she had taken a lover or two, and then had been unable to get out of the habit, for she loved easily, and there were so many handsome men at court. 'But,' explained Margot to her women, 'I am always faithful to Monsieur de Guise when he is at court.' And now the thought of him made her eyes shine and the laughter bubble to her lips.

'Go to the window, Charlotte,' she commanded. 'Tell me, can you see him? Describe him to me.'

A young woman of infinite grace rose from her stool and sauntered to the window. Charlotte de Sauves could not obey a command such as the Princess had just given, without seeming to proclaim to all who watched her that she was the most beautiful woman at court. Her long, curling hair was magnificently dressed, and her gown was almost as elaborate as those worn by Claude and Margot; she was fair, her eyes were blue and she was two or three years older than Margot; her elderly husband occupied the great position of Secretary of State, and if his duties left him little time to bestow on his wife,

11

there were many others ready to take over his conjugal responsibilities. Margot's reputation was slightly tarnished, but that
of Charlotte de Sauves was evil, for when Margot strayed, she
loved, however briefly, and for her that love was, temporarily
'the love of her life'; Charlotte's love affairs were less innocent.

'I see him,' said Charlotte. 'How tall he is!'

'They say he is at least a head taller than most of his followers,' commented Claude.

'And how he sits his horse!' cried Charlotte. 'It is not surprising that the Parisians love him.'

Margot rose and went swiftly to the window.

'There is no one like him,' she said. 'Ah, I could tell you
much of him. Oh, Claude, do not look so shocked. I shall not do
so, for I am not as indiscreet as Charlotte and Henriette.'

'You should tell us,' said Charlotte, 'or some of us may be
tempted to find out for ourselves.'

Margot turned on Charlotte and, taking her ear between her
finger and thumb, pinched it hard. It was a trick Margot had
learned from her mother, and she knew from personal experience what pain it could inflict.

'Madame de Sauves,' she said, every bit the Princess now,
'you will do well to keep your eyes from straying in the direction of Monsieur de Guise.'

Touching her ear very gently, Charlotte said: 'My lady Princess, there is no need to fear. I have no doubt that Monsieur de
Guise is as faithful to you as . . . you are to him.'

Margot turned away and went back to her chair; it did not
take her long to forget her anger, because already she was
anticipating a reunion with Henry of Guise; those about her
knew her well, and they were fond of her, for, with all her
faults, she was the most lovable member of the royal family.
Her temper rose quickly but it fell with equal speed and she
was generous and goodhearted; she could always be relied
upon to help anyone in distress; she was vain and she was
immoral; there had in fact been unpleasant rumours concerning her affection for her brother Henry, the Duke of Anjou;
she had at one time admired him greatly; this was when he was
seventeen and the hero of Jarnac and Montcontour, and

12

Margot's love, whether for cousin or brother, held nothing back that might be asked. But beautiful as she was, both gay and learned, so eager always to talk of herself, to make excuses for her conduct, she was an enchanting companion, a joy to be with, and greatly she was loved.

Now, because of the words of Charlotte de Sauves, she must justify herself in the eyes of her women. She shuddered and rocked herself gently to and fro. 'To think,' she murmured, 'that each passing minute brings me nearer to a marriage which I hate!'

They tried to comfort her.

'You will be a Queen, dearest sister,' said Claude.

Others added their balm. 'It is said that Henry of Navarre, although lacking the beauty of Monsieur de Guise, is not without his attractions.'

Charlotte joined them, still tenderly fingering her ear. 'You would find many women ready to testify to his attractiveness,' she murmured. 'He is a little rough, they say, a little coarse; but it would be difficult to find another as affectionate *and* as elegant as Monsieur de Guise. Duke Henry is a king among men; and the King of Navarre, it is said, is just a man . . . among women.'

'Be silent, Charlotte,' said Margot, beginning to laugh. 'Oh, but my heart bleeds. What shall I do? I declare I'll not be married to this oaf. I hear he has a fondness for peasant girls.'

'Not more than for great ladies,' said Charlotte. 'He just has a fondness for all.'

'It may be,' said Margot, 'that the Pope will not send the dispensation. Then there can be no marriage. I pray each hour that the Pope will refuse to allow the marriage to take place. And then what can we do?'

Her ladies smiled. They were of the opinion that the Princess' mother, who desired the marriage, would not allow it to be prevented by a mere Pope. But they said nothing; it was the fashion to share wholeheartedly in Margot's fables. As for Claude, she did not wish to add to her sister's distress.

'Then there will be no wedding,' continued Margot, 'and all these men and women can go back where they belong. But it is exciting to see so many people in Paris. I must confess I like it. I like to hear the shouts of the people all through the night. They have turned night into day – all because they have gathered here to see me married to that oaf Henry of Navarre, whom I will never marry, whom I have sworn never to marry.'

There was a knock on the door.

'Enter!' cried Margot; and her face changed when she saw Madelenna, her mother's confidential Italian attendant. Claude shivered; she invariably did when there was a prospect of her being called to her mother's presence.

'What is it, Madalenna?' asked Margot.

'Her Majesty, the Queen Mother, desires the immediate presence of Madame de Sauves.'

All except Charlotte showed their relief, and she gave no indication of what she was feeling.

'Go at once,' said Margot lightheartedly. 'You must not keep my mother waiting.'

There was silence when Charlotte had gone. After a pause Margot went on to talk of her hated marriage, but her eyes had lost their sparkle and the animation had left her face.

∗

Charlotte de Sauves knelt before Catherine de' Medici, the Queen Mother of France, until Catherine, waving a beautiful white hand, bade the young woman rise.

Catherine was fifty-three years of age at this time; she had grown very fat in the last years, for she was very fond of good food; she was dressed in black – the mourning which she had worn since the death of her husband, Henry the Second, thirteen years before. Her face was pale, her jowls heavy, her large eyes prominent; her long black widow's veil covered her head and fell over her shoulders. Her carmined lips were smiling, but Charlotte de Sauves shivered as many did when they were in the presence of the Queen Mother, for in spite of a certain joviality of manner, her sly secret nature could not be, after so many years, completely hidden; and it was such a short time since the death of Jeanne of Navarre, the mother of the bride-

14

groom-to-be, who had, much against her inclination, been persuaded to come to court to discuss the marriage of her son with Catherine's daughter. Jeanne's death had been swift and mysterious and, as it had occurred immediately after she had done what Catherine required of her, there were many in France who connected the death of Jeanne of Navarre with Catherine de' Medici. People talked a good deal about the strange ways of the Queen Mother, of her Italian origin, for it was recognized that the Italians were adepts in the art of poisoning; it was suspected that her perfumer and glove-maker, René the Florentine, helped her to remove her enemies as well as her wrinkles, supplied her with poisons as well as perfumes and cosmetics. There had been deaths other than that of Jeanne of Navarre – secret murders of which this widow in black had been suspected. Charlotte thought of them now as she stood facing her mistress.

But Charlotte, young, bold and beautiful, was by no means of a timid nature. She enjoyed intrigue; she was delighted to exploit the power which was hers through her unparalleled beauty. She had found favour with Catherine because Catherine always favoured those who could be useful to her; and she had her own way of using beautiful women. She did not keep a harem to satisfy her erotic tastes as her father-in-law Francis the First had done. The women of Francis' *Petite Bande* had been his mistresses whose task was to amuse him with their wit and their beauty; Catherine's women must possess the same qualities; they must be able to charm and allure, to tempt husbands from their wives and ministers of state from their duties; they must wheedle secrets from those who possessed them, and lure foreign ambassadors from their Kings. All the women of the *Escadron Volant* belonged to Catherine, body and soul; and none, having entered that esoteric band, dared leave it. Charlotte, like most young women who had joined it, had no wish to leave it; it offered excitement, intrigue, erotic pleasure; and there was even a certain enjoyment to be had from the more unpleasant tasks. No woman of virtue would have been invited to enrol in that band, for women of virtue were of no use to Catherine de' Medici.

Charlotte guessed the meaning of this summons. It was, she

was sure, connected with the seduction of a man. She wondered who this might be. There were many noble and eminent men in Paris at this time, but her thoughts went to the young man whom she had seen on horseback from the window of Princess Margot's apartment. If it were Henry of Guise she would enter into her task with great delight. And it might well be. The Queen Mother might wish to curb her daughter's scandalous behaviour; and as Margot and Henry of Guise were in Paris at the same time there was bound to be scandalous behaviour, although he was another woman's husband and she a bride-to-be.

Catherine said: 'You may sit, Madame de Sauves.' She did not go immediately to the point. 'You have just left the Princess' apartments. How did you find her?'

'Most excited by the tumult in the streets, Madame. She sent me to the window to look at the Duke of Guise as he rode by. Your Majesty knows how she always behaves when he is in Paris. She is very excited.'

Catherine nodded. 'Ah well, the King of Navarre will have to look after her, will he not? He will not be hard on her for her wantonness. He himself suffers from the same weakness.' Catherine let out a loud laugh in which Charlotte obsequiously joined.

Catherine went on: 'They say he is very gallant, this gentleman of Navarre. He has been so ever since he was a child. I remember him well.' Charlotte watched the Queen Mother's lips curl, saw the sudden lewdness flash into her eyes. Charlotte found this aspect of Catherine's character as repelling as anything about her; as cold as a mountain-top, she had no lovers; and yet she would wish her *Escadron* to discuss their love affairs with her, while she remained cool, aloof, untouched by any emotion and yet seemed as though she enjoyed their adventures vicariously. 'Old and young,' went on Catherine. 'It mattered not what age they were. It only mattered that they were women. Tell me what the Princess Marguerite said when she sent you to the window to watch Monsieur de Guise.'

Charlotte related in detail everything that had been said. It was necessary to forget nothing, for the Queen Mother might question another who had been present and if the two accounts

16

did not exactly tally she would be most displeased. She liked her spies to observe with complete accuracy and forget nothing.

'She is not so enamoured of the handsome Duke as she once was,' said Catherine. 'Why, at one time . . .' She laughed again. 'No matter. An account of such adventures would doubtless seem commonplace to you, who have had adventures of your own. But those two were insatiable. A handsome pair, do you not think so, Madame de Sauves?'

'Your Majesty is right. They are very handsome.'

'And neither of them the faithful sort. Easily tempted, both of them. So my daughter was a little jealous of the effect your interest might have on the gallant Guise, eh?'

Charlotte touched her ear reminiscently, and Catherine laughed.

'I have a task for you, Charlotte.'

Charlotte smiled, thinking of the handsome figure on horseback. He was, as so many agreed, the handsomest and the most charming man in France.

'I wish to make my daughter's life as pleasant as I can,' went on Catherine. 'This wedding of hers is distasteful to her, I know, but she likes to see herself in the role of injured innocent, so she will, in some measure, enjoy playing the reluctant bride. The young King of Navarre has always been one of the few young men in whom she has not been interested; and as I wish to make life easy for her, I am going to ask you to help me do so.'

'I have one wish, and that to serve Your Majesty with all my heart.'

'Your task will be an easy one. It is well within your range, and as it involves attracting a gallant gentleman and seeking to hold his affections, I am sure you will accomplish it with ease.'

'Your Majesty may rest assured that I will do all that is possible to please you.'

'It should not be unpleasant. The lover I propose for you has a reputation as colourful as your own. I have heard it said that he is as irresistible to most women as I know you are to most men.'

17

Charlotte smiled. She had long desired the handsome Duke of Guise. If she had never dared to look his way it was because Margot guarded her lovers as a tigress guards her cubs; but if the Queen Mother commanded, then Margot's anger would be of little importance.

'I see that you are excited by the proposal,' said Catherine. 'Enjoy yourself, my dear. I feel sure you will. You must let me know how you progress.'

'Is it Your Majesty's wish that I should begin at once?'

'That is not possible.' Catheine smiled slowly. 'You must wait until the gentleman arrives in Paris. I should not like your courtship of him to be conducted by letter.'

'But, Madame . . .' began Charlotte, taken off her guard.

Catherine raised her eyebrows. 'Yes, Madame de Sauves? What did you wish to say?'

Charlotte was silent, her eyes downcast.

'You thought I referred to a gentleman who is now in Paris . . . who has just come to Paris?'

'I . . . I thought that Your Majesty . . . had in mind . . . a gentleman who is already here.'

'I am sorry if I disappoint you.' Catherine looked at her beautiful hands, kept young and supple by René's lotions. 'I do not wish your love affair to advance too quickly. I wish that you should remember while you court this gentleman that you are a dutiful wife. You must tell him that your respect for the Baron de Sauves, my Secretary of State and your loving husband, prevents your giving what he will, ere long I doubt not, be asking for with great eloquence.'

'Yes, Madame.'

'That is all. You may go.'

'Your Majesty has not yet told me the name of the gentleman.'

Catherine laughed aloud. 'A serious omission on my part. It is, after all, most important that you should know. But have you not guessed? I refer, of course, to our bridegroom, the king of Navarre. You seem surprised. I am sorry if you had hoped for Henry of Guise. How you women love that man! There is my daughter doing her best to refuse a crown, for Monsieur de Guise; and I declare you were almost overcome by excitement

18

when, for a moment, you thought that my orders were to take him for your lover. No, Madame, we must make life easy for our young married pair. Leave Monsieur de Guise to my daughter, and take her husband.'

Charlotte felt stunned. She was by no means virtuous, but there were times when, confronted by the designs of the Queen Mother, she felt herself to be in the control of a fiend of Hell.

*

Sadness brooded over the lovely old Château of Châtillon. There should not have been this sadness, for in the castle there lived one of the happiest families in all France; but for the preceding weeks, the head of the house, the man whom every member of the great family revered and loved deeply, had been restless and uneasy. He would busy himself in his gardens, where now the roses were making a magnificent show, and spend many happy hours with his gardeners discussing where they should plant the new fruit trees; he would chat with the members of his family or walk through the green alleys with his beloved wife; he would laugh and jest with his family or read aloud to them. This was a home made for happiness.

But it was precisely because there had been such happiness that the anxiety was with them now. They did not speak to one another of that dear friend, the Queen of Navarre, who had recently died so mysteriously in Paris, but they thought of her continually. Whenever the court, the King or the Queen Mother were mentioned, Jacqueline de Coligny would cling to her husband's arm as though, by so doing, she could keep him at her side and out of harm; he would merely press her hand and smile, though he knew he could not grant her mute request; he could not promise not to go to court when the summons came.

Gaspard de Coligny had been singularly blessed, but being beloved by the Huguenots, he must be hated by the Catholics. He was now fifty-three years of age; ever since his conversion to 'the Religion', which had come about when he had been a prisoner in Flanders, he had been entirely devoted to it; he had sacrificed everything to it as now he knew that he might be called upon to sacrifice his happiness with his family. He did

19

not fear the sort of death which had overtaken Jeanne of Navarre, but he was perturbed at the thought that his family might be left to mourn him. That was at the root of his sadness. He lived dangerously; he had faced death many times during his lifetime and he was ready to face it many more. Only recently he had narrowly escaped being poisoned at – he guessed – the instructions of the Queen Mother. He should not trust that woman; yet if he did not trust her, how could he hope for a solution of all the problems which beset him? He knew that the mysterious deaths of his brothers, Andelot, the Colonel-in-Chief of the Infantry, and Odet, the Cardinal of Châtillon, had probably been ordered by Catherine de' Medici. Odet had died in London; Andelot at Saintes. The spies of the Queen Mother were everywhere and she poisoned by deputy. Yet if he were called to court, he must go, for his life belonged not to him, but to his party.

As he strolled along the paths of his garden, his wife Jacqueline came to him. He watched her with great tenderness; she was pregnant – a fact which was a great joy to them both. They had not been long married and theirs had been a romantic match. Jacqueline had loved him before she had seen him; like many a Huguenot lady, she had admired him for years, and on the death of his wife she had determined to comfort him if he would let her do so. She had made the long journey from Savoy to La Rochelle, where he had been at that time, and, touched by her devotion, the lonely widower had found irresistible that comfort and adoration which she had offered. It was not long after Jacqueline's arrival in La Rochelle that Gaspard had entered into the felicity of a second married life.

'I have come to see your roses,' she said, and she slipped her arm through his.

He knew at once that some new cause for anxiety had arisen, for he could sense her uneasiness. She was never one to hide her feelings, and now that she was carrying the child she seemed more candid than ever. The way in which her trembling fingers clung to his arm set him guessing what had happened. He did not ask what troubled her; he wished to postpone unpleasantness, just for a little while.

'Why, you saw the roses yesterday, my love.'

'But they change in a day. I wish to see them again. Come. Let us go to the rose gardens.'

Neither of them looked back at the grey walls of the Château. Gaspard put an arm about his wife.

'You are tired,' he said.

'No.'

He thought: it must be a summons from the court. It is from the King or the Queen Mother. Jacqueline will weep and beg me not to go. But I must go. So much depends on my going. I must work for our people; and discussions and councils are better than civil wars.

He had long dreamed of that war which was to mean freedom for the Huguenots of France and Flanders, the war which would bring freedom of worship, that would put an end to horrible massacres like that of Vassy. If he could achieve that, he would not care what became of him – except for the sorrow his death would cause his dear ones.

His two boys, Francis and Odet, aged fifteen and seven, came out to join them. They knew the secret; Gaspard realized that at once. Francis betrayed nothing, but little Odet could not stop looking at his father with anxious eyes. It seemed sad that fear and such apprehension must be felt by one so young.

'What is it, my son?' asked Gaspard of Odet; and even as he spoke he saw the warning glances of Jaqueline and his elder son.

'Nothing, Father,' said Odet, in his shrill boy's voice. 'Nothing ails me. I am very well, thank you.'

Gaspard ruffled the dark hair and thought of that other Odet who had gone to London and never returned.

'How pleasant it is out here!' he said. 'I confess I feel a reluctance to be within walls.'

He sensed their relief. Dear children! Dearly beloved wife! He almost wished that God had not given him such domestic happiness since it broke his heart to shatter it; that he had not been chosen as a leader of men, but rather that he might give himself over to the sweeter, more homely life.

His daughter Louise, with Téligny, the husband whom she had recently married, came into the garden. It was a pleasure to see those two together, for they were very much in love; and

Téligny, that noble young man, was more to Gaspard than a son, for Téligny, a staunch Huguenot, had become one of the most reliable leaders of the movement, a son-in-law of whom Gaspard de Coligny, Admiral of France and leader of the Huguenot cause, could be proud.

Jacqueline and the boys knew that they could no longer keep the secret from Gaspard.

Téligny said: 'There are summonses from court.'

'From the King?' asked Gaspard.

'From the Queen Mother.'

'The messenger has been refreshed?'

'He is eating now,' said Louise.

'My orders are to return to court as soon as possible,' said Téligny. 'Yours, sir, are doubtless the same.'

'Later we will go and see,' said Gaspard. 'For the time being it is pleasant here in the garden.'

But the evil moment could not long be put off, and even as he dallied in the gardens, it was obvious to Jacqueline that her husband's thoughts were on those dispatches. She was foolish, she knew, to think that they could be cancelled merely by refusing to speak of them or to look at them. Téligny had had his orders; her husband must expect similar ones.

And so it was. There was a command from the Queen Mother for him to come to court.

'Why so gloomy?' asked Gaspard, smiling at his wife. 'I am invited to court. There was a time when I thought never to receive such an invitation again.'

'I wish that you never had,' said Jacqueline vehemently.

'But, my dearest, you forget that the King is my friend. He is good at heart, our young King Charles. It is my belief that he is the most benign sovereign that ever mounted the throne of the *fleur-de-lis*.'

'I was thinking of his mother, and so my thoughts went to our dear friend, Queen Jeanne of Navarre.'

'You should not think of the Queen Mother when you are reminded of Jeanne's death. Jeanne was sick and she died of her sickness.'

'She died of poison and that poison was administered by . . .'

But Gaspard had laid a hand on his wife's arm. 'Let the people of Paris whisper such things, my love. We should not. From them they are gossip; from us they would be treason.'

'Then is truth treason? Jeanne went to buy gloves from the Queen Mother's poisoner and ... she died. That tells me all I wish to know.'

'Caution, my dearest. You think that I am in danger. That may be fancy. Do not let us make of it a real danger.'

'I will be cautious. But must you go to court?'

'My dear, I must. Think what this means to us ... to our cause. The King has promised help to the Prince of Orange. We will overcome Spain and then those of our religion will be able to worship in peace.'

'But, Gaspard, the Queen Mother cannot be trusted. Jeanne used to say that, and she knew.'

'We are dealing with the King, my dear. The King has a good heart. He has said that the Huguenots are as much his subjects as the Catholics. I am full of hope.'

But to his son-in-law Téligny he was less optimistic. When they were alone, he said to him: 'Sometimes I wonder whether some of our party are worthy of God's help; I wonder whether they are aware of the solemnity of our mission. Do they realize that it is time for them to establish "The Religion" in our land so that generations to come may be born to it? Sometimes it seems to me that the bulk of our people have no real love for "The Religion". They use it to quarrel with their enemies, and they would rather argue over dogma than lead good lives. The men of our country do not take kindly to Protestantism, my son; not as do the men of Flanders, England and the German Provinces. Our people love gaiety and ritual; they consider it not amiss to sin, receive pardon, and sin again; as a nation, the quiet, peaceful life does not appeal to them. We must remember that. The two religions have been, to many as yet, a reason for fighting one against the other. My son, I am uneasy. There is a coldness in these summonses of ours which was not shown when I was at court. But I am determined to fulfil my promises to the Prince of Orange, and the King must be made to keep his word.'

'All that you say is true,' said Téligny. 'But, my father, if the

King refuses to keep his word to Orange, what can we do?'

'We can try to influence him. I feel I can do much with the King, providing I am allowed to see him alone. Failing his help, we have our followers, our soldiers, our own persons . . .'

'The help of Châtillon would seem small, when the help of France had been promised.'

'You are right, my son; but if France fails to keep her word, Châtillon must not do likewise.'

'I have had warning letters from friends at court. Father, they beg us not to go. The Guises plot against us, and the Queen Mother plots with the Guises.'

'We cannot stay away because of warning letters, my son.'

'We must take great care, sir.'

'Rest assured we will.'

At the communal meal nothing was said of the departure, but, from Jacqueline and Gaspard at the head of the table to the servants at the other end, all were thinking of it. Gaspard was greatly loved throughout the neighbouring countryside, for all were aware that there was food for any who needed it at the Château de Châtillon; it was the Admiral himself who had instituted these communal meals which began with a psalm and were followed by grace.

Gaspard was now thinking, as he sat down at the long table, of the struggle which lay before him and those men who were pledged to help him. There was the young Prince of Condé, so like his gay and gallant father who had died fighting for the cause; but the young Prince, for all his valour, was scarcely a strong man. There was the young King, Henry of Navarre, who, at nineteen, was a brave enough fighter but a light liver, a man who thirsted after pleasure rather than righteousness. He could not resist the blandishments of women; he was fond of roystering, of good food and drink; he was too gay a Prince to devote himself to a religious cause. Téligny? It was not because he was so closely related that Gaspard's hopes rested in that young man. In Téligny Gaspard recognized his own determination, his own devotion. There was also the Duc de la Rochefoucauld, dearly beloved of King Charles; but he was young yet and untried. There was the Scot, Montgomery, whose lance had accidentally killed King Henry the Second. Montgomery

24

was the man who would probably lead the Huguenots if death overtook the Admiral, but he was no longer young, and it was among the young that they must look. In the natural course the leadership would fall to the young King of Navarre.

It was foolish to think of his own death; it was the frightened glances of his family and friends which had sent his thoughts in that direction. Even the servants threw fearful glances at him. They were all silently begging him to ignore the dispatches, to refuse to obey the command of the Queen Mother.

Only Téligny was unafraid; and Téligny knew, as the Admiral knew, that they must leave as soon as possible for the court.

Gaspard talked; he talked lightheartedly of the coming marriage, which was not merely the union of a Catholic Princess and a Protestant Prince but, he hoped, the union of all Catholics and Protestants throughout France.

'If the King and the Queen Mother were not ready to favour us, would they have wished for this marriage? Has not the King himself said that if the Pope will not give the dispensation, the Princess Marguerite and King Henry shall be married *en pleine prêche*? What more could he say than that? He is our friend, I say. He at least is our friend. He is young and he is surrounded by our enemies; but when I go to court I shall be able to assure him of the righteousness of our cause. He loves me; he is my dear friend. You know how I was treated when I was last at court. He consulted me on all matters. He called me Father. He wishes to do good and he wants peace in the kingdom. And, my friends, do not doubt that I will help him to attain it.'

But there were murmurings along the table. The Italian woman was at court, and how could she be trusted? The Admiral had forgotten how at one time she had set one of her spies to poison him when he was in camp. That might easily have been accomplished. The Admiral was too forgiving, too trusting. One did not forgive, nor did one trust, a serpent.

Étienne, one of the Admiral's grooms, wept openly. 'If the Admiral leaves us he will never return to us,' he prophesied.

His fellows stared at him in horror, but he persisted in his gloomy prognostications. 'She will succeed in her evil plans this time; evil will triumph over good.'

He was silenced, but he sat there dropping tears into his cup.

When the cloth was removed one of the ministers – there were usually one or two at the Admiral's table – gave the benediction. Then the Admiral and his son-in-law shut themselves up together to talk of their plans and to prepare dispatches which must be sent to court to announce their coming.

When they rode out a few days later, Étienne was in the stables. He had been waiting there since early morning, and when the Admiral mounted his horse, he flung himself on his knees and wailed like one possessed.

'Monsieur, my good master,' he implored, 'do not go to your ruin, for ruin awaits you in Paris. If you go to Paris you will die there . . . and so will all who go with you.'

The Admiral dismounted and embraced the weeping man.

'My friend, you have allowed evil rumours to upset you. Look at my strong arm. Look at my followers. You must know that we can take care of ourselves. Go to the kitchens and tell them they are to give you a cup of wine. Drink my health, man, and be of good cheer.'

He was led away, but he continued to mourn; and the Admiral, riding with his son-in-law to Paris, could not dismiss the scene from his thoughts.

*

Having dismissed Charlotte de Sauves, Catherine de' Medici gave herself up to reflection. She had no definite plans yet for the young King of Navarre, but she guessed that it would be well to have Charlotte working upon him as soon as he arrived; it would not be advisable for him to make a prior attachment which might prove a stronger one than that which she intended to forge. She was sure that Henry of Navarre was another such as his father, Antoine de Bourbon – a man to be ruled by women; and she was determined that the woman who ruled her prospective son-in-law should be her spy. He must not be allowed to fall in love with his bride. That was hardly likely,

26

since Margot would be as ungracious as she could, and Henry of Navarre, who had never lacked admirers, was not likely to fall in love with a wife who spurned him. But she could not trust Margot. Margot was a schemer, an intriguer, who would work for her lover rather than for her family.

As she sat brooding, her son Henry came into the room. He came unannounced and without ceremony. He was the only person at court who would have dared to do that.

She looked up and smiled. Tenderness sat oddly on her face. The prominent eyes softened, and the faintest colour shone beneath her pallid skin. This was her beloved son; and every time she looked at him she was irked by the thought that he was not her first-born, for she longed to take the crown from his brother and place it on that dark, handsome head.

She had loved Henry her husband through years of neglect and humiliation, and she had called this son after him. It was not the name which had been given to him at his baptism; that was Edouard Alexandre; but he had become her Henri; and she was determined that one day he should be Henry the Third of France.

Francis, her first-born, was dead; and when he had died she had wished fervently that Henry might have taken the crown instead of mad ten-year-old Charles. It was particularly irritating to reflect that there was a year between their births. Why, she had so often asked herself, had she not borne this son on that June day in 1550! If that had been so she would have been spared many an anxious moment.

'My darling,' she said, taking his hand – one of the most shapely in France and very like her own – and carrying it to her lips. She smelt the scent of musk and violet powder which he brought into the room. He seemed the most beautiful creature she had ever seen, in his exaggeratedly fashionable coat of mulberry velvet slashed to show pearl-grey satin; the border of his linen chemise was stiff with jewels of all colours; his hair was curled and stood out charmingly beneath his small jewelled cap; his long white fingers were scarcely visible for the rings which covered them; diamonds sparkled in his ears and bracelets hung on his wrists.

'Come,' she said, 'sit close to me. You look disturbed, my

27

dearest. What ails you? You look tired. Not too much love-making with Mademoiselle de Châteauneuf?'

He waved a hand languidly. 'No, not that.'

She patted the hand. She was glad that he had at last taken a mistress; the public expected it and it pleased them. Moreover, a woman would not have the influence with him which was enjoyed by those frizzed and perfumed young men with whom he liked to surround himself. Renée de Châteauneuf was not the sort to meddle with what did not concern her and she was the kind Catherine would have chosen for her son. Yet she was a little worried about his love-making with Renée, because it tired him, and afterwards he would have to take to his bed for a day or two in sheer exhaustion while his young men waited on him, curling his hair, bringing to him the choicest sweet-meats in the palace, reading poetry to him and fetching his dogs and parrots to play their tricks and amuse him.

He was a strange young man, this son of hers. Half Medici, half Valois, he was tainted in mind and body as were all the sons of Henry the Second and Catherine de' Medici. They had had little chance from their births; the sins of the grandfathers – Catherine's father as well as Henry's – had fallen upon them.

People said it was strange that a young man such as this Henry, Duke of Anjou, could have been that great general which the battles of Jarnac and Montcontour seemed to have proved him to be. It seemed impossible that this fop, this languishing, effeminate young man who painted his face, curled his hair and at twenty-one must take to his bed after making love to a young woman, had fought and beaten in battle such men as Louis de Bourbon, the Prince of Condé. Catherine, the realist, must admit to herself that at Jarnac and Montcontour Henry had been blessed with a fine army and excellent advisers. Moreover, like all her sons, he matured early and declined rapidly. At twenty-one he was not the man he had been at seventeen. Witty he would always be; he would always possess an appreciation of beauty, but his love of pleasure, his perverted tastes which he petulantly indulged were robbing him of his energy. It was certainly not the general who stood before his mother now. His lips were curled sullenly and Catherine thought she understood why.

She said: 'You should not concern yourself with the Queen's pregnancy, my son. Charles' child will never live.'

'There were times when you said he would never have a son.'

'Nor has he yet. How do we know what the sex of the child will be?'

'What matters that? If this should be a girl, it does not alter the fact that they are young and will have more children.'

Catherine played with her talisman bracelet which was made up of different coloured stones. On these stones were engravings said to be devils' and magicians' signs; the links of the bracelet were made of parts of a human skull. This ornament inspired awe in all who saw it, as Catherine intended that it should. It had been made for her by her magicians and she believed it to have special qualities.

As he watched her fingers caress it, Anjou felt some relief. He knew that his mother would never let anyone stand in his way to the throne. Still, he thought it had been rather careless of her to let Charles marry, and he intended to let her know that he thought so.

'They will not live,' said Catherine.

'Can you be sure of that, Mother?'

She appeared to be studying her bracelet with the utmost concentration. 'They will not live,' she repeated. 'My son, soon you will wear the crown of France. Of that I am sure. And when you do you will not forget the gratitude due to the one who put you on the throne, will you, my darling?'

'Never, Mother,' he said. 'But there is this news from Poland.'

'I confess I should like to see you a King and that without delay.'

'A King of Poland?'

She put an arm about him. 'I should wish you to be King of France *and* Poland. If you were the King of Poland alone, and that meant you would have to leave France for that barbarous country, then I think my heart would break.'

'That is what my brother wishes.'

'I would never let you stay away from me.'

'Let us face the facts, Mother. Charles hates me.'

'He is jealous of you because you are so much more fitted to be King of France than he is.'

'He hates me most because he knows that you love me most. He would wish to see me banished from this country. He has always been my enemy.'

'Poor Charles, he is both mad and sick. We must not expect reason from him.'

'Yes. A fine state of affairs. A mad King on the throne of France.'

'But he has many to help him govern.'

They laughed together, but Henry was immediately serious. 'Yet what if this child should be a boy?'

'It could not be a healthy boy. Believe me, you have nothing to fear from your brother's sickly offspring.'

'And what if he should demand my acceptance of the Polish throne?'

'It is not yet vacant.'

'But the Queen is dead and the King dangerously ill. My brother and his friends are angry because I refused to marry the Queen of England. What if they now insist that I take the crown of Poland?'

'We must see that you are not banished from France. I would not endure that; and surely you do not believe that any such thing could happen if I did not wish it?'

'Madame, I am as sure that you rule this realm as I am that you sit here.'

'Then you have nothing to fear.'

'Yet my brother grows truculent. My lady mother, forgive me when I point out that of late there have been others about the throne whose influence with him would seem to increase.'

'They can be taken care of.'

'Yet they can be dangerous. You remember my brother's attitude concerning the Queen of Navarre.'

Catherine remembered it very well. The King, like many people in France, had suspected that his mother had had a hand in the murder of Jeanne of Navarre, yet he had ordered an autopsy. Had poison been found, the execution of René, the Florentine poisoner and servant of the Queen Mother, would have been inevitable. Charles, believing his mother to have been involved, had not hesitated in his wish to expose her. She would not forget such treachery from her own son.

'We know who was responsible for his attitude,' said Catherine. 'And once the cause is known it can be removed.'

'Coligny is too powerful,' said Anjou. 'How long shall he remain so? How long will you allow him to poison the King's mind against you . . . against us?'

She did not answer, but her smile reassured him.

'He is on his way to court,' said Anjou. 'This time he should never be allowed to leave it.'

'I think that when Monsieur de Coligny comes to court, your brother may not be quite so enamoured of him,' said Catherine slowly. 'You talk of the Admiral's influence with your brother, but do not forget that when the King is in any trouble it is to his mother that he has been wont to turn.'

'That was once so. Is it so now?'

'Coligny is wise. That righteousness, that stern godliness have had their effect on the King. But this happened because it did not at once occur to me that the King could be so bemused by his Huguenot friend. Now that I have learned the power of the Huguenot and the folly of Charles, I shall know how to act. I am going to see Charles now. When I leave him I think he may be a little less trustful towards his dear good friend Coligny. I think that when the mighty Admiral arrives in Paris he may find a cold reception waiting for him.'

'I will come with you and add my voice to yours.'

'No, my darling. Remember that the King is jealous of your superior powers. Let me go alone and I will tell you every word that passes between us.'

'Mother, you will not allow me to be sent to that barbarous country?'

'Did I send you to England? Have you forgotten my indulgence to you when you so ungallantly refused the Queen of England?' Catherine burst into laughter. 'You insulted her and she might have gone to war with us on that account. You know what a vain old baggage she is. I shall never forget that wicked suggestion of yours that if you married the Earl of Leicester's mistress, it would be fitting for Leicester to marry yours. You are quite mischievous and I adore you for it. How could I endure my life without you near me to make me laugh? Was it not all but intolerable when you were away at the wars? No, my darling, I shall not allow him to send you to Poland . . . or anywhere else which is away from me!'

He kissed her hand while she touched his curled hair, gently because he did not like it to be disarranged.

*

Charles, the King, was in that part of the Louvre where he enjoyed being – the apartments of Marie Touchet, the mistress whom he loved.

He was twenty-two, but he looked older, for his face was wrinkled and his skin pallid; he had not had eight consecutive days of health in his life; his hair was fine but scanty, and he stooped as he walked; he was, at twenty-two, like an old man. Yet his face was a striking one and at times it seemed almost beautiful. His wide-set eyes were golden brown, and very like his father's had been; they were alert and intelligent, and when he was not suffering a bout of madness, kindly and charming; they were the eyes of a strong man, and it was their contrast with that weak, almost imbecile mouth and receding chin that made his face so unusual. Two distinct characters looked out of the King's face; the man he might have been and the man he was; the strong and kindly humanist, and the man of tainted blood, bearing through his short life the burden which the excesses of his grandfathers had put upon him. Each week the trouble in his lungs seemed to increase; and as his body gave up its strength, it became more and more difficult for him to control his mind. The bouts of madness became more frequent as did the moods of melancholy. When, in the dead of night, he would feel that frenzy upon him, he would rise from his bed, waken his followers, put on his mask and go to the lodgings of one of his friends; the pack would catch the young man in his bed and beat him. This was a favourite pastime of the King's during his madness; and the friends he beat were the friends he loved best. So it was with the dogs which he adored. In his sane moments he shed bitter tears over the dogs which, in his madness, he had beaten to death.

He was in a continual state of bewilderment and fear. He was afraid of his brothers, Anjou and Alençon, but particularly of Anjou, who had his mother's complete devotion. He was well aware that his mother wanted the throne for Henry and he was continually wondering what they plotted between them. At this time he was sure that the pregnancy of the Queen was a matter which caused those two much concern.

He was afraid also of the Guises. The handsome young Duke was one of the most ambitious men in the country; and to support him there was his uncle, the Cardinal of Lorraine, that sly lecher whose tongue could wound as cruelly as a sword; there were also the Cardinal's brothers, the Cardinal of Guise, the Duke of Aumale, the Grand Prior and the Duke of Elboeuf. These mighty Princes of Lorraine kept ever-watchful eyes on the throne of France, and they never lost an opportunity of thrusting forward their young nephew, Henry of Guise, who, with his charm and nobility, already had the people of Paris behind him.

But there were some whom the King could trust. Strangely enough, one of these was his wife. He did not love her, but his gentleness had won her heart. Poor little Elisabeth, like many another Princess sacrificed on the altar of politics, she had come from Austria to marry him; she was a timid creature who had been terrified when she had learned that she was to marry the King of France. What must that have suggested to her? Great monarchs like Charles' grandfather, Francis the First, witty, amusing and charming; or Henry the Second, Charles' father, strong, stern and silent. Elisabeth had imagined she would come to France to marry such a man as these; and instead she had found a boy with soft golden-brown eyes and a weak mouth, who had been kind to her because she was timid. She had repaid his kindness with devotion and now she had amazed France by promising to become the mother of the heir to the throne.

Charles began to tremble at the thought of his child. What would his mother do to it? Would she administer that *morceau*

Italianizé for which she was becoming notorious? Of one thing the King was certain: she would never willingly let his child live to take the throne. He would put his old nurse Madeleine in charge of the child, for Madeleine was another whom he could trust. She would fight for his child as she had tried to fight for him through his perilous childhood. Yes, he could trust Madeleine. She had soothed him through the difficult days of his childhood, secretly doing her best to eliminate the teachings of his perverted and perverting tutors — but only secretly, because those tutors had been put in charge of him by his mother in order to aggravate his madness and to initiate him into the ways of perversion; and if Catherine had guessed that Madeleine was trying to undo their work it would have been the *morceau* for Madeleine. Often, after a terrifying hour with his tutors, he had awakened in the night, trembling and afraid, and had crept into the ante-chamber in which Madeleine slept — for he would have her as near him as possible — to seek comfort in her motherly arms. Then she would rock him and soothe him, call him her baby, her Charlot, so that he could be reassured that he was nothing but a little boy, even though he was the King of France. Madeleine was a mother to him even now that he was a man, and he insisted on her being at hand, day and night.

His sister Margot? No, he could no longer trust Margot. She had become brazen, no longer his dear little sister. She had taken Henry of Guise as her lover, and to that man she would not hesitate to betray the King's secrets. He would never trust her absolutely again, and he could not love where he did not trust.

But there was Marie — Marie the dearest of them all. She loved him and understood him as no one else could. To her he could read his poetry; he could show her the book on hunting which he was writing. To her he was indeed a King.

And then Coligny. Coligny was his friend. He never tired of being with the Admiral; he felt safe with him, for although some said he was a traitor to France, Charles had never felt the least apprehension concerning this friend. Coligny, he was sure, would never do anything dishonourable. If Coligny intended to work against him he would at once tell him so, for

Coligny had never pretended to be what he was not. He was straightforward; and if he was a Huguenot, well then Charles would say that there was much about the Huguenots that he liked. He had many friends among the Huguenots; not only Coligny, but Madeleine his nurse was a Huguenot, and so was Marie; then there was the cleverest of his surgeons, Ambroise Paré; there was his dear friend Rochefoucauld. He did wish that there need not be this trouble between Huguenots and Catholics. He himself was a Catholic, of course, but he had many friends who had accepted the new faith.

One of his pages came in to tell him that his mother was approaching, and Marie began to tremble as she always did when she contemplated an interview with the Queen Mother.

'Marie, you must not be afraid. She will not harm you. She likes you. She has said so. If she did not, I should not allow you to remain at court. I should give you a house where I could visit you. But she likes you.'

Marie, however, continued to tremble.

'Page,' called the King, 'go tell the Queen, my mother, that I will see her in my own apartments.'

'Yes, Sire.'

'There,' said the King to Marie, 'does that please you? *Au revoir*, my darling. I will come to you later.'

Marie kissed his hands, relieved that she would not have to face the woman whom she feared, and the King went through the passages which connected his apartments with those of his mistress.

Catherine greeted him with a show of affection.

'How well you look!' she said. 'I declare the prospect of becoming a father suits you.'

The King's lips tightened. He was filled with numb terror every time his mother mentioned the child the Queen was carrying.

'And how well our dear little Queen is looking!' went on Catherine. 'I have to insist on her taking great care of herself. We cannot have her running risks now.'

Charles had learned to dread that archness of hers. The Queen Mother was fond of a joke and the grimmer the joke the

35

better she liked it. People said she would hand the poison cup to a victim with a quip, wishing him good health as she did so. This trait of hers had led some people to believe that she was of a jovial nature; they did not immediately see the cynicism behind the laughter. But Charles knew her better than most people, and he did not smile now.

Catherine was quick to notice his expression. She told herself that she would have to keep a close watch on her little King. He had strayed much further from her influence than she had intended he should.

'Have you news for me?' asked the King.

'No. I have come for a little chat with you. I am disturbed. Very soon Coligny will arrive in Paris.'

'The thought gives me pleasure,' said Charles.

Catherine laughed. 'Ah, he is a wily one, that Admiral.' She put the palms of her hands together and raised her eyes piously. 'So good! Such a *religious* man! A very clever man, I would say. He can deceive us all with his piety.'

'Deceive, Madame?'

'Deceive indeed. He talks of righteousness while he thinks of bloodshed.'

'You are mistaken. When the Admiral talks of God he thinks of God.'

'He has discovered the kindness of his King – that much is certain – and made good use of Your Majesty's benevolence.'

'I have received nothing but benevolence from him, Madame.'

'My dear son, it is not for you to receive benevolence, but to give it.'

The King flushed; she had, as ever, the power to make him feel foolish, unkingly, a little boy who depended for all things on his mother.

'I have come to talk to you of this man,' said Catherine, 'for soon he will be here to cast his spells upon you. My son, you have to think very clearly. You are no longer a boy. You are a man and King of a great country. Do you wish to plunge this country into war with Spain?'

'I hate war,' said the King vehemently.

'And yet you encourage those who would make it. You offer

your kingdom, yourself and the persons of your family to Monsieur de Coligny.'

'I do not. I want peace ... peace ... peace ...'

She terrified him. When she was with him he would remember scenes from his childhood when she had talked as she had now, dismissing all his attendants; on those occasions she had described the torture chambers and all the horrors which had been done to men and women who were powerless in the hands of the powerful. He could not shut out of his mind the thoughts of blood, of the rack, of mangled, bleeding limbs. The thought of blood always sickened him, terrified him, drove him to that madness, when, obsessed by that thought of it, he must see it flow. His mother, more easily than those Italian tutors whom she had set over him, could arouse this madness in him. When he felt it rising and while some sanity remained with him, he must fight it with all the strength he possessed.

'You want peace,' she said, 'and what do you do to preserve it? You hold secret councils with a man who wishes for war.'

'No! No! No!'

'Yes. Have you not held secret meetings with the Admiral?' She had risen and stood over him; he could see nothing but her heavy face with those glittering, prominent eyes.

'I ... I have had meetings with him,' he said.

'And you will hold more?'

'Yes. No ... no. I won't.' He looked down, trying to escape from those hypnotic eyes. He said sullenly: 'If I wish to hold meetings with any of my subjects I shall do so.'

There spoke the King, and Catherine was secretly perturbed by this show of strength. He had made too many friends among the Huguenots. At the earliest possible moment Coligny must be killed, and Téligny would have to follow, with Condé and Rochefoucauld. But Coligny was the most dangerous.

She changed her tone and, covering her face with her hands, she spoke with sadness. 'After all the trouble which I have taken to bring you up and to preserve your crown – the crown which Huguenots and Catholics alike have tried to snatch from you – after having sacrificed myself for you and run a thousand dangers, how could I ever guess that you would reward me so miserably? You hide yourself from me – from your own mother! – in order to take counsel of your enemies. If you intend to work against me, tell me so, and I will return to the land of my birth. Your brother too must escape with me, for he has spent his life in preserving yours, and you must give him time to fly from those enemies to whom you are preparing to give the land of France.' She laughed bitterly. 'Huguenots who, while they talk of war with Spain, want only a war in France – the ruin of our country so that they may flourish on those ruins.'

'You would never leave France,' he said.

'What else could I do? As for you yourself, when they had you in the torture chambers, when they had left you to rot in a dungeon, or, worse still, disposed of you in the Place de Grève . . .'

'What do you mean?'

'You cannot imagine they intend to let you live?' She lifted those large eyes to her son's face. Although he did not believe she would ever leave France, although he knew that his brother Anjou had never been devoted to anything but his own ambitions, he was hypnotized by this strange mother of his, as he had been so many times before. Realizing that her son was no longer the pliable boy, Catherine did not intend to press her point too far; at the moment she only wished to plant distrust for the Admiral in her son's mind.

She took his hand and kissed it. 'Dearest son, know this: everything I say and do is for your good. I do not ask you to exile the Admiral from court. Indeed no. Receive him here. Then it will be easier for you to discover his true nature. Ah, he has bewitched you. That is understandable. He has bewitched many before you. All I ask is that you should be wary, not too trusting. Am I right, my son, in asking that this should be so?'

The King said slowly: 'As usual you are right. I promise you I will not be too trusting.'

'And if, my dear son, you discover that there are traitors about you, men who plot against you, who work for your death and destruction?'

The King was biting his lips and there were flecks of red in the whites of his eyes. 'Then,' he said savagely, while his fingers pulled at his jacket, 'then, Madame, rest assured that there shall be no mercy for them ... no mercy ... no mercy!'

His voice had risen to a shriek, and Catherine smiled, certain that she had gained her point.

*

The Duke of Alençon had finished a game of tennis and had retired to his apartments to brood moodily on his future.

He was a very dissatisfied young man; he could imagine no worse fate than his – to be born the fourth son of a King. There were few who could hold out any hope of his mounting the throne, and he ardently desired to do so.

He was sullen because he believed life had been unfair to him. As Hercule, the youngest of the royal children, he had been such a pretty boy, so spoilt, so pampered – except by his mother – but when he was four years old, he had caught the smallpox, and that delicate skin of his had become hideously pitted; he had not grown so tall as his brothers; he was squat, thickset and swarthy; it was said at court that he was a true Italian, which meant that the French did not like him. But which of his brothers did they like? Sickly Francis? No, they had despised him. Did they love mad Charles? Certainly they did not. And would they love the perfumed, elegant Henry? No. They would hate him more than any. Then why should they not love Francis of Alençon? They had changed his name from Hercule to Francis when his eldest brother had died. He had been delighted at the time, Francis was a King's name. But his mother had maliciously said, with that cynical laugh of hers, that Hercule was not a suitable name for her *little* son. He hated her for that; but then he hated her for so many things. Well, then, why should the people of France not take another Francis for their King?

He thought of the marriage with the English Queen, which they were proposing for him, and such thoughts made him very angry. He could not bear ridicule and he knew that courtiers often smirked behind their hands when the subject of his marriage was discussed. The Queen of England was an old woman, a virago, who amused herself by playing tricks on those who came to woo her. She should play no tricks on him. And why

39

should he, a young man of eighteen, be married to a woman of thirty-nine?

One day he would show them all what he would do. They would cease to treat him as a person of no importance then. One day they would have a surprise. He had his friends who would follow whither he led.

He looked from the window of his apartment towards the Tour de Nesle; he let his eyes wander to the three towers of Saint-Germain-des-Prés. He saw the people crowded together, Huguenot and Catholic. There was much roystering in the streets and many a secret counsel in the palace; yet he, the King's brother, the son of Henry the Second and Catherine de' Medici, was kept outside the excitement, because he was considered too young and of too little importance!

And as he stood there he saw a cavalcade come riding through the streets. Another great personage come to attend the wedding of his sister. He called to one of his attendants: 'Who is this riding into the city?'

'It is the Admiral de Coligny, sir. He is a fool to come riding into Paris thus.'

'Why so?'

'He has many enemies, sir.'

The Duke nodded. Yes, there were plots against the Admiral, he doubted not. His mother would have discussed that man when she was closeted with his brothers; but she never discussed her plots with him. He bit his lips until the blood came. He was treated as a child – the youngest son who could never come to the throne, little Hercule who had become Francis because Hercule was the name of a strong man; and he was not even handsome because his skin was so hideously pitted. His mistresses told him he was more handsome than his brother Henry, but that was because although he was the youngest he was still the son of a royal house. He had many mistresses; but any man in his position might have the same number. He was squat and ugly; he was of no importance; and when his mother called him 'her little frog' she did not mean to be affectionate. She despised him and had no place for him in her schemes. She wanted him safely out of the way in England.

He laughed aloud at that fool of an Admiral who was riding

straight into a trap. He hated the Admiral – not for political or religious reasons – but merely because he was tall and handsome and of great importance.

He saw that the Huguenots in the city had formed a procession about the Admiral and his men, marching along beside them as though to protect them. Catholics stood about sullenly; some shouted abuse. It would take very little to start a conflagration which would lay waste the entire city of Paris.

They were crazy to have arranged this marriage and, arranging it, to have brought together in the capital so many of the Huguenot faith. But ... were they? Was this the result of some plan of his mother's?

His brothers would know. Henry of Guise too would doubtless know. All men of importance would know. But they kept Francis of Alençon completely in the dark. It was more than a Prince of the Blood Royal could be expected to endure.

He bit his lip afresh and tried to imagine that those shouting voices called for a new King, and that that King's name was Francis.

*

As soon as he was in the presence of the King, Gaspard de Coligny knew that his enemies were working against him. The King's attitude towards him seemed to have changed completely. When the Admiral had last seen Charles, the young man had embraced him warmly, dispensing with all ceremony. 'Do not call me Majesty,' Charles had said. 'Do not call me Monseigneur. Call me Son and I will call you Father.' But here was a different monarch. The golden-brown eyes had lost their warmth; they were coldly suspicious. Henry of Guise and his uncle, the Cardinal of Lorraine, were at court, and they were enjoying the favour of the Queen Mother. Yet, during the ceremonial greeting, Gaspard thought he caught a hint of apology in the King's eyes; but the Queen Mother stood beside her son, and although her greeting might be warmer than that of any other present, still the Admiral trusted her less, and he was sure that the animosity which he sensed emanated from her.

The Admiral came fearlessly to the purpose of his visit: the

41

question of aid for the Prince of Orange and war with Spain.

Catherine spoke for her son. 'You have been long in coming to Paris, Monsieur l'Amiral. Had you come earlier you might have been present at the military council which I called together to settle this question of war.'

'A military council, Madame?' said Coligny aghast. 'But of what members did this council consist?'

Catherine smiled. 'Of the Duke of Guise, of the Cardinal of Lorraine . . . and others. Do you wish to hear their names?'

'That is my wish, Madame.'

Catherine mentioned the names of several noblemen, and all of them were Catholics.

'I understand, Madame,' said Coligny. 'These councillors would naturally suggest that we should not keep our promises. Such men would never support any expedition of which I was the leader.'

'We were not, Monsieur l'Amiral, considering a question of leadership; we but considered the good of France.'

The Admiral turned from the Queen Mother and knelt to the King. He took Charles' hand and smiled up into his face.

Catherine, watching closely, saw the faint flush under Charles' pallid and unhealthy skin; she saw the affection in his glance. Charles was only free from this man's influence when the latter was away from court. There was real danger here. The Admiral must not, on any account, be allowed to live many more weeks. Whatever disaster followed on his death, he must die.

'Sire,' Coligny was saying, 'I cannot believe that you will break your promise to the Prince of Orange.'

Charles said very quietly and in a voice of shame: 'You have heard the result of the council's deliberation, Monsieur l'Amiral. It is to them that you should address your reproaches.'

'Then,' said Coligny, 'there is nothing to be said. If the opinion contrary to mine has won the day, that is the end. Oh, Your Majesty. I am as certain as I kneel here that if you follow the advice of your council you will repent it.'

Charles began to tremble. He put out a hand as though to detain the Admiral; he seemed as though he were about to speak, but his mother's eyes were on him and he lapsed completely into her power once more.

Coligny went on: 'Your Majesty must not be offended if I, having promised aid to the Prince of Orange, cannot break *my* word.'

Charles flinched and Coligny waited; but still the influence of Catherine was greater than that of the newly arrived Admiral, and although Charles seemed once more about to speak, no words came.

'This,' added Coligny, 'will be done with my own friends, my relations and servants, and with my own person.' He turned to Catherine. 'His Majesty has decided against war with Spain. God grant that he may not be involved in another from which he cannot retreat.'

Coligny bowed and took his leave.

There were letters waiting for him in his apartments. One said: 'Remember the commandment which every Papist obeys: "Thou shalt not keep faith with a heretic". If you are a wise man you will leave the court at once. If you do not, you will soon be a dead one.'

'You are in acute danger,' wrote another. 'Do not be deceived by the talk of marriage between the Queen of England and the Duke of Alençon. Do not be beguiled by this marriage of Marguerite and Navarre. Get away as quickly as you can from that infected sewer which is called the Court of France. Beware the poisoned fangs of the Serpent.'

'You have,' said another, 'won the regard of the King. That is sufficient reason for your death.'

He read through those letters, and as the dusk crept into his apartment, he found that the least rustle of the hangings set his heart beating faster. He touched the walls gingerly with his fingers and wondered whether here, where the wood was uneven, there was a secret door. Was there a hole up there among the ornate carving of the ceiling through which an eye watched him? Any moment might be his last.

*

Charles was soon under the spell of the Admiral. Since Gaspard had come to court, Charles felt bolder, less afraid of his mother. He kept Gaspard with him, and there were many interviews at which none but the King and the Admiral were present. But Catherine was aware of what took place at those interviews. There was a tube from her secret chamber adjoining her apartments which was connected with the King's, and by means of this she was able to hear most of what took place. It was enough to alarm her.

The proposed war with Spain was continually under discussion, and the King was wavering. 'Rest assured, my dear Admiral,' he had said, 'that I intend to satisfy you. I will not budge from Paris until I have utterly contented you.'

There must be no delay in putting the murder of the Admiral into effect, but it must be after the wedding. If the Admiral suddenly died now, there might be no wedding. Catherine found a pleasure in watching her victim; it was like fattening up a pig for the kill. There he was, puffed up with pride and confidence; he thought he only had to come to court to gain the King's goodwill; he had only to persuade and his plans would be put into action.

Well, let him enjoy his last weeks on Earth. Let him continue to think he was a power in the land . . . for a few weeks.

The Admiral had no finesse, and like most blunt soldiers he needed lessons in statecraft and diplomacy. He rarely stopped to consider his words; he said what he thought, which, in a court such as this where artificiality was a fine art in itself, was the height of folly.

At one of the council meetings, he brought up this matter of the Polish throne.

'There are several claimants,' he said, 'and there can be no doubt that very shortly it will become vacant. If that throne is to fall to France it is very necessary for the Duke of Anjou to leave for Poland at once.'

The King nodded with enthusiasm, since there was little he would like better than to see his hated brother out of the country. Catherine was furious, but she calmly appeared as though she were considering the matter. As for Anjou, his rage was almost uncontrollable; the hot colour flamed in his face and the earrings quivered in his ears.

'It seems to me that Monsieur l'Amiral interferes in matters which do not concern him,' he said coldly.

'This matter of Poland is of vital concern to France, Monsieur,' answered Gaspard with his habitual frankness.

'That is true enough,' supported the King.

'And if,' went on Gaspard, 'Monsieur who would have none of England by marriage, will have none of Poland by election, he should say outright that he does not desire to leave France.'

The council broke up and as soon as possible Anjou sought out his mother.

'What think you of such insolence, Madame?' he demanded. 'Who is this Admiral to address me thus?'

Catherine soothed her beloved son. 'My darling, do not distress yourself. Do not take the words of such a man too much to heart.'

'Such a man! You know he is the close friend of the King. Who can guess what they will hatch up between them? Mother, will you let them plot against me?'

'Have patience,' said Catherine. 'Wait until after the wedding and you will see.'

'The wedding! But when can this be? I know they are all here ... all the nobles of France and their followers, but that old fool, the Cardinal of Bourbon, will never perform the ceremony without the dispensation from the Pope; and will he give it, do you think? Will he allow a marriage between our Catholic sister and the Huguenot to take place? Why, soon we shall hear that he forbids the marriage and Paris will be in an uproar.'

'You are young yet, my love, and you have not learned that there are ways of working miracles. We shall manage without Monsieur Gregory, never fear.'

'One cannot think that the Bourbon will perform the ceremony against the wishes of the Pope.'

'He will not know the wishes of the Pope, my son. I have written to the Governor of Lyons that no posts must be allowed to come from Rome until after the ceremony.'

'Then we shall wait in vain for the Pope's dispensation.'

'Better that than that we should receive word from Rome that the wedding must not take place.'

'How will you get him to perform the ceremony without the Pope's consent?'

'Leave that to your mother. Ere long your sister will be united to Navarre. Never fear. I can manage the old Cardinal. Have patience, my dearest. Wait . . . just wait until the wedding is over and then you shall see.'

Anjou's dark Italian eyes gleamed as he looked askance at his mother. 'You mean? . . .'

She put her fingers to her lips. 'Not a word . . . even between us. Not yet. But have no fear.' She put her mouth close to his ear. 'Monsieur l'Amiral has not long to live. Let him strut as much as he likes through his last hours on Earth.'

Anjou nodded, smiling.

'But,' whispered his mother, 'it is necessary for us to employ the utmost caution. Planning the end of such a man is full of dangers. He is no little fish. We have our spies everywhere and they tell us that he receives warnings of what is about to happen to him. How this becomes known it is beyond my knowledge to understand. It is necessary to lay the net very carefully in order to trap the salmon, my son. Make no mistake about that.'

'My mother, I have no doubts of your powers to achieve what is necessary.'

She kissed him tenderly.

*

In the closet which led from her bedchamber, the Princess Marguerite entertained the Duke of Guise. She lay beside him on the couch which she had ordered should be covered in black satin as the perfect contrast to her beautiful white limbs. She smiled at him, for the moment sleepily content. No man delighted her, nor she believed ever could, as did her first lover, Henry, Duke of Guise.

'It has seemed so long,' she said. 'I had forgotten how wonderful you are.'

'And you, my Princess,' he answered, 'are so wonderful that I shall never forget you.'

'Ah!' sighed Margot. 'If only they had let us marry! Why, then you would not be another woman's husband and I should not be close to the most odious marriage that was ever made. Oh, Henry, my love, if you only knew how I pray each day, each night, that something will happen to prevent this marriage. Is it possible, my love? Is there something which can be done?'

'Who knows?' said Guise gloomily. 'There is that in the air of Paris which makes one wonder what will happen next.' He took her face in his hands and kissed it. 'There is only one thing certain in the whole world, and that is that I love you.'

She embraced him feverishly; her arms were about him, her lips warm and demanding. She never failed to astonish him, although he had known her and loved her all his life. He looked at her as she lay back, stretching out her arms to him, her black hair loose, those wonderful dark eyes glowing in her lovely, languorous face; she was already eager for their next embrace. She was irresistible and very beautiful; the heaviness of her nose which was an inheritance from her grandfather, and the thickness of her jaw which had come from her mother, were not apparent now.

'Margot,' said Guise, with passion, 'there is no one like you.'

They lay content behind the locked door of the closet, happily secure. In tender reminiscence they recalled that night when they had been discovered – Margot in the fine clothes in which she had greeted her suitor, Sebastian of Portugal. They both recalled the fury of the King and the Queen Mother on that night when they had beaten Margot almost to death for her share in the adventure; as for Guise, he had narrowly escaped with his life. 'Ah,' said Margot, 'you emerged from that danger with a wife, but I came out of it with a broken heart.' She had said that at the time, but now she knew that hearts which broke one day were mended the next; and the wife of Henry of Guise could not prevent his being Margot's lover. There were other men in the world, Margot had found – not so handsome nor so charming, it was true – and she could not exist without a lover.

How pleasant it was to lie in this man's arms and to lure him

47

to fresh frenzies of passion, and to think sadly, when passion brought temporary − a very temporary − satisfaction: ah, how different it would have been had I been allowed to marry the man whom I loved. We should have been faithful to one another and ours would have been the perfect union! This self-pitying role was Margot's favourite one; she would indulge her desires and then she would say: 'But how different I should have been if I had been allowed to marry the only man I ever loved!' She had only to tell herself that and she could, with a good conscience, indulge in any amusement.

There was a sudden knocking on the door of the closet and the voice of Charlotte de Sauves was heard. Margot smiled. Charlotte would know whom she was entertaining in her closet, and Charlotte would be just a little jealous. That was pleasing. Charlotte, because of her beauty and her importance in the *Escadron*, gave herself too many airs.

'Who is there?' asked Margot.

'It is I. Charlotte de Sauves.'

'And whom do you want?'

'But to ask if you have seen Monsieur de Guise. The Queen Mother is asking for him. She grows impatient.'

Margot laughed. She rose and went to the door. 'When I next see Monsieur de Guise I will tell him. Have no fear, that will be very soon.'

'Thank you. I will go to Her Majesty and tell her that Monsieur de Guise is coming.'

Margot turned to her lover, who had already put on his coat and was adjusting his sword. She felt angry at his impatience to leave her.

'You seem very eager to be gone.'

'My darling, that was a summons from your mother.'

Margot put her arms about him. 'Let her wait awhile.'

He kissed her, but she knew that he was thinking of the interview with the Queen Mother.

'The ambitious head of the House of Guise and Lorraine first,' she said lightly. 'The lover second. Is that not so?'

'No,' he lied. 'You know it is not so.'

Her black eyes flashed. There were occasions when she wanted to quarrel with him. With her, love was everything;

48

and she could not bear to think that this was not the case with him.

'Then kiss me,' she said.

He did so.

'Kiss me as though you were thinking of me and not what you will say to my mother. Oh, Henry, five minutes more!'

'Dearest, I dare not.'

'You dare not! It is always "I dare not" with you. It was "I dare not!" when you let them marry you to that stupid wife of yours.'

'Margot,' he said, 'I will be back.'

'Why do you think she sends for you now? It is because she knows we are together and it delights her to tease us. You do not know my mother.'

'I know that when she summons me, I must obey.'

He had turned the key in the lock, but Margot still clung to him, kissing him passionately. 'When will you return?'

'As soon as it is possible to do so.'

'You promise that?'

'I promise.'

'Then kiss me again ... and again ... and again.'

*

Catherine dismissed all her attendants; she would not even allow her dwarf to remain; she was preparing to receive the young Duke of Guise.

She watched him approach, thinking that it was not surprising that Margot found him irresistible. He was a handsome creature. Twenty-two was not very old, but in a few years he would be as wily as his father had been; and even now, since he had that old fox his uncle, the Cardinal of Lorraine, at his elbow, she must be wary of this man.

When he had greeted her ceremoniously, she said: 'I have much to say to you, Monsieur de Guise. We are alone, but keep your voice low when you speak to me. It is not easy to talk secretly in the palace of the Louvre.'

'I understand, Your Majesty.'

'The presence of one at this court, I feel, must anger you as much as it does me, my dear Duke. You know of whom I speak?'

'I think I do, Madame.'

'We will not mention his name. I refer to the murderer of your father.'

He was very young and unable yet completely to hide his emotion. He looked a little tired, which was no doubt due to the hour he had spent with Margot. That baggage would tire out anyone! From whom had she inherited such habits? Not from her mother; that much was certain. From her father? Indeed not. He had been a faithful man . . . faithful to the wrong woman, it was true; but Margot would never be faithful. She had had many lovers, though she was not yet twenty. It must be her grandfather, Francis I, or perhaps Catherine's own father. They had both been insatiable, so it was said. But she had sent for this young man to discuss important affairs, not his love-making with her daughter.

'Yes, Madame,' he said bitterly; he had always believed that Gaspard de Coligny had murdered his father, and he would never be completely happy until he had avenged Francis of Guise.

'We cannot tolerate his presence here at court,' said Catherine. 'His influence is bad for the King.'

Guise's heart began to beat more quickly. He knew that Catherine was hinting that he should help her arrange the murder of Coligny. His fingers closed over his sword and his eyes filled with tears as he remembered how they had carried his father into the castle near Orléans. He saw afresh Duke Francis' noble face with the scar beneath the eye, which had earned for him the name of *Le Balafré*; he remembered seeing that beloved face for the last time, and remembered too how he had sworn vengeance on the man who he believed had murdered his father.

'Madame,' said the Duke, 'What are your instructions?'

'What?' said Catherine. 'Do you need instructions to avenge your father?'

'Your Majesty doubtless had some suggestion in mind when you sent for me.'

'This man walks about the court; he commands the King; he

50

threatens not only your family, but mine, and you ask me for instructions!'

'Madame, I promise you that he shall not live a day longer.'

She lifted a hand. 'Now you go too fast, my lord Duke. Would you plunge this city into bloodshed? I wish this man to attend the wedding of my daughter and the King of Navarre. After that . . . he is yours.'

The Duke bowed his head. 'It shall be as Your Majesty wishes.'

'My dear Duke . . . why, you are almost a son to me. Did you not spend the greater part of your childhood with my own family? And you have grown to love them, have you not . . . some more than others? Well, that is natural. But I love you as a son, my dear boy; and it is for this reason that I wish you to have the joy of avenging your father.'

'Your Majesty is most gracious to me.'

'And would be more so. Now listen. Do nothing foolhardy. I would not have you challenge the man. Let the shot that kills him be delivered by an unknown assassin.'

'I have always believed that it is my mother who should fire the shot that kills him, Madame. That, I feel, would be justice indeed. She is a good shot and . . .'

Catherine waved a hand. 'You are young, my dear Duke, and your ideas are those of a boy. If a shot were fired at the man and he were to escape, what an uproar there would be! No, let the first shot find its mark. Let us not make of this matter a bit of play-acting. That man has a way of avoiding his fate. Sometimes I think some special magic preserves him.'

'It shall not preserve him from my vengeance, Madame.'

'No. I feel sure that it will not. Now keep this matter secret, but discuss with your uncle what I have said. Find some means of hiding an assassin in one of your houses, and as your father's murderer passes along the street on his way from the Louvre, let the shot be fired. No play-acting. Let us have a skilled marksman, not a nervous Duchess. This is life . . . and death, Monsieur, not a drama to be acted for the amusement of the court. Go, and when you have a plan, bring it to me. But do not forget . . . *after* the wedding. Is that clear?'

51

'It is perfectly clear, Madame.'

'Now, back to your pleasures, and not a word of this to anyone — except, of course, your worthy uncle. I know that I can trust you.'

'Your Majesty can have complete trust in me.'

He kissed her hand and retired. He was too excited to return to Margot. He sought out his uncle, the Cardinal of Lorraine, to tell him of his interview with the Queen Mother.

As for Catherine, she was pleased; it suited her serpentine nature to bring about her desires by such circuitous means.

*

The bridegroom was riding to Paris at the head of his men, and although he was dressed in deepest mourning — for it was less than three months since his mother had died mysteriously in Paris — there was a Gascon song on his lips.

He was a young man of nineteen, not by any means tall, but of good proportions; there was an immense vitality about him; his manner was bold and frank, and there was often laughter on his lips; but his eyes were veiled and shrewd, and it was as though they belied the character which the rest of his face betrayed. In those eyes was a hint of something deep, something which was at the moment latent and which he had no intention of showing to the world. He had inherited much of his mother's shrewdness, but little of her piety. He was a Huguenot because his mother had been a Huguenot, but on religious matters he was a sceptic. 'By God,' he would say, 'a man, it seems, must have a faith; and as the good God decided He would make a Huguenot of me, so let it be.' But he would yawn during sermons and at times openly snore; and on one occasion he had hidden himself behind a pillar and while eating cherries had shot the stones up into a preacher's face.

His men were fond of him. They considered him a worthy Prince to follow. He would be coarsely familiar with them, and he was easily moved to tears and laughter, but there was little depth in his emotions. The veiled, cynical eyes belied the facile emotions, and it was felt that while he wept he had already done with tears.

His love affairs had already been so numerous that even in a

52

land where promiscuity seemed natural enough he was remarkable. He had been brought up in a practical manner by his
mother, who had discouraged him from imitating the fanciful
manners of the Valois Princes. He was coarse in his manners
and not over-careful about his appearance; he was as happy in
a peasant's cottage as in a royal palace, providing the peasant's
wife or daughter could amuse him during his stay.

So he came riding into Paris, seducing the women of
Auvergne and Bourbonnais, Burgundy and Orléans as he
came.

He was thinking of the marriage shortly to be celebrated
between himself and the Princess Marguerite. He had known
from his earliest childhood that such a marriage would probably take place, for it had been arranged by Margot's father,
Henry the Second, when Navarre was two years old and
Margot a few months older. It was a good marriage – the best
possible for him, he supposed. His mother had wanted it because it brought him nearer to the throne. Navarre shrugged
his shoulders when he thought of the throne of France. There
were too many between; there were Henry of Anjou and
Francis of Alençon, not to mention any children they might
have; and Charles' wife was at present pregnant. Navarre
doubted very much whether a King of France could enjoy life
more than he did; and what he was bent on at the time was
enjoying life.

Still, the marriage had been arranged and it was as good a
marriage as any could be. Margot had always been antagonistic
towards him, but what did he care? What did he want of a wife
when he could so effortlessly find so many women to give him
what he desired? He would be quite content to leave Margot to
her affairs, and he would see that she left him to his.

As soon as it had become known that he was to go to Paris
he had had to listen to many warnings. 'Remember what happened to your mother,' he was told. "She went to Paris and
never returned.' They did not understand that he was not
seriously perturbed by the thought of danger, and that he
looked forward with eagerness to being at that court of intrigues. His mother had died and that had shocked him; bitterly
he had wept when the news was brought to him, but he had

soon discovered that, even while he wept most bitterly, he was thinking of the freedom which he would consequently enjoy. His mother he had always known to be a good woman, and he was ashamed that he could not love her more. She was a saint, he supposed; and he was, at heart, a pagan. She would have been disappointed in him if she had lived, for he could never have been the pious Huguenot she had tried to make of him. And her death brought with it more than his freedom; he had become of great importance – no longer merely a Prince, but a King of Navarre. There were no longer irksome restrictions, no more sermons from his mother; he was gloriously free, his own master, and that was a good thing to be at nineteen years of age when a man was virile, full of health and effortlessly attractive to all women.

So as he rode he sang a song of Gascony; and although now and then a friend would whisper to him a word of warning, that could only excite him the more. He was eager for adventure, eager for intrigue.

And when, with his numerous followers, he was but a short distance from Paris, King Charles himself rode out to meet him. The young King of Navarre was gratified to be embraced by the King of France, to be called brother, to receive such a show of friendship.

The Queen Mother had ridden with the royal party, and she too made much of the newcomer, embracing him, telling him how she rejoiced to see him again, tenderly touching his black sleeve, while she lowered her eyes in assumed regret for his mother.

But what delighted Navarre more than the royal welcome were the ladies who rode with the Queen Mother. He had never before seen so much beauty, for every one of these ladies, seen singly, would have dazzled him with her charms. His half-veiled eyes studied them and from one of them – it seemed to him the most beautiful of them all – he received a smile of what he considered to be definite promise. She was a beautiful creature with fair hair and blue eyes. No other woman, he realized, had the grace and the elegance of these court beauties; and what a delightful change they made after the more homely charms of his dear little friends in Béarn!

The King of France rode beside him as they made their way into the capital.

'It pleases me,' said Charles, 'to think that you will soon be my brother in truth.'

'Your Majesty is gracious indeed.'

'You will find the city full of my subjects who have come from the four corners of France to see you married to my sister. Do not be afraid that we shall delay the wedding. The Cardinal of Bourbon is making difficulties. He is an old bigot. But I shall not allow him to waste much more of that time which belongs to you and my sister Margot.'

'Thank you, Sire.'

'You look well and sturdy,' said the King enviously.

'Ah, it is the life I lead. I spend much time on pleasure, so they say, but it would seem that it agrees with me.'

The King laughed. 'My sister will be pleased with you.'

'I trust so, Sire.'

'I hear,' said Charles, 'that you have little difficulty in pleasing women.'

'I see that rumour concerning me has reached Paris.'

'Never fear. Parisians love such as you, brother.'

Was that true? Navarre was aware of glowering faces in the crowds that surged close to the cavalcade as it went through the streets.

'*Vive le Roi Charles!*' cried the people. And some added: '*Vive le Roi Henri de Navarre!*' But not many, and there was a hiss or two to counteract the cheers.

'There are many Guisards in the streets today,' said Navarre.

'There are all sorts,' answered the King. 'The followers of the Guise and the followers of my dear friend the Admiral mingle together now that you and my sister are to marry.'

'It would seem as though the whole of France were gathered here . . . Huguenot and Catholic.'

'It would indeed seem so. I have heard that so many are in Paris that there is no room for them to sleep. The inns are full and at night they sprawl on the cobbles of the streets. It is all for love of you and Margot. My dear friend, the Admiral, will be filled with delight to see you here. He has a right good welcome waiting for you.'

Navarre smiled his pleasure while he glanced sideways at the King. Was the King, with his continual references to his dear friend the Admiral, trying to tell him that he was favouring the Huguenot cause after all? What of Catherine de' Medici, who many believed had been responsible for the death of his mother? What did she intend for him?

He rarely concentrated on anything for long at a time, and as he saw the Louvre with its one arm stretching along the quay and the other at right angles, he looked up at its tower and narrow windows and remembered the young woman he had seen riding with the Queen Mother.

He said: 'I noticed a very beautiful lady riding with Her Majesty, the Queen Mother. Her eyes were of a most dazzling blue, more blue than any eyes I have ever seen.'

The King laughed. 'My sister's eyes are black,' he said.

'The most beautiful eyes in France, so I have heard,' said the bridegroom. 'Yet I wonder to whom the blue ones belonged.'

'There is a lady in my mother's *Escadron* who is remarkable for the colour of her eyes, and they are blue. I think, brother, that you refer to Charlotte de Sauves.'

'Charlotte de Sauves,' repeated Navarre.

'My mother's woman, and wife to the Baron de Sauves – our Secretary of State.'

Navarre smiled happily. He hoped to see a good deal of the owner of the blue eyes in the weeks to come, and it was rather pleasant to learn that she had a husband. Unmarried ladies sometimes made difficulties which it would be trying for a young bridegroom to overcome.

And as he came into the great hall and idly gazed through the windows at the Seine flowing peacefully by, as he mounted the great staircase of Henry the Second, he thought with extreme pleasure of Madame de Sauves.

*

On a Turkey rug in his apartments the King lay biting his fists. He was greatly troubled and none dared approach him. Even his favourite falcons on their perches set up in this room could not delight him. His dogs slunk away from him; they, no less than his servants, detected the brooding madness in him. He was worried, and when he was worried it was usually because he was afraid. Sometimes when he stood at his window he seemed to hear a murmur of warning in the cries of the people which floated up to him. He felt that mischief was brewing and that he was threatened.

He could not trust his mother. What mischief did she plan? He watched the thickening body of his young wife with disquietude. His mother would never let the child live to stand in the way of her beloved Henry's coming to the throne. And if she longed to see Anjou on the throne, what did she plot for her son Charles?

There were horrible silences in the streets, broken by sudden tumult. Of what did the huddled groups of people talk so earnestly? What did they mean – those skirmishes in taverns? It had been madness to bring Huguenots and Catholics into Paris; it was inviting trouble; it was preparing for bloodshed. He saw pictures of himself, a prisoner; he smelt the evil smell of dungeons; he saw his body tortured and his head severed from his body. He wanted to see blood flow then; he wanted his whips so that he could attack his dogs; and yet because some sanity remained to him he must remember the remorse which would follow such actions; he remembered the horror that was his when he looked on a beloved dog which he had beaten to death.

Someone had come into the room, and he was afraid to look up in case he should encounter his mother's smile. They said she had secret keys to all the rooms in the palaces of France, and that often she would silently open a door and stand behind curtains, listening to state secrets, watching the women of her *Escadron* making love with the men she had chosen for them. In all his dreams, in all his fears, his mother played a prominent part.

'Charlot, my little love.'

He gave a sob of joy, for it was not his mother who stood close to him, but Madeleine, his old nurse.

'Madelon!' he cried, as he used to when he was a little boy.

She took him into her arms. 'My little one. What ails you, then? Tell Madelon.'

He grew calmer after a while. 'It is all these people in the streets, Madelon. They should not be there. Not Huguenots *and* Catholics together. And it is I who have brought them here. That is what frightens me.'

'It was not you. It was the others.'

He laughed. 'That was what you always said when there was trouble and I was accused. "Oh, it was not my Charlot; it was Margot or one of his brothers." '

'But you were never one for mischief. You were my good boy.'

'I am a King now, Nurse. How I wish I were a boy again, and that I could slip out of the Louvre, out of Paris, to some quiet spot with you and Marie and the dogs and my falcons and my little pied hawk to bring down the small birds for me. To escape from this . . . with you all. How happy I should be!'

'But you have nothing to fear, my love.'

'I do not know, Nurse. Why cannot my subjects be at peace? I care for them all, be they Huguenots or Catholics. Why, you yourself are a Huguenot.'

'I wish that you would pray with me, Charlot. There would be great comfort for you in that.'

'Perhaps I will one day, Madelon. But it is all this hate about me that frightens me. Monsieur de Guise hating my dear Admiral, and the Admiral cold and haughty with Monsieur de Guise. That is not good, Madelon. They should be friends. If those two were friends, then all the Huguenots and all the Catholics in Paris would be friends, for the Catholics follow the Duke, and the Huguenots the Admiral. That is it! That is what I must do. I must make them friends. I will insist. I will demand it. I am the King. By the good God, if they will not give each other the kiss of friendship, I will . . . I will . . .'

Madeleine wiped the sweat from his brow. 'There! You are right, my little King. You are right, my Charlot. You will insist, but now you will rest awhile.'

He touched her cheek lightly with his lips. 'Why are not all the people in Paris gentle like you, dearest Nurse? Why are they not all like Marie and my wife?'

'It might be a dull world made up of such as I,' she said.

'A dull world, you say. Then it would be a happy one. No fears ... no death ... no blood. Go, Nurse darling, go and tell Marie to come, and I will talk to her and see what she has to say about a friendship between Monsieur de Guise and Monsieur l'Amiral.'

*

Catherine's benign expression hid the cynicism she felt as she witnessed the farce which was now being enacted before her.

The kiss of peace which Henry of Guise was giving Coligny! Her mind went back to a similar scene which had taken place six years before in the château at Blois. She herself had organized that scene and with the two same actors. Of course, at that time Guise had been a boy, completely without subtlety, unable to hide the blushes which rose to his cheeks, unable to quell the fire in his eyes. Then he had said: 'I could not give the kiss of friendship to a man who has been called my father's murderer.'

How the years change us! she thought. Now this Duke – no longer a boy – was ready to take the Admiral in his arms and plant on his cheeks the kisses of friendship, even while he was plotting to kill him.

'How good it is,' murmured Catherine 'when old enemies become friends!'

Madame de Sauves, who happened to be near her, whispered: 'Indeed yes, Madame.'

Catherine allowed herself to smile graciously on the woman. She was playing her part well with the bridegroom, playing both the seductress and the virtuous wife. Catherine had said: 'The Baron de Sauves would be proud of his wife if he could see the way in which she repulses that young rake of Navarre.' At which the woman had smiled demurely and lifted those wonderful blue eyes of hers to the face of the Queen Mother, as though asking for fresh instructions. But there were no further instructions ... yet.

Catherine was seriously worried. That old fool, the Cardinal of Bourbon, was hedging. He could not, he declared, perform the ceremony until he had the Pope's consent. And how could he receive word from the Pope when Catherine herself had arranged that no mail should come from Rome! She and Charles would have seriously to threaten the old man if he held out much longer.

He could be coerced, she was sure. He was getting old now, and, after all, he was a Bourbon. His brothers had not been noted for their strength. Both Antoine de Bourbon and Louis de Condé, brothers of the Cardinal, had been successfully tempted from the path of duty by members of Catherine's *Escadron*. Not that the Cardinal could be seduced in *that* way; but there were other methods.

And when he had consented, it would be necessary to let the people of Paris believe that the Pope had agreed to allow the marriage to take place. That would be simple.

But still she was worried. The grey shadow which haunted her life seemed more ominous than ever – that man who had been her son-in-law. In his gloomy *Escorial* he would be aware of all that was happening in France, and if he did not like what happened he would blame the Queen Mother. His ambassadors were spies and she was well aware that they sent long accounts of her activities to their master.

Alva had sent a special agent to inquire into her intentions. She admitted that in Spain's eyes she must appear as an enemy. There was an alliance with England, recently signed; she was trying hard to bring about the marriage of her son Alençon with Elizabeth of England; there were signs that Coligny had almost persuaded the King to keep his word and support the Netherlands against Spain and now there was the marriage of the Princess of France with the Huguenot Navarre. She doubted not that Philip of Spain was thinking of war ... war with France; and a war, with Spain's powerful armies and mighty armadas, was the bogey which haunted Catherine's days and nights. She saw in it disaster – disaster to herself and her sons, and that which she dreaded more than anything on Earth, the fall of the House of Valois. To keep her sons on the throne she had followed a devious policy, twisting this way and that in order to seize every advantage, never sure today which way she would go tomorrow, supporting Catholics, favouring

Huguenots, so that with good reason they likened her to a snake, with poisonous fangs, since, when she schemed for the sake of the House of Valois, she did not hesitate to kill.

She remembered a conversation which she had had at Bayonne, whither she had gone in great state to meet her daughter, the Queen of Spain; but more important than her encounter with her daughter had been that with the Duke of Alva, deputy for Philip, with whom she had had that important conversation.

Then it had been necessary to make promises, to declare herself a staunch Catholic, and she had begged Alva not to be misled when for purposes of policy she appeared to support their enemies. She had offered Alva the heads of all the Huguenot chiefs — but at the right moment. 'It must happen,' she had said, 'as though by accident, when they are gathered in Paris; for what reason, as yet we cannot say.'

She wanted this marriage between the King of Navarre and her daughter because she knew that any power she enjoyed in France must come to her through her children. In the event of a civil war, resulting in a victory for the Huguenots, the crown of France might be placed on the head of the Bourbon King of Navarre; the daughter of Catherine de' Medici would then be the Queen of France. Catherine need not, therefore, lose her position as Queen Mother. She would, naturally, do all in her power to prevent such a calamity overtaking the House of Valois; she would not hesitate to use assassins or the deadly *morceaux*. But it was well to consider all eventualities. Margot would not be so easy to control as Charles had been and as she hoped her beloved Henry would be; but she would still be Catherine's daughter. This marriage then was an insurance against possible future mishap, for Catherine had seen great Huguenot victories in her time; and the sight of all those followers of Coligny — Téligny, Rochefoucauld, Condé, and young Navarre — confirmed her opinion that she was wise in changing her course as it suited her.

The marriage must take place soon, although afterwards it would be imperative and urgent to pacify Philip of Spain; and if she were fortunate it might be that the murder of Coligny, whose death His Most Catholic Majesty had long desired, would be sufficient to satisfy him. And if not? Vividly there came to her memories of that conversation with Alva at Bayonne. '. . . the right moment . . . when all the Huguenots are gathered in Paris on some pretext or other . . .'

Was this the pretext? Was this the right moment?

*

The King was being dressed for the wedding, and there was a certain dismay among his friends and attendants, for his mouth was working in a way which all had seen before, and the whites of his eyes were shot with red. What would be the result of this wedding which was the talk of Paris, the talk of France?

'This wedding will be blood-red,' said the people of Paris. And the King knew that they whispered those words.

The Cardinal of Bourbon had been persuaded to perform the ceremony; he had been shown that he would find extreme disfavour in the eyes of the King and, what was more serious, in those of the Queen Mother if he did not comply with their wishes. Charles and his mother had had the news spread through Paris that the Pope's dispensation was in their hands. So there was nothing now to delay the ceremony.

So the King trembled, and as he was dressed in the most magnificent garments yet seen – for his clothes, with his jewelled cap and dagger, alone cost six hundred thousand crowns – those about him wondered how long he would be able to smother his smouldering madness and whether it would break out before the wedding was a *fait accompli*.

*

Busy as she was, Catherine found time to admire her darling. How beautiful he was! More beautiful than any, and more magnificent than the King himself. His dark beauty was set off by a hundred sparkling jewels; and he was as delighted with himself as his mother was.

Catherine admired the cap with its thirty pearls, each one weighing twelve carats. How soft the pearls looked in contrast with the sapphires and rubies and the hard glitter of diamonds – and how they became her darling!

She kissed him tenderly.

'If I could have one wish granted, my dear,' she whispered, 'it would be that you were King of France this day. To think that you were born one year too late hurts me deeply.'

'But one day, Mother ...' he murmured, his long eyes alight with ambition.

'One day, my darling. Your brother looks sickly today,' she added.

'He has looked sickly for so long.'

'Have no fear, my darling. All will be well.'

She smiled, but, in spite of outward calm, she was uneasy. She felt like one who, imagining herself to be a goddess, had stirred up a troublous sea, only to find that she was no goddess, but merely a frail human being in a flimsy craft. She was determined to steer to safety. Let them get the wedding over and then, as compensation, Philip should be offered Coligny.

'The marriage at least was not of my making,' she would say, as though to imply: 'And that other deed was. I did it to show you that I am your friend.' That would satisfy Philip. But would it? Fanatic he might be, but he certainly was no fool.

She was never one to think more than a move or two ahead, and today she must think only of the wedding and Coligny. After that? ... There were gathered here in Paris a mighty force of Huguenots and Catholics. She had said: 'When the time comes, I shall know what to do.' And she *would* know. She had no doubt of that. So much for the present.

*

The bride was haughty, pale-faced and sullen. She stormed at her women.

'I have prayed all these nights and days. I have begged the Virgin and the saints to help me. Is it all of no avail? It must be that this is so, for here is this most hateful day, the day of my wedding. I have spent my nights in weeping ...'

Her women soothed her. They knew that her nights had been spent in love-making with the Duke of Guise, but Margot often managed to convince others as she convinced herself. Now she saw herself as the reluctant bride, the tool of her brother and her mother, forced to marry a man whom she

63

hated. Did she hate Henry of Navarre? He was not without his attraction. She had felt mildly interested when he had cocked a shrewd eye at her and winked in an extremely vulgar and provincial manner. Perhaps she did not exactly hate him; but it was far more dramatic to hate than to feel mildly indifferent, therefore she must declare she hated Henry of Navarre.

For all her misery she could not help but delight in her own appearance. She touched the crown on her head. How well it became her! By this marriage she would be a Queen, and even her beloved Henry of Guise could not have made her a Queen; yet this coarse fellow whom she hated was a King. She put on her cape of ermine; then she stood still admiring herself while the blue cape glittering with the crown jewels was put about her. She looked over her shoulder at the long train which would need three to carry it – and they must be Princesses. Nothing else would be suitable for a Queen. She laughed with pleasure, and then remembered that she was a most reluctant bride.

The 18th of August, she thought, and my wedding day . . . the day I shall become the Queen of Navarre. She had left behind her that girl who had thought her heart was broken when they took her lover from her and married him to Catherine of Clèves. She thought fleetingly of that girl – only a little younger than the bride of today, but how different, how innocent! She wept a real tear for that girl, for now she recalled something of that desolation which had come to her when she had known that the dream of her childhood, that dream of marriage with the most handsome man in France, was ended. That girl was a charming, tragic ghost who watched the women preparing her for a wedding which would make her a Queen.

'Your Majesty, we must go,' whispered one of her women.

The ghost retired and the actress was there in her place. 'You are premature,' she said coldly. 'I am not yet a Queen to be addressed thus.'

The girl's eyes filled with tears and Margot kissed her.

'There, let there be no more tears. Those I have already shed will suffice.'

As she walked along the platform which was draped with cloth of gold and which led from the Bishop's Palace to Notre

Dame, she held her head high. She could see the masses of people below, and she knew that many were dying of suffocation in that crowd, and that before the ceremony was over many would be trampled to death. And all for a glimpse of a royal wedding, and in particular for a bride who was noted not only for her beauty, but her profligacy. She knew what they would be saying about her, and yet they would not be unkindly. They knew of her love affair with their hero, and the Catholic population would murmur together because she was being married, not to Catholic Henry of Guise, but to Huguenot Henry of Navarre. There would be coarse jests about her. She could imagine their saying:

'Oh, it was not only Monsieur de Guise, you know. There was Monsieur d'Entragues and a gentleman of the King's body-guard, Monsieur de Charry. Some say there was also the Prince de Martigues.'

It seemed impossible to keep one's affairs from the public. Were the walls of the châteaux no protection at all?

Ah well, she would amuse them; and the people of Paris loved those who amused them – although they might not be pleased with her infidelity to their beloved Duke.

Yes, Margot had no doubt that she was providing gossip for the streets and markets of Paris today.

They did not enter the church, because it had been agreed that the bridegroom should neither hear Mass nor cross the threshold of Notre Dame for the ceremony; the crowd murmured loudly at this and there were jeers and cries of 'Heretic!' But it was soon seen that it was more interesting to have the ceremony performed outside the church than inside, since it could be seen by more people. So, before the western door of the church, Margot knelt by the side of Henry of Navarre.

The bridegroom looked handsome enough, magnificently attired as he was, but his bride was quick to notice the lack of elegance to which she was accustomed in the gentlemen of the court and which even cloth of gold and jewels could not give. He wore his hair *en brosse, à la Béarnais*; no delicate perfume hung about the man; and yet with his lazy smile and his cynical eyes he was not altogether unattractive.

But as she knelt beside him, Margot caught sight of her

lover, and it seemed to her that never had he looked so handsome as he did today. She knew that the shouts of enthusiasm which she had heard as they walked along the platform had not been so much for her and her bridegroom as for her lover. In his ducal robes he was magnificent. He towered above those about him, and the August sunshine turned his hair and beard to a ruddy gold. Memories came back to Margot and she was once more a broken-hearted girl. Oh, why had they not married her to the man of her choice? If they had let me marry Henry of Guise, she thought, there would have been none but he. D'Entragues and de Charry and even the Prince of Martigues – what did I care for them? It was only because my heart was broken and they had taken my true love away that I turned to them.

How distasteful was this man beside her! She would not marry him. She belonged to the golden giant, the beloved of the Parisians. He had been her first love and he would be her last.

The ceremony had begun. Henry of Navarre had taken her hand.

I will not. I will *not*! she thought. Why should I not marry whom I choose? Why should I be forced to a marriage with this oaf? I will have Henry of Guise. I will have none of Henry of Navarre.

They were waiting for her responses and she felt the silence all about her. She must say that she agreed to marry the man beside her. But mischief had caught her; her love of drama overcame everything else. The whole of Paris should know that at the very last moment she had refused to marry the man they had tried to force on her.

The Cardinal was repeating his questions. Margot's lips were tightly pressed together. I will not. I will *not*! she thought.

Then from behind she felt a hand on her head.

'Speak!' said the savage voice of the King in her ear, and defiantly she shook her head.

'Fool!' went on Charles. 'Bend your head or I will kill you.' He roughly forced her head forward; and she heard him mutter to the Cardinal: 'That's good enough. The nod will do.

Our bride is too shy to speak. The nod means that she agrees.'

But many had seen what had happened, and they marvelled at the courage of the Princess; and so the ceremony proceeded while the bridegroom turned his cynical smile upon his bride.

*

Now for the rejoicing, the feasting, the balls and the masques.

Coligny longed for the quiet of his home at Châtillon. How he wished that he might join his family, even while he knew he must stay in Paris! He reproached himself, reminding himself that he should be grateful that his influence with the King had been rekindled.

As soon as was possible he escaped from the tumult and the lavish shows to his apartment, there to write a letter to Jacqueline.

'Dearest and well-beloved Wife,' he wrote, 'today was completed the marriage of the King's sister with the King of Navarre. The next three days will be passed in pleasure, in banqueting, masques, ballets and tourneys; after which the King, so he assures me, will give up several days to the hearing of divers complaints which arise in many parts of his kingdom. I am therefore constrained to labour to the utmost of my power; and although I have the greatest wish to see you, I think we should both of us feel a strong remorse if I failed in my duty. But I shall get leave to go forth from the city next week. I would far rather be with you than sojourn at the court, but we must think of our people before our private happiness. I shall have other things to tell you when I see you, the which joy I desire night and day.

'And now dearest and well beloved, I pray God to have you in His keeping.

'Written at Paris this 18th day of August, 1572. Rest assured that amid all these feastings and gaiety, I shall not give offence to any — least of all to God.'

As he sat alone, he could hear the music from the palace, the laughter and the singing. From the streets he could hear the sounds of the roystering of the people, and the air seemed full of their shouting.

＊

Catherine noticed the absence of Coligny. Our revels give such a pious man little delight, she thought. She knew that he was in his apartments writing – doubtless to his equally pious wife. That matter should be discovered later. It would be amusing to read the love letters of such a man. Well, let him write as long a letter as he pleased and as full of passion as he could manage. With luck it would be the last he would write.

She watched the ballet. Margot was dancing with the Duke of Guise, and Henry of Navarre with Charlotte de Sauves. Catherine could not help smiling cynically as she surveyed those four. Well, one thing was certain: neither bride nor bridegroom was in a position to blame the other for infidelity. The cynical pair! It was perfectly obvious that they were both considering the violation of their marriage vows on the very night of their wedding! It was a situation worthy of the pen of Boccaccio or of Margot's namesake, that other Queen of Navarre.

For a few days she could rest content. The marriage was effected. In the remote possibility of a Huguenot ascendancy over Catholics and a suppression of the House of Valois by that of Bourbon, she would have a daughter who was Queen of France. She had managed to get a foot in both camps – she would be the Queen Mother whether Catholic Valois or Huguenot Bourbon sat on the throne of France.

As for Philip, he must have Coligny. The Governor of Lyons had been instructed not only to let no mail into France, but to let no mail out. Philip and the Pope should not know that the wedding had taken place until she could also send the news of the Huguenot leader's death.

Imperceptibly, she lifted her eyebrows, for Coligny had entered the great hall.

Catherine made her way to him.

'Dear Admiral, how delighted I am to see you join our foolish revels. They are gay and a little silly, are they not? But I doubt not that you were amused by such things when you were the age of these young people – just as I was. It is pleasing to see our young pair so fond – so charming, is it not? And, Admiral' – she laid her delicate white hand on his arm – 'Admiral, I know you pray with me that this marriage will bring to an end the strife in our land.'

'Amen, Madame,' said Coligny.

'I rejoice to see the influence you have with my son. His Majesty, I know, consults you in all things. Ah, my dear Admiral, you have a mother's gratitude. Promise me you will stay with us ... stay long and use your benign influence to bring peace to our land.'

She looked up into the noble face, at the widely set eyes, the fine high brow, the firm lips and the clearly moulded features. It was, she thought lightly, his nobility of countenance which made the Admiral such a handsome man. I will send his head to Rome. It should arrive almost as soon as the news of the wedding.

*

They had been put to bed in royal state – the cynical groom and the indifferent bride. His Huguenot gentlemen had now retired; so had her Catholic ladies; and they were alone.

The candlelight flattered him, Margot thought; but she did not believe she could endure him near her. She did not wish those thick hands to touch her; the coarse hair reminded her of the soft natural curls of Henry of Guise by their very contrast. Why did he not use some perfume as he did not appear to be over-particular with his toilet?

He was watching her, determined to match her indifference with his own.

'Well, you see,' he said at length, 'the marriage did take place. I remember long ago, when we rode to Bayonne together, you pulled my hair and swore that you would die rather than marry me.'

'I am not sure,' she answered with a touch of melancholy, 'that I would not rather be dead than here at this moment.'

He laughed aloud. 'You . . . dead! And *before* the ceremonies are over!'

She laughed suddenly. 'Well, perhaps I should have said immediately after.'

Some understanding seemed to be established between them at that moment. She betrayed a humour which matched his, a humour so strong that she had been unable to suppress it and to play the role which she had planned for herself.

'I never saw one less melancholy than you in the dance this night.'

'I have learned to play many a part which has been forced upon me. Your pursuit of Madame de Sauves was disgraceful. It was noted, I assure you, by many. That is not a seemly manner in which to behave on your wedding night, Monsieur. At least not in Paris. Perhaps in your remote state of Béarn . . .'

'Which is now your state, Madame.'

'Perhaps in *our* remote state of Béarn, courtesy, elegance and the manners of a courtier do not count; but here in Paris, I would have you treat me with respect. I have become your wife.'

'Most reluctantly,' he reminded her.

'And Queen of Navarre.'

'Less reluctantly,' he put in, and she permitted herself to smile.

'I would have you know that this marriage ceremony of ours was, as far as I am concerned, performed but to please the King and my mother, and it is my wish that it should be a marriage of state only . . . by which I mean . . .'

'Your meaning is perfectly clear to me,' he said, resting on his elbow to look at her.

'I trust that you will respect my wishes.'

'Have no fear on that score, Madame. May I wish you goodnight?'

'Goodnight,' she said.

She was angry with him. He might at least have shown some sign of regret, even if he had made no attempt at persuasion; he had no manners; he was an oaf, a provincial. It was an insult to have married her to such a man even though he was a King.

She looked at the ornate curtains of the bed while she trembled with anger.

He said, after a pause: 'I perceive your inability to remain still, Madame. Should I attribute this to anger at my unworthiness to occupy this place in the bed, or may I put it down to your desire for me?'

'You may certainly not put it down to the latter,' she said sharply; but she was glad he had started to talk again.

'Do not be too harsh with me, I beg of you,' he pleaded. 'We of royal blood cannot choose our wives and husbands, and it is well to make the best of what are chosen for us.'

'Make the best! What do you mean?'

'To smile instead of fume. To enjoy friendship, since love is out of the question.'

'So you feel friendship for me?'

'If you will but extend the hand of friendship, I shall not refuse it.'

'That,' she agreed, 'would, I suppose, be better than being enemies. But is friendship possible between us? We are of different faiths.'

He lay back on his satin pillow and folded his arms behind his head. 'Faith?' he said with a laugh. 'What has faith to do with us?'

She sat up startled. 'I do not understand you, Monsieur. You are a Huguenot, are you not?'

'I am a Huguenot,' he said.

'Then you know what I mean by faith.'

'I am a Huguenot,' he continued, 'because I am my mother's son. My dear Marguerite, had you been her daughter, you would have been a Huguenot. Had I been your father's son I should have been a Catholic. It is as simple as that.'

'No,' she said, 'some change their faiths. Your mother did. Why, even Gaspard de Coligny was a Catholic once.'

'These fanatics may change their faiths; but, my dear wife, such as you and I were not meant to be fanatics. We are not unlike in our love of life. We mean to enjoy it, and faith can stand in the way of enjoyment. So our faith is a little thing. You are a Catholic; I am a Huguenot. What of it? You know what you want from life and you get it. I am the same. Our faiths are not our lives, Marguerite. They are things apart.'

'I have never in the whole of my life heard any talk thus!' she declared. 'Is this the Huguenot way?'

He laughed. 'You know better than that. Why, they are more fanatical than the Catholics, if that be possible. It is just *my* way . . . and perhaps yours.'

'But I had thought you . . . as the son of your mother . . .'

'I am many men, Marguerite. I am one man to the King, another to your mother, and yet another to Monsieur de Coligny; and ready to be yet another to you, my friendly wife. You see, when I was a baby I had eight different nurses and was reared on eight different kinds of milk. There are eight different men inside this body, which alas! does not find favour in your sight. I am sorry for your sake that I am not as tall and handsome as Monsieur de Guise.'

'And I am sorry I do not possess the blue eyes and golden hair of Madame de Sauves.'

'It is true yours are black,' he said with mock regret. 'Yet,' he added maliciously, 'they are not unattractive. But we stray from the point. We talk of lovers and I would speak of friends.'

'You are suggesting that as I cannot love you as a husband I might as a friend?'

'I am suggesting that it would be folly for us to work against each other. I am the King of Navarre; you are the Queen. We should be allies. You, as a good wife, should watch my interests; as a wise wife you should do this, because, my dear Margot, my interests happen to be yours from this day on.'

'Interests?'

'Oh, come! You know we live in a web of intrigue. Why have your brothers and mother brought me here?'

'In order that you might marry me.'

'And why should they wish for this marriage?'

'Surely you know . . . to unite Huguenots and Catholics.'

'Is that the only reason?'

'I know of no other.'

'And if you did, would you tell me?'

'That would depend.'

'Yes. It would depend on whether it was to another's interest

72

that I should be told. But your interest is my interest now, my Queen. If I lose my kingdom, you lose yours.'

'That is true.'

'Then you will help me to preserve that which you share with me?'

'Well,' she said, 'I think I might.'

'You will find me a lenient husband. It is necessary, of course, that we should stay together this night – the etiquette of your royal house demands it – or, in my leniency I should leave you. But it is only one night in our married life. You understand me?'

'You mean that I shall not interfere with you nor you with me. That seems sound enough.'

'Ha,' said the King of Navarre, 'if all people were as sensible there would be many more happy marriages in the land. I will make no attempt to stop your friendship with Monsieur de Guise, but you, while so fondly admiring his handsome person, his charming manners, and his elegance, will remember, will you not, that the gentleman, while the friend of the Princess Marguerite, might well be the enemy of the Queen of Navarre?'

She answered coldly: 'Madame de Sauves has beautiful eyes; she has charming golden hair; but you know, do you not, that she is my mother's chief and most trusted spy?'

He took her hand and pressed it. 'I see that we understand each other, my dear wife.'

The candles guttered as she murmured: 'That is a great consolation.'

He answered: 'There might be other consolations.'

She was silent and he leaned over her to kiss her.

'I would rather you did not,' she said.

'Believe me, it was merely a matter of etiquette.'

Margot laughed. 'Some of the candles have gone out,' she said. 'In the dimmer light you seem different.'

'And you, my love,' he told her.

They were silent for a while and he moved closer.

'On my part,' she told him, 'it would merely be because we are a King and Queen and etiquette makes its demands upon us.'

'And for mine,' he replied, 'it would be because I find it so ungallant to be in bed with a lady and resist ... the demands of gallantry, you understand?'

She moved away, but he had caught her.

He whispered: 'The gallantry of Béarn and the etiquette of France ... together, my love, they are irresistible.'

Two

In the Louvre the ballets and masques continued. Outside the common people gathered in groups. They looked up at the lighted windows and said: 'What does it mean? Huguenots and Catholics dance together; they join hands; they sing; they watch the same tourneys, the same nymphs and shepherds. They are joined in amity . . . and yet, what does it mean?'

The days were hot; there was not a breath of wind. When it was dark the stars seemed big in the sky; and all through the night the sounds of revelry could be heard throughout the city. People danced in the streets and when they were exhausted lay on the cobbles, since Paris could not provide beds for so many visitors. It was all gaiety and celebration and yet there was hardly a person in the city who did not feel that there was something false, a little unreal, about these wedding festivities.

Least concerned of any was perhaps the bride. She danced wildly; she seemed more fascinating than ever, more alluring; the reluctant bride enjoying her role, too absorbed in her own affairs to think of anything that might be happening about her.

She was the most enchanting figure in that ballet which Henry of Guise with his two brothers and sisters had devised for the entertainment of the court. 'The Mystery of the Three Worlds' they called it, and it was a brilliant charade into which they had infused a certain mockery, a certain defiance of their enemies. Henry of Navarre and that other Henry, the Prince of Condé, had been dressed as knights and had been shown as entering Paradise, where they found among others such beauteous nymphs as Marguerite, the bride, and Charlotte de Sauves. They danced together rapturously to the applause of the onlookers; but it seemed that this was not the end of the ballet, for quite unexpectedly the King and his brother Anjou appeared, more richly dressed than Navarre and Condé, and there was a mock battle between the four knights which Navarre and Condé realized they must lose, for none – even in play – must overcome the King of France. And so Navarre and Condé were driven from the women; and there appeared numbers of courtiers dressed as devils who made sport with Navarre and Condé and drove them into the company of more courtiers in similar dress; curtains were parted to show a great fire, and it was understood immediately that the Huguenot Princes had been driven to Hell.

The Catholics cheered wildly as the King and Anjou danced with the ladies while the 'devils' pranced wildly about the bewildered Navarre and Condé, prodding them towards the fire.

The Huguenots watched in silence and with apprehension. Only the King of Navarre seemed to be enjoying himself, having a riotous time in Hell, trying to fight his way back to Paradise and almost succeeding in wresting Madame de Sauves from Anjou and carrying her to Hell with him.

Afterwards, dancing with Henry of Guise, Margot said to him: 'You spoil the fun with such masques as that.'

'Nay,' said Guise. 'All enjoyed it.'

'The Catholics jeered,' said Margot, 'but the Huguenots were uneasy.'

'Then perhaps they will change their ways before they are driven to Hell in very truth.'

'I wish that you were less of a fanatic. Fanaticism is folly.'

He looked at her sharply. 'Who has been counselling you?'

'No one. To whose counsel do you think I would listen? I am sickened by this strife between Huguenots and Catholics.'

'Not long ago you were a firm Catholic. Has this marriage of yours anything to do with the change?'

'I am still a firm Catholic, and my marriage has not changed me in the least.'

'Are you sure of that? It seems to me that you do not view your husband with the same disfavour.'

'What is the use now that I am married to him? You are jealous?'

76

'Maddeningly. What do you imagine my feelings have been these last days and nights?'

'Ah!' sighed Margot. 'It was when I looked at you that I could not make the responses.'

'I know.'

'Henry, do something for me.'

'Anything in the world.'

'Then stop this baiting of Huguenots. Let us be peaceful for a change. That stupid masque of the Three Worlds, and that one in which you made my husband and Condé Turks and my brothers Amazons to beat them in battle . . . in such you go too far. All remembered how the Turks were beaten at Lepanto, and they knew what insults you intended to convey. It is tasteless and inelegant.'

'Marriage has made you tender to these Huguenots.'

'Huguenots! Catholics! Let us think of something else. But you cannot, can you? Even now when you talk to me, talk of love, your thoughts are elsewhere. Do I not know it? What are you thinking of? What are you hatching?'

She had moved closer to him and as she looked up into his brilliant eyes, just for a second she saw distrust in them. They had been passionate lovers; but although he desired her as she desired him, he would not trust her with his secrets, for now she was the wife of a Huguenot, and nothing – desire, passion, love – could make him forget that the Huguenots were his bitterest enemies.

'I am thinking of *you*,' he said.

She laughed, a trifle scornfully. Still, he was very handsome and to be near him was to realize afresh his charms; his vitality matched that of her husband, but how different he was. He was beautiful, elegant; he moved with grace; his manners were perfect; he was skilled in chivalry. How could she compare such a man with her coarse provincial husband, quick-witted and amusing though he might be? Henry of Guise and Henry of Navarre! As well compare an eagle with a crow, a swan with a duck. Henry of Guise was serious; Henry of Navarre careless. Henry of Guise looked for greatness and honour; Henry of Navarre for women to give him pleasure.

I cannot be blamed for loving Henry of Guise, thought Margot.

'I must see you alone,' she said.

'Why yes,' he answered, but his eyes had strayed beyond her, and she noticed that they had settled on someone in the crowd about the door of the hall. Angry jealousy beset her; but it was quickly turned into curiosity, for it was not a woman at whom he looked but a man whom she recognized as one of his old tutors, the Chanoine de Villemur.

The Chanoine's eyes met those of Guise, and the two men exchanged glances which seemed to Margot full of meaning.

'Well,' she demanded, 'when?'

'Margot,' he said, 'I will see you later. I must have a word with the old man over there. Later, my darling . . .'

She stood angrily watching him as he went across the hall. She saw him pause and mutter something to the old man before the two of them were lost in the crowd; but a few seconds later she saw the old man alone, saw him hesitate for a while and then slip quietly out of the hall; but although she looked for Henry of Guise she could not see him.

How dared he! He had made an excuse to leave her. Doubtless he had some assignation with a woman. That she would not endure. She looked about her and was faintly relieved to see Charlotte de Sauves chatting animatedly with Henry of Navarre.

*

When Henry of Guise left the Louvre he went hurriedly to the house of the Chanoine de Villemur, which was situated nearby in a narrow street leading to the Rue Béthisy, where Coligny had his house.

Guise let himself into the house, shut the door quietly behind him and mounted the wooden staircase.

In a candlelit room several members of his family were waiting for him; among these were his brothers, the Duke of Mayenne and the Cardinal of Guise, and his uncle, the Duke of Aumale. There was a stranger with them, a dark, swarthy man, whose appearance suggested that he had recently undertaken a long journey.

'Toshingi has arrived,' said Mayenne, pushing the man forward.

Toshingi knelt and kissed the hand of the young Duke.

'Welcome,' said Guise. 'Did any see you enter Paris?'

'None, sir. I came disguised and in the dark.'

'You know what is expected of you?' asked Guise.

'We have told him,' said the Cardinal, 'that his victim is a man of some importance.'

'That is so,' said Guise. 'I will tell you more. The man you must kill is Gaspard de Coligny. Have you the stomach for the deed?'

'I have stomach for any deed you should command me to do, sir.'

'That is well. We are making careful provisions for your escape.'

'I thank you, sir.'

'The shooting will not take place from this house. Next door there is an empty house. If you wait at one of the lower windows you will catch him as he passes through the street on his way to the Rue Béthisy. It is imperative that you do not miss.'

'Sir, you know my reputation.'

'There is not a better marksman in Paris,' said Mayenne. 'We have the utmost confidence in you, Toshingi.'

'Thank you, sir. I shall see that it is deserved.'

'A horse will be saddled ready for you in the Chanoine's stables. Immediately after firing the shot you must, with all speed, make your way to the back of the house, over the low wall and into the stables. Now, let us go through to the empty house. Let us make sure that everything is in order so that nothing can stand in the way of our success.'

The small party descended the wooden staircase and went into the empty house next door.

*

The council meeting was over and the King wished for a game of tennis.

'Walk with me, Father,' he said to Coligny. 'Walk with me to the tennis court, and then go home and rest, for you are tired.

79

Guise and Téligny will join me in a game, will you not, my friends?'

Both Guise and Téligny expressed their delight to share a game with the King.

A group of gentlemen accompanied them to the courts and, after watching the game for a while, Coligny expressed his intention of returning to the house in the Rue Béthisy. Some dozen of his followers left with him.

Gaspard only vaguely heard their conversation as they walked behind him; he himself was in no mood for talk; the King, he guessed, was ready to grant his requests, but there were many of the councillors who were against him. He remembered the masques and ballets with their mockery of the Huguenots. It was clear enough that the new friendship which the Catholics in Paris had feigned to feel for the Huguenots during the celebrations of these nuptials, was an entirely false friendship.

He began to read one of the papers in his hand; he had moved a little ahead of his friends and was deep in the study of the papers when a sheet fell from the packet he carried and fluttered to the ground. He had no sooner stooped to pick it up than a bullet whizzed over his head and was embedded in the wall of one of the houses. He turned and saw a man at one of the windows of a nearby house. He pointed and as he did so another shot was fired; it carried off Coligny's finger, grazed his arm and became embedded in his shoulder.

He shouted: 'That house. Through that window.'

Some of his followers obeyed; others clustered about him. The sleeve of his jacket was saturated with his blood and he felt dizzy from its loss.

'The king . . .' he said. 'Tell him . . . at once . . .'

Merlin, one of his ministers, realizing that the Admiral was fainting from the loss of blood, put an arm about him.

'Let us get to your lodging,' he said. 'In all haste . . .'

'Ah,' murmured Coligny leaning against Merlin, 'this will be the work of the Guises. What a noble fidelity was intended when the Duke made his peace with me . . .'

Very slowly and now quiet painfully, the Admiral, surrounded by those friends who had not gone in search of the assassin, went into his house in the Rue Béthisy.

*

When the news was taken to the King, he was still playing tennis.

'Sire, the Admiral has been shot. It happened while he was on his way to his home. The shot came from an empty house.'

Charles stood still, clutching his racquet. He was afraid. He looked at Guise; the man was impassive, betraying nothing; he was aware of the anguish in Téligny's eyes.

'Sire, give me leave to go to him.' That was Téligny speaking.

Charles said nothing. He continued to stare before him. There was no peace anywhere. No one was safe. There was no peace.

'Shall I never have a moment's peace?' he sobbed.

'Sire, Sire, I beg of you . . . leave to go to him.'

'Go, go!' cried Charles. 'Oh, God in Heaven, what have they done to my friend?'

Guise was at his elbow. 'Sire, it would be well to send doctors. Something may yet be done.'

Charles' voice rose to a scream. 'Yes, yes. Send them all. Send Paré. Paré will save him. I myself will go. I . . .'

He was sobbing as he ran into the palace.

*

Catherine was sitting quietly in her apartments when Madalenna came running in with the news.

'Madame, the Admiral has been shot.'

'Shot?' she was exultant, but her eyes expressed horror, 'Madelenna, you lie. It cannot be.'

'Oh yes, Madame. He was on his way to the Rue Béthisy from the palace when a shot was fired through the window of an empty house.'

'But this is terrible.' She did not move; she was thinking: I will send the head to Rome. It should arrive almost as soon as

81

news of the wedding. 'And ... who fired the shot? Have you discovered that, Madelenna?'

'It is not yet known, Madame, but the house is next to that of the Chanoine of Saint-German l'Auxerrois, and the Chanoine was once a tutor of the Guises.'

'And ... have they caught the assassin?'

'I do not know, Madame.'

'Then go and see what you can discover. Go into the streets and hear what people are saying.'

Catherine was ready to meet the King when he came into the palace. His eyes were wild and she noted the familiar twitching of the lips, the foam on the mouth.

'Have you heard? Have you heard?' he shouted to his mother. 'They have tried to kill my dear friend, the Admiral. They have tried to kill the great Gaspard de Coligny.'

'If they have tried and failed, my son, let us be thankful. If he is not dead we must save him.'

'We must save him. Paré! Paré! Where is Paré? Do not stand staring at me, dwarf. Go ... go and bring Paré to me. Let all go ... All go and find Paré. There may not be a moment to lose. When you have found him send him to the house of the Admiral. Tell him to lose no time ... or he shall answer to me. Mother, I must go there at once. I must tell him to live ... to live ...'

'My son, you must calm yourself. You cannot leave in this state, my darling. You must be guided by me. Wait ... wait until there is more news. Send Paré by all means, but do not yet go yourself. You do not know how ill he is. Wait awhile, I beg of you. You cannot suffer more shocks this day.'

He was tearing at his coat; he was sobbing wildly. 'He was my father. I trusted him. They have killed him. He must have suffered cruelly. Oh my God, how he suffers. There will be blood ... *his* blood ...'

'And you must not see it,' soothed Catherine. 'Wait, my son. Ah, here is Paré. Paré, the King's orders are that you go immediately to the house of the Admiral and ... save his life. Go ... go at once.'

'Yes, Paré, go ... *go*! Do not delay, but go now.'

Catherine said to her dwarf: 'Call Madeleine and Mademoiselle Touchet. Tell them to come to the King's apartments at once.'

Between them they did their best to soothe the tortured King.

*

All the chief Huguenots were assembled at the house in the Rue Béthisy. Téligny, Henry of Navarre, the Prince of Condé, the Duke de la Rochefoucauld waited in an outer chamber. Nicholas Muss, Gaspard's oldest and most faithful servant, and Merlin, his minister, remained in the sick-room. A message had been sent to Montgomery at Saint-Germain. Outside the house a crowd of Huguenots were gathered; there were angry murmurings in that crowd and the name of Guise was repeated again and again.

A cheer of hope went up when Ambroise Paré, the greatest surgeon in Paris and a Huguenot, was seen hurrying to the house. The crowd parted to make a way for him.

'The good God aid you, Monsieur Paré. May you snatch the life of our great leader from these wicked men who would murder him.'

Paré said he would do his best and hurried into the house.

He found the Admiral very weak. The wound in itself did not appear to be a mortal one, but Coligny had lost a good deal of blood and there was a possibility that the bullet, which was lodged in his shoulder, might be poisoned.

Navarre and Condé, Téligny and Rochefoucauld followed Paré into the room.

'Messieurs,' said Paré, 'it may be necessary to take off the arm. If that could satisfactorily be done, the danger would be considerably lessened.'

Coligny had heard. 'If that is your opinion,' he said resignedly, 'then let it be done.'

Paré examined the arm more thoroughly, washing the stains away and prodding the tissue. He smiled. 'Not so bad as I at first thought,' he said. 'The arm is sound enough. If I remove what is left of the finger and extract the bullet, that may be all that is necessary.'

It was going to be an excruciating ordeal, for there was no

opium available, and Coligny must look on while Paré performed the operation with a pair of scissors. Muss and Téligny held the Admiral who, with his pale face and bloodless lips already had the appearance of a corpse; yet it was Téligny who groaned; it was Muss who sobbed.

'Have courage, my friends,' said the Admiral. 'The pain is not yet such as cannot be borne, and it will soon be over. All that comes to us is through the will of God.'

Merlin whispered: 'Yes, my friends. Let us thank God for sparing the Admiral's life, for sparing his head and his understanding, rather than reproach Him for what has happened.'

The stump of forefinger was at length amputated, and after several very painful attempts, Paré extracted the bullet. The Admiral lay back fainting in the arms of Muss and Téligny. He longed for unconsciousness to escape the pain, but he had disciplined himself for so long, and the needs of his body had always been sacrificed for the good of the cause. He was afraid — not so much of his own sufferings, but of what this attempted assassination meant to all his friends and followers now assembled in Paris.

He murmured: 'I have now ... no real enemies ... but the Guises. But remember, my friends, it may not have been they who struck this blow. We must be sure before making accusations.

He heard a murmur about him. Someone said: 'We will go and kill the Guises. Shall they escape punishment for what they have done to the Admiral?'

Coligny tried to lift a hand and groaned. 'Nay ... I beg of you. No bloodshed ... now. That would indeed be the ruin of France.'

Paré whispered: 'Leave him now. He must rest.'

All left but Téligny, Muss, Paré and Merlin.

There were moments during that pain-racked morning when Coligny could not remember where he was. At one time he thought he was at Châtillon with his first wife, and that Andelot had just been born. Then the child seemed to be François, not Andelot. Now he was hearing of the death of that other Andelot. Then he was with Jacqueline and Jeanne of Navarre in his rose gardens.

'Rest, rest!' begged Paré. 'That is what you must do. You are strong, Monsieur l'Amiral, but you need rest for you have lost much blood.'

But the Admiral could not rest; and when those staunch Huguenots, and Maréchal de Cossé with Damville and Villars, called to see him, he remembered what had been worrying him.

'I am afraid, my friends, afraid, but not of death.' And then it seemed to him that his dazed consciousness was granted clarity. In his mind's eye he saw the young King, the bewildered madness in his eyes, and holding him by the hand was the woman in black with the smiling, evil face.

He must warn the King. That was what he had to do. He must free the King from her whom he knew to be his evil influence.

'I am not afraid to die,' he said, 'if die I must. But before doing so I must see the King. It may be that some will try to keep him from me. But my greatest wish is that I may see the King before I die . . . and see him alone.'

*

Charles waited in gloomy apprehension for something to happen. His mother refused to leave him; he knew that she was determined that he should do nothing without her consent.

His first visitors were the King of Navarre and the Prince of Condé, who had come to the Louvre direct from the Admiral's bedside.

'What news? What news?' demanded Charles.

'Bad news, Sire.'

'He is . . . dead?'

'No, Sire, but badly wounded. Monsieur Paré thinks that there may be a faint hope that he will pull through. But he has lost much blood.'

'Thank God he is not dead,' said Catherine.

The King wept. 'It is I who am wounded,' he moaned.

'It is the whole of France,' said Catherine. 'Ah, Messieurs, who is safe? They will come and attack the King in his own bed soon.'

Her eyes were on her shuddering son. Leave this to me, said those eyes. You are in danger, but all will be well if you leave this to me.

'Sire,' said the Prince of Condé, 'we found the gun in that empty house. It was still smoking. And it belonged to one of the guards of the Duke of Anjou.'

Catherine gasped. 'It must have been stolen,' she said. 'And to whom does this house belong?'

'I do not know, Madame, but what we have discovered is that it was next door to that of the Chanoine de Villemur.'

'And how did the assassin get away?'

'The doors of the Canon's stables were open; a horse must have been ready saddled and waiting for him.'

The King cried out: 'The Canon is the servant of the Guises. I'll have their heads. They shall not escape my vengeance. Go now. Bring the Canon to me. Bring the Duke and his uncles and his brothers. They are the leaders. The people of Paris shall see what happens to those who harm my friends.'

'The people of Paris,' said Catherine ironically, 'would not stand by and see Your Majesty harm *their* friends. Your Majesty is overwrought by this terrible tragedy. Let us be calm. Let us wait and see what happens, and meanwhile we will pray for the Admiral's recovery.'

'Madame,' said Henry of Navarre, 'my cousin Condé and I feel that trouble might be avoided if we left Paris for a while.'

'No,' cried the King. 'You will stay.'

Catherine smiled. 'My lords, we could not let the new bridegroom leave us. Why, the marriage is only a few days old. You must stay with us for a little while yet.'

She heard the sound of voices in an outer chamber and sent an attendant to see who had come and what fresh news had been brought.

Damville and Téligny were ushered in.

'The Admiral?' cried Charles.

'He is resting peacefully, Sire,' said Téligny, 'and he has asked if you would do him the great honour of calling on him, since he is unable to come to you.'

'That I will!' cried the King; and Catherine knew that she

could do nothing to stop him. 'I will come this instant.'

Téligny said: 'Sire, he has asked that you shall come alone.'

Catherine put in quickly: 'We shall accompany the King – his brothers and I, for we are as anxious as he is to tender our best wishes to the admiral in person.'

Charles wanted to protest, but Catherine had already ordered that Anjou and Alençon should be sent to her; and when the party set out she arranged that it should be followed by a group of noblemen, all of whom had worked against Coligny; and so the Maréchal de Tavannes, the Duke of Montpensier, the Count of Retz and the Duke of Nevers, with certain gentlemen of their suites, followed the King's party to the house in the Rue Béthisy.

Catherine was uneasy. She was aware of the murderous looks which were thrown at her train by the groups of people in the streets, and she knew that their anger was directed against herself more than any other; she caught those words which she had heard so many times during her life in France – Italian Woman – and she was well aware of the suspicion which they were meant to convey. She heard the name Guise again and again. If the Admiral died, the Huguenots, she was sure, would rise against the Catholics. She heard the jeers directed against her beloved son. Pervert! they called him. Murderer! Italian! She was glad that a strong Catholic party followed close behind.

As they came nearer to the Rue Béthisy they found that the crowd was more dense. It had formed outside the Admiral's house as though to protect him from further attempts on his life. These were the Huguenots who had come to Paris for the wedding. Who would have thought there could be so many? The royal House of Valois and, above all, the King and the Queen Mother were in danger.

As Catherine and their followers passed through the lower rooms of the house the Protestants who were assembled there showed them little respect.

'My friends,' said Catherine, 'we pray with you for the recovery of this great good man. Let us pass, for our beloved Admiral himself has asked us to come.'

They made way suspiciously, and the King went straight to the Admiral's bed, where, kneeling, he wept bitterly.

'Sire,' said Gaspard, 'you are kind indeed to come to me.'

'Oh, my Father,' sobbed Charles, 'you have the wound but I have the perpetual pain. Do not call me Sire. Call me Son, and I will call you Father. I swear by God and all the saints that I will renounce salvation if I do not take such vengeance on those who have brought you to this pass ... such vengeance, my Father, that the memory of it shall never fade.'

'Speak not of vengeance, my dear Son,' said the Admiral with tears in his eyes. 'My regret is that my wounds should deprive me of the great happiness which working for you can give me.'

Catherine was now standing by the bed and Gaspard was aware of her. She seemed to him like a black vulture who waited eagerly for his death.

'Oh, my Son,' he said, 'people have tried to tell you that I am a disturber of the peace, but I swear before God that all my life long I have been Your Majesty's faithful servant. God will decide between me and my enemies.'

'My Father, you shall not die. I will not allow it. I am the King ... remember that.'

'There is a greater King than you, Sire, and it is He who decides such matters. But I must speak to you.' He looked imploringly at Catherine, who smiled gently, refusing to see the plea in his eyes.

'I was always faithful to your father,' said Gaspard to Charles, 'and I will be to you. And now I feel it my duty – it may be my last duty – to implore you not to lose the great opportunity which will mean the salvation of France. The war in Flanders has already begun. You must not disown it; if you do you forfeit peace in your kingdom. You expose France to great dangers. Purge your council of the servants of Spain, Sire.'

'Dear Admiral,' said Catherine, 'you excite yourself. You must not, for Monsieur Paré's orders are that you should rest.'

'She is right,' said the King. 'You must not disturb yourself, dearest friend.'

'Sire, Sire, you must not break your promises. Every day your promises to bring peace to our provinces are broken.'

'Dear Admiral, my mother and I will put that right. We have already sent our Commissioners into the provinces to keep the peace.'

'That is so, Monsieur l'Amiral,' said Catherine. 'You know it is true.'

'Madame,' said Gaspard, 'I know it is true that you have sent Commissioners into the provinces who are offering rewards for my head.'

'Do not be distressed,' said Catherine as the King looked at her with horror. 'Others who are above suspicion shall be sent.'

'You are so hot,' said Charles, touching the Admiral's brow. 'This talk does you no good. I will do all you ask and, in return, you must do what I ask, which is that you should rest. You must get well.' He called to Paré to bring the bullet which had wounded the Admiral. 'I would like to see that villainous object,' he said.

It was brought and the King stared at it, his lips twitching. Catherine took it and weighed it in her white hand.

'Such a little thing to do so much harm,' she said. 'How glad I am that it was extracted. Do you remember, Monsieur l'Amiral, when Monsieur de Guise was shot near Orléans? Of course you do. Who does not remember the death – some call it murder – of that great man? The doctors told me at the time that, even though the bullet was poisoned, if it had been removed there might have been a chance of saving the life of Monsieur de Guise.'

The King kept staring at the bullet. He demanded to see the Admiral's coat.

'Do not look at it, my son,' warned Catherine.

But he stubbornly demanded that it should be brought, and when he saw the bloodstains on the sleeve be began to sob.

'Let us return,' said Catherine. 'No good can come of such weeping.'

'My Father,' cried the King, 'you must come with us. You shall have the apartments next to mine own. I will look after you. My sister of Lorraine shall give her apartments to you. Please! I insist.'

But Gaspard refused. He must cling to life. He must fight death with all his might, for his work was not finished. Should he go to the Louvre to walk into a trap? Should he expose himself to the woman in black – the Italian woman – who was now eagerly urging him to accept the King's invitation?

Paré came hastily forward and said that the Admiral could not possibly be moved.

'Very well,' cried the King. 'I will have this house surrounded by followers – your followers, my Father. You shall rest in peace and safety while I find those who sought to murder you, and do to them what they would have done to you.'

He rose, but Gaspard whispered: 'Sire, stay awhile. I greatly wish . . . I greatly desire . . .'

'Speak, dear Father. Any wish of yours shall be immediately granted.'

'It is that I may speak with you alone.'

Charles looked at his mother. She smiled, bowing her head, but she was furious. The very thing which she had determined to avoid had happened.

'Come, Monsieur Paré,' she said. 'You and I will wait outside.'

When they were alone the King knelt by the bed.

'Speak to me, my Father. Tell me what it is that you wish to say to me.'

'Sire, I love you . . . not only as a King, but as my son in very truth.'

Tears poured down Charles' cheeks. He kissed the coverlet. He was beside himself; he could not stop thinking of the torn sleeve of the Admiral's coat and the stains of blood on it.

'Oh, my Father, what a terrible world it is we live in. You must not die. You must not leave me . . . for I am afraid.'

'You must not be afraid, my beloved son. You are the King of this realm and it is in your hands to save it from disaster. You must be strong. You must be brave. Calm yourself, dear Sire. Listen to me, for we may not have long together alone. Reign by yourself. Use your own judgement. There is one above all others whom you must not trust. This is hard for me to say, but I must say it.' He lowered his voice and whispered: 'Beware of

90

your mother. Do not trust her. Reign without her. Many of the ills which have come to our poor suffering country have come through her work. She is your evil genius, my son. You must escape from her. You are a man. You are of an age to govern. Be strong. Be brave. And pray God that you may receive His guidance in the difficult tasks ahead of you.'

'You are right,' whispered the King. 'I must rule alone. I must rule alone.'

'Be strong. Be worthy. Give freedom of worship to all. Do not use religion for reasons of state. Religion and diplomacy should be things apart. Keep your promises. Lead a good life and pray continually for the help of God. And above all, my son . . . above all . . .'

The King was sobbing now. 'Gaspard, my father, I cannot bear this. You talk as though you will never speak to me again.'

'Nay, it may well be that I shall recover. There is much life in me yet. Keep your promises to Orange. Remember you are in honour bound to do so. Do not follow your mother's guidance. Follow the word of God, never the example of Machiavelli. You can make your reign a good one, Sire, so that when you come to your last hours, you can thank God that He called you to rule this land.'

'I keep seeing the blood on your coat. Such rich, red blood. The blood of the greatest Admiral France has ever known. What shall we do without you?'

'Do not weep, I beg of you. I am still here. Remember . . . oh remember what I have said. And above all remember what I have said about . . . your mother.'

The door had opened quietly and Catherine was standing on the threshold watching them. The King caught his breath in fear. He knew that he was terrified of her and that she was the source of all his fear.

'This will never do,' said Catherine briskly. 'Our dear Admiral is worn out. He must rest. Come, Your Majesty must leave him now. Monsieur Paré, he is worn out. Is that not so?'

'He needs rest,' said Paré.

'Then leave me now, Sire,' said the Admiral.

'I will come again,' said the King; and he whispered: 'I shall remember all that you have said to me.'

On the journey back to the Louvre, Catherine seemed serene, but she was deeply aware of her son beside her.

*

No sooner were they back at the Louvre than she dismissed all attendants and shut herself in with the King.

'And what had our Admiral to say to you, my son?'

The King turned his tear-stained face away from her. 'It was between ourselves,' he said with dignity.

'Matters of state?' asked Catherine.

'Matters of state between a King and his Admiral, Madame.'

'I trust he was not urging you to folly.'

'Only to wisdom, Madame. I pray to God that he may recover, for what this land will do without him, I dare not think.'

'When one great man dies there is another to replace him,' said Catherine. 'Why, when one King dies there is another to take the throne.'

'Mother, I have much to do and I would wish to be allowed to proceed with it.'

'What did that man say to you?' she asked.

'I have told you it was a matter between us two.'

'You little fool!' she cried.

'It would be well for you to remember to whom you speak, Madame.'

'I do not forget. I speak to a man who is scarcely more than a boy, and who is so foolish that he allows his enemies to deceive him.'

'Madame, I have allowed you too much power ... too long.'

'Who said so?'

'I say so. I say so. I ...'

'You have never said anything but what you were told to say.'

'Madame, I will ... I will ...'

He faltered and she laid her hands on his shoulders. 'Do not hang your head, my son. Look into my eyes and tell me what you will do. Tell me what the Admiral ordered you to do . . .'

'He ordered nothing. He respects me as his King, as . . . as others do not. All I do, I do because I wish to.'

'So all that time you were alone with him he told you nothing, gave you no orders?'

'What was said was between us two.'

'You are bemused by all that piety. Did he say, "Pray for God's guidance, Sire, Pray, Pray."? Of course he did. And by God's guidance he means his own, for in the estimation of Monsieur l'Amiral, Monsieur l'Amiral is God.'

'You blaspheme, Madame.

'Nay, it is he who does that. What else did he tell you?'

'I wish to be left alone.'

'You saw what his enemies had done to him, did you not? How would you feel if his friends did the same to you? I heard what happened when they took off his finger. The pain of it! You have no idea. Two men had to hold him while Monsieur Paré got to work with a pair of scissors. You would never have been able to endure that, my son. And did you see the blood on his coat? He was but slightly wounded. Men have suffered more than that. Did you notice the scowls of the people as we passed along the streets to his house? Did you hear their murmurings? They murmured against me, did they not? But who am I? I am merely the mother. It is you at whom they would strike. Oh, what a dangerous world we live in! There is bloodshed all around us. Great men die. Kings die too; and as Kings live more grandly than ordinary men, so they die more fearfully.'

'Mother . . .'

'My son, when will you learn that you are surrounded by your enemies? How can you say, "This is my friend? . . ." How can you know *who* is your friend? This Admiral . . . this Huguenot . . . has no friendship to give you. He has only his faith. He would see you torn limb from limb for the sake of the Huguenots. He is a brave man; I grant you that. He does not care if he suffers . . . if he dies . . . for his cause. Do you think that, caring so little for himself, he would care for you? He would lead you to your death; he would run a sword through your heart . . . for the good of his cause. He would put you on the rack; he would stretch your limbs, break your bones . . . he would lop off your head for the sake of his cause.'

The King was staring straight in front of him and she laid a hand on his trembling arm. 'But the mother who bore you has a tenderness for you which none but a mother can feel. A King you may be, but you are still her son. You are the baby . . . the child she suckled at her breast. A mother never forgets that, my son. She would die for her children's happiness. And if they should be Kings, she is the only one they should trust. Others? What do they care? They care only for power. They would laugh to see you tortured. "The King is dead," they would say. "Long live the new King." Oh, you are a fool indeed to allow yourself to be deceived by a man who, great though he may be, has no thought but to see the Huguenots rule this realm . . . a Huguenot King on the throne. He will strive to put him there, even though he wades through your blood to do so. Tell me, what did he say to you? What advice did he give?'

Charles plucked at his coat with shaking hands. He turned his tortured eyes on his mother.

She embraced him tenderly. 'Tell me, my darling,' she whispered. 'Tell your mother what he said.'

'I cannot . . . I cannot . . . It was between us two.'

'Did he mention . . . your mother?'

The King glared at her in silence, his eyes bulging, his lips awry.

'What did he say of me, my son?' she coaxed.

'You torture me,' cried the King. 'Leave me. I would be alone.'

He flung her off, and throwing himself on to a couch began biting one of the cushions. 'I will not tell. I will not tell. Leave me. He was right when he said you were evil . . . my evil genius. He was right when he said I must rule alone. I will, I tell you. Leave me . . . Leave me . . .'

Catherine bowed her head; he had confirmed her suspicions. She called Madeleine and sent her to soothe the King. Anjou was waiting for her in her apartments. He had caught the general fear, for he had seen the looks which the people had cast at the royal party in the streets.

'Mother,' he said, 'what now?'

'The first thing we must do,' she said, 'is to kill off that tiresome Admiral, and without delay.'

'And how shall this be accomplished? He has a talisman . . . a greater magic than ours. It seems impossible to kill the man.'

'We will find a way,' she said grimly.

*

Charles, having recovered under the tender care of Madeleine, had made up his mind.

He had sworn to take revenge on those who had attempted to take the Admiral's life and he was determined to fulfil his oath.

Without consulting his mother, he ordered the arrest of several servants of the Guises, among them the Chanoine de Villemur.

'By God,' cried the King, 'if Henry of Guise is implicated, even he shall lose his life.'

Catherine sought an early opportunity to be alone with the King.

'Ah, my son,' she said sadly, 'how ill-advised you are to talk thus against Henry of Guise. Do you not yet know the power of that man? Had you talked thus at Blois or Orléans, Chambord or Chenonceaux, I should have said you spoke without thinking; but to utter such threats here in Paris is to commit the greatest folly. If you dared lay a hand on the Duke, you would have the whole city against you, for Paris does not follow you, it follows Guise. He has but to lift a hand and this city rallies to his cause. You may be King of France, but he is King of Paris.'

But the King would not be diverted from his purpose. He remembered the words of his friend, Coligny. He was going to avenge Coligny; he had sworn to avenge him, and if that meant the death of Guise, then it should be the death of Guise, no matter what the consequences.

She tried to reason with him. 'At such times as this we must resort to diplomacy. You can easily find a scapegoat for your Admiral. One of your brother's men would do very well as they say the gun belonged to one of his guards. The Chanoine himself . . . if you must. But, I warn you, if you wish to remain King of France, do not touch the King of Paris!'

'Madame,' said the King, in an unusually calm voice, 'my mind is made up.'

She smiled serenely, but she was far from serene.

She left the King and, dressing herself in the clothes of a market woman, she slipped into a little-known passage which led out of the Louvre, and made her way through the crowded streets to the Rue St Antoine. The atmosphere in the streets was unhealthy. Everywhere, it seemed, people were discussing the attempt on the Admiral's life – the Catholics with gratification, the Huguenots with horror. She slipped into a back entrance of the Hôtel de Guise and told one of the lower servants that she had a message for the Duke; she was amused to see that she was unrecognized.

'It is imperative that I see the Duke,' she said. 'I come from the Queen Mother.'

She was at length taken to the Duke, who was with his brother Mayenne; and when Henry of Guise saw who his visitor was he immediately dismissed all attendants.

As soon as the doors were shut, Catherine said: 'Are you sure that we cannot be overheard?'

'It is quite safe to speak, Madame,' said Guise.

She turned on him angrily. 'Here is a pretty state of affairs. It seems it would have been better to have employed the Duchess after all. That bungling fool should have his hands chopped off for this.'

'Your Majesty must realize,' said Mayenne, 'that it was no fault of the man's. A better shot does not exist in France.'

'Madame,' put in Guise, 'it was not his fault the Admiral stooped when he did. It was Fate.'

'Ah!' said Catherine, and her fingers closed over her bracelet. 'I have always feared that some great magic protects him. Why . . . why should he have stooped at that moment?'

'And merely to pick up a paper which had fluttered to the ground,' said Guise gloomily. 'But for that, he should no longer be troubled with him.'

'Listen,' said Catherine. 'The King has arrested some of your servants, as you no doubt have heard. That fool left his gun behind him. It is known that he escaped on a horse from one of your friends' stables. The King swears vengeance on you. You must leave Paris at once.'

Guise smiled. 'But, Madame, that would indeed be folly. Leave Paris now? That would be to admit our guilt.'

'I think,' said Mayenne, 'that Her Majesty has some plan to lay before us.'

'You are right. Matters cannot rest as they are. Those Huguenots stand about the streets muttering threats. They dared insult me when I was on my way to the Admiral's house. They simmer, Messieurs, and they are ready to boil over.'

'Let them,' said Guise, putting his hand on his sword. 'Let them boil all over Paris, and they will see what Paris thinks of them.'

'We cannot have civil war in Paris, Monsieur. I would wish this trouble to be put right before it grows beyond our control.'

Catherine's eyes were gleaming and there was the faintest colour under her skin. She saw now that the time had come, the moment for which she had said she would wait, when she had paced the gallery of the palace of Bayonne with Alva.

Here was the moment. It was inescapable. There must be no *fighting* between the Catholics and Huguenots in Paris. If there was, Guise would assume the role of King, and who knew what outcome that would have? Ironical it would be if the Catholics won and decided they would put their hero on the throne! He was a Prince; he had a slight claim. It might be that, in spite of the stoppage of the mail, the news of the Catholic-Huguenot wedding was already carried over the border and into Spain . . . into Rome. If what she planned could be brought to pass, she would have more heads than that of Coligny to send to Rome. And the news she would send would make both Philip and Gregory forget all about a mere marriage.

'I do not mean that you should leave Paris in *fact*, Messieurs. No. Pretend to leave Paris with the members of your family who are here with you. Ride out by the Porte St Antoine . . . ride a little way out . . . then assume a disguise and, at dusk, come riding back. Keep yourselves hidden for a little while . . . here in this house, so that none but your trusted followers know that you are here. I could not have you leave Paris, my friends, for you will be needed for the task which lies ahead of us.'

'And the task, Madame?' asked Guise.

'To rid France of these pestilential Huguenots for ever . . . and at one sweep.'

*

Later that day the city was seething with excitement. The Guises had left Paris! They had, it appeared, almost slunk out without ceremony and without followers, as though they were eager to escape from the city at the greatest possible speed. The Catholics were aghast; the Huguenots were jubilant. What could this mean, they asked each other, but that the Guises were in disgrace? The King then was siding with the Huguenots. If this were so, said the Huguenots, all that the Admiral had suffered was not in vain.

There was an incident in the Tuileries gardens; a Huguenot started trouble with a member of the King's Guard who had refused him entry, whereupon Huguenots rushed into the gardens and demanded justice. Téligny, with great wisdom, managed to avert disaster, but the tension had increased.

Catherine had now determined to act quickly. She called a meeting, but it was a secret gathering, and it took place in the shady alleys of the Tuileries gardens, whither her fellow conspirators came to join her and Anjou, who had her confidence in this matter. All these conspirators were Italian, and she had selected them because she believed that her fellow countrymen were more skilled in the art of murder than the French. There were Retz and Birago, those two whom she had set to tutor the King; Louis of Gonzaga, the Duke of Nevers; and the two Florentines, Caviaga and Petrucci.

'My friends,' whispered Catherine when they were all assembled, 'the Admiral must die and die speedily. You can see there will be no peace in this land until he is dead.'

It was agreed that what she said was true.

'And now,' she said, 'we must decide which are the best means to employ.'

And while she talked she was alert for the arrival of a man

whom she had employed more than once in delicate matters, and who, she had arranged, should on this occasion burst in on them with news of a plot which he had just discovered; for she had decided that she would need great justification for what she was about to propose, and the alleged discovery by this man would provide that justification.

His entrance was perfectly timed.

He had the alert eyes of the spy, this Bouchavannes. Installed in the house in the Rue Béthisy ever since the Admiral had been in Paris, it had been his duty to repeat to the Queen Mother all that he had heard and seen during his sojourn there. Now he had a startling story to tell. The Huguenots, he declared, planned revolt. They were going to rise and take possession of the Louvre, kill every member of the royal family, set Henry of Navarre on the throne of France and subdue the Catholics for ever.

'Messieurs,' said Catherine, 'now we know what we must do. There is only one path open to us.'

'What are Your Majesty's plans?' asked Retz.

Catherine replied calmly: 'To destroy, monsieur, not only the Admiral, but every Huguenot in Paris ... before they destroy us. We must preserve absolute secrecy. Only those who are with us and whom we can trust must know our plans. And, Messieurs, we must get to work at once, for there is little time to be lost if we would strike at them before they strike at us.'

'Madame,' Nevers reminded her, 'it would be necessary to obtain the consent of the King before such a matter could be undertaken. It must have a seal of authority. If Guise were in Paris we could rely on him to rally every Catholic in Paris to the cause.'

Catherine permitted herself a smile. 'Have no fear. Monsieur de Guise will be here at the right moment. As for the King, leave him to me. Monsieur de Retz, you were his tutor and you know him well. I may need your help in persuading him.'

'Madame,' said Retz, 'the King has changed. He is not the pliable boy we once knew. He is now obsessed by the idea of avenging the Admiral.'

'Then we must jerk him out of his obsession.' She turned her cold stare on Retz, and looked from him to the others. 'We must meet again. We must call together all those whom we can trust. I will see that Monsieur de Guise and his family are with us. As for the King – we must get to work on him at once.'

*

Together, Retz and Catherine worked on him; but the King showed unwonted determination, and the influence of the Admiral was aggravatingly apparent.

'Madame,' he shouted at Catherine, 'I have sworn to bring to justice those who would have murdered him, and this I will do.'

'You are a fool,' said Catherine. 'You do not know what he plans for you.'

'He is my friend and I trust him. Whatever happened, the Huguenots would never harm me. He is their leader and he loves me as a son.'

'He has bewitched you with his fine words.'

Retz said: 'Sire, you are misled by this man. He would sacrifice you if the need arose. You remember what I told you of atrocities committed by Huguenots against Catholics. Let me remind you . . .'

'There is no need to remind me. You may go, Comte. I have matters to attend to.'

The Comte hesitated, but the King was eyeing him sternly. Catherine signed to Retz to go, and when he had left, Charles turned to Catherine.

'You also, Mother,' he said; but Catherine was not going to be dismissed as easily as that.

'My dear son,' she said, 'I must speak to you of certain matters which are for your ear alone and which I would not discuss even before a faithful servant like the Comte de Retz. News has been brought to me – news of which you should be made aware at once.'

'And this news is?'

'Of a Huguenot plot to murder you.'

The King shrugged his shoulders impatiently. 'I have seen the Admiral. I know that he wishes me nothing but good. Would he allow such a plot to be made?'

'Yes, he would; and he is the ringleader. I see that you do not

100

believe your mother who has worked so assiduously for your good. Perhaps others may be able to impress you.' She pulled a bell rope and when an attendant appeared, asked that Bouchavannes should be sent to her.

'Bouchavannes?' said the King. 'Who is this?'

'A good friend to Your Majesty, and one who, at great peril to himself, took a post in the Admiral's house, that he might watch your interests. He will tell you what he heard while he was there.'

Bouchavannes entered.

'Ah, Monsieur,' said Catherine, 'I have brought you here that you may tell the King in person what you have discovered in the house of his enemy.'

Bouchavannes kissed the King's hand while Charles scowled at him.

'Speak, man,' growled the King.

'Your Majesty, there is a plot against your life. The Huguenots under the Admiral are about to rise. It is for this reason that they are here in Paris. They plot to take your family, to kill your mother, your brothers and sisters, in most brutal fashion. Yourself they will keep in confinement. They will tell the people that they are offering you a chance to keep the throne if you become a Huguenot. They will torture you; they will say it is to make a Huguenot of you, but it will not matter if you do change your religion, for they do not wish you to reign. They propose to set up their own King in your place.'

'It is a lie!' cried the King.

'I can only say, Sire, that this is what I heard in the Admiral's house where there were constant meetings and councils. I listened at doors. I kept my eyes and ears open . . . for love of Your Majesty and the Queen Mother who has always been my friend. Your Majesty, be warned in time.'

The King's fingers were twitching. 'I do not believe a word of this.' He turned to his mother. 'Ring for the guards. I will have him arrested. I will confront him with the Admiral and we will see if he can tell his lies then. Ring! Ring! Or shall I do it myself?'

Catherine signed for Bouchavannes to leave them; she herself restrained the King, but he struggled in her grasp and she was alarmed. He was not strong, but his strength seemed to grow when his mad moods were on him, and she noticed with dismay that one was threatening now. She must keep him balanced on the side of sanity that she might terrify him utterly and so make sure of his obedience to her wishes.

'Listen to me, my son. You give in too easily. Horrible death awaits you. That is true. The good God only knows what diabolical torture they are planning for you. All we know is this: it will be more terrible than that meted out to ordinary men. It is not every day that they have a King to torture. Oh, my darling, do not tremble so. Here, let me wipe the sweat from your poor brow. You must not give in. Do you think your mother will allow them to hurt her son, her little King?'

'How . . . could you stop them? They will kill you too.'

'No, my son. All these years since the death of your father, I have fought the enemies of our family. I . . . single-handed, a weak woman. Your brother was King until he died, poor boy; then you were King, and for twelve years I have kept the throne for you in difficulties and against odds such as you cannot yet understand. When my history is written it will be said: "There was a woman who lived for her sons alone. There is the most devoted mother the world has ever known, for in spite of plots and treachery, in spite of the suspicion of her own children, she won their rights for them, and she *held* their rights; she sacrificed her life for them." That is true, is it not, my son? Have you not been King since the death of your brother Francis? And that in spite of all the wicked men who have sought to dethrone you!'

'Yes, Mother, it is true.'

'Well then, will you not listen to your mother now?'

'Yes, Mother, yes. But I cannot believe that Coligny would be treacherous towards me. He is such a good man. He is so brave.'

'He is a good man according to his lights as a Huguenot. He is undoubtedly brave. But he is not your man, my son. To his enemies we know he is ruthless, and you, perforce, are his enemy.'

'No! I am his friend. He loves me as a son. He would not lie to me when it might well be that he is about to face his God.'

102

'He would think he did right to lie for the sake of his faith. That is his way, my son. It is the way of them all. Oh, be guided by your mother. Do not let them drag you from your family. Do not let them take you to the torture chambers, stretch your poor limbs, mutilate your dear body. I would not let Boucha-vannes tell you of all the things they threaten to do to you.'

'You know then! You . . . you must tell me.'

'It is better not to know, my son. If you are determined to sacrifice yourself and your family for the Admiral, then for the love of God do not ask me to tell you of the tortures they are preparing for you. Have you ever seen a man roasted to death over a slow fire? No. You could not face it. Have you ever seen flesh torn with red-hot pincers and molten lead poured into the wounds? Nay! You could never bear to see such things.'

'They have said . . . they will do . . . these things to *me*!'

She nodded.

'I do not believe it. Men like Coligny . . . Téligny . . . my dearest Rochefoucauld!'

'My darling, the mob takes matters out of the hands of such men. When the mob rises the leaders must give them a free hand with the prisoners. Do you remember Amboise and the executions there? I made you look on, did I not, because I wished you to know of such things. You and your brothers and sisters looked on and saw men's limbs cut off . . . saw them die a hundred deaths . . . quick and slow.'

'Do not speak of it!' cried the King.

He had flung himself down. He was biting his fists and she saw the saliva foaming at his lips. She did not want him to lose complete control, for then he demanded blood. She must keep him in a state of terror as he was at such times when he hovered between sanity and madness.

'Charles, control yourself. It is not too late. You have many friends. I have called some of them together. They are waiting to see you now.'

He stared at her with wide bewildered eyes.

'Your friends, my dear son,' she said, 'Those who would stand between you and the horrible fate these traitors are preparing for you. Pull yourself together, my dearest. We must fight this and we will emerge triumphant. Do you think your mother would let them hurt her boy? Already she has laid her plans against your enemies, and your friends are ready to help her. These traitors make plans; but the real friends of the King also make plans. Come, my darling. Get up.' She stroked his cheek with her fingers. 'There, that is better, is it not? Your mother, who has always protected you, has protected you now, and when I take you to the council who are now waiting for you, you will see gathered together the great men of France, all ready, with their swords at their sides, to fight the traitors who would harm their King. You will be heartened, dear son, by what you see. Will you come to the meeting now?'

'Yes, Mother.'

'And will you believe what I and my friends have discovered as a result of working unfalteringly for you?'

'Yes, Mother.'

'Come, my darling. We will rid you of that spell which your enemies have laid upon you.' He was faltering and she went on. 'It is difficult, I know. The Admiral has some magic to help him. He stooped at that moment when the shot was fired. His devils were at his elbow, you see. They are with him now. But we will fight them with magic of our own, my son; and you know this: there is some magic in a mother's love for her son, in the loyalty of good friends. That is good magic, and evil spirits are afraid of good.'

She was leading him to the door. He was now hypnotized by her as he had been so many times during his childhood. He did not trust her; she terrified him; but he had to follow her; he had to obey.

In the council chamber the first person he noticed was Henry of Guise.

Guise bowed low. 'I have returned, Sire,' he said, 'hearing that Your Majesty had need of my sword.'

His brothers and his uncles were there. They each had a few words to say on their loyalty to the King. They had risked his displeasure, they assured him, solely that they might be at hand if needed.

The King saw that the members of the council were all Catholics. They talked of the plot against the King and the royal family which, so they said, had been discovered by their spy.

They talked of the need for immediate action; they but asked the consent of the King.

Charles looked round at the group of men and wanted to fling himself on to the floor and give way to the paroxysm that he felt was so close. He wanted to lose consciousness of reality, in his mad, fantastic world. He did not know how long he would be able to restrain himself. He felt the mad pumping of his heart; it was difficult to breathe. And as he stood there, he thought of the stern yet kindly face of the Admiral, of the last words he had spoken to him: 'Beware of your evil genius . . .'

And there, close to him, stood this evil genius . . . his own mother, her eyes large, the largest things in the room . . . so large that he could not escape from them; and as he looked at them he seemed to see there all the horrors of which she had talked to him; it seemed to him that he was not in this room, but in the torture chambers; they had taken off his clothes; they were putting him on the rack; and the torturer was bending over him. The torturer had the stern and noble face of Gaspard de Coligny.

He heard his own voice; it sounded faint, but that was only because of the pounding of the blood in his head which made such a noise; he knew that he was shouting.

'By the death of God, since you have decided to kill the Admiral, then I consent. My God . . . but then you must kill every Huguenot in France, so that none is left to reproach me with that bloody deed after it is done!'

He was aware of his mother's triumphant smile. He turned from her. He was trembling violently and the foamy saliva spattered his velvet jacket.

He stared at Catherine. His evil genius! 'This is your wish!' he said. 'To kill . . . kill . . . kill!' He ran to the door of the chamber. He shouted: 'Kill . . . kill then . . . kill them all. That is it. Death . . . blood . . . blood on the cobbles . . . blood in the river . . . Kill them all, for that is what you wish.'

He ran sobbing to his apartments while the councillors looked from one to another in dismay. They had rarely seen even the King in such a sorry state.

Catherine turned on them sharply. 'Gentlemen,' she said,

'you have heard the command of the King. There is little time to be lost. Let us make our plans.'

*

And so discussion went on in the council chamber.

'Monsieur de Guise, it is only right that to you should be left the destruction of the Admiral, his suite and all his noblemen in the quarters about Saint-Germain l'Auxerrois.'

'Madame, you may safely leave my father's murderer and his followers to me and mine.'

'Monsieur de Montpensier, you should make yourself responsible for the suite of Condé.'

'Madame,' said Montpensier, 'what of the young Prince himself?'

Guise said: 'Did not the King say, "Kill every Huguenot"? Why should you wish to exclude the Prince of Condé, Monsieur? *Every* Huguenot was the King's command; and by that is included Condé, Navarre, Rochefoucauld and all Huguenots.'

Catherine was silent. Here was an old problem. She looked at them, these Princes of the House of Guise and Lorraine. They were full of arrogance and ambition. Henry of Guise was already in command of Paris; what if all the Bourbon Princes were destroyed? Why, then there would be no one between the House of Valois and the House of Guise and Lorraine. The men of Valois were not strong; they did not enjoy the rude physical health of the Guises. She had only to compare Henry of Guise with the mad King, or even with her own Henry, beautiful though he was. Even her beloved Henry could not compare with Henry of Guise for virility and strength of body. The Guises were irrepressible; they were natural leaders. Even now this Henry of Guise was ready to take over the management of the massacre as though he had been its instigator. Remove the Bourbons, and the House of Guise and Lorraine would know no restraint whatsoever.

She decided then that Navarre and Condé must not die.

The Duke of Nevers, whose sister had married the young Prince of Condé, had no wish to see his brother-in-law killed. Catherine glanced at him and with a look encouraged him to plead for young Condé, which he did with eloquence.

106

Catherine said: 'Let us give Condé and Navarre the chance of changing their religion.'

'That,' said Guise, 'they will never do.'

'In that case,' she promised him, 'they must go the way of the others. But I insist that they shall be given the chance to change. Now to more practical matters. What shall the signal be? Let the bell of the Palais de Justice give the signal. You must all be ready when it is given. I suggest it shall be when the first sign of dawn is in the sky. How many men can we rely on in Paris?'

An ex-*prévôt* answered her. 'Twenty thousand at this time, Madame. Later we could call in thousands more.'

'Twenty thousand,' repeated Catherine. 'They would all be ready to follow the Duke of Guise?'

The Duke reassured her that this would be so.

He gave instructions to the *prévôt* who was then in office. 'Monsieur le Charron, it will be necessary to close all city gates so that none may leave or enter. There must be no movement of boats on the Seine.'

Catherine, visualizing revolt, insisted that all the artillery should be moved from the Hôtel de Ville.

'Later, Monsieur le Charron,' she said, 'you will learn where it is to be placed.'

Le Charron was aghast. He had come to the council expecting to discuss the dispatch of a dangerous enemy, and now he found himself confronted with a plan for wholesale murder. Catherine saw his hesitancy and it terrified her. She had caught her son's fears. This was, she knew, the most dangerous period she had yet lived through. One false move and the tables could be turned; it might be herself, her sons, the royal House of Valois, who were massacred in place of the Huguenots.

She said sharply: 'There will be no orders given until the morning; and, Monsieur le Charron, all traitors to our Catholic cause need expect no mercy.'

'Madame,' said the terrified le Charron, 'I am at your command.'

'That is well for you, Monsieur,' she said coldly, but she was shaken.

They went on with their plans. Each Catholic should wear

107

about his arm a white scarf, and there should be a white cross in his hat. Everything must be planned to the minutest detail. There must be no false moves.

Finally the council broke up and the nerve-racking period of waiting began.

*

It seemed to Catherine that the night would never come. She did not believe she had ever before experienced such fear. Up and down her apartment she paced, her black garments flowing about her, her lips dry, her heart pounding, her limbs trembling, while she sought in vain that calm which she had maintained in the course of so many dangerous years.

All those in the secret were awaiting the signal, but first there was a night to be lived through, a night of suspense and fear. Guise and his family with their followers were in their hôtel waiting for the hours to pass. Instructions had been given to trusted friends. But who could still be trusted? She had seen the revulsion in the face of le Charron, the *prévôt.* Could le Charron be trusted?

Never had time passed so slowly for the Queen Mother. This was the most critical, the most important night of her life. It must be successful. It must put an end to her fears. It must convince Philip of Spain that she was his friend, and in such a way that he would never doubt her again. He would know she was keeping a promise which she had made long ago at Bayonne. But would the dawn never come?

What could go wrong? The *prévôt* could be trusted. He was a man with a family; he could be trusted not to put them in danger. A Catholic never betrayed Catholics to Huguenots. She rejoiced that, for the time being, she and the Guises were allies. She could rely on them. There was no greater hater of Huguenots than Henry of Guise, and there was nothing he wished for more than the death of the Admiral. All those who, she had feared, might not be trusted, knew nothing of the venture. Alençon was in the dark. He had flirted with the Huguenot faith – oh, just out of perversity, for that youngest son of hers was as mischievous as Margot. Margot herself had been told nothing of what was to take place, because she was

108

married to a Huguenot and seemed to be on better terms with him since her marriage than she had been before; and Margot had previously shown that she was not to be trusted. There was nothing to fear ... nothing ... nothing. But the minutes would not pass.

If only Henry were King in place of Charles! Henry was as eager for this as Guise, and she could trust Henry. But Charles? 'Kill every Huguenot!' he had cried; but that was while the madness was on him. What when it faded? She was terrified of what he might do. She sent for the Comte de Retz.

*

Retz went to the King. Charles was pacing up and down his apartment, his bloodshot eyes staring wildly about him.

Retz asked the King to dismiss all his attendants that he might speak with him alone.

'How long it seems,' said Charles when this had been done. 'Too long to wait. I am afraid, Comte, that they will start before we do. What then? What then?'

'Sire, we are controlling everything. We need fear nothing.' But he thought: except the King.

'Sometimes I think I should go to the Admiral, Comte.'

'Nay, Sire. You should do no such thing,' cried Retz in horror. 'It would ruin all our plans.'

'But if there is a plot against us, Comte, it would be against the Guises. It is they whom they accuse of trying to kill the Admiral.'

'That is not so, Sire. They accuse also your mother and the Duke of Anjou. And rightly, because, Sire, your mother and your brother knew that it was necessary to kill the Admiral to protect you. That is not all. It is believed that you also were involved in the plot. That is why they make their plans to ... remove you. Nothing you could say to the Admiral would convince him and his friends that you had no hand in the attempt to assassinate him. There is no way out of this other than the way we plan.'

'When blood flows,' said the King, 'I am always so sorry afterwards. And then ... people will say that King Charles the

109

Ninth of France shed the blood of Huguenots who came in
innocence to his sister's wedding. They will say it for ever . . .
they will remember it always . . . And they will blame me . . .
the King!'

Retz was alarmed. He knew the King's moods as well as his
mother did. A return to complete sanity would be disastrous at
this point.

'Sire,' he said, 'I beg of you to recall what they have planned
to do to you. As for recriminations, why, all will know that it is
the result of a feud between the Houses of Guise and
Châtillon. Henry of Guise never forgave the murder of his
father. You are outside this, Sire. It is no fault of yours. Henry
of Guise is the man behind it. The blame will be placed on him;
to you it will mean safety.'

'To me it will mean safety,' said the King; and he began to
sob.

•

While the long night progressed the King took fright suddenly.
He went in great haste to the apartments of Marie Touchet. His
appearance alarmed her.

'What ails you, Charles?'

'Nothing, Marie. I shall lock you in tonight. You will be
unable to get out. No matter who comes to the door . . . remember you are not to answer.'

'What has happened? Why do you look so strange?'

'It is nothing . . . nothing, Marie. But you must stay here.
Promise me you will stay here.' He laughed madly and cried:
'You will have no choice. I shall lock you in. You will have to
stay.' He laughed gleefully. 'You are my prisoner, Marie.'

'Charles, what is wrong? Tell me.'

'Nothing is wrong. All is well. After tonight it will be well
indeed.' His face crumpled. 'Oh, Marie, I forgot. There is Madeleine.'

'What of Madeleine?'

'I cannot tell. I shall lock you in now. You are my love, my
prisoner. Tomorrow you will know.'

When Marie was alone she began to cry. She was very

frightened. She was to have the King's child, and this fact half delighted, half terrified her.

*

'Madelon,' cried the King. 'Where are you, Madelon? Come here to me at once.'

Madeleine was in her own small chamber close to the King's apartments; she was singing a Huguenot hymn.

'Do not sing that. Do *not*! I forbid it. You must not sing it, Madeleine.'

'But, Sire, it is just one of the hymns which you have heard me sing many times. I used to sing you to sleep with it. You will remember it. It was a favourite of yours.'

'Not tonight, Madeleine. Dearest Madelon, be silent. Come with me. You must come with me.'

'Charlot, what ails you? Is it the strangeness again?'

He stood still and his face puckered. 'Yes, Madelon, it is the strangeness. Here . . . in my head.' His eyes had grown wild. There was excitement in them now as though he looked forward to something with most joyful anticipation 'Come, Madelon. Come at once. Marie needs you. You must stay with her tonight.'

'Is she ill?'

'She needs you. She needs you. I command you to go to her. Go at once. You must stay with her all through the night, Madelon. And you must not leave her apartment. You will not be able to. Madelon, you must not sing that hymn . . . or any of your hymns . . . not tonight. Swear you will not tonight, Madelon.'

'Charlot, Charlot, what ails you? Tell Madelon . . . you know how that used to help.'

'It would not help now, Madelon. Nor do I need help.' He took her roughly by the arm and pushed her towards Marie's apartment.

Marie was at the door when he unlocked it. He pushed Madeleine in, and stood there watching them. He put his fingers to his lips – a gesture he had learned from his mother.

'Not a sound from you. Only I have a key to this room. Rest

111

assured it shall not leave my possession. No singing. No sound
... or it will be death ... death ...'

He locked the door and the two women looked at each other
with puzzled apprehension.

'He sent me because you were ill,' said Madeleine.

'But I was not ill, Madeleine.'

'He must have thought you would need me.'

Marie sank on to her bed and began to cry bitterly.

'What ails you, my little one?' asked Madeleine. 'Tell me, for
he has sent me to comfort you. There has been some quarrel?'

Marie shook her head. 'Oh, Nurse, I am so frightened sometimes. What is it? What is happening? Everything seems so
strange tonight. I am frightened ... frightened of his strangeness!'

'It is nothing,' said Madeleine. 'It is only some wild notion
that he has got into his head. He thinks we are in danger and
he wishes us to protect each other.'

But Marie, feeling the child within her, could not be so easily
comforted.

*

Retz tried to calm the King, but the King was in a frenzy.

'Marie!' he cried. 'Madeleine! Who else?'

He remembered Ambroise Paré; and, ignoring Retz, he
rushed to the door of his apartment shouting to his attendants:
'I wish Ambroise Paré brought to me at once. Find him. Lose no
time. And when you have found him send him to me ... at once
... at once ...'

An attendant ran off, spreading the report that the King was
ill and calling for his chief doctor.

Retz begged the King to go with him into a small private
chamber, and when they were there he locked the door.

'This is madness, Sire. You will betray the plan.'

'But I cannot let Paré die. Paré is a great man. He does much
good in France. He saves lives. Paré must not die.'

'You will betray us, Sire, if you act thus.'

'Why does he not come? Fool that he is! He will be caught.
It will be too late. Paré, you fool, where are you? Where are
you?'

In vain did Retz try to soothe the King. He was unsure of what method was needed to keep Charles balanced between madness and sanity. If he were quite mad, there was no knowing what he might do; yet if he were wholly sane he would not agree to the massacre.

Paré arrived, and when Retz let him into the chamber, Charles fell on him, embracing him, weeping over him.

'Sire, are you ill?'

'No, Paré. It is you ... you ... You will stay here. You will not move from this room. If you attempt to, I will kill you.'

Paré looked startled. He expected guards to enter the chamber and arrest him. He could not imagine of what he was about to be accused.

Charles laughed with abandon to see the terror in Paré's face and to guess its reason.

'My prisoner!' he cried in hysterical mischief. 'There will be no escape for you tonight, my friend. You shall stay here under lock and key.'

Laughing wildly, he allowed Retz to lead him away, leaving the bewildered and alarmed surgeon staring at the locked door.

*

Margot was disturbed. Henry of Guise had failed to meet her as they had planned. What could have happened to detain him?

She had been occupied all that day with the thoughts of two men – Henry of Guise and Henry of Navarre. This was a piquant situation such as she delighted in. This husband of hers was not such an oaf after all. He could be amusing; she was even a little jealous of his pursuit of Madame de Sauves, though she could counter that by continuing her liaison with Henry of Guise. But where had her lover been this night, and why had he not kept his appointment?

It was certainly disturbing. She had met him coming from a council meeting when she had thought he was not even in Paris. She had noticed his discomfiture on meeting her, and he told her somewhat shamefacedly that he had hurried back to the capital in some secrecy. She had accepted that explanation at the time, but now when he did not keep his promise to meet her she began to wonder what was meant by this secret coming and going.

It was now time for her mother's *coucher*, which she must, of course, attend, and this night there seemed more people than usual in the bedchamber. Margot was suddenly alert. There was something different about these people tonight, some tension, some excitement. Little groups seemed to be whispering animatedly, but it seemed to her that when she approached, the conversation which had previously been so lively became dull and commonplace. Could it be that there was some new scandal in the court of which she knew nothing and which they were keeping from her? Could it be concerned with Guise's failure to keep his appointment?

She sat down on a coffer and looked about her, watching the ceremony of the *coucher*.

Her mother was now in bed and several people were talking to her.

Then Margot noticed her sister, the Duchess of Lorraine, and she saw that she looked sad and frightened rather than excited.

Margot called to her sister and patted the coffer.

'You look sad tonight, my sister,' said Margot; and she saw that Claude's lips were trembling as though she had been reminded of something which was terrifying.

'Claude, what is it? What is the matter with you?'

'Margot . . . you must not . . .' She stopped.

'Well?' said Margot.

'Margot . . . I am frightened. Terribly frightened.'

'What has happened, Claude? What has happened to everybody tonight? Why do you persist in this secrecy? Tell me!'

Charlotte de Sauves was beside them.

'Madame,' she said to Claude, 'the Queen Mother desires you to go to her at once.'

Claude went to the bed, and Margot, watching, saw the angry glance her mother gave her sister, saw Claude bend her head and listen to Catherine's whispered words.

It was bewildering. Margot noticed now that some of those present watched her with concern.

'Marguerite,' called Catherine. 'Come here.'

114

Margot obeyed. She stood by the bed, aware of her sister's terrified eyes still fixed upon her.

'I did not know that you were here,' said Catherine. 'It is time you retired. Go now.'

Margot wished her mother goodnight, but even as Catherine waved her impatiently away, she was conscious of her sister's eyes which had not left her. When Margot reached the door Claude darted after her and seized her arm.

Tears ran down Claude's cheeks. 'Margot!' she cried. 'My dearest sister.'

'Claude, are you *mad*!' cried Catherine.

But Claude was overcome by her fears for her sister. 'We cannot let her go,' she cried wildly. 'Not Margot! Oh, my God! Oh, dear dear Margot, stay with me this night. Do not go to your husband's apartments.'

Catherine had raised herself from her pillows. 'Bring the Duchess of Lorraine to me this instant . . . this instant . . .'

Margot stood by, watching Claude almost dragged to their mother's bedside.

She heard her mother's whispered words: 'Have you lost your senses?'

Claude cried: 'Would you send her off to be sacrificed? Your daughter . . . my sister . . .'

'You *have* lost your senses. What has come over you? Do you suffer from your brother's malady? Marguerite, your sister suffers from delusions. I have already told you it is time you retired. Pray leave us and go to your husband immediately.'

Margot went out, apprehensive and bewildered.

*

In the King's apartment, where his gentlemen attended his ceremonial *coucher*, Catholics mingled with Huguenots; there was not, as there had been in his mother's apartments, that atmosphere of secrecy and suspense, and Catholics chatted amicably with Huguenots as they had done each night since they came to Paris for the wedding.

The King felt worn out by the events of the day. He wanted to rest; he wanted to forget everything in sleep.

'How tired I am!' he said; and the Comte de Retz, who had

not left his side for many hours, was there to soothe him.

'Your Majesty has had a busy day. You will feel better after a night's rest.'

But, thought Charles, it was no use trying to pretend that this day was just like any other. Tomorrow? How he longed for tomorrow. Then it would be over and done, the rebellion quelled, and he would be safe. He would let Marie and Madeleine out of their little prison. He would release Monsieur Paré. How they would thank him for saving their lives!

His head was throbbing and he could scarcely keep his eyes open. Had there been some drug of his mother's in the wine Retz had brought him, something to make him spend the next hours in sleep?

Huguenot and Catholic! Looking at them, who would believe in this great animosity between them! Why could they not always be friends as they seemed to be now?

Soon the wearisome ceremony would be over, the curtains drawn about his bed, and sleep ... gentle sleep ... would come. But what if he dreamed! He had reason to dread his dreams. Dreams of torn flesh ... mutilated bodies ... the agonized cries of men and women ... and blood.

The Duc de la Rochefoucauld was bending over his hand. Dear Rochefoucauld! So handsome and so gentle. They had long been friends; the Duke was one of the few whom Charles really loved; he had always been happy in his company.

'Adieu, Sire.'

'Adieu.'

'May only the pleasantest of dreams attend Your Majesty.'

There was tenderness in those eyes. There was real friendship there. Even if I were not the King he would love me, thought Charles. He is a true friend.

Rochefoucauld was moving towards the door. He would leave the Louvre and go through the narrow streets to his lodgings, accompanied by his followers: he would laugh and joke as he went, for there was none so fond of a joke as dear Rochefoucauld. Dear friend ... and *Huguenot*!

No, thought the King. It must not be. Not Rochefoucauld!

He threw off his drowsiness. ' 'Foucauld,' he cried urgently, ' 'Foucauld!'

The Duke had turned.

'Oh, 'Foucauld, you must not go tonight. You may stay here and sleep with my *valets de chambre*. Yes, you must. You will be sorry if you go, my friend, my dearest 'Foucauld.'

Rochefoucauld looked surprised; but Retz had darted forward.

'The King jests,' said Retz.

Rochefoucauld gave the King a smile and inclined his head slightly while Charles watched him with dazed eyes. He was murmuring under his breath: ' 'Foucauld, come back. 'Foucauld ... oh, my dear friend ... not my 'Foucauld.'

Retz drew the curtains about the King's bed.

The *coucher* was over.

Tears fell slowly down the cheeks of the King of France and there was silence in the Louvre.

*

Catherine lay in bed counting the minutes as they passed. Two hours, and then she would rise, but she could not lie there waiting. She thought bitterly of that fool Claude, who must have aroused suspicions in Margot's mind. She thought of stupid Charles who, according to Retz, had done his best to warn Rochefoucauld. What if Rochefoucauld had got an inkling? He was one of the Huguenot leaders. What would he do? What would any sane man do if he realized what was afoot? Make counter-plans, of course.

She could not endure it. It was not yet time to rise, but she could not stay in bed. She could not wait for disaster to overtake her. She must act. While she was active she could endure the suspense.

She rose and dressed hastily; she went stealthily along to Anjou's apartment, and drawing the curtain close about his bed, shut herself in with him.

He had not slept for his fear was far greater than hers. She saw the sweat glistening on his forehead; and his hair was uncurled.

'My darling, you must get up and dress,' she said. 'There are some hours yet. But it is better to be dressed.'

'Mother, it is just past midnight, and the bell of the Palais de

117

Justice is not to ring until an hour before daybreak.'

'I know, my son, but I am afraid. I wonder if the folly of your brother and your sister may have disclosed our intentions. I wonder if our enemies plan to strike first. I will give other orders. We must start earlier in case we have been betrayed. We must surprise them. Now rise and dress and I will awaken the King. We should not waste more time in our beds. I must get a message through to Monsieur de Guise. If he knows of the change in our plans, the procedure can be safely left to him.'

'But, Mother, is it wise to change at this late hour?'

'I fear it may be unwise not to. Come.'

This was a better than lying in bed waiting. Action was always more stimulating than idleness. She sent Bouchavannes with a message to the Hôtel de Guise, and Retz to awaken the King and send him to her.

She had chosen a position at one of the windows where she might have a good view of what was happening outside; and here the King arrived, bewildered and agitated.

'What means this, Madame?'

'Our plans had to be changed. We have discovered a further and most devilish plot. It is necessary to advance ... delay is dangerous.'

Charles covered his face with his hands. 'Let us give up this affair. I have had enough of it. If there is a plot against us by the Huguenots there are many Catholics to defend us.'

'What! You would let them come and murder us here in the Louvre!'

'It seems there will be murder in any case.'

His mother and Anjou looked at him in horror. He was mad. He was unaccountable. They had been right not to trust him. How did they know what he would plan from one minute to the next? Delay was dangerous and it was largely due to this unstable King that it was so.

'There must be killing, I know,' sobbed Charles. 'There must be bloodshed and murder. But do not let us start it.'

'Do you realize,' said Catherine quietly, 'that the Huguenots attack our Holy Church? Is it not better that their rotten limbs should be torn asunder, than that the Church, the Holy Bride of Our Lord, should be rent?'

118

'I do not know,' cried the King. 'I only know that I wish to stop this bloodshed.'

The tocsin of Saint-Germain l'Auxerrois opposite the Louvre began to ring out; and almost immediately it seemed as though all the bells in Paris were ringing.

Noise broke forth. Shouts; screams; laughter that was cruel and mocking; the agonized cries of men and women mingled with their pleas for mercy.

'It has begun then . . .' said the King in a whisper.

'God in Heaven!' murmured Anjou. 'What have we done?'

He looked at his mother and he saw in her face that which she had rarely allowed him to see – fear . . . such fear that he never hoped to see in any face again.

She repeated his words softly as though to herself: 'What have we done? And what will happen now?'

'All Hell is let loose!' screamed the King. 'All Hell is let loose.'

'Stop it,' entreated Anjou. 'Stop it before it goes too far. Before we are destroyed . . . stop it, I say!'

Catherine did then what she had never done before: she panicked.

She muttered: 'You are right. We must stop it. I will send a message to Guise. The Admiral must not die yet . . .'

But although the dawn was not yet in the sky, all Paris had awakened to the Eve of St Bartholomew.

*

The Admiral was in too much pain for sleep. Paré had wanted to give him an opiate. but he would not take it. He had much to think of. In an ante-chamber his son-in-law was sleeping, lightly, he surmised, eager to answer his slightest call. Dear Téligny! God had been good to allow him to give his daughter into such hands.

Nicholas Muss, the Admiral's faithful servant, was dozing in a chair. Merlin, his pastor, sat in another. He had many faithful servants in his house; he had many friends in Paris. The Prince of Condé and the King of Navarre had visited him earlier in the evening, but they had now left for the palace of the Louvre. Ambroise Paré, who had made such great efforts to save his

119

life, had been with him until a few hours ago; he had been reluctant to leave him and would not have done so but for an urgent command from the King himself.

What disquiet there was all through Paris! If only the King would throw off the influence of his mother and his brother Anjou, together with that of the Guises, what good could be achieved! The Admiral knew that they hated him; he knew that when the Queen Mother had uttered her condolences and spoken of her sympathy, she was furiously angry because the shot from the gun of the Guise hireling had failed to kill him outright. He knew that when the King had ordered a guard to protect this house, Anjou and his mother had seen to it that the men who arrived had been led by a certain man named Cosseins, and this man was an old enemy of the Admiral and the Huguenot cause. This was ominous and he knew that danger was all about him and his friends.

How quiet it was tonight! There had been so many nights of feasting and roystering during the celebrations of the wedding that on this night the silence seemed all the more impressive.

He wondered fitfully if he would ever see Châtillon again. Had news reached Jacqueline of his accident? He trusted not. She would be beside herself with anxiety, and that would be so bad for her and the child. He was glad that François and Andelot were safe at Châtillon, and Louise with them. Perhaps, if he recovered, as Paré assured him that he would, he would be in Châtillon in a few weeks' time . . . perhaps by the end of September. The roses would not be all gone. What joy to wander in the alleys once more, to gaze at the grey walls of the castle and not care whether he went in or stayed out, since there could be no dispatches waiting for him!

Who knew, perhaps he would be home by the end of September, for it was now nearing the end of August. Today was the . . . yes, the 23rd. St Bartholomew's Eve.

He started suddenly; the sound of bells crashed on the air. Whence did it come? Who was ringing the bells at this hour?

Muss started up from his chair; Merlin opened his eyes.

'Is it morning then?' asked Merlin. 'What mean these bells?'

'I wonder,' said the Admiral. 'Bells before daybreak! What can it mean?'

'And they startled you from your sleep master,' said Muss.

'Nay, I was not sleeping. I was lying here thinking – oh, thinking most happily, of my wife and family and my roses at Châtillon.'

Téligny had come into the room.

'You heard the bells, my son?' asked the Admiral.

'They awakened me, Father. What is the reason for them? Listen. Do you hear? The sound of horses' hoofs ... coming this way.'

The men looked at each other, but none spoke his thoughts. A great terror possessed them all except the Admiral. For hours now he had lain in pain, expectant, waiting for death; and if this were death it would merely mean that the end of his pain was at hand.

'Muss,' he said, 'go to the window, my friend. Tell us what you see below.'

The man went and, when he drew back the hangings, the room was filled with the wavering light from the torches and cressets below.

'Who is there, Nicholas?' asked the Admiral.

Téligny was at the window. He turned his pale face towards the Admiral and stammered: 'Guise ... and ten ... twenty more mayhap.'

Gaspard said: 'They have come for me, my friends. You must help me to dress. I would not care to receive my enemies thus.'

Téligny ran from the room and hurried down the staircase.

'Be on guard!' he shouted to the men who were posted on stairs and in corridors. 'Our enemies are here.'

As he reached the main door, he heard Cosseins shout: 'Labonne, have you the keys? You must let this man through. He has a message from the King to the Admiral.'

'Labonne!' shouted Téligny. 'Let no one in!'

But it was too late. The keys were already in Cosseins' hands. He heard Labonne's shriek; and he knew that that faithful friend had been murdered.

'Fight!' cried Téligny to the men. 'Fight for Coligny and the cause!'

He ran back to the bedchamber, where Merlin knelt in prayer while Muss was helping the Admiral to put on a few clothes. The sound of shots and shouts could now be distinctly heard in the room.

Suddenly a Huguenot soldier burst in upon them. 'Monsieur l'Amiral,' he cried, 'you must fly. You must waste no time. The Guisards are here. They are breaking down the inner door.'

'My friends,' said the Admiral calmly, 'you must go . . . all of you. For myself I am ready for death. I have long expected it.'

'I will never leave you, Father,' said Téligny.

'My son, your life is too precious to be recklessly thrown away. Go . . . go at once. Remember Louise. Remember Châtillon, and that it is for such as you to live and fight on. Do not be over-troubled because I must die. I am an old man and my day is done.'

'I will fight beside you,' said Téligny. 'We may yet escape.'

'I cannot walk, my son. You cannot carry me. It is folly to delay. I hear them on the staircase. That means they are coming over the dead bodies of our faithful friends. Go, my son. Jacqueline will know much sorrow, for this night she will be a widow. If you love my daughter do not subject her to the same fate. You grieve me. I am most unhappy while you stay. Give me the joy of knowing that you have escaped these murderers. Son, I beg of you. There is yet time. The roofs . . . through the *abat-son*. Now . . . for the love of God, for the love of Louise . . . for Châtillon . . . I beg of you . . . go!'

Téligny kissed his father-in-law and sobbed: 'I will, Father. I will . . . since it is your wish. For Louise . . .'

'I beg of you, make haste. To the attics . . . to the roofs . . .'

'Goodbye, my father.'

'Goodby, my dearest son.'

Gaspard wiped the sweat from his brow, but he was smiling as he saw the last of his son-in-law. He turned to Merlin. 'You too, my dearest friend, go . . .'

122

'Dear master, I have no wife to make a widow. My place is here with you. I will not leave you.'

'Nor I, master,' said Muss. 'I have my sword and my arm is strong.'

'It is certain death,' said the Admiral wearily. 'We are so few, they so many.'

'But I would not wish for life, master,' said Muss, 'if I left you now.'

'Dear friends, I would not have those who hold you dear, reproach me with your deaths. You would please me if you went. Merlin, you can do much good elsewhere. Go . . . Follow my son-in-law to the roofs. Listen. They are on the staircase now. Merlin . . . I entreat you. I have learned to pray. I can pray without you. You waste a life . . . a Huguenot life. I beg of you. I command you . . .'

The pastor was persuaded that he could do no good by remaining, but old Nicholas Muss was resolutely standing by the bed, his sword in hand, and Coligny knew that nothing he could say to his servant would make him leave his side.

Then Coligny knelt by the bed. He began to pray. 'Into Your hands, oh God, I commend my soul. Comfort my wife. Guide my children, for they are of such tender age . . . Into your hands . . . into your hands . . .'

The door was burst open. Cosseins and a man whom the Admiral recognized as an enemy and whose name was Besme, rushed into the room. Behind them came others, among whom were the Italians, Toshingi and Petrucci. They all wore white scarfs about their arms and crosses in their hats.

They fell back at the sight of the old man kneeling by the bed. Hastily they crossed themselves. The serenity of the Admiral's face and the calm manner in which he lifted those noble eyes to their faces temporarily unnerved them.

'You are Gaspard de Coligny?' said Toshingi.

'I am. And you have come to kill me, I see. Do what you will. My life is almost over and there is little you can do.'

Nicholas Muss lifted his sword in defence of his master, but the blow was parried by Toshingi, while Petrucci thrust his dagger into the old man's chest. The others crowded round to finish what Toshingi had begun, and Muss fell groaning beside the bed.

'So perish all heretics!' cried one of the men.

This was the signal; together they rushed on the prostrate Admiral. Besme thrust his sword through the body of the noble old man, while all in turn stabbed him with their daggers, each eager to anoint his blade with the most distinguished of the blood that they had promised themselves they would shed that night.

Coligny lay stretched out before them, and they stood silently looking down at him, none willing that his companions should see that look of shame which he feared he might be weak enough to show.

Besme went to the window and opened it.

'Is the deed done?' called Henry of Guise.

'Yes, my lord Duke,' answered Besme.

The Chevalier of Angoulême, bastard of Henry the Second and half-brother to the King, who was below with Guise, shouted: 'Then fling him out of the window that we may see that you speak truth.'

The assassins lifted the body of the Admiral.

'He still lives,' said Petrucci.

'He will not live for long after he has made contact with the courtyard below,' answered Toshingi. 'Ah, my good friend, my noble Admiral, if you had not stooped to pick up a paper when I took a shot at you, what a lot of trouble you might have saved yourself . . . and us! Hoist him, my friends. What a weight he is! Steady . . . Over!'

The Admiral made a feeble effort to grasp the window-sill; one of the men pricked his hand with his dagger and then . . . Gaspard de Coligny was lying in the courtyard below.

The Chevalier d'Angoulême, who had dismounted, said to Guise: 'It is not easy to see that it is he. His white hair is red tonight. It is as though he has followed Madame Margot's fashion and put a wig of that colour on his head.'

Henry of Guise knelt to examine the body. 'It is he,' he said: and he placed his foot on the Admiral. 'At last, Monsieur de Coligny,' he said. 'At last you die, murderer of my father. You

124

have lived too long since you bribed a man to kill Francis of Guise at Orléans.'

Angoulême kicked the body and ordered one of his men to cut off the head.

A cheer went up as the head was held high by the blood-stained hair.

'Adieu, Coligny!' the shout went up.

'Adieu, murderer of François de Guise!' cried the Duke; and those about him took up the cry.

'You may take the head to the Louvre,' said Angoulême. 'A gift for the Queen Mother, and one which she has long coveted.'

'What of the body, sir?' asked Toshingi.

'A gift to the people of Paris to do with what they will.'

It was at that moment that a messenger came galloping up.

'From the Queen Mother, my lord Duke. "Stop," she says. "Do not kill the Admiral." '

'Ride back with all speed,' said the Duke. 'Tell the Queen Mother that you came too late. Come, my men. Death to the heretics! Death to the Huguenots! The King commands that we kill . . . kill . . . kill.'

*

Téligny, from the roofs, looked down on the city. Lights had sprung up everywhere, and there were torches and cressets to pick out the horrible sights. The air was filled with the cries of dying men and women – hoarse, appealing, angry and be-wildered.

Which way? Which way to safety and Louise? He knew that the Admiral had no chance of survival, and he must reach those loved ones at the Château de Châtillon to comfort them, to mourn with them.

He could already smell the stench of blood. What was hap-pening on this mad, most fantastic of nights? What were they doing down there in the streets? What were they doing to his friends?

He was too young to die. He had not yet lived. The Admiral had known adventure, love, as well as devotion to a cause; he

125

had known the joy of rearing a family; but Téligny as yet knew little of these things. He thought of the fair face of Louise, of walking with her in the flower gardens, through the shady green alleys. How he longed for the peace of Châtillon, how he longed for escape from this nightmare city!

He would wait here on the roof until all was quiet. He would escape through one of the gates of the city. Perhaps he could disguise himself, for if they were murdering the friends of the Admiral, they would never let him live; and he *must* live; he must get to Châtillon . . . and Louise.

A bullet whined over his head. He heard a shout from below. They had seen him. They had picked him up by the light from their cressets.

'There he goes . . . On the roof . . .'

There was a hot pain in his arm. He looked about him, bewildered.

'I must escape,' he murmured. 'I must reach Châtillon . . . and Louise . . .'

The torchlight showed him the outline of the roof. He saw the way he had come; the blood he had shed lay behind him in pools like dark, untidy footprints. He could hear the malignant shouting as more shots whined about him.

He clambered on. He was weak and dizzy. 'For Louise . . .' he panted. 'For Châtillon . . . and Louise . . .'

He was still murmuring 'Louise' when he rolled off the roof.

The mob, recognizing his quivering body, fell upon him and called to one another that Téligny was dead. They tore his clothes to shreds to keep as mementoes of this night.

*

Margot had gone uneasily to her bedchamber. Her husband was already there. He lay in bed and was surrounded by members of his suite.

She retired to an ante-chamber, called her women to help her disrobe and, when this was done, joined Navarre in the bed.

It seemed that he, like herself, was disinclined to sleep.

She could not forget her sister's words, nor the anger which

126

they had aroused in her mother. Something threatened her, she was sure. She longed for the gentlemen to depart so that she might tell her husband what had taken place, but the gentlemen showed no signs of departing, and Navarre showed no sign of wishing them to do so.

They were excitedly discussing the shooting of the Admiral, and what the outcome would be.

'In the morning,' said Navarre, 'I shall go to the King and demand justice. I shall ask Condé to accompany me, and I shall demand the arrest of Henry of Guise.'

Margot smiled cynically. Her husband had much to learn. Here in Paris Henry of Guise was of as great importance as the King. No one – not even her mother or brother – would dare accuse Guise in Paris.

They went on talking of Coligny, of the audience they would demand, of the justice for which they would ask. Margot listened. She was tired, yet she could not sleep while the men remained, and her husband did not dismiss them. So the long night dragged on, and at length, declaring that it would soon be day, Navarre announced that he was going to play tennis until the King should wake up. 'Then,' he said, 'I shall, without delay, go to him and demand audience.' He turned to his men. 'Let us go and prepare ourselves for a game. I shall not sleep until I have won justice for Coligny.'

He leaped out of bed and Margot said: 'I will sleep till daybreak. I am tired.'

They drew the curtains about her and left her, and it was not long before she slept.

She was suddenly awakened. In the streets bells were ringing and people were shouting. She sat up in bed listening in amazement, and now she realized that what had awakened her was a repeated hammering on her own door. Immediately she remembered the strange events of the previous evening.

The hammering on her door persisted; it was accompanied by loud cries. She listened. 'Open ... Open ... For the love of God. Navarre! Navarre!'

'Who is there?' cried Margot. She called to one of her women who came running in from the ante-chamber. 'Someone knocks. Unlock the door.'

The woman stumbled to the door. Margot, her bed-curtains parted, saw a man rush into the room. His face was deathly pale, his clothes spattered with blood; the blood dripped on to the carpet.

He saw the bed. He saw Margot. He staggered towards her with his arms outstretched.

Margot had leaped out of bed, and the intruder, flinging his arms about her knelt and, lifting his agonized face to hers, cried: 'Save me . . . Navarre . . . Navarre . . .'

Margot, for once, was completely bewildered. She had no idea who this man was, why he should be in such a condition and why he should thus break into her bedchamber; but even as he knelt there, his blood staining her nightgown, four men rushed into the room, their bloodstained swords in their hands, their eyes like those of wild animals lusting for the kill.

Ever emotional in the extreme, Margot was roused to pity, anger and indignation all at once. With a quick gesture she released herself from the clinging hands of the man and stood in front of him; her black hair in disorder, her black eyes flashing, she faced those bloodthirsty men in such a manner that even in their present mood they were aware that they stood in the presence of a Queen.

'How dare you!' she cried. 'How dare you come thus into *my* chamber!'

The men fell back, but only a pace. Margot felt a twinge of fear, but only enough to stimulate her. She called to her women: 'Bring the Captain of the Guard to me immediately. As for you, cowards . . . bullies . . . murderers . . . for I see you are all three . . . stay where you are or you will suffer.'

But on this night of bloodshed, such killers as these were not going to be over-impressed by nobility or even royalty. One of them had, ten minutes before, stained his sword with the blood of a Duke. And who was this . . . but the wife of a Huguenot!

She saw the fanatical gleam in their eyes and haughtily she held up her hand.

'If you dare come a step nearer, I will have you beaten, tortured . . . and put to death. Down on your knees! I am the Queen, and you shall answer for this unless you give me immediate obedience.'

But they did not fall on their knees, and she saw now, in those four pairs of eyes, lust for herself mingled with their lust for blood. She realized that terrible things were happening about her; and she knew that she was in great danger, that these men were of the mob and that on nights such as this, a Queen meant nothing more than a woman.

How long could she hold them off? How long before they dispatched the poor half-dead creature who lay behind her? How long before they dealt with her?

But here, thank God, was Monsieur de Nançay, the Captain of the Guard, handsome, charming, a man on whom Margot had bestowed smiles of warm regard and promise.

'Monsieur de Nançay!' she cried. 'See what indignity these rogues put me to!'

She noticed that he, like the intruders, wore a white cross in his hat.

He shouted to the men: 'What do you here? How dare you enter the apartments of our Most Catholic Princess?'

One of them pointed to the man whom Margot was trying to hide in the folds of her nightgown.

'He ran in here, sir, and we but followed. He escaped after we had caught him.'

'You followed him here! Into the apartments of Her Majesty! It will be well for you if you make yourself scarce at once before Her Majesty has time to note your evil faces.'

'Shall we take the heretic, sir? He is making a mess in the lady's bedchamber.'

Margot said haughtily: 'I will deal with him. You have heard what Monsieur de Nançay said. You will be wise to go at once.'

When they had gone, reluctant and almost sheepish, de Nançay's lips began to twitch.

'You will help me to get this man into my *ruelle*, Monsieur,' said Margot coldly. 'And while you do so perhaps you will tell me why you are amused at your low soldiers' daring to insult me.'

'Madame, Your Majesty's pardon,' said de Nançay, lifting the semi-conscious man in his arms, 'but Your Majesty's kindness is well known, and if I seemed to smile, it was because I

129

was thinking that this man might have heard of it.'

'Take him to my *ruelle* at once.'

'Madame, he is a Huguenot.'

'What of that?'

'The King's orders are that no Huguenot shall survive this night.'

She stared at him in horror. 'My ... husband? His ... friends?'

'Your husband will be safe, together with the Prince of Condé.'

Now she understood the meaning of the terrible noises in the streets below. She was nauseated. She hated bloodshed. They were all concerned in this – her mother, her brothers ... her lover.

De Nançay spoke gently to her. 'I will take this man away, Madame. He shall not defile your chamber further with his blood.'

But Margot shook her head. 'You will obey me, Monsieur, and take him to my *ruelle*.'

'But, Madame, I beg of you to remember the King's orders.'

'I am not accustomed to having *my* orders disobeyed,' she said. 'Take him in there at once. And, Monsieur de Nançay, you will tell none that he is here. And you will obey me, or I will never forgive your insolence of this night.'

De Nançay was very gallant and Margot was very charming. What, he asked himself, was one Huguenot among thousands?

'I promise you, Madame,' he said, 'that none shall know you keep him here.'

He laid the man on the black satin-covered couch, while Margot called to her women to bring her ointments and bandages; she had been a pupil of Paré's and was more skilled than most in the use of these things. Tenderly she bathed and bandaged the wounds, and, as she did so, determined that here was at least one Huguenot who should not die.

❋

The Duc de la Rochefoucauld had been sleeping soundly, a smile on his fresh young face; but he had awakened suddenly, and was not sure what had awakened him. He had dreamed he was at a masque, the noisiest masque he had ever known, and the King was calling to him not to leave his side. He heard the voice distinctly: ' 'Foucauld. 'Foucauld, do not go tonight.'

What noise there must be in the streets tonight! It was as bad as it had been during the wedding celebrations. It would be well when all the visitors had gone back to their homes. But these were strange noises. Bells at this hour? Screams? Shouts? Cries?

He turned over and tried to stop up his ears.

But the noise would not be shut out. It came nearer. It seemed as though it were in his own house.

He was right. It was. The door was flung suddenly open. Someone was in his room; several people seemed to have called on him.

He was fully awake now that they had parted his bed-curtains.

He grinned. He thought he understood. This was why the King had advised him to stay in the palace. Here *was* the King with his merry followers prepared to play that game of beating his friends. In a moment he would hear the voice of the King. 'Your turn tonight, 'Foucauld. Do not blame me. I asked you to stay in the palace.'

'Come on!' he cried. 'I am ready.'

A dark figure with a white cross in his hat had darted forward and de la Rochefoucauld felt the sharp pain of a dagger. Others closed in on him and he saw the gleam of their weapons.

'Die . . . heretic!' said one; and Rochefoucauld, the favourite of the King, lay back moaning, while his life-blood stained the bedclothes a vivid scarlet.

*

Now that the massacre was in full swing, Catherine's fear had left her. It was apparent that the Huguenots had been taken completely by surprise and that there was no danger of serious retaliation. She was safe; her family was safe; and she would

131

have the best possible news for Philip of Spain, to counter-balance that unpleasant pill, the Huguenot marriage of her daughter; and this marriage, the gloomy monarch would readily see, had been a necessity, a bait to catch his enemies in one big trap. She had kept her word; the promise she had made to Alva at Bayonne was fulfilled. Now she could rest, assured of her temporary safety in an unsafe world; for temporary safety was the best for which she could hope.

The head of Coligny had been brought to her, and she, sur-rounded by members of her Flying Squadron, had gloated over it.

'How different the Admiral looks without his body!' said one of those cynical young women.

'But death has somewhat impaired his beauty!' tempered another.

'Ah, my big salmon!' cried Catherine exultantly. 'You were hard to catch, but now you will give us no further trouble.'

She was laughing, and her women noticed that the excite-ment made her look years younger. She was as energetic as ever, remembering those who must die tonight, mentally tick-ing them off as news of their deaths was brought to her. 'Ah, another name to cross off my list!' she would cry. 'My *red* list!'

Trophies were brought to her. 'A finger of Monsieur de Téligny, which was all the mob would let us have, Madame.'

'A little part of Monsieur de la Rochefoucauld . . . for one of your ladies who did so admire him.'

There was ribald laughter and many a joke between the women, for some had known the victims very well indeed. There was great hilarity when the mutilated body of a certain Soubise was brought in, for this gentleman's wife had sued him for a divorce on account of his impotency. The *Escadron Volant* amused its mistress with its clowning over his body.

Catherine, watching them, burst into loud laughter which was largely the laughter of relief.

*

Through the streets rode the Duke of Guise accompanied by Angoulême, Montpensier and Tavannes, urging the excited

132

Catholics to fresh slaughter. They were determined that no Huguenot should survive.

'It is the wish of the King!' cried Guise. 'It is the command of the King. Kill all heretics. Let not one of these vipers live another hour.'

Not that such exhortation was necessary. The bloodlust was rampant. How simple to wipe off old scores; for who would doubt that Monsieur So-and-So – a business rival – was a Huguenot in secret, or that the too-fascinating Mademoiselle Such-and-Such who had been receiving the attention of another's husband, had been a convert to 'The Religion'?

Ramus, the famous Greek scholar and teacher, was dragged from his bed and put to lingering death. 'He is a heretic. He has been practising heresy in secret!' was the cry of the jealous scholar who had long coveted the professorial chair of Ramus.

There was rape and brutality in plenty that night. It was so simple to commit the crime and kill afterwards, to leave no evidence of villainy. Bewildered Huguenots, running for shelter to the Admiral's house or the Hôtel de Bourbon, were shot down or run through with swords. They lay where they fell, dead and dying heaped together.

Tavannes cried: 'Let them bleed, my friends. The doctors say that bleeding is as beneficial in August as in May.'

Priests walked the streets, carrying swords in one hand, crucifixes in the other, making it a solemn duty to visit those quarters where there was a falling-off of bloodshed, a lack of enthusiasm to kill.

'The Virgin and the saints watch you, my friends. Your victims are an offering to Our Lady who receives it with joy. Kill . . . and win eternal joy. Death to the heretic!'

The trunk of Coligny was being dragged through the streets, naked and mutilated. No obscenity was too vile, no insult too degraded to be played on the greatest man of his times. Finally, the remains of the Admiral were roasted over a slow fire, and the mob surrounding the spectacle, screaming and shouting at each other like the savages they had become, laughed at the sight of the distorted flesh, jocularly commented on its odour as it burned.

Men and women were murdered in their beds during that night of terror; heads and limbs severed from their bodies, fell from the windows. Nor were babies spared.

Lambon, the Catholic reader to the King, as great a bigot as lived in Paris at that time, on witnessing the horrible death of Ramus the scholar, was overcome by horror and died of the shock.

'I cannot tell you what happened on that night,' said an old Catholic in writing to another. 'The very paper itself would weep, if I wrote upon it all I have seen.'

The poor King was lost in his madness. He could smell blood; he could see it flow. He stood at the windows of his apartments, shouting to the murderers, urging them to commit more horrible atrocities.

When he saw men and women trying to get into a boat which had been overlooked and was moored on the banks of the Seine, he himself fired at them and, missing, was in a raging frenzy lest they should escape; he called his guards and ordered them to shoot the people, and he laughed with glee when he saw the boat capsize and heard the cries of the victims as they sank in the bloodstained water.

Madness had come to Paris, and the light of morning showed up in hideous clarity the terror of the night before. Bodies were piled high in the streets; the walls were splashed with the blood and remains of what had been human beings; everywhere was the stench of the night's carnage; and all through the day the horror continued, for that which it had been so easy to start, it was found impossible to stop.

*

The King of Navarre and the Prince of Condé stood before the King. The King's eyes were bloodshot; there were flecks of foam on his clothes and his hands twitched.

The Queen Mother was with the King; several guards stood close by and all attendants were armed.

'You are here, Messieurs,' said Catherine, 'for your own safety.'

The King shouted: 'There must be one religion in France from now on. I will have only one religion in my kingdom. It is

134

the Mass now . . . the Mass or death.' He began to laugh. 'You have perchance seen what is happening out there, eh? You have passed through the streets. The bodies are piled high. Men have been torn limb from limb . . . women too . . . babies . . . little girls, little boys. They were all heretics in my kingdom. The Mass . . . or death . . . Death or the Mass.'

Catherine said: 'You, Messieurs, have been more fortunate than others who have not had the choice which is offered to you.'

Henry of Navarre looked shrewdly from the mad face of the King to the impenetrable one of the Queen Mother; he was aware of the guards who were posted, not only in the apartment, but in the corridors. He would be careful; he had no intention of losing his life over a mere matter of faith.

Condé had folded his arms. Poor Condé! thought his cousin of Navarre; he was emotional – sentimental – brave as a lion, and as stupid as an ass.

'Sire,' said Condé in a cold remote voice as though he faced death a hundred times a day and therefore to him such a situation was commonplace, 'I will be faithful to my creed though I die for it.'

The King's fingers closed about his dagger. He came close to Condé and held the weapon against the Prince's throat. Condé stared up at the ornate hangings as though the King had merely asked him to admire them, and poor Charles lost his nerve before such a display of cool courage. His trembling hand fell to his side, and he turned to Navarre.

'And you . . . you?' he screamed.

'Sire,' said Navarre evasively, 'I beg of you, do not tamper with my conscience.'

The King frowned. He suspected his uncouth kinsman of cunning; he had never understood him and he did not understand him now; but the look on Navarre's face suggested that he was in fact ready to consider changing his religion, but that he did not wish to appear to do so readily. He needed time to consider how he might adjust his conscience.

Condé cried out: 'Most diabolical things have been done. But I have five hundred gentlemen ready to avenge this most lamentable massacre.'

'Do not be so sure of that,' said Catherine. 'Have you had a roll-call lately? I doubt not that many of those fine gentlemen will never again be in a condition to serve the Prince of Condé.'

The trembling King felt his frenzy passing; he was close to that mood of deep melancholy which often followed his more violent bouts. He said almost piteously to Navarre: 'Show good faith and I may show you good cheer.'

At that moment there came hurrying into the room a beautiful girl with her dark hair loose about her shoulders. Margot knelt before the King, and taking his trembling hands in hers kissed them.

'Forgive me, brother. Oh, Sire, forgive me. I heard that my husband was here, and I have come to ask you to spare his life.'

Catherine said: 'Get up, Marguerite, and leave us. This affair is none of yours.'

But the King held his sister's hands and the tears ran fast down his cheeks.

'My husband is in danger,' said Margot turning to her mother. 'That, it seems, should be an affair of mine.'

Catherine was furious. She had no intention of letting Condé or Navarre die, but she was angry that her daughter as well as her son should dare to defy her; she was annoyed also by this display of what seemed to her yet another of Margot's dramatic tricks. A little while ago the girl had hated that husband of hers; now she was making a spectacle of herself, as she said, to save his life. It was her love of drama not of Navarre that made her act so, Catherine was sure; but it was the effect on the King which was important.

'I have offered him his life,' said the King. 'He only has to change his religion. "The Mass or death", is what I said to him. "Death or the Mass . . ." '

'And he has chosen the Mass,' said Margot.

'He will,' said Catherine sardonically.

'Then he is safe!' cried Margot. 'And, Sire, there are two gentlemen who have begged me to help them . . . gentlemen of my husband's suite – De Mossans and Armagnac. You will give

136

them this chance, Sire? Dearest brother, you will let them make this choice between death and the Mass?'

'To please you,' said Charles, embracing his sister hysterically. 'To please my dearest Margot.'

'You may leave us, Marguerite,' said Catherine.

As Margot went out her eyes met those of her husband. His seemed to signal: 'Effective but unnecessary. Can you doubt that I would choose the Mass?' But there was also a twinkle in those eyes, a smile of approval about his lips which seemed to add: 'This means that we are friends, does it not? It means that we are to work together?'

When Margot had left, the King turned to Condé. 'Give up your faith!' he cried. 'Accept the Mass. I give you an hour's grace, and then if you will not accept the Mass, it shall be death. I will kill you myself. I will kill . . . kill . . .'

The Queen Mother signed to the guards to take Navarre and Condé away; then she gave herself up to the task of soothing the King.

*

Charles was weary. He lay on his couch, and the tears rolled down his cheeks. 'Blood . . . blood . . . blood,' he murmured. 'Rivers of blood. The Seine is red with blood, the cobbles are red with it. It stains the walls of Paris like the leaves of creeping plants in autumn. Blood! Everywhere blood!'

His Queen came to him; her face was distorted with grief. The awkward gait which proclaimed her pregnancy made the King's tears flow more copiously. Their child would be born into a cruel world. Who knew what would happen to it?

She knelt before him, 'Oh, Sire, that terrible night! This terrible day! Do not let it go on. I beg of you. I cannot bear to hear the cries of the people. I cannot bear it.'

'I cannot bear it either,' he moaned.

'They say you yourself are going to kill the Prince of Condé.'

'It is all killing,' he said. 'It is all blood. It is the only thing which will make us safe.'

'Oh, my lord, do not have murder on your soul.'

137

The King burst into loud laughter while his tears continued to flow. 'All last night's murders will be on my soul,' he said. 'What is one more?'

'It was not your fault. It was others. Do not kill Condé. I beg of you, do not kill him.'

He stroked her hair and thought: poor little Queen. Poor little stranger in a strange land.

'It is a sad life we live,' he said, 'we Princes and Princesses. They married you, poor child, to a King of France who is a madman.'

She kissed his hand. 'You are so kind to me . . . so good to me. You are not a murderer. You could not do it. Oh, Charles, give *me* the life of Condé. It is not often that I ask for a gift, is it? Give me Condé's life now, dearest husband.'

'I will not kill him, then,' he said. 'Let him live. Condé is yours, my poor sad little Queen.'

Then she lay down beside him and, like two unhappy children, they wept silently together, wept for the terrible things which were happening in the streets below them, and for the terrible fate which had made them a King and a Queen in this cruel age.

*

The nightmare days went on. At noon, on St Bartholomew's Day, le Charron the *prévôt*, came to the palace and begged Catherine to stop the massacre. Both Catherine and the King attempted to do this, but without success. That which had been started with the ringing of the bell of Saint-Germain l'Auxerrois could not be stopped, and all through that day and the next night the carnage continued.

The King's madness returned and he called for fresh bloodshed. He was the instigator of those expeditions to witness the vilest executions. He made a pilgrimage, with priests and nobles, to that gibbet where they had now hung Coligny's body after they had taken it out of the Seine; it had been thrown there following the roasting.

On the 25th a hawthorn in the Cemetery of Innocents unexpectedly blossomed. This, cried the excited Catholics, was a sign of Heaven's approval. Any who said that hawthorn had been known to blossom in all other seasons, ran the risk of being named 'Heretic', which meant instant death, for it was so comforting to stifle any pangs of conscience by calling attention to Heaven's approval. Solemn pilgrimages were made to this cemetery, led by the dignitaries of the Church. The chanting voices of the priests, singing praises to God and the Virgin, mingled with the screams for mercy, with the groans of the dying.

Charles had aged considerably since the Eve of St Bartholomew; he now looked more than ever like an old man; his moods were various and sadness came to him suddenly, to be dispersed in wild hilarity when he shouted for more excitement. He would be proud of the carnage at one hour; he would be deeply ashamed the next. In a moment of melancholy, he declared his innocence of responsibility for the massacre and announced that it had been brought about because of a feud between the House of Guise and Lorraine and that of Châtillon, a feud which had been simmering for years and which he had been unable to prevent boiling over.

Guise, who would not allow this, publicly declared that he had but obeyed the orders of the King and the Queen Mother. The Duke and his adherents brought such pressure to bear on the King that he was forced to declare before an assembly of his ministers that he, and he only, was responsible for what had taken place. He was nervous and exhausted; in turn humble and truculent, belligerent and repentant. He stooped more than usual and his breathlessness had increased. He seemed perpetually to be tottering on the brink of complete insanity.

Catherine on the other hand looked, so many remarked, ten years younger. Energetic, eager to take her place at all ceremonies, she was in the forefront of the religious processions that paraded the streets and entered the churches to sing Te Deums of praise, and the Cemetery of the Holy Innocents to rejoice at Heaven's sign of approval. She herself rode out to see Coligny's remains; she made a point of being present at executions whenever possible.

*

The King talked continually of the massacre. He longed, he said, to put back the clock, to live again through that fateful day of August the 23rd. 'If I had that chance,' he would sigh, 'how differently I should act!'

Yet he was persuaded that the murder of Huguenots in Paris was not enough; so throughout the whole of France Catholics were ordered to commit murders and atrocities similar to those which had taken place in the capital. Readily the Catholics of Rouen, Blois, Tours and many other towns in the tortured land obeyed the commands that came from Paris.

There were some who protested, for there were Catholics in the provinces as humane as le Charron, the *prévôt* of Paris; chief among these were the Governors of Auvergne, Provence and Dauphiné together with the Duc de Joyeuse of Languedoc, who refused to obey such command which came by word of mouth and would not kill until they received written orders from the King. In Burgundy, Picardy, Montpellier and in Lyons the governors declared that they had learned to take life for justice of war, but that cold-blooded murder was something with which they did not care to burden their souls.

This seemed like rebellion, and Catherine and her council were uncertain how to act until they decided on sending priests down to the rebellious provinces to explain to the citizens that St Michael, in a vision, had ordered the massacre.

This was accepted as the certain will of Heaven, and so the bloody orgy continued, and for weeks after the Eve of St Bartholomew thousands were slaughtered all over France.

*

When Philip of Spain heard the news he laughed aloud – as many said – for the first time in his life. Charles, he said, had now truly earned the title of the 'Most Christian King'; he sent congratulations to Catherine for having brought up her son in her own image.

The Cardinal of Lorraine, who was in Rome at that time, gave the messenger who brought him news of the massacre a great reward. Rome was especially illumined to celebrate the death of so many of its enemies; Te Deums were sung, and the cannons of Castel St Angelo were fired in honour of the massacre. The Pope and his Cardinals went in special procession to the Church of St Mark, there to call God's attention to the good and religious work of the faithful; and Gregory himself proceeded in state on foot from St Mark's to St Louis'.

But if there was rejoicing in the Catholic world, there was deep consternation in England and Holland. William the Silent, who had been hoping for the help of France, through Coligny, was overcome with grief. He said that the King of France had been most evilly advised and that his realm would be plunged into fresh trouble ere long. The slaughtering of unsuspecting innocents, he went on, was no way in which to settle the differences of religion.

'This,' said Burleigh to the Queen of England, 'is the greatest crime since the Crucifixion.'

A few weeks after the massacre, the King was in his apartments, which were full of members of the court, and they were trying to regain something of that gaiety which had once been theirs. It was not easy. There was no forgetting. Names were casually mentioned, and it would then be remembered with a shock that that person was no more. Such a short while ago he had been alive, full of gaiety; now he was dead, and there, among them, was his murderer. The massacre haunted them like some evil spectre which they had called up from the underworld and which would not now be banished.

As they sat or stood about, talking loudly, giving vent to laughter which was, more often than not, unnatural, a great croaking was heard outside the windows of the Louvre, and the croaking was accompanied by a flapping of wings.

There was a sudden silence in the apartment followed by a susurration. 'It was as though,' someone remarked afterwards, 'the angel of death hovered over the Louvre.'

Catherine, deeply disturbed, for she was as superstitious as any present, hurried to the window and, looking out, saw a flock of ravens flying just above the palace. She cried out and everyone ran to the windows to watch the birds. They flew round, cawing; they perched on the building; they flew against the windows; and they remained in the vicinity of the palace for a long time.

Although some assumed that the birds had been attracted by

141

the carnage, all were unnerved that night.

Many believed that the birds were the spirits of those whom they had murdered come to haunt them and to remind them that their days also were numbered, that horrible death such as they had meted out to others might well await them.

Catherine called René and the Ruggieri brothers to her and demanded spells to protect her from impending evil.

The King called wildly to the birds: 'Come . . . whoever you be. Come and kill us . . . Do to us what we did to them.'

Madeleine and Marie Touchet did their best to soothe him.

Alençon, who had been sulking because he had been told nothing of the proposed massacre and had not been allowed to have a part in it, was relieved and able maliciously to watch the effect of the birds on those about him. Margot and Navarre watched with a good conscience. Anjou went shuddering to his mother and would not leave her. Henry of Guise was unperturbed. If the birds were the spirits of dead Huguenots, he was sure that the spirit of his father would protect him. He had but kept the vow to avenge him which he had made on his father's death.

But the King suffered most of all; and in the night he awakened from his sleep and ran screaming through the palace.

'What is all the noise in the streets?' he demanded. 'Why do the bells ring? Why do the people shout and scream? Listen. Listen. I can hear them. They are coming to kill us . . . as we killed them.'

Then he fell on to the floor, his limbs jerking in his terror; he bit his clothes and threatened to bite any who came near him.

'Stop them!' he cried. 'Stop the bells. Stop the people. Let us have done with bloodshed.'

Madeleine was brought to him. 'Charlot,' she whispered, 'all is well. All is quiet. Charlot . . . Charlot . . . you must not distress yourself.'

'But, Madelon, they will come for me . . . They will do to me what was done to them.'

'They cannot touch you. They are dead and you are the King.'

'They could return from their graves, Madelon. They have

come as black birds to torment me. They are in the streets now, Madelon. Listen. Listen. They shout. They scream. They are ringing all the bells . . .'

She led him to the window and showed him a quiet and sleeping Paris.

'I heard them,' he insisted. 'I heard them.'

'It was only in your dreams, my love.'

'Oh, Madelon, I am responsible. I said so at the meeting. I . . . I did it all.'

'You did not,' she said. 'It was not you. *They* did it. They forced you to it.'

'I do not know, Madelon. I can remember it . . . parts of it. I can remember the bells . . . the shouting and the blood. But I cannot remember how it came about. How did it come about? My headpiece knows nothing of it.'

'You knew nothing of it, my darling. You did not do it. It was they who did it.'

'They . . .' he stammered. 'She . . . my evil genius, Madelon. It was my evil genius . . .'

Then he began to sob and declare once more that he could hear noises in the streets.

He kept Madelon with him, there at the window, looking out over the sleeping city.

Three

The memory of those terrible days and nights continued to hang over Paris. Many of those who had taken part in the massacre were so troubled by conscience that they took their own lives; others went mad and ran screaming through the streets; some thought they were pursued by ghosts. So many were guilty. They could find some consolation in speaking together with venom and hatred of the woman whom they considered to have conceived the idea, to have inflamed them – the Italian woman. She was behind all the misery of France. Everyone knew that. The King was mad and he was controlled by that woman. He suffered more deeply than any; but there was no sign that Catherine suffered the slightest pangs of remorse.

Nor did she. She was not going to break a lifelong habit. She had learned not to look back, and she would not look back now. The massacre had been a necessity when it was committed, and it was no use regretting it after it was done. She was growing fatter; she looked in better health than she had for some time. An ambassador wrote to his government that she had the appearance of a woman who had successfully come through a bad illness. The illness had been her fear of Philip of Spain, and the cure was the massacre which had begun on St Bartholomew's Eve.

She had rarely felt so safe as she did during the winter of 1572 and the spring of the next year. Navarre and young Condé had become Catholics – Navarre cynically, Condé shamefully. The stock of these two Princes stood very low throughout the country, although most Huguenots who remained alive were resolute, more determined than ever. They seemed to embrace hardship and flourish under persecution. It was always so with fanatics. They had lost Coligny, Téligny and Rochefoucauld. Montgomery had been warned and had been able to fly from Saint-Germain before he could be caught. Navarre had succumbed almost immediately and accepted the Mass. But the Huguenots would not have hoped for much from Navarre. It was the defection of Condé which had been the bitterest blow to them. They were on the defensive now in that stronghold, La Rochelle, and were bent on making trouble; they had, however, suffered a severe blow and were temporarily helpless. As for Catherine, she was now recognized as the woman who planned the whole massacre.

Cynically she disguised herself and mingled with the people of Paris that she might hear what was said about her. She knew that it was their guilty consciences which made them so critical of her. They enumerated her crimes, often accusing her of murders in which she had had no hand.

'Who is this murderess, this poisoner, this Italian who rules France?' one merchant demanded of her as she stood by his stall, her shawl over her head, her soiled petticoat trailing below her shabby gown. 'She is not royal. She is the daughter of merchants. Ah, I knew what evils would come to France when she married the son of King Francis.'

'It is not fitting, Monsieur,' she agreed, 'to take a foreign upstart and make her Queen of France. For this Italian woman rules France, Monsieur. Make no mistake about that.'

'She rules France indeed. Our poor mad Charles would not be so bad without her to guide him . . . so they say. But he is no King. It is she who rules. She poisoned the Cardinal of Châtillon and the Sieur d'Andelot; she poisoned the Queen of Navarre. She is responsible for the death of Monsieur de Coligny,' went on the merchant. 'She is responsible for this bloody business. They say that she killed her son, Francis the Second . . . that he died before he should have done. And Monsieur d'Alençon was ill with fever, and they say that was her work. Do you remember the Duke of Bouillon, who was poisoned at Sedan? His doctor was hanged for that crime, but we know whose was the real guilt. Monsieur de Longueville, the Prince of Poitien, Monsieur Lignerolles . . . There is no end to the list, Madame; and then add to it all those who died at her command at the St Bartholomew. It is a long list of murders, Madame, for one woman to answer for.'

'Even for an Italian woman,' she admitted.

'Ah, Madame, you have spoken truly. I hope that one day there will be slipped into *her* wine that *morceau Italianizé.* That is what I wish, Madame. It is the wish of all Paris.'

She came away smiling. Better to win their hatred than their indifference. She wanted to laugh aloud. The Queen Mother ruled France. She was glad they realized that.

They were singing a song about her in the streets of Paris now. It was insolently sung even under the windows of the Louvre itself.

> *'Pour bien sçavoir la consonance*
> *De Catherine et Jhésabel,*
> *L'une, ruyne d'Israel,*
> *L'autre, ruyne de la France:*
>
> *'Jhésabel maintenoit l'idolle*
> *Contraire à la saincte parolle,*
> *L'autre maintient la papaulté*
> *Par trahison et cruaulté:*
>
> *'Par l'une furent massacrez*
> *Les prophètes à Dieu sacrez,*
> *Et l'autre a faict mourir cent mille*
> *De ceux qui suyvent l'Evangille.*
>
> *'L'une pour se ayder du bien,*
> *Fist mourir un homme de bien,*
> *L'autre n'est pas assouvie*
> *S'elle n'a les biens et la vie:*
>
> *'Enfin le jugement fut tel*
> *Que les chiens mengent Jhésabel*
> *Par une vengeance divine;*
> *Mais la charongne de Catherine*
> *Sera différente en ce point,*
> *Car les chiens ne la vouldront point.'*

Well, words could not hurt her. She herself sang the song. 'It is pleasant to think,' she said to her women, 'that the people of

Paris have no intention of throwing my flesh to the dogs.' She laughed loudly. 'Ah, my friends, these people are really fond of me. They like to think of me. Have you noticed that that wicked old lecher, the Cardinal of Lorraine, is now regarding me with some affection? He never did before. But now, he is not so young, and he is terrified of death, for that man was always a coward. He still wears a suit of mail under his clerical robes. But he looks at me with love because he says to himself: "I cannot live many more years. Soon I must face God." The Cardinal, my friends, is a very devout man, and when he thinks of the life he has led he trembles. And then he looks at me and says to himself: "Ah, compared with the Queen Mother, I am as innocent as a babe." And for this reason he grows fond of me. So it is with the people of Paris. Did I ride through the streets brandishing a sword on those August days and nights? No, I did not. But they did. Therefore it is comforting for them to recount my wickedness. They can then say: "Compared with Queen Jhésabel, we are innocent indeed." '

One day Charlotte de Sauves brought a book to Catherine.

'I think Your Majesty should see it,' she said, 'and that those who are guilty should be taken and punished.'

Catherine took the book, which was called *The Life of St Catherine*, and turned over the leaves. When she discovered that the title was an ironical one and the St Catherine was herself, she began to chuckle. There were hideous caricatures of her, only just recognizable in which she appeared quite gross. In these books were enumerated all the crimes of which the people of France accused her; everything evil that had happened in France since she, a little girl of fifteen, had ridden into the land to marry the King's son, were, according to the authors of this book, due to her.

Charlotte stood by, waiting for an outburst of wrath, but instead there came a loud guffaw.

Catherine called her women about her and read aloud to them.

'This is the story of your mistress, my friends. Now listen.' And she read until she was so overcome by mirth that she had to put the book away from her.

'It is well,' she said, 'that the French should know that they have a strong woman to rule them. Why, had I been given notice that such a book was about to be written, I could have told the authors many things of which they know nothing; I could have reminded them of much which they have forgotten. I could have helped them to make a bigger, finer book.'

Some of the women turned away that she might not see the looks of horror on their faces. They were depraved enough, since they were her creatures, but sometimes she revolted them. They realized that she, this Italian woman, this strange mistress of theirs, was different from others. She cared only for keeping power. She did not think beyond this life. This was why she could kill, and laugh at her killing, even be proud of it; she had no conscience to worry her.

Some of them remembered two boys they had seen among those pilgrims who had gone to look at the remains of Coligny, which had been hung on a gibbet at Montfaucon. One of those boys – he was only about fifteen years old – had broken down suddenly and flung himself on the ground while bitter sobs shook his body. The younger of the boys had stood very still, bewildered and frightened, too numbed by grief to weep as his brother did. When one knew that the fifteen-year-old boy was François de Coligny, and the younger one was his brother Andelot, that was an unforgettable tableau. One remembered too that Jacqueline de Coligny, in spite of her condition, had been carried off from Châtillon and put in a prison at Nice. Such matters haunted the memory. Moreover, these women were beset by superstitious fear. They remembered the miracle of Merlin, about which the Huguenots talked continually. Coligny's pastor had escaped on that night of terror. He had lain on the roofs after Téligny had been shot, and at length, weary beyond endurance, had clambered down from the roof to find himself beside a barn. Here he hid, and each day a hen came and – by the Grace of God, said the Huguenots – laid an egg beside him. This nourished him and kept him alive until the massacre was over.

Such stories were alarming, for it seemed that God was sometimes on the side of the Huguenots, even though the Virgin *had* made a hawthorn flower in the Cemetery of the Innocents.

148

Catherine laughed when she heard the story of Merlin and the eggs. It was she who recalled the flowering of the hawthorn.

'The good God preserve us from Heaven,' she cried, 'if when we get there we are going to find the Huguenots and Catholics still warring with one another.'

It was all very well to joke about such matters under the eye of the Queen Mother; but later came fears.

Catherine went on reading the book. She kept it with her, reading it at odd moments; and she was heard singing in her apartments:

> *L'une ruyne d'Israel,*
> *L'autre, ruyne de la France.*

*

After the massacre, Guise and Margot were no longer lovers.

Margot, like so many others, could not forget the massacre. She believed, as did most people, that her mother had inspired it and that, more than any person in France, she was responsible for it; but she could not forget the part her lover had played in it.

She had actually seen him, riding through the streets urging people to kill, and, she told herself impetuously, she could never love him again. He had changed, as she had; he was no longer the charming boy, but a man whose ambition meant far more to him than love ever could. He had known that she, as the wife of a Huguenot, must have been in danger, but he had neglected her. All that she had once so ardently loved in him – his beauty, his charm, his virility, and even his ambition, for she had believed then that a man must be ambitious to prove his manhood – now increased her indifference towards him.

He came to her after the massacre was over.

She said: 'You keep your appointment, Monsieur, but are you not a little late?'

He did not know that she had decided to finish with him. 'But, Margot, you understand how I have been occupied.'

'Too occupied in shedding blood to think of love!' she said.

'It had to be.'

149

She studied him closely. He had grown older. She thought: he will age quickly. Then she smiled, thinking of Monsieur de Léran, the man who had burst so dramatically into her bed-chamber; he was still weak, but, thanks to her, he would recover. He was very handsome, tender and grateful. One did not always want such self-satisfied, such arrogant and self-sufficient lovers as the man who stood before her now. There were some on whom too many gifts were showered; and such people knew little of gratitude for services rendered – and gratitude could be a delightful thing.

He came to her and put his arms about her. She did not repulse him yet; she laughed up at him.

'And now,' she said, 'there is time for love?'

'My darling,' he answered, 'it has been long, but love keeps; and can be all the more sweet for the waiting.'

'Sometimes it turns sour,' said Margot.

'You are annoyed, my darling?'

'Oh no, Monsieur. I could only be annoyed when I cared deeply.'

He did not understand. He had too high an opinion of himself. This was Margot, he thought, as he had known her so many times before – piqued, eager to be wooed into that abandonment of passion which was habitual to her.

'My dearest,' he began, but she interrupted.

'Ah, Monsieur de Guise,' she said, 'I have discovered that you are a better murderer than a lover, and you know I would be satisfied with nothing but the best. If I need a murderer, I may ask for your services. But when I need a lover, I shall not come to you.'

She saw at once that he was not only perplexed, but suspicious. She was involved with the Huguenots and therefore might be his enemy.

She laughed. 'Oh, be cautious, Monsieur de Guise. Remember that you are seeking a mistress from the Huguenot camp. Why do you not take your sword and kill me! You suspect me of friendship for Huguenots. That is sufficient reason to kill me, is it not?'

'Have you gone mad?' he demanded.

'No. I have merely ceased to love you. You do not look so handsome in my eyes as you once did. You arouse no desire in me whatsoever.'

'That cannot be true, Margot.'

'It must be difficult for you to believe it. But it is true. You may go now.'

'Dearest,' he said soothingly, 'you are angry because I have stayed from you too long. Had it been possible I should have come long ere this. You must understand that if we had not killed the Huguenots, they would have killed us'

'They would not!' she said vehemently. 'There was no Huguenot plot. You know as well as I do that the so-called Huguenot plot was an invention of my mother's. She wanted an excuse to murder.'

'Why do we concern ourselves with such unpleasant matters? Have you forgotten all that we are to one another?'

She shook her head. 'But it is over now. We must look elsewhere for our pleasures.'

'How can you talk so! All your life you have loved me.'

'Until now.'

'When did this end?'

'Perhaps on St Bartholomew's Eve.'

He put his arms about her and kissed her. She said, with dignity: 'Monsieur de Guise, I beg of you, release me.' And she laughed delightedly to find that she was quite unmoved by him.

He was the haughty one now. He was unaccustomed to being repulsed. It hurt his dignity, the dignity of Guise and Lorraine.

'Very well,' he said, releasing her. But he was hesitating, waiting for her to laugh, to tell him she loved him as much as ever and that her fit of temper was over.

But she stood still, smiling mockingly; and at length he turned angrily away and left her.

In the corridor he almost collided with Charlotte de Sauves, for Charlotte had not expected him to come out so quickly; she had thought that Margot would call him back and that there

151

would be one of those intense and passionate scenes to be reported to the Queen Mother.

He caught her as she gave a little cry and pretended to be almost knocked off her feet.

'Madame, I crave your pardon.'

She smiled up at him, flushed, aware that he must be noticing how beautiful she was. 'The fault was mine, Monsieur de Guise. I . . . I was about to go to Her Majesty . . . and I had no idea that anyone could come out so quickly.'

'I trust I did not hurt you?'

'No, Monsieur. Indeed not.'

He had smiled and passed on. Charlotte stood still, watching him.

She did not go into Margot's apartment at once, but stood outside, thinking deeply. Had Margot really meant what she had said? Was she really finishing her love affair – this most passionate of all love affairs, the most discussed at the court? Suppose this was so. Charlotte smiled. A woman should be allowed to please herself sometimes. She was weary of this game she must play with Navarre, keeping him desirous yet unsatisfied. Perhaps it would be as well to say nothing to the Queen Mother of this little scene. She might receive definite instructions regarding the Duke of Guise if Catherine were told, for there was no doubt that the Queen Mother had an uncanny knack of discovering the inner thoughts and yearnings of her *Escadron Volant*.

No. Charlotte would say nothing of what she had discovered; and if the handsome Duke was in need of a little comfort – Charlotte had received no direct instructions from her mistress to deny him.

❀

Catherine's satisfaction could not last long; and if she did not regret her increased unpopularity throughout France and that her evil reputation was spreading abroad, she was perturbed to see how far the King was straying from her influence. She had thought that, having destroyed the influence of Coligny, she would be able to restore that relationship which had existed between herself and Charles before he had fallen under the spell of the Admiral; but this was not so. Charles was weaker in physical health; his bouts of madness were more frequent; but it was obvious that, tormented by the memory of those fateful August days and nights, he, like the rest of the world, blamed Catherine for the massacre, and his great desire now was to escape from her domination.

He continually remembered the words of the Admiral: 'Govern alone. Evade the influence of your mother.' And he intended to do that, as far as his poor weak mind would allow him.

Catherine knew this and it disturbed her greatly. If, as many people said, it was true that her real motive in murdering Coligny had been to leave herself in sole command over her son, she had completely failed to achieve that desired result; for Charles was further from her control than he had ever been.

Spain, now that it had ceased to exult over the massacre, hinted that since so many Huguenot leaders were now dead – and Philip understood that the marriage had been necessary to bring the unsuspecting victims into the trap – there was no reason why that marriage should not be dissolved.

Catherine had at first felt indignant. 'My daughter, a bride of a few months ... just beginning to love her husband ... and now it is suggested that the marriage should be dissolved!'

The Spanish ambassador smiled cynically. 'The gentleman of Navarre is not such a good *parti* now, Madame, despised as he is by both Catholics *and* Huguenots. Not a very grand marriage for a daughter of a royal house!'

Catherine pondered that and, after a while, it seemed to her that there was much in what he said. Even in the event of civil war – which seemed remote now that the ranks of the Huguenots were so depleted – it was hardly likely that the people of France would wish to see a man who could change sides so easily – and a noted *bon vivant* and philanderer at that – on the throne.

She knew to whom the people of France would look if by some dire misfortune – and Catherine herself would fight to the death to avoid that misfortune – the sons of the House of Valois were robbed of their prior claim to the throne. He was that young man who, in Paris at least, could do no wrong. He

153

had been the leader, one might say, in the massacre, but no one in Paris blamed him. It was said that he but obeyed the orders of the King and the Queen Mother. What a good thing after all was the popularity of the mob! It excused your faults and extolled your virtues.

Yes, Paris would delight to see its hero on the throne, even though his right to it was a little obscure.

She pondered deeply. One must adjust one's policy to events; and circumstances altered cases. Now it seemed that it might not have been so very unwise to have allowed Margot to marry Henry of Guise when those two had so desired; although it had appeared quite wrong at the time. But in view of the turn of events, and of Navarre's recent record, a marriage between Margot and Guise had now become more desirable than that between Margot and Henry of Navarre. The Pope naturally would raise no difficulty, and Philip of Spain would be pleased. Guise was known to Spain and Rome as one of the most loyal Catholics in France. Why not a double divorce? Guise divorced from his wife; Margot from her husband; and those two, who were so passionately in love, might marry after all! Catherine smiled ironically. This seemed to be one of those occasions when the chief parties concerned could all be happy and sensible at the same time.

She discussed the matter with the Spanish ambassador. He was favourably impressed. So Catherine next sent for her daughter, and there took place one of those secret interviews with which the children of Catherine were very familiar.

'My daughter, you know that I have always had your well-being at heart ... your position ... you future ... You did not know, did you, that I also concerned myself with your happiness?'

Margot was inclined to be truculent. She too had changed. As a married woman and a Queen she seemed to have moved from her mother's influence, even as her brother the King had done. 'No, Madame,' she said, insolence carefully veiled. 'I did not know that.'

Catherine would have liked to slap the saucy young face.

'Well, you shall know it now. This marriage, which was so necessary, has been a tragic affair. But you do understand, do you not, my daughter, that it was a necessity at the time it took place.'

'Yes, Madame,' said Margot. 'The unsuspecting Huguenots had to be drawn into the trap, and for that reason the marriage and its ceremonies were very necessary.'

Catherine was determined to show no anger. 'My dear daughter, you repeat the scandals of the court, and you should be clever enough to know that scandals are but half-truths; and surely you are wise enough not to believe all you hear. Now I have good news for you. That man, to whom it was necessary to marry you, is unworthy of you. He is provincial, coarse . . . Really, his manners shock me.' Catherine gave her sudden laugh. 'And you, who are forced to live with him in intimacy, must be doubly shocked, I'm sure.'

'One adjusts oneself,' said Margot.

'And what an adjustment must be necessary, my poor dear child! You are elegant. You have charm and beauty. You are of Paris. It is intolerable that you should have to endure the caresses of the boor of Béarn. There is one who is worthy of you. A man who, many in France would tell you, is the most revered . . . next your King and your brothers, of course. You guess to whom I refer?'

'To Monsieur de Guise. But . . .'

'My dear, you need feel no shame. Your mother knows of your relationship with that gentleman, and quite understands it. In fact she has always understood it. He is a Prince and you are a Princess. What more natural than that you should love?'

Margot was watching her mother closely; she could not guess the meaning of this interview. That her mother was preparing her for some dark scheme she was sure; but what?

'It is your happiness that I now seek, my child,' said Catherine. 'You have served your country by marrying for reasons of state. You will understand that I speak truth when I say I seek nothing but your happiness, when I tell you that I am now going to arrange that you shall marry for love.'

'Madame, as I am already married, I do not understand.'

'My dear child, my obedient daughter! You married most reluctantly, did you not? Ha! I remember how you refused to

155

make the responses at the ceremony. That was a very brave thing to do. And he was so close, was he not, the man you loved? Well, now I have decided that you shall live in torment no longer. You shall have Henry of Guise for your husband.'

Margot was stunned by this revelation. 'Madame . . . I . . . I do not see how that can be. I . . . I am married to the King of Navarre. Henry of Guise is married to Procien's widow . . .'

'Then you shall be "unmarried" and . . . marry each other!'

Catherine waited for the joyful tears, the expressions of gratitude; instead Margot's face had become cold and hard.

'Madame,' she said, 'I am married to the King of Navarre, and that marriage took place against my will; but now it would be against my will to . . . as you say . . . "unmarry" him.'

'Oh come, Margot, your rank as Queen of Navarre is not such a good one. How will you like going with him to that miserable little kingdom when the time comes? There are some Duchesses who are in positions superior to some Queens . . . and the Duchess of Guise would be one of them.'

'That may be so,' said Margot, 'but Henry of Guise does not please me, and I would not marry a second time against my wishes.'

'This is sheer perversity!' cried Catherine angrily. 'You to talk like this! You who have made a spectacle of yourself over that man!'

'You are right, Madame,' said Margot coolly. 'But one grows out of one passion and into another. I have grown out of love with Monsieur de Guise, and nothing would induce me to marry him; and since you have told me that nothing but your desire for my happiness prompts you to make this suggestion, there is no more to be said. For, quite simply, I am not in love with Monsieur de Guise. Have I your leave to retire now?'

'It would be advisable for you to do so,' said Catherine grimly, 'before you tempt me to do you some mischief.'

When Margot left her she sat in furious silence. She found it impossible to believe that Guise and Margot were no longer lovers. They had been so ever since she could remember. Was a woman ever before cursed with such a family? The King had turned against her; Alençon she had never liked nor trusted;

156

Margot was too clever, too shrewd – a little spy, not averse to working against her family; only Henry could be trusted.

She instructed one of her spies to watch Margot and Guise very closely. It was true that they had ceased to be lovers. In the course of these investigations Catherine made a discovery which resulted in her sending for Charlotte de Sauves. She was very angry with that young woman.

'Madame,' she accused, 'you seem to be very friendly with the Duke of Guise.'

Charlotte was startled, but Catherine was quick to sense a certain smugness. 'I did not know that Your Majesty would frown on such a friendship.'

Catherine stroked one of the charms on her bracelet. So this was the explanation. Guise was indulging in a love affair with Charlotte, and Margot was piqued and jealous.

She said sharply: 'There must be no love-making with the Duke, Charlotte. If there were, it would displease me greatly. I can speak frankly to you. The Queen of Navarre is greatly enamoured of the Duke.'

'Your Majesty . . . that is no longer so. I understand that the Queen of Navarre has declared that she no longer feels friendship towards the Duke.'

'Because you have been playing tricks, I suppose.'

'Oh no, Madame; she gave him his *congé* before he looked my way. Monsieur de Guise is of the opinion that she has become enamoured of the King of Navarre.'

'Margot and Guise must make up their quarrels,' said Catherine. 'As for you, Madame, you will keep away from the Duke. There must be no love-making.'

'Madame,' said Charlotte slyly, 'I fear your command comes too late.'

'You sly slut!' cried Catherine. 'I thought I had given you instructions regarding Navarre.'

'But only to attract him, Madame. That was all; and there was no word in Your Majesty's instructions regarding Monsieur de Guise.'

'Well, you have my instructions now.'

Charlotte looked at Catherine from under those thick eyelashes of hers. 'Madame,' she said, 'it will be necessary for you to instruct Monsieur de Guise, for I fear that, no matter how I tried to avoid him, I could not succeed. It would therefore be necessary to give him Your Majesty's personal instructions. Otherwise I fear there could be no stopping what has already begun. Monsieur de Guise would take orders from none ... except, of course, Your Majesty.'

Catherine was silent, thinking angrily of the arrogant Duke. How could she say to such a man: 'Your affaire with Madame de Sauves must stop immediately!' She could imagine the haughty lift of the eyebrows, the courteous remark which would imply that his affaire was no concern of hers.

She laughed suddenly. 'Go away,' she said. 'I see that this matter must take its own course. But, in future, Madame, you will ask my permission *before* you enter into such a liaison.'

'Madame, never fear that I shall offend again.'

Catherine sat back, thinking of Charlotte de Sauves. It was galling to think that that sly little harlot's love affairs could turn the Queen Mother from a line of policy which she had intended to adopt. But such things could happen occasionally. Catherine therefore decided that there was nothing to do for the moment but to shelve the idea of 'unmarrying' her daughter.

*

Civil war between Catholics and Huguenots had broken out again, and an army under Anjou was sent to besiege the Huguenots' stronghold of La Rochelle.

With the Catholic army were Guise and his uncle, the Duke of Aumale; and Catherine felt comforted to think of those two supporters of her beloved son, for Catherine – even as far as Henry was concerned – had a habit of looking facts in the face, and it was hard, even for her, to believe that Henry, with his effeminacy and his unstable ways, had really the character of a great general. It was true that the credit for Jarnac and Montcontour had gone to him; but would he have succeeded but for those brilliant soldiers who had shared the campaign? As the Prince of Valois, brother of the King, and the most illustrious general in the army, he had received the credit; but Catherine knew that credit did not always go to those who most deserved it. It pleased her though that he should take the glory and so win the approval of the people. To him should go the honours of the victory which must surely come about at La Rochelle. Guise and Aumale were great men of battle; and Guise could inspire – effortlessly as his father had done – that blind devotion which led men to victory.

It was, therefore, rather amusing to send with the army those two converts to Catholicism, Navarre and Condé. It was a situation tinged with that special brand of irony which amused Catherine; and to think of those two 'converts' fighting against their one-time friends delighted her. Alençon was also sent with the army, for it was time that young man won his spurs, and the adventure should keep him out of mischief for a time.

She had high hopes of the early surrender of La Rochelle, but in this she was disappointed. The recent massacre had strengthened the determination of the people in that town, with the result that the heroic few were able to stand up to superior numbers. The besieging army was more disturbed by the spirit of the people within the walls of La Rochelle than harassed by the missiles of war which flew from the battlements; and it was as though those gallant people were on the offensive instead of, as was obviously the case, in such a precariously defensive position.

Guise and Aumale had the additional problem of keeping the peace in their own camp. In view of the difficult task of subduing La Rochelle, it had been folly to allow Navarre and Condé to accompany them, for neither of these had any heart for the fight. Condé, who had had some reputation as a fighter, seemed lethargic and useless; while Navarre was lazily cheerful, spending too much time with the women who had followed the camp.

As for Alençon, he was actually a menace. Truculent in the extreme, anxious always that he should receive his share of adulation which his close relationship to the King demanded, he was utterly conceited and no help at all.

All day long the sound of singing could be heard from behind the walls of La Rochelle – the singing of hymns. It

159

seemed that religious services were being conducted continually. The superstitious Catholics were unnerved, and as the siege dragged on, they became more so. The news circulated that great quantities of fish had been caught off the shores of La Rochelle and that the Huguenots took this as a sign that God intended to preserve them.

Guise persuaded Anjou that the best thing to do was to attack the town and take it by force of overwhelming numbers before the besieged had completed their preparations for its defence; this idea that God was on the side of the Huguenots must not be allowed to demoralize the Catholic army.

Anjou agreed, and there followed that historic attack in which a few Huguenots triumphed over the great Catholic army through sheer determination not to surrender and an unwavering belief that they were receiving Divine help. Those who took part in the attack never forgot it. The citizens had hung a hawthorn on the ramparts to remind the Catholics of their contempt for that hawthorn which had flowered in the Cemetery of the Innocents – flowered at the Devil's command, said the Huguenots.

The fight began, but the city's walls stood firm; and the women themselves mounted the towers and poured boiling pitch on the soldiers below. And as soon as there was a lull in the fighting, the citizens of La Rochelle could be heard singing praises to God.

'Let God arise, and let His enemies be scattered; let them also that hate Him flee before Him . . .

'Like the smoke vanisheth, so shalt Thou drive them away; and like as wax melteth at the fire, so let the ungodly perish at the presence of God . . .'

To the superstitious men below, this was terrifying; particularly as it seemed to them that the walls of La Rochelle had stood more assault than a city's walls could, without Divine assistance.

And so the battle for La Rochelle was a defeat for the Catholic army, and the walls of the city continued to stand firm against all attack. The Catholics counted their dead and wounded to the sound of triumphant singing within the city's walls.

Alençon swaggered into his brother's tent and, throwing himself unceremoniously on to Anjou's bed, began to taunt him with the loss of the battle.

'Here's a pretty state of affairs!' mocked Alençon. 'A great army defeated by a few men and women behind city walls. I tell you, brother, the mistake was yours. You were too noisy in your preparations. *I* should have smuggled men into the city somehow. *I* should have sent spies among them.'

'Fool!' cried Anjou. 'What do you know of battle? Would you have given your spies wings to fly over the city's walls?'

'I would ask you not to call me "Fool", brother, but to remember to whom you speak.'

'Have a care lest I put you under arrest, Monsieur,' said Anjou coldly.

But Alençon would not heed him. He was the brother of the King, just as Anjou was, and he had been neglected too long.

'Brother,' he teased, 'you are more successful at court than on a battlefield. You choose your men for their beauty rather than for their military ability.'

'Your lack of beauty, brother, is not the only reason why I do not confide in you,' said Anjou languidly.

Alençon was sensitive about his shortness of stature and pock-marked skin. He flushed angrily and began to shout, calling his brother a conceited popinjay who looked more like a woman than a man.

Anjou said: 'If you do not remove yourself in ten seconds I will put you under arrest.'

Then Alençon thought it better to go quickly. He knew that his mother would approve of anything that Anjou planned for him; and he would certainly find himself a prisoner if he were not careful.

As he came out of his brother's tent, he encountered Navarre, who seemed to be lounging about outside. Navarre smiled in a sympathetic fashion, and Alençon was ready to accept sympathy from anyone at that moment.

'You heard?' demanded Alençon fiercely.

'It was impossible not to. The insolence! He forgets that if he is a Prince of Valois, so are you.'

'It is pleasant to know that some remember it,' muttered Alençon.

Navarre smiled at the little figure beside him. There were many who thought Alençon rather ridiculous, but Henry of Navarre knew that since the massacre he himself had been in a very precarious position, and a man as wise as Henry of Navarre, when in such a position, does not despise friendship.

'My lord,' said Navarre, 'they would be fools to forget it when it is possible that one day you may be King over us all.'

The thought pleased Alençon; and coming from Navarre, who was after all a king – if somewhat eclipsed at the moment – it was doubly pleasant.

'I am many steps from the throne,' he mused smiling.

'Not so. The King's son did not live . . . nor would any child of his, I am thinking. And when the King dies . . .'

'There is my arrogant brother whom you so recently heard insult me.'

'Yes. But he is hardly likely to produce progeny. And then . . .' Henry of Navarre administered a Béarnais slap on the back which almost knocked Alençon off his feet; but the little Duke did not mind such boisterous behaviour when accompanied by words which were so gratifying. If one could forgive the crude manners of a provincial, he thought, he is not such a bad fellow, this Henry of Navarre.

They walked in friendly silence for a few paces.

'And so,' continued Navarre at length, 'your time will come. I am sure of that, my lord Duke.'

Alençon looked up into the shrewd face of his kinsman.

'You are happier now that you have become a Catholic?' he asked.

Then Henry of Navarre did an astonishing thing. He closed one eye and opened it swiftly. There was something worldly about Navarre, something experienced, which made Alençon long to be like him. Alençon chuckled. He knew that Navarre was hoodwinking such people as the King, Anjou and the Queen Mother in just the way which he, Alençon, longed to do. He found himself returning the wink.

'So . . . you are not truly Catholic?' he asked.

'I am Catholic today,' said Navarre. 'Who knows what I may be tomorrow?'

Alençon laughed conspiratorially. 'I myself have been attracted to the Huguenot faith,' he ventured.

'It may well be,' said Navarre, 'that, like me, you intend to be a Huguenot-Catholic.'

Alençon laughed with Navarre; and then they began to talk of women, a subject which Alençon found almost as exciting as Navarre did.

They were very quickly the best of friends. Navarre showed that right mixture of respect for a man who might be a King one day, and *camaraderie* for a fellow who he recognized as just such another as himself.

Those were uneasy weeks before La Rochelle. Anjou and Guise noticed the growing friendship between the mischievous pair and wondered what it foreboded; Condé and Navarre, encouraged by Alençon, who was now their recognized ally, threatened to desert. The army seemed about to disintegrate when Catherine and the council in Paris decided it was time to make peace. The King of Poland had died, and Anjou had been elected by the Poles as their new King; it was therefore necessary to recall him to Paris without delay. So the town of La Rochelle must be left in peace for a spell. The Huguenots were promised liberty of worship and the right to celebrate marriages and christenings in their own houses if no more than ten people were present. The war had come to another uneasy pause.

*

Riding to the hunt, Catherine watched her son, and asked herself how much longer he could be expected to live. His lung complaint had grown so much worse that he was continually out of breath. He blew his horn more frequently than was necessary, and such a strain on his lungs, Paré had warned him, should be avoided.

But when Charles was in one of his violent moods he never thought of what was good or bad for him.

He cannot live much longer, thought Catherine.

However, the position was alarming although there was one bright side to it. Charles' son had died, as she had guessed he would. From the day of the child's birth she had known she could safely leave it to its fate; but, strangely enough, he had a healthy son now by Marie Touchet, and the Queen was pregnant again. What if the Queen were to produce a healthy child as Marie had done! Then on the King's death there would have to be another regency – and worse still, an end to her darling Henry's hopes of the throne. She would never allow that to come about.

'My son,' she said, knowing full well that comments on his health could irritate him when he was in certain moods, 'you tire yourself.'

He turned angry eyes upon her. 'Madame, I am the best judge of that.'

He was at the beginning of one of his violent moods. She, who knew him so well, could see it encroaching on his sanity. In a short while that whip of his would descend on his horse, on his dogs and on his huntsmen as they happened to come within his range. She saw the foam on his mouth and heard the familiar hysteria in his voice.

'What is the matter with you all?' he shouted. 'My horse slackens speed. My dogs seem asleep, and my men are a lazy good-for-nothing lot. By God!' Down came the whip on his horse's flank.

Catherine watched, smiling a little. That is well, she thought. Beat the creature to madness. May it bolt and throw you, and let that be an end to your madness and you, for I am heartily sick of you, and it is time Henry was King.

He caught her eyes fixed on him, and fearing that he might have read her thoughts she said quickly: '*Hé*, my son. Why do you get so angry with your dogs and horses and these poor men whose delight it is to serve you, while you are over-meek with your enemies?'

'Over-meek!' he cried.

'Why are you not angry with those wretches in La Rochelle who are causing death and suffering to so many in your army?'

The King's brow puckered. He said: 'Wars ... wars ... It is

all wars. It is all bloodshed in this land.' He glared at Catherine and began to shout. 'And who is the cause of it all? Tell me that.' He shouted to his men: 'Tell me! Who is the cause of this, eh? You . . . you tell me. Who is the cause of all the misery of this land? Answer me. Have you no tongues? We will see . . . we will see . . . and if you have, we will have them out, since they appear to be no use to you.' He lifted his whip and slashed his dogs. 'Who is the cause of all our misery, eh?' Then he turned his fierce, mad eyes again on his mother. 'We know!' he cried. 'All know. My God! It is you . . . *you*, Madame . . . you are our evil genius. You are the cause of it all.'

Then, digging his spurs into his horse, he turned and galloped madly away from them – back the way they had come.

The huntsmen looked at Catherine in dismay, but she was calm and smiling.

'His Majesty is out of humour today,' she said. 'Come, let us ride on. We have come to hunt, so let us hunt.'

And as she rode on she was thinking: this is rebellion. He flouts me . . . even before his lowest servants. It cannot be allowed to continue. I will not be treated thus. Assuredly, my son Charles, you have lived too long!

And when she returned to the palace it was to find that ambassadors from Poland had arrived.

*

Anjou was sulky. He could not bear the thought of being sent away to Poland. How could such as he was endure life in the barbarous country which Poland must be? Since he had tired of Renée de Châteauneuf, he had formed an attachment with the Princess of Condé, young Condé's wife. He could not, he now declared, endure the thought of parting from her.

The situation was alarming, for the King had made it clear that he intended Anjou to accept the Polish throne. Their mother would do all in her power to frustrate the King, but Anjou was fully aware that Catherine's influence with Charles was waning fast. Charles looked upon Anjou as his enemy, and wished to exile him as soon as possible; moreover, it was said that the King would not be greatly disturbed if the Queen Mother decided to accompany her favourite son to Poland.

Catherine went to Anjou, who was fuming in his apartments, surrounded by three of his young men. The three young men were in tears at the prospect of losing their benefactor or, failing that, accompanying him far from the civilized land of France to the barbarous one of Poland.

'The King is obstinate,' said Catherine. 'He declares you must go. It is no use bewailing. We must think of something that we can do.' Her eyes alighted on her son's table with its bottles of perfume and pots of cosmetics. She looked at the sprawling yet completely elegant figure, and she thought: what will those barbarians think of his elegance, of his young men, and his preoccupation with his own beauty?

Then she laughed suddenly. 'Why, my son,' she said, 'you will appear to these men of Poland as strange, unlike themselves. I think they will not wish you to show yourself to your Polish subjects. They will wish you to send a lieutenant to rule for you – someone coarse, crude, more like themselves. I have it. We will make you even more elegant than usual – if that be possible. Let us paint your face more vividly; let us perfume your body; let us curl your hair. We will show them that you could not live among them. Then I will bring forth one of our big rough men and show him to them . . . a man such as these savages would understand.'

Anjou smiled. 'My dearest mother, what should I do without you?'

They embraced warmly and Catherine was momentarily happy.

He wore his jacket open at the throat and a string of pearls about his neck. He loaded his ears with pearls; his hair was curled in a most elegant fashion; his face more vividly painted than usual.

The young men clapped their hands and declared that he had but enhanced his beauty.

Catherine chuckled. 'I shall enjoy seeing their faces when they set eyes on you.'

When Anjou was presented to the Polish ambassadors, they stared in astonishment, for the moment completely forgetting the etiquette of greeting their new King.

Anjou smiled sardonically while the King looked on with

anger; some of the courtiers could not restrain a titter. Never before had Anjou looked so completely unlike a King, and never, said some, more like a female courtesan.

But now the Poles had recovered from their astonishment and were bowing low over the scented hand. It was obvious that they had never before seen anyone like their new King, and yet, instead of being disgusted by his appearance, they were delighted with it. They could not take their eyes from him; they laughed with pleasure every time he spoke to them. They whispered together that never, in the whole of their lives, had they seen such a glorious creature.

Catherine watched in dismay.

'A King in very truth,' said one of the Poles in his odd French.

'Our people will never let such a man go, Madame,' said another to Catherine. 'They have never seen any like him. They will love this King.'

And they continued to gaze at him with delight, certain that such a wonderful creature must receive the admiration of all who beheld him.

•

Anjou was *distrait*; Catherine was furious; but Charles was adamant. Here was a Heaven-sent opportunity to rid himself of the brother whom he hated; and no pleading, no threats from Catherine, no sarcasm from Anjou, would make any difference to the King's decision. Anjou was to go to Poland.

Anjou declared that if he were parted from the Princess of Condé his heart would be broken. His natural wit seemed to have deserted him; he could do nothing but bemoan his cruel fate.

Catherine made her preparations calmly enough, successfully hiding her fury from all but her intimates.

When the royal party set out to accompany Anjou to the border, the King declared his intention of going with it. He wanted, he said to his friends, to have the great joy of seeing Anjou leave the soil of France.

Marie Touchet begged the King to take care; Madeleine joined in her entreaties.

'What do you fear?' asked Charles. 'Anjou knows he must obey his King, and do not doubt that he will.'

Neither Marie nor Madeleine dared say that it was not Anjou whom they feared.

Catherine rode beside Anjou, who noticed that she seemed to be unconcerned at the prospect of their parting. He was inclined to be petulant. 'I cannot understand you,' he said. 'You seem to contemplate my departure with the same pleasure as does my brother who hates me.'

Catherine shook her head and said in a low voice: 'To contemplate parting with you, as you must know, could bring me nothing but grief.'

'Madame, you have a strange way of expressing your grief.'

'Oh my darling, have you not yet learned that I am an adept at masking my feelings?'

'I feel that this departure of mine seems to you like one of the court comedies which you so much enjoy.' He turned to smile at her. 'No doubt your joy seems so sincere because it is real joy. Dear mother, you are an adept at providing the drama or the comedy as well as wearing the mask.'

'Ah, I knew your ready wit would tell you something of this.' She leaned towards him. 'You may go to Poland, my darling, and . . . on the other hand . . . you may not.'

'What? Can plans be changed at this late hour?'

'Surely you can imagine circumstances in which they might be.'

He caught his breath, and there was silence between them for a few seconds. Then Catherine continued: 'If you did, by some ill-chance, reach that barbarous land, you may be sure that your stay in it would be a short one.'

Madeleine overheard those words and trembled. Madeleine was surprised to find what a good spy she had become. It was, she guessed, because the good God endowed mothers with some special sense when their little ones were in danger; and she had always looked upon herself as mother to the King.

Now she began to watch what was brought for the King to eat or drink; but it was not possible for her to taste everything that he took. How could she, his nurse, take her place at the banqueting table in the various castles at which they stayed? She became so anxious that at last she decided to speak to him of her fears.

She asked that she might be quite alone with him and indulgently he granted that permission.

'Sire,' she said, 'you know that I love you.'

He kissed her hand tenderly. 'I have no doubt of that, dear Madelon.'

'Then you will listen with attention to what I have to say. I believe there are some in this company who are trying to shorten your life.'

He was startled. The fear of death was stronger than it had ever been. 'What have you discovered?' he asked.

'I cannot say that I have actually discovered a plot. It is some sense . . . that warns me. I am as a mother to you, Charlot, and I sense that you are in danger.'

'You think that someone is trying to poison me, Madelon?'

'I am sure of it. I am not always with you to supervise what you eat and drink, and this gives me great cause for anxiety. It occurs to me that it would be an easier matter to kill you on a journey like this than at home, at court, where you are surrounded by friends and doctors.'

'Madelon, speak frankly to me.'

'There are some who are grieved that Monsieur d'Anjou is leaving us, and moreover do not intend that he should. There are some who would like to see him in your place, and those would be pleased if you were no longer with us.'

Charles flung himself into his nurse's arms. 'Oh, God,' he cried, 'I am afraid of her. I know you speak truth, dearest Nurse. I would that you were my mother in truth. What can I do? Oh, Madelon . . .' He looked furtively round him. 'Monsieur de Coligny was my friend. He said she was my evil genius. He warned me, as you do now. Would I had taken his advice. Then I should not have been led to that wicked slaughtering of innocents . . . that bloodshed. I cannot escape from it, Madelon. It pursues me . . . continually.'

'You must banish it from your mind, my darling. It was no fault of yours. But let us think of this danger which now lies before us.'

'Madelon, what can I do? If it is decided that there shall be a *morceau Italianizé* for me, then so it will be, I fear. Those who are marked down never escape.'

'It shall not be,' said Madelon. 'You are the King. That is a fact which you often forget, my little one. Let us, with those whom we trust, ride back to Paris. You must announce our intentions to leave at once. The Queen Mother, her women and her friends, will go on with Monsieur le Duc to Lorraine. And we will ride back, safe and happy. Do that, my Charlot, to please your old Madelon, who loves you as her own son, and whose heart would break if aught ill should happen to you.'

'Oh, Madelon,' he sobbed, 'how good it is to have true friends. I am not alone, am I? There are some who love me. There is blood on my hands, and some say that I am mad, but I have good friends, have I not?'

'You will always have Madelon to love and watch over you,' said his nurse.

❋

Catherine bade farewell to her beloved son.

'My darling,' she said, 'you must go, but believe me when I tell you it shall not be for long. You should not have gone at all if I had had my will.'

Anjou had to be content with that. He guessed that the King's sudden decision not to accompany the party farther than Vitry-sur-Marne, and his immediate return to Paris with a few friends, meant that one of the latter had discovered his mother's plans. This brought home to him afresh the fact that his mother was not all-powerful. People had become more suspicious of her than ever.

He wept dramatically and declared himself to be the most unhappy man in the world.

'I must leave the Princess whom I love; I must leave my mother, who is my good friend; I must leave my home and my family. Oh, what a sad fate it is to be a King!'

He had desired above all things to be a King, but a King of France, not of Poland. However, he could not but enjoy the role of exile; he played it delicately and with tears which were not

170

allowed to spoil his complexion or redden the lids of his long dark eyes.

But when he had left the French border and was travelling through Flanders – which he was forced to do in order to reach Poland – he began to realize that a really uncomfortable stage of his journey had begun. He entered a small town with his *entourage* and, expecting to be admired as he had been during the first stages of his journey, he prepared himself to smile graciously on the assembled townsfolk who must, his gentlemen assured him, be as enchanted by the sight of him as those of his Polish subjects who had already seen him had undoubtedly been.

To his horror, he found that numbers of those people in the streets were not foreigners; they were French – men and women who had recently fled from France to escape the Catholic persecution in which he himself had played so prominent a part.

They shouted after him as he rode by: 'Ah, there he goes, the fop! The dandy! But not too foppish, not too much the dandy to stain his hands with the blood of martyrs. Where were you, Monsieur, on the night of August the 23rd . . . the 24th . . . the 25th? . . . Answer. Answer.'

He look at those people and shuddered. They threw mud and dung at him, and he was horrified to see and smell it on his beautiful clothes. There was nothing he and his followers could do but dig their spurs into their horses' flanks and ride away to the ironical laughter of the French refugees.

It was a most uncomfortable journey. Anjou dreaded entering the towns; he hated the discomfort of such travel. He longed for his charming mistress; he longed for the luxurious comfort of Paris.

'And whither are we bound?' he complained. 'Only for some foreign land. How can such as I *exist* among savages! My mother promised that I should not be away from home for long, but how can she prevent it? My brother ignores her now. How discourteously he left us to continue our journey! She no longer has any power over him. He is jealous of me . . . so he banishes me. It may be . . . for ever!'

171

But there were worse shocks awaiting the unhappy Anjou. The Elector Palatine received him courteously; he could do nothing else, since he was not now at war with France; but Anjou, remembering his reception by the French refugees and some of the natives of this Protestant land, had one wish, and that was to reach Poland as soon as possible.

'You honour us indeed,' said the Elector; but he did not act as though this were an honour he greatly appreciated. He and his fellow countrymen in their simple dress managed to make Anjou feel ill at ease and ridiculous as he never did at home; and while these people entertained him with all the honour due to him, they made him realize that they did not forget the St Bartholomew for one moment and blamed him as one of those responsible for the massacre.

The Elector himself, when the banquet in Anjou's honour was over, conducted the Duke to his chamber. It was dimly lighted and it was only when Anjou was alone – but for a few attendants – that he noticed the murals. Taking a candle to study them more closely, he uttered a scream of horror, and almost dropped his candle. He was looking at a picture of a Paris square, and in that square were bodies piled one on top of the other. There was a headless corpse in the forefront of the picture; and looking on, smiles on their faces – which must have been the most diabolical ever depicted – were men and women, all of whom wore hats with white crosses on them.

Anjou shuddered and turned away, but his eyes were immediately held by another picture. Here was Paris again, showing horrors more terrible than the first. From this he went to a picture of Lyons and then to another, on the same subject, of Rouen.

All four walls of the apartment were painted with pictures of the massacre of the St Bartholomew and, so lifelike were they, so realistic, that Anjou could not avoid the feeling that he stood in those streets depicted there, and that the horrors were still going on.

He turned to his young men, but they were as shocked as he was and could offer no comfort.

'What do they intend to do to us?' whispered one of them.

172

'They are attempting to unnerve us!' cried Anjou. 'To let us know that they remember. As long as that is all, no harm can come to us.'

He threw himself on to his bed, but he was in no mood for sleep. He ordered that all candles should be snuffed out; but when the apartment was in darkness the pictures seemed more vivid than before, since imagination, aided by memory, could conjure up scenes more readily than the excellent artist whom the Elector had employed for the discomfiture of the guest he hated.

'Light the candles!' cried Anjou. 'I cannot endure the darkness. How many hours till morning?'

There were many hours to be lived through before he could leave this accursed place, he knew.

He could not keep his eyes from the pictures.

'I feel that I am there . . . in Paris . . . looking on . . . seeing it all. Oh, my friends, it was even more terrible than that. But how real the blood looks in the pictures! . . . Oh, what blood we shed in Paris! It will never be forgotten.'

His friends assured him that he had not been to blame. 'Others were responsible. There was nothing you could have done to prevent it.'

But if Anjou lacked courage, he did not lack imagination, and those pictures recalled too many memories for his peace of mind. There was no sleep for him that night. He lay tossing and turning on his bed, calling to his friends not to sleep, but to talk to him, amuse him. He had them snuff out the candles; then he had them relighted. He could not make up his mind whether he would rather see the pictures or imagine them springing to life in the darkness.

A few hours before dawn, he got up. 'I cannot rest,' he said, 'and I do not think I ever shall until I have written down what happened on that night. The world should know. So, I will write a confession. I will not excuse myself, for I am as guilty as most, of that horrible crime. I will write now . . . this instant. I cannot bear to wait.'

When writing material had been brought to him, he took one of the lighted candles and opened the door of a closet.

'I shall write in here,' he said, 'and by the time I have

finished, perhaps it will be morning. Then we will leave this place and ride on to Cracow with all speed.'

He stared, and fell backwards. It seemed to him that a man stood in the closet, a tall man of noble countenance, who looked down on him with stern and haughty eyes.

'Coligny!' screamed Anjou, and he fell on his knees, dropping the candle, which was extinguished. 'Oh ... Coligny ...' he gasped, 'come back from the dead ... to haunt me ...'

His friends rushed to him, bearing lights. They grew pale when they saw what Anjou had seen. Some covered their eyes with a hand to shut out the vision. But one man, bolder than the rest, lifted his candle high and looked full into the face of what the others had believed to be the Admiral's ghost.

'*Mon Dieu!*' he cried. 'It is the Admiral to the very life. But ... it is only a picture.'

Anjou went back to the main apartment, and spent the rest of the night in writing what he called his confession.

The next day he left the town in haste; he had no wish to stay in a land where such cruel tricks were played upon him.

But he had learned something. The massacre of St. Bartholomew would never be forgotten while men lived on Earth, and those who had taken part in it would be held in horror and dismay by countless millions of their fellow men.

Anjou was in a high fever by the time he reached Cracow.

*

Margot was restless. Her love affair with Monsieur Léran, who had been so charmingly grateful since she had saved his life on the night of the massacre, was palling; and Margot was discovering that, although she could remain faithful to Monsieur de Guise for years, she could not be so for long to any other. At times she still hankered after the handsome Duke, and she would have taken him back but for his attachment to Charlotte de Sauves. She knew Charlotte too well; Charlotte never released a man until she was tired of him, and Margot had an idea that Charlotte was going to love Guise as constantly as she herself had. Surprisingly, it seemed that Charlotte could be in love, for she had changed, growing more softly beautiful; and Margot, sensing this had a good deal to do with Henry of

174

Guise, was jealous, but her pride remained stronger than her jealousy.

She knew that in refusing to allow herself to be divorced from Navarre and married to Guise she had wounded her former lover deeply. He would never, she knew, forgive the slight; he would remember it against her as he had remembered his father's death against Coligny. He no longer looked her way; he no longer sent those appealing and tender glances towards her. If he noticed her at all, it was to let her know how deeply absorbed he was in his new love affair, how delightful he found Charlotte de Sauves.

Dissatisfied, jealous and bored, Margot looked about her for fresh excitement. Perhaps she needed a new lover. But who was there? There was none who specially pleased her; if she selected one for his charming manners, for his handsome face, she would, before she realized what she was doing, find herself comparing him with Henry of Guise, and there would begin once more that battle between desire and pride.

She supposed it was not too late to ask for that divorce and to marry him. He would undoubtedly consent; it was ambition first with Monsieur de Guise; but should she marry him to satisfy his ambitions? And what if he continued his liaison with Charlotte de Sauves after their marriage!

No, she had sworn to have finished with Henry of Guise, and finished she had. She must find another lover, or some excitement. But now ... what excitement was there? Masques, ballets ... all commonplace to her; she could no longer be excited by a new gown, by a new wig or an exaggerated hair-style. As for lovers, she must first be in love; and how could she fall in love at will?

It was while she was in this state of restlessness that one of her women, Madame de Moissons, who had always been anxious to serve her since Margot had saved her husband's life at the time of the massacre, came to her and asked if she might have a word with her in private.

Madame de Moissons, who had suffered great mental torture when the life of her husband had been at stake, was a woman who lived in continual terror of further risings; it was this fear which had now caused her to seek the help of Margot.

175

'I would speak with Your Majesty alone,' she said, 'if you would grant me that honour.'

Margot, guessing from the woman's demeanour that she was deeply perturbed, immediately granted the request.

When they were alone, Madame de Moissons burst out: 'I do not know if I do right in telling you what I have discovered, but I think Your Majesty may know how to act. It concerns the King of Navarre and the Duke of Alençon. They plan to escape, join a Huguenot force and take the offensive against the Catholic army.'

'They cannot be so foolish.'

'Indeed yes, Madame. That is what they plan. Madame, can you plead with them, stop them? They will plunge France into civil war once more. There will be more bloodshed and when it starts who knows where it will end?'

'They are like irresponsible children,' said Margot. 'And when is this plot to be put into effect?'

'As soon as is possible, Madame. But the King of Navarre finds it difficult to tear himself away from Madame de Sauves, to whom, as you know, he is deeply attracted.'

Margot was seized with a jealous fury, but she managed to say calmly to Madame de Moissons: 'Leave this to me. I will see that this plot is foiled.'

'Madame, I would not care to bring trouble on the King of Navarre, who has always been so good to my husband.'

'He will be safe enough,' said Margot; and she dismissed the woman.

When she was alone she threw herself on to her bed and thumped the cushions angrily. She, Marguerite, the Princess of France and the Queen of Navarre had, she considered, been most vilely used. Her lover had deserted her for Madame de Sauves; and her stupid husband made dangerous plots and then hesitated to put them into action for love of the same woman. Henry of Guise had sworn to love her for ever and it seemed as though he had forgotten her; she and her husband were to have been allies, if not lovers, and he, with Alençon, had made this plot without her knowledge. She did not know who angered her most – Guise, Navarre or Charlotte de Sauves.

She acted impulsively as she always acted; and, rising from her bed, she went to the King.

He was with their mother and she asked if she might speak with them alone.

'I have discovered a plot,' she said.

They were alert. Neither of them trusted her, but they could see that she was not only excited but angry.

'Tell us, my dear,' said Catherine, and the sound of her mother's voice sobered Margot. What was she doing? She was betraying her husband and her brother. She took fright. She had no wish to harm either of them; she discovered in that moment that she was quite fond of them both.

She temporized. 'If I tell you what I have discovered, will you promise me that no harm shall come to the two people who are most deeply involved?'

'Yes, yes,' said Catherine.

'Charles,' said Margot, 'I want your word. I have discovered something which it is my duty to tell you, but I cannot do so until you promise me, on your sacred honour as King of France, that you will not harm those two involved.'

'I give my word,' said the King.

Catherine smiled sardonically. So her word was not good enough! It seemed that all her children were banding together against her.

'My husband and Alençon plan to escape from Paris, to join their friends and form an army which they intend to use against yours.'

The King began to sweat, his fingers to twitch.

'You have proof of this?' asked Catherine.

'No. I have only heard of it. If you search their apartments, doubtless you will find evidence.'

'We will have their apartments searched at once,' said Catherine. 'You have done well, daughter.'

'And your promise not to harm them is not forgotten?'

'My dear Marguerite, do you think I would hurt my own son and him who has become my son through his marriage with you ... mischievous as they may be! Now, there is no time to be lost.'

Catherine was as energetic as ever. She made Navarre and

Alençon her prisoners as a result of what she discovered; but they were not confined to dungeons, and continued to live, under guard, at the palace.

*

Henry of Guise faced the Queen Mother.

'Their friendship,' he said, 'began at the siege of La Rochelle. I cannot understand it. They are an ill-assorted pair. Something must be done to separate them. They are full of mischief, both of them. This plot of theirs proves that. Madame, something must be done immediately.'

Catherine studied him. She feared him, as much as she feared anyone in France, and yet that cool courage of his, that handsome presence, inspired admiration even in her. A surprisingly disloyal thought came to her then. She wished that this Henry had been *her* Henry. She would have loved him then with a great devotion and together they would have shared all the power in France. But he was not her son and because this was the case she resented that arrogance of his, that insolent manner of telling her what should be done, as though he were the master and she a favoured servant.

In accordance with her usual habit, she hid her resentment and wore an expression of humility. 'You are right, Monsieur de Guise,' she said. 'You may rest assured that after this scare I will do something to spoil their unnatural friendship.'

'Madame,' said Guise, 'I do not trust the King of Navarre. I do not think he is such a fool as he would have us believe. He poses as a frivolous man, thinking of nothing but women.'

'Ah,' said Catherine, 'a man can think of women *and* politics at the same time, can he not?'

Guise ignored the barb and went on: 'His manner, I feel sure, is a pose. He should be kept under strict surveillance. And as for the Duke of Alençon . . .' Guise shrugged his shoulders.

'You may speak out,' said Catherine. 'Though he is my son, I know him as a man who is full of mischief and who must be watched.'

'But for our good fortune in discovering this plot, these two might have made good their escape. There are still enough

178

Huguenots in the country to cause us trouble, Madame.'

'It is indeed fortunate that we discovered the plot in time. We owe it to Madame de Sauves, did you know?'

The Duke raised his eyebrows, and Catherine, who knew him so well, realized that his heart had begun to beat a little faster at the mention of his mistress in this connexion.

'The King of Navarre, as you know,' went on Catherine, 'is more interested in women than in politics. He found it difficult to tear himself away from the lady – otherwise he would have escaped before we realized what he was about. His hesitation betrayed him, Monsieur.'

'We must be grateful for that, Madame.'

'Very grateful indeed to that fair lady, who is, I am told, irresistible to so many.'

'Madame, the first thing we must do is to drive a wedge between Navarre and Alençon.'

'Leave that to me, Monsieur.'

'How will you accomplish it?'

'As yet I am unsure, but I am giving the matter my deepest consideration. You will see how I intend to separate those two, and you will see it in a very short time. Now, if you will forgive me, I must ask you to leave me, as I have much to do which I dare neglect no longer.'

As soon as he had left her, alone as she was, she began to laugh.

'Ah, Monsieur de Guise,' she chuckled, 'you will soon see how I plan to separate those two.'

She went to the door, called her dwarf and sent him in search of Madame de Sauves.

'And see,' she added, 'that when she arrives, she is left alone with me.'

Charlotte came immediately.

'You may sit, my dear,' said Catherine. 'Now tell me: how progresses your affair with the King of Navarre?'

'Just as Your Majesty commanded it should.'

'You must be a witch, Charlotte, to keep such a man dancing attendance on you without receiving any satisfaction.'

'I have behaved in accordance with Your Majesty's instructions,' said Charlotte.

'Poor Navarre! He will be sad this night. You have heard that he has been playing tricks which we shall have to punish. I think it might be a charming idea if you enlivened his captivity this night.'

Charlotte grew pale. 'Madame . . . I . . .'

'What! Another engagement! I promise you you need have no fear. I will see that the Baron, your husband, is kept busy and that he asks no embarrassing questions.'

'Madame,' faltered Charlotte, 'could I not? . . .'

Catherine burst out laughing. 'What! An assignation with a gentleman *not* your husband!'

Charlotte was silent.

'Tell me, Charlotte, is it Monsieur de Guise? He is so charming, and from the way in which he is pursued by you women it appears he must be an adequate lover. But I have always made you understand, have I not, that duty comes before pleasure?'

'Yes, Madame.'

'Well, tonight you must make it your duty to enliven the poor captive King of Navarre. Now . . . no more. I have spoken. You may go, Charlotte.'

When Charlotte was at the door, Catherine called her back. 'And come to me tomorrow, Charlotte. I shall have further instructions for you then.'

Charlotte ran along to her own apartments, and when she reached her bedchamber she drew her curtains about her bed, upon which she lay down and began to weep bitterly. For the first time in her life she was disgusted with the *Escadron* and wished to escape from it. She lay weeping for some time, lost in her wretched thoughts until, uncannily conscious that she was being watched, she turned her head and shrank in startled horror from the parted bed-curtains. Catherine stood there, looking at her, and her gaze seemed diabolical; but when she spoke her voice was almost tender and belied the cruel glitter of her eyes. 'You should not grieve, Charlotte. Monsieur de Guise must learn to understand as readily as does Monsieur de Sauves. And by night one man is very like another – so they tell me.'

The curtains were drawn together again, and Catherine went away as silently as she had come.

*

Margot looked down at her husband, who was lying sprawled across his bed. The door was locked and outside it were members of the King's Guard. Margot felt angry with him. He looked so inelegant lying there; he had no grace; his hair, which looked none too clean, would doubtless stain that beautiful cushion.

'You should not be allowed to use beautiful things,' she told him. 'You should live in a stable.'

'Stables can be very comfortable,' he said reflectively, 'and a horse is often a more amiable companion than a wife.'

She lifted her head haughtily. 'Not only are you coarse and crude – that I accept; that I forgive – but your folly is beyond forgiveness.'

'I was certainly a fool not to realize I had a spying wife.'

'It was for your own good, you fool, that I stopped your folly.'

'You call it folly because it failed. If it had succeeded it would have been very clever. And but for you, it would not have failed. *Ventre de biche!* I have a mind to thrash you for this.'

'You would find yourself in a less comfortable prison if you were as foolish as that.'

'Have no fear. I am far too lazy. To thrash such a spitfire as you, would take a good deal of energy, and I am not inclined to spend mine on you.'

'Pray keep your coarse manners for your peasant women.'

'I will, if you will allow me to. Why do you not take yourself off to a more comfortable apartment?'

'Because I wish to talk to you.'

'I am expecting a visitor.'

'A wife of one of the gardeners, or one of the kitchen wenches?'

'Guess again,' he said.

'I am not inclined to waste my energy on that! Gardener's wife or kitchen woman, it matters not to me. I am not

181

interested in your crude amours. What angers me is that you should have entered into such a plot as this and told me nothing of it.'

'It did not concern you.'

'It concerns Navarre, of which I am Queen.'

'Only as long as I allow you to be.'

'How dare you!'

'Madame, you astonish me. You play the spy; you place your husband and his kingdom in jeopardy, and then you come here and tell me that my kingdom is yours.'

'I had thought that we two had decided to be allies.'

'We had, but you show yourself to be a very doubtful ally.'

'And you plot such things without consulting me!'

'If I had been successful, I should have come back for you. And how can you talk of our being allies when you so callously betray me?'

'You are indolent as well as foolish. You do not seem to know what forces would be brought into action against you.'

'You overrate Monsieur de Guise,' said Navarre. 'We who would pit ourselves against him and his Catholics do not hold him in the same reverence as you do. You involve yourself too deeply in your love affairs, my dear. You look upon your lover as a god. He is but a man. Why, is it not for that very reason that you love him? You will never be happy in love until you learn to love as I do. I have had a hundred love affairs and never a pang of remorse or wretchedness on account of any of them. Yet you . . . you are all passion, all hate, all desire. When we have more leisure you and I must compare experiences, but tonight I am expecting a visitor.'

'You are a provincial boor,' she cried, 'and as for discussing my love affairs with you, I would as soon discuss them with a stable boy.'

'Or a kitchen wench, or a gardener's wife?' he taunted.

She went to him and, taking his stiff hair in her hands, shook him angrily. He was almost apoplectic with laughter, and to her annoyance she found herself laughing with him.

'There, you see,' he said, 'we cannot be bad friends. You betray me and I forgive you. Why, I even forgive you for spoiling the set of my hair which, although not elegant like that of

182

your brothers, or softly curling like that of one whom it would be provincial, boorish, coarse and crude to mention at this point . . .'

She gave him a stinging blow on his cheek, which delighted him.

'Oh, Margot,' he cried, catching her by the arms suddenly and holding her so tightly that she cried out, 'I almost wish that I had not this visitor coming to me tonight, for I find you extremely attractive in this fighting mood.'

He released her and she stood up, for she had heard a movement in his closet.

'Who is there?' she asked.

'No one,' he answered; and turning to look at him she believed that he was as surprised and startled by that sound as she was. There followed immediately a light tap on the door of the closet.

'May I come in?' said a voice which both of them recognized.

'This is my visitor,' said Navarre. 'I did not expect her to have secreted herself in my closet. She must have had a key to come in that way, no doubt from your mother. Come in!' he called.

Margot stepped back so that the curtains of the bed hid her.

Charlotte de Sauves walked to the bed. She was holding a key. 'I managed to acquire a key to the small chamber,' she said. 'It seemed better to come in that way.'

Navarre said: 'Her Majesty is most helpful, and so generous with her personal keys. But, my dear, it matters not how you come, as long as you come.'

Margot stepped out, and Charlotte stared at her in dismay.

'Do not be afraid of me, Madame de Sauves,' said Margot. 'I was just about to leave.'

Charlotte looked from the husband to the wife. 'I . . . I did not know that Your Majesty would be here . . . If I had . . .'

Margot waved a hand. 'You must obey the royal command, must you not?' she said; and she threw a contemptuous glance at Navarre, which implied that she despised him since, knowing this woman was her mother's spy, he could yet receive her.

'I was just about to go,' she added. 'I wish you joy, Madame. A very goodnight to you both.'

'And a very goodnight to you, my dear wife,' said Navarre, smiling at her cynically. Margot walked out, aware that he scarcely waited for her to reach the door before pulling Charlotte down beside him.

Margot was angry. One did not expect a husband to be faithful; but one expected a certain show of good manners.

She was bored; the monotony of her life was more than she could endure. She decided that, for the want of something better to do, she would go and make her peace with her brother; for he, like her husband, would be annoyed with her, and lacking the humour of Navarre, would not be so inclined to find humour in the situation.

She went into his apartments, and the King's Guards made way for her. In an ante-chamber, a tall slim young man was sitting, and as Margot approached he leaped to his feet and bowed low.

Margot smiled at him charmingly, for she noticed immediately that he was an exceptionally handsome young man, and it was obvious from his expression that he was as impressed by her charms as she was by his. Indeed, this kind of adoration was just what Margot needed most at this moment. She was at once enchanted by this young man.

She studied him closely. He was, she guessed, in his mid-twenties, a few years older than herself; his hair was dark and he wore it long and curling; his eyes were a deep shade of blue, and Margot found the contrast of eyes and hair striking. His moustache could not hide the sensitive lips, and if his expression was one of melancholy, although somewhat relieved by his delight in looking at her, it was such a contrast to the crude boisterousness of the man she had just left, that it was enchanting. Bowing, he had placed a white hand on his velvet doublet which was a deep shade of blue that matched his eyes and was decorated with black jet.

'I do not know you, Monsieur?' she said.

His voice was low and melodious. 'There, Madame, I have the advantage of Your Majesty.'

'So you are in no doubt as to my identity?'

184

'Madame, who does not know the Queen of Navarre?'

'You must have seen me when I have not seen you.'

'Yes, Madame; and, having seen you, could never banish your image from my mind.'

Margot was excited. 'And, Monsieur, why should there be need for such banishment?'

His melancholy eyes, of such a startling blue, supplied the answer she expected, and his lips endorsed it. 'That, Madame, I could not tell you. I beg of you not to embarrass me by commanding me to answer.'

'I see you are in my brother's service. I should therefore have no power to command you.'

'Madame, any request of yours would be a command.'

She smiled. 'You are from Provence,' she said. 'I realize that, for you have the soft speech. But you have learned to flatter like a Parisian.'

'You are mistaken, Madame. There was no flattery.'

'What is your name?' asked Margot.

'La Mole, Madame.'

'La Mole? Just that . . . nothing more?'

'Count Boniface de la Mole, Madame, at your service.'

'You mean at the service of the Duke of Alençon?'

'If I could find some means of serving his sister, I should be completely happy.'

'Well, you may do so at once. I wish to see my brother.'

'He is engaged at the moment, Madame, and is likely to be for some hours.'

'It would seem that he is gallantly engaged.'

'That is so, Madame.'

'In that case I shall not disturb him. It would go ill with you if you interrupted him merely to tell him his sister wished to see him.'

'Madame,' he said, bowing and laying his hand on the hilt of his sword, 'if you were to command me, I would willingly face death.'

She laughed lightly. 'Nay, Monsieur le Comte, I would not have you face death. I think I should find you more amusing alive than dead.'

She extended her hand for him to kiss; he did this with a

mingling of reverence and passion which delighted Margot.

'Adieu, Monsieur.'

'You will think me bold, Madame, but I will say what is in my heart. *Au revoir*, Madame. I shall live for our next meeting.'

Margot turned and left the chamber. She was smiling, for she had ceased to be bored.

*

Catherine summoned Charlotte de Sauves to her presence.

'Well, Charlotte, I trust Navarre pleased you?'

Charlotte was silent.

'You must not mind,' said Catherine softly, 'that I witnessed your grief yesterday. I thought how sad you looked when you left me, so I followed. Never try to lock your door against your Queen, Charlotte. It is useless. I do not like to see you looking so sad. I hope you were not sad when with Navarre. Poor man! He has waited so long. I should not have wished him to be disappointed.'

'Madame,' said Charlotte, 'I have done what you commanded.'

'That is well. I trust there was not too great a quarrel with Monsieur de Guise? However, it will do that young man good to learn that he is only about half as important as he imagines himself to be. You see, Charlotte, my dear, when you joined the *Escadron*, you agreed, did you not, to put aside all sentimentality. But let us not go into that. You have done well with Navarre. I do not wish your love affair with him to progress too rapidly. Navarre must not expect you to give all your spare time to him. There are others on whom you must bestow your smiles.'

Charlotte waited apprehensively.

'I was not referring to Monsieur de Guise. If you patch up your quarrel with him, he must be made to understand that he can only gladden your leisure hours. You have serious work to do, and this does not include dalliance with the charming Duke. No, Charlotte! For there is another who needs your attention. I refer to my little son – my youngest, poor little Alençon.'

'But, Madame, he has never looked my way.'

'Whose fault is that? None but your own. He is susceptible to female beauty. You have only to smile on him a little, to flatter him a good deal, and he will be your slave.'

'I am not sure, Madame. He is deeply enamoured of . . .'

'Never mind of whom. I'll wager that within a few days he will be deeply enamoured of Charlotte de Sauves if that lady intends to make him so. I expect to hear in a very short time that the King of Navarre and the Duke of Alençon have fallen out because they have both fallen into love with the same lady, and she is distributing her favours equally between them to keep the quarrel warm.'

'Madame, this is a difficult task . . .'

'Nonsense! It will be easy for you. You already have Navarre at your feet. Alençon . . . that one is a simple matter. I expect results, and I know that you are too wise a woman to disappoint me. Go now.'

When she was alone Catherine smiled to herself. Intrigue, as well as being stimulating. was often amusing if one had the right sort of humour to appreciate that fact. Monsieur de Guise had rather arrogantly suggested that she should have a wedge driven between Alençon and Navarre; he had almost dared to give an order to the Queen Mother. She had found it necessary to follow that suggestion, but Monsieur de Guise should not be allowed to come out of this matter without some discomfiture. As soon as Alençon began to hanker after Charlotte, and when he and Navarre began to regard each other with jealousy and suspicion, Guise would realize that she had used his mistress as that 'wedge'. It was very amusing, but she doubted whether Guise would enjoy the joke; he had not the humour of young Navarre.

But she did not laugh long. There were other matters which were not so amusing. Her beloved son was far away in Poland and she yearned for him. Charles was becoming more obstinate, more suspicious of his mother every day. So that situation gave her little to laugh at.

Charles must die. She had promised herself and Henry that. But the death of the King would have to be a slow one. Heaven knew she had everything on her side. His physical state was such that, when speaking of it, Monsieur Paré was very grave. He coughed incessantly and spat blood. His violent moods would often end with those fits of coughing. When she watched him, writhing on the floor, his jacket stained with blood, she would assure herself that it could not now be long.

His wife had given birth to a girl. That was a blessing. Surely he would never have the strength to give the Queen another child. But one could not be sure, and while Charles lived there was great cause for anxiety.

Why should he live? In her private closet she had many powders and potions which had solved such problems for her before and would do so again. But slow deaths were not so easy to achieve as quick ones. If it had just been a matter of giving one dose, that could have been achieved . . . if not at one time, then at another. But when there must be continual doses, it was not so easy.

Neither René, nor Cosmo, nor Lorenzo would be anxious to assist at the death of a King. Moreover Charles was surrounded by certain women, and, ironical as it was, each of these women, while being in herself quite insignificant, unimportant and altogether meek, seemed to stand by the side of the King like an angel with a flaming sword. There was his mistress, the mild Marie Touchet, his wife, the milder Elisabeth, and Madeleine, his nurse. All suspected the King's mother of trying to shorten his life, and all were prepared to die to save him from her.

And, always hovering close to the King, was Monsieur Paré, the Huguenot, who should have been dispatched during that fateful August and who, owing his life to the King, was determined to pay his debt of gratitude by prolonging the King's life.

But it was those three women who were the worst obstacles. They were more effective than an armed guard. And what could one do? Remove them? She had not the power to do that, for the King would not allow it; he was the master now. They had succeeded in turning him away from his mother.

And so the King grew weaker, and there were rumours throughout Paris that his mother was responsible for his low state of health. But he continued to live, to the delight of those three women who loved him and to the chagrin of his un-natural mother.

*

Margot's friend, the flighty little Duchesse de Nevers, had a new lover. Little Henriette was so much in love that Margot was inclined to be envious.

Henriette whispered to Margot of her experiences. 'He is so charming ... so different. So handsome! So bold! And he is in the service of your brother, Monsieur d'Alençon.'

Margot was alert. 'Indeed! I would hear more of this.'

'He has a fair complexion and the most splendid white teeth. You should see them flash when he smiles ... and he smiles continually.'

'His name?' demanded Margot.

'Annibale. Le Comte Annibale de Coconnas.'

Margot sighed with relief.

'I like the sound of him. So he is in the service of my brother. How odd that Poor Alençon, who is so unprepossessing him-self, should have such handsome men in his service! Tell me more.'

'He is very quick to anger, Madame, and his hair is reddish rather than brown. His eyes seem golden. I am asking him to my apartments to supper. Would Your Majesty honour us by coming tonight?'

Margot's eyes sparkled. 'What if you were discovered? Mon-sieur le Duc de Nevers ...'

'Has his own affairs to attend to, as Your Majesty well knows.'

'I do not think that I should come,' said Margot, deciding at once that she would not miss this for anything, and that it was just what she needed to relieve the monotony of her days. Any gentleman of Alençon's suite was of interest to her as she might be able to talk to him of that most fascinating La Mole.

'If you do not come, there will be no supper ... for it is to be arranged solely on Your Majesty's account.'

'What does this mean?' demanded Margot.

'I suppose I must tell you, although it is supposed to be a

189

secret. A friend of Monsieur de Coconnas is so enamoured of you that he is plunged in deepest melancholy and can neither eat nor sleep until he speaks with you. My Annibale is a most warm-hearted man, a most compassionate man and he . . .'

'Enough of your Annibale, Henriette. We know *he* is charming. Tell me of the melancholy gentleman.'

'He is very handsome, and it seems that he saw you and spoke to you, and you to him. You seemed so gracious that he has imagined that his wildest dreams may not be without some hope of fulfilment, and his name is . . .'

'Le Comte Boniface de la Mole!' said Margot.

'You knew then, Madame?'

'As you said, Henriette, we met. He is charming and your Annibale is coarse compared with him. That melancholy of which you speak . . . it is very deep. One feels he must be a poet, a dreamer. One *longs* to chase away his gloom. His eyes are startlingly blue. He is like a beautiful Greek statue. Already I think of him as my Hyacinth.'

'If you will but attend our supper party, Madame, you will make your Hyacinth very happy.'

'I will consider it.'

'He intends to go to Cosmo Ruggieri this very afternoon to ask, first for some charm which will make you decide to attend the party, and then for another which will make you regard him favourably.'

'But this is insolence!' cried Margot delightedly.

'You must forgive him, Madame. He is so much in love. And when a man cannot eat or sleep, Your Majesty must understand that he cannot go on like that.'

'These are the tales they tell us, Henriette.'

'But, Madame, this is true. Annibale swears it. La Mole has seen you often. He never misses a chance of seeing you. But he loved from afar . . . and then . . . when you spoke to him . . .'

'Henriette, this afternoon, we will go to Ruggieri, and we will make him hide us, so that we may look at this young man and hear what he says.'

The two frivolous young women could not stop laughing. Margot embraced her dear friend, Henriette. Margot was delighted by the prospect of a love affair which she was sure would be one of the most charming she had ever experienced. It was just what she needed to keep intact her pride and annoyance with the Duke of Guise.

●

Heavy cloaks concealing them, Margot and Henriette de Nevers left the Louvre for the house of the Ruggieri brothers.

Margot allowed Henriette to lead the way into the shop, as she felt that she was more likely to be recognized by the apprentice than was Henriette.

The shop was small and dark and it smelt of the perfumes and cosmetics which were sold to any who cared to buy them. The secret business of these sinister brothers was carried on beyond the shop.

The apprentice came forward, bowing, for in spite of their cloaks, it was obvious that these ladies were of the quality.

'My mistress wishes to see your master,' said Henriette, at which the young man, nodding gravely, announced that he would carry the news of the ladies' arrival to his master. In a few moments he returned with Cosmo Ruggieri.

Margot threw back her cloak and Cosmo said at once: 'Please come this way.'

When the two young women were with him on the other side of that door which led from the shop, he locked it, and asked them to follow him, which they did. He led the way up a staircase and unlocking a door in a corridor ushered them into a small room, the walls of which were hung with tapestry of a not very elaborate kind.

'What can I do for Your Majesty?' asked Cosmo.

The two of them were laughing so much that they could scarcely tell him. At length Margot said: 'There is a young Count coming here this afternoon to ask you for a charm. He is in love, and we want to overhear what he says to you. You can put us somewhere where we can look on without being seen. I know you often hide my mother here. I know there are numerous secret hiding-places and holes in the wall through which it is possible to watch what goes on in some of your chambers. You must take this young man to a room which is fitted with one of these secret places, and the Duchess and I will look on. If you refuse I shall know that you do not wish to please me.'

As Cosmo certainly did wish to please the young Queen of Navarre, who was too important a person to be flouted, he smiled deprecatingly and said: 'It is possible, if you two young ladies do not mind waiting in rather cramped quarters, perhaps for some time, as I shall have to secrete you in your hiding-place before the gentleman arrives.'

'Conduct us to the hiding-place at once,' said Margot.

Cosmo bowed and led them along a corridor and up a short staircase to a small apartment. As they entered this room, Henriette gripped Margot's arm and Margot smiled at her scornfully, noting her superstitious fear. Margot herself was merely enchanted with what lay before them.

They were in the laboratory of the Ruggieri brothers. Its walls were panelled and strewn about the room were strange and gruesome objects. On one bench lay a human skeleton from which Henriette found it difficult to take her eyes. The signs of the Zodiac adorned the ceiling; and on the wooden panels were carefully drawn cabalistic signs. A huge murky mirror hung on one wall and the two young women saw their reflections, grey and ghostlike beneath two human skulls which seemed to be hanging from the ceiling. Over a fire a cauldron was steaming and the smoke swirled about the room, so it appeared to Margot and Henriette, in fantastic shapes. On a large table were pictures of the stars and the planets, a balance, strange instruments, wax figures, several jars in which could be seen the bodies of small animals, or parts of their bodies, in various stages of decomposition. The light from two oil lamps which were fixed on brackets in the wall did not succeed in lighting the corners of the room, so that it seemed to extend farther than their eyes could see. The scented oil in the lamps fought, not quite successfully, with the unpleasantly odorous objects in the room.

Cosmo opened a door in the wall which had been so cleverly made that it had not appeared to be a door at all.

'You may wait in there,' he said. 'I will show you the shutter which will enable you to see and hear what is said in this room.'

They stepped into the cupboard and he shut the door on them. He touched one of the panels to open the shutter. Henriette was giggling with excited pleasure; and she and Margot whispered together during the twenty minutes they had to wait for the arrival of La Mole.

Cosmo had meanwhile sought out his brother Lorenzo.

'The Queen of Navarre and the Duchess of Nevers are here,' he said. 'They are waiting in the cupboard in the small laboratory for a young man, who I gather is a lover of the Queen's. It may be just another of her love affairs, but the Queen Mother will expect to be informed. As soon as the interview is over, I will go to the Louvre and tell her all that has taken place.'

*

Cosmo was smiling as he brought Boniface de la Mole into his laboratory. Margot watched him with delight. He was more handsome than she remembered; and how elegant he looked against the gruesome background of the alchemist's workshop.

Cosmo said: 'You wish to consult me about the future, Monsieur?'

'I wish you to work some magic for me,' said the Count.

'Ah! First I must know your name.'

'Is that necessary?'

'It is indeed, Monsieur. We are secluded here within four walls, and you will be telling none who would bring it against you that you dabbled in magic for the sake of love. It is for love, Monsieur?'

'It is for love,' said the young man mournfully.

'Do not be so sad. I have no doubt that we shall be able to ensure your success. Your name, Monsieur?'

'Comte Boniface de la Mole.'

'And the name of the lady whom you wish to influence?'

'That I cannot tell you.'

'Very well, sir. We will see what can be done without her name. Your wishes?'

'I wish you to use your magic to ensure that I see her tonight. There is some entertainment at which I wish her to be present.'

Cosmo stirred what was in the cauldron and, looking into the rising smoke, said: 'You will see her tonight. She will be at the entertainment.'

The Comte's melancholy lifted. 'That is wonderful. That is delightful.' But he was soon sad again. 'She is of high rank. She will never look my way.'

'You give up too easily, Monsieur. There are ways of touching the heart of the hardest female.'

'You mean? . . .'

'Let us make an image of your loved one. You may pierce her heart, and then I think you may be sure of success.'

'I beg of you to make this image quickly.'

'It is easily done, Monsieur le Comte. Pray be seated.'

Cosmo took a piece of wax, melted it in a pot he kept for this purpose, and moulded it into a human shape.

'Now, Monsieur le Comte, that is not really like your lady, is it? May we add some distinguishing feature? We must be sure that you pierce the heart of the right woman. Tell me, how shall I distinguish her from other ladies?'

'There is no one so beautiful.'

'Beauty is not sufficient, I am afraid. In the eyes of the lover the one he loves is always the most beautiful in the world.'

'But there is no mistaking this lady's beauty. She is . . .'

'Words seem to elude you, Monsieur. Perhaps I could distinguish her by some garment . . . some ornament. Look. I will put a royal cloak about her. I will put a crown on her head.'

'Monsieur,' cried the Count, 'you are truly a man of magic.'

Cosmo laughed whilst he moulded the cloak and crown.

'Now we have our lady. I will take this pin.' Cosmo took the pin and gripping it in a pair of tweezers, thrust it into the fire. 'It will take very little time to become red hot. Now. Yes, it is ready. Take it, thrust it into the lady's heart and whisper your wish to yourself.'

La Mole took the pin and thrust it into the waxen figure.

'There, Monsieur. That is all. Keep the figure. While you have it with you, the pin safe in its heart, you cannot fail.'

La Mole wrapped the figure in a silk kerchief and slipped it reverently inside his jacket.

'I am deeply indebted to you,' he said.

'Then let us go to my sitting-room and discuss payment,' said Cosmo. 'I am a poor man and cannot give my skill for nothing.'

Five minutes later Henriette, led by Margot, slipped into the street; and shortly after that Cosmo went to the Louvre and asked for an audience with the Queen Mother. It appeared to be a matter of little importance, he told her when he was alone with her, but as she liked to be informed of what went on about her, he had thought it wise to let her know who had come to his house this day. The Comte de la Mole was deeply enamoured of Queen Margot and had been given a waxen image of her which he had pierced to the heart.

'Another lover,' said Catherine with a spurt of laughter. 'Jesus! That daughter of mine astonishes even me. And Boniface de la Mole! He is, I believe, a gentleman of the Duke of Alençon's suite. Thank you, Cosmo. A matter of slight importance doubtless, but you are right to assume that these gallant little matters amuse me.'

*

Margot was happy. She was in love. The supper party had been a great success, and had been the forerunner of many meetings. She was kept fully occupied; there were so many clandestine meetings to be arranged, so many love letters to be written.

Catherine was less contented. The King continued to live and she was uncertain what to do. It was very unfortunate that Henry should be in Poland; when she thought of that, her anger against Charles, who had insisted on his going, was so great that she felt inclined to diverge from her habitual caution. But that even was difficult while Charles was surrounded by his three meek guardians.

Charlotte de Sauves had not had the great success which Catherine had expected in the Navarre-Alençon affair. The little Duke was enamoured of the woman, as Catherine had guessed he would be, but the ultimate desired effect had not been realized. Though the two men were both attracted by the same woman, their friendship seemed to remain unimpaired. It might be that there was something in progress, something so vital that it could not be touched by jealousy concerning a love affair.

Guise had been right to be suspicious of Navarre. There were two sides to the latter's nature. One showed a pleasure-loving young man, lazy and amorous; but there was the other side to be considered. Was it ambition that secretly fermented behind those shrewd eyes? His love affairs were light-hearted. He cared deeply for no one and he had no religion. Catherine fancied that she saw some of her own characteristics in the King of Navarre, and that made him seem formidable. For what did he hope? After Henry and Alençon – if they had no children – Navarre would certainly be King of France. Could even a lazy provincial be indifferent to such a prospect? Was it likely that a son of Jeanne of Navarre could be nothing more than a pleasure-loving fool? What did he plot with Alençon? It was safe to assume that Alençon was up to mischief, for mischief was as necessary to a man of his nature as women were to one of Navarre's. Catherine was certainly uneasy on account of this friendship.

Margot fortunately was fully occupied with La Mole. Catherine felt that she understood her daughter: give her a lover and she was content. Margot was clever, perhaps the cleverest member of the family; and she could learn quickly; she was sharp-witted, but her sensuality betrayed her with its incessant demands, and she misused her ability by scheming and intriguing with her numerous lovers. Margot was a little wanton – as shameless now with La Mole as she had been with Guise. She exercised no restraint. She should have made some attempt to keep this new love affair secret. Those notes she sent to her lover were very revealing, as everything Margot wrote seemed to be. Margot ought to know by now that her mother liked to see all notes which passed between people of the court, even if they were only the outpourings of lovers.

Catherine had her spies in Alençon's suite; she had her spies among Margot's women. She had, as a matter of routine, read all the notes which had passed between them ever since

Ruggieri had told her of La Mole's infatuation for her daughter.

One of her women who had been a mistress of Alençon's, and was now – since Alençon's growing infatuation for Madame de Sauves – courting one of Alençon's men who took messages from La Mole to Margot, came to her and asked if she might have audience with the Queen Mother.

Catherine granted it and when they were alone, the woman put several letters into Catherine's hands.

'More letters!' said Catherine. 'Our melancholy Hyacinth is as enamoured of his pen as of our daughter.'

'Madame, my friend was given some of these letters by Monsieur de la Mole and some by Monsieur de Coconnas. There is one for the Queen of Navarre from La Mole, and one for Madame de Nevers from Coconnas. The others are to be taken to people outside Paris.'

'What! Have our young gallants involved themselves in other love affairs! It will go ill with them when our two young ladies discover their infidelities. I will look through them and return them to you, resealed, in a very short time. You may go now. Let nothing, however seemingly trivial, be allowed to pass without my scrutiny.'

'Everything shall be brought to Your Majesty.'

Left alone Catherine started on the letters. It was a pleasant pastime – reading letters which were intended for other people. Here was a letter from La Mole to Margot, professing undying devotion and hope for the future. She was to meet him this afternoon at a house on the corner of the Rue de la Vannerie and the Rue Monton. He was all impatience. And here was another letter. This was for Madame de Nevers from Coconnas, expressing *his* undying devotion, *his* adoration, *his* hope for the future; he begged Madame de Nevers to remember that she was meeting him at a house on the corner of Rue de la Vannerie and the Rue Monton this afternoon . . .

Catherine laughed. Ah well, let the foolish creatures frivol their time away. It kept them from meddling in state affairs.

And now for the letters which were to be taken out of Paris. These too were in the handwriting of La Mole and Coconnas. Catherine broke the seals and read, and as she did so, a cold fury took possession of her. She had been foolish; she had read their stupid love letters when letters such as these must have been passing out of the palace without her knowledge. It was clearly due to a little carelessness on the part of the lovers that these letters had fallen into her hands. How long had they been deceiving her? These were not the outpourings of lovesick suitors, but the clear, concise phrases of conspirators; and they were not addressed to foolish young women, but to none other than the Marshals Montgomery and Cossé.

She read on, and although her expression did not change, there was murder in her mind. This was treason. This explained that friendship between Alençon and Navarre which Charlotte could not break. Those two were together in this. They were plotting – those two whom she had kept in semi-captivity – to escape, to join Montgomery and Cossé, and to get together a Huguenot army to march on Paris.

Conceited Alençon no doubt thought that his brother could not live long and, with Henry away in Poland, here was his chance to seize the throne. Navarre doubtless was prepared to play a waiting game and meanwhile ally himself with Alençon.

Catherine's anger cooled. This was great good luck. How grateful she was to her dear Cosmo and Lorenzo Ruggieri, who had aroused her interest in the lover of her daughter!

*

Margot and Henriette, wrapped in their cloaks, slipped out of the Louvre to the house at the corner of the Rue de la Vannerie and the Rue Monton. They took off their masks as soon as the concierge let them in.

'The gentlemen have arrived?' demanded Margot of the woman.

'No, Madame. They are not yet here.'

They went upstairs to a room in which a table was laid for four; on this were the choicest delicacies, and the best wines that France could offer. A banquet fit for a Queen and her friends. Margot looked at the table with pleasure, but she was uneasy.

'There is no message to explain why they have been delayed?' she asked of the woman.

'No, Madame.'

When Margot had dismissed her, Henriette said: 'Margot, you don't think they have ceased to love us!'

'If they had,' said Margot, 'they would have been very early. They would have been most chivalrous, most eager to assure us of their fidelity.'

'They were most eager to assure us of that last time we met.'

'I cannot believe my Hyacinth could deceive me. Something has happened to detain them . . . nothing more.'

'Your brother would not detain them. He knows they come to meet us, and he is most friendly to you and eager to please you.'

'It may have been some other small matter. Come, drink a cup of wine, and you will feel better.' Margot poured out the wine and handed it to Henriette.

'I shall be most piqued when they do come,' said Henriette. 'Margot, you do not think, do you, that it is your husband who may have detained them?'

'Why should he?'

'Jealousy.'

'He does not know the meaning of jealousy. "Do not stand in the way of my pleasure," he says, "and I will not stand in the way of yours!" ' She turned to her friend. 'Perhaps the Duke of Nevers . . .'

'But he would have stopped only Annibale. That does not excuse La Mole. They are both late. Could it be Monsieur de Guise?'

Margot was pleasurably excited at the possibility of her former lover's jealousy. She dismissed such thoughts hastily. Must it always be so? Must she always wonder how her actions were going to affect that man!

'Nonsense!' she said. 'That is finished. Listen. Someone is coming up the stairs.'

'They are very quiet, Margot.'

'Hush! They creep in order to surprise us.'

There was a tap on the door.

'Enter!' said Margot; and to her intense disappointment and also that of Henriette, it was the *concierge* who entered, not their lovers.

'Madame, there is a lady downstairs who says she must speak with you at once. Shall I allow her to come up? She says it is of the utmost importance. She has news for you.'

'Send her up at once,' said Margot; and in a few seconds one of her attendants came into the room. The woman's face was pale and it was obvious from her expression that the news which she brought was not good.

She knelt before Margot and cried: 'Madame, I regret to be the bearer of such news. The Comte de la Mole and the Comte de Coconnas cannot come to you.'

'Why not?' demanded Margot. 'Why have they sent you instead?'

'They are prisoners, Madame. They are already in the dungeons of Vincennes, whither the Duke of Alençon and the King of Navarre have also been sent. It is said that the Marshals Montgomery and Cossé have been arrested. There is said to have been a plot which the King discovered.'

Henriette fell on to a couch, covering her face with her hands. Margot stared blankly before her. Why, why could they not leave their foolish plots; why could they not be content with love?

*

Margot lost no time in driving to Vincennes. She knew that she would not be allowed to visit her lover in the dungeons below the castle, but it would be a simple matter to have a word with her husband, who was lodged in apartments there.

Navarre was nonchalant.

'What could have possessed you to be so foolish?' she demanded.

'My dearest wife, it was not I who was foolish. It was those lovesick idiots of yours and Henriette de Nevers. It was through their carelessness that notes, not intended for her, reached your mother's hands.'

'Do you think you can escape punishment this time?'

'That question gives me cause for reflection.'

'What a fool you were to attempt escape a second time!'

'There might have been no need for a second time but for

200

your interference. Your brother and I might be free men now but for you.'

'You are so irresponsible, both of you. You have involved these two men in your schemes, and they will be the ones to suffer for your misdeeds.'

'Dear Margot!' he said. 'Always so solicitous on behalf of your lovers! You make me wish that I were one of them myself.'

'Do not let us waste time. What can we do?'

He shrugged his shoulders and she stormed at him. 'Do not stand there smiling as if this was of no account. Other people have been led into danger.'

'Say "La Mole", not "other people". It is so much more friendly . . . and is after all what you mean.'

'You must admit that you and my brother are responsible for this.'

'It is not entirely true, my dear. There was a letter in La Mole's handwriting; there was also one in that of Coconnas. These letters show these two men to be deeply involved and quite knowledgeable as to what we planned should take place.'

'You *must* save them,' said Margot.

'You may be sure I shall do what is possible.'

'We must deny there was a plot. That is possible, is it not?'

'We can always deny,' said Navarre. 'Even when confronted with proof, we can deny.'

'I do not think you care for your own life or for any one else's.'

'It may be that it is better to die young than to grow old. I often wonder.'

'You madden me. Listen to me. I am going to draw up a document which I shall present to the Commissioners if there is any sign of your being brought up for questioning.'

'*You* . . . write *my* defence!'

'Why not? I am your wife. I am also a writer of some ability. I swear that I can present your case with such sympathy and understanding that I will make those who believe you to be guilty believe in your innocence.'

He smiled at her. 'Why, Margot, I think there may be something in this. You are a clever little chronicler. When I read your accounts of what happens here at court I find myself believing you to be a poor, innocent, misjudged and virtuous woman. And that in spite of all that I know! Yes, if you can tell such pretty stories about yourself, why not about me? Come, draw up this document. I put myself in your hands. I will say what you advise.'

One of the guards was knocking at the door.

'Come in,' said Margot.

'The Queen Mother is coming this way,' she was told.

'She shall not find me here,' said Margot. 'But remember what I say. Confess nothing. It is imperative that you remember that although you and my brother may escape punishment, those two poor men, whose services you have so carelessly used, may not.'

'My love,' said Navarre, kissing her hand, 'you may trust me to remember.'

*

Now that Catherine had decided how she should deal with the further rebellion of her son and son-in-law, she lost no time in putting her plan into action. She did not intend that this plot should be generally known. There must, she knew, be a certain leakage, but she was going to do all in her power to make it as small as possible.

Montgomery and Cossé were under arrest and could do no more damage for the moment. She was thinking that it might be a good idea to ensure that they never did again. They could be murdered while they were in jail. Not yet, of course. It would be necessary to employ great caution with such well-known men. She would have the news that they were ill circulated, and later on it could be said that they had died of their illness.

She did not wish the Huguenots to know how nearly the plan of their leaders had succeeded. She did not wish them to know that Alençon and Navarre considered themselves as Huguenot leaders. They had been represented as having changed their faith, and she wished the Protestant population of France to continue to regard them with contempt. Therefore the plot must be kept secret as long as possible.

But it must not be taken for granted that men could enter into treachery against the King and the Queen Mother, and escape merely because it was not wise to let the country know of their plots. She would make an example; and she had the scapegoats in mind. They were La Mole and Coconnas. Those in the immediate entourage of Alençon and Navarre would know why disaster had overtaken these two men. But the outside world must think that it was for some other reason.

What wisdom there was in obtaining information regarding every little detail! For how could one be sure that the little thing, which seemed so trivial, might not supply the key for which one was looking?

When she had ordered the arrest of La Mole and Coconnas, she had said to her guards: 'Arrest these two men. On the person of the Comte de la Mole you will find a small wax figure. This wax figure will be wearing a cloak which, it will be apparent, is a royal cloak; and there will be a crown on that figure's head. If this figure is not on the person of La Mole, then search his lodgings until you find it.'

The figure had been found on the person of the amorous Count, and now, wrapped in a silk kerchief, it was in Catherine's possession.

When it was brought to her she lost no time in going to the King.

Charles was failing more than ever, and each day showed a difference in him. He could not walk now, but had to be carried in a litter. Every time she saw him, she thought: shall I send a message to Poland? If only she could have been sure of dealing with him as she had long desired to do, she could have sent that message to Poland long ago. But the King kept those three women at his side and would not allow them to leave him, even if they would. Either Marie Touchet, the Queen, or Madeleine was always with him. Nothing touched his lips unless one of them had superintended its preparation. What a terrible position for a great Queen to be in – the mother of the King, and to be treated so by these insignificant women!

The little wax figure gave her just what she needed; it

justified her in what she was about to do. It would put into her hands the lives of those two men who she had decided should die, and it would explain to the Touchet and that stupid old nurse as well as to Charles' wife, why the King's health had declined so rapidly.

'I must speak to you, my son. It is of the utmost importance.'

She looked at Marie, who quailed before her; but Charles clung to his mistress' hand.

'You are not to go, Marie,' he said.

Catherine gave the trembling girl her cold smile.

'No, you must not go, Marie, for you love my son even as I do myself, and for that reason I love you too. And you will be needed at hand to comfort him, to assure him of our love when I tell him of this wicked plot against his life.'

'What plot is this?' asked the King suspiciously.

For answer she took out the silk kerchief and, unfolding it, held out its contents to the King.

'A wax figure!' said Marie.

'Do you see whom it represents?' asked Catherine.

'It wears a crown,' cried the King. 'It is myself!'

'You are right. And you see this pin which pierces the figure's heart? You know what that means, my son. You know why, during these last weeks, your state of health has declined so rapidly.'

'It is magic!' said the King. 'Someone has been trying to kill me.'

'You have not always trusted your mother,' said Catherine. 'Your enemies have whispered about her and it has pleased you to believe them. Well, Charles, I forgive you. I only ask you to remember that it is your mother who, through her zealous efforts on your behalf, has discovered this plot against you.'

His lips began to tremble and the tears ran down his cheeks; soon he was sobbing in Marie's arms.

'Take courage, my dear lord, my darling,' whispered Marie. 'Her Majesty has discovered this plot, and doubtless she will also have discovered its perpetrators.'

'You speak truth there, Marie. I have the wicked men under arrest,' said Catherine.

'Who are they?' asked Charles.

'The Comte de la Mole and the Comte de Coconnas.'

'They shall die,' said Charles.

'Assuredly they shall,' promised Catherine. 'This is treason. We will bring them to trial for conspiring against your life. Though there is little need of a trial. These men are guilty. This image was found on the person of La Mole when he was arrested.'

'They shall all die,' agreed Charles. 'All ... all concerned with this wicked plot against me.'

Catherine watched him; he was too weak for violence nowadays. He slumped in his chair like an old man, his lips twitching, the mad light in his eyes and the tears running down his cheeks.

She left Marie to comfort him and went immediately to Vincennes. There she had Alençon brought into Navarre's apartments and the rooms cleared of all guards and attendants. She faced the two of them, smiling coldly.

'So, Messieurs, your further infamy has been uncovered. Here is a pretty state of affairs. What do you plan? A civil war? You are mad. You pretend to be friends, do you not? My son, why does Henry of Navarre assist you, do you think? Why does Alençon work with you, son-in-law? What a pair of featherbrained fools you are! Now to business. You should be wiser than to enter into such fruitless plotting, such absurd folly. Now I wish you to tell me that, if any has said you were involved in such a plot, they have lied. You two were unaware of any plot, were you not?'

Alençon could not understand her. He began to shout. 'There was a plot! I am kept in semi-captivity. Do you think I will endure that? I am the brother of the King and I am treated as a nobody. I will not endure it, I swear. I will not have it. I am determined to take my due. One day I may be King of this realm; then, Madame, you shall see ... you shall see ...'

'As ever,' interrupted Catherine, 'thoughtless, speaking without care. So you will be King of France, will you, my son? Make sure first that your brothers – your *two* brothers – do not see that you pay the penalty of treason.'

She turned to Navarre. That insolent young man was more

likely to see reason; already she noticed the shrewd look on his face. He had grasped her intentions. Here is a way out of trouble, said Navarre's twinkling eyes; let us seize it!

'False reports have been circulated about you,' said Catherine.

Navarre bowed. 'Yes, Madame. False reports have been circulated about us.'

'I see that you at least are not without sense, Monsieur,' said Catherine, 'and for that I am thankful. I have with me a document, and I wish you both to put your names to it. It disavows your connexion with any plot, if plot there was. You will sign it here. Come, my son, you also.'

Navarre took the document and studied it.

'We should sign,' he said to Alençon at length, 'for if a plot fails, the wiser course is to disown it.'

*

Margot was suffering acute anxiety.

The realization of what was happening had been the more terrible because it had come upon her suddenly. The rumours of the plot which Alençon and Navarre had made against the crown had spread too much to be ignored, and there had had to be an inquiry. Navarre had come out of this with ease, thanks to the clever defence which his wife had prepared for him. All Margot's frivolity could be banished on occasions, disclosing the bright intelligence which it obscured. But for her intense preoccupation with her lovers, she would have made as shrewd a statesman as most at court. But always she was governed by her emotions; and when she had penned that most lucid document – she was always most clever when her pen was in her hands – she had done so, not for love of her husband, whom she knew her mother would not at this time wish to see out of the way, but of the handsome Count with whom she was in love.

Navarre and Alençon had been cleared, but were still kept in semi-confinement. Margot had therefore expected the immediate release of her lover.

But this had not happened; and to her horror she had learned that La Mole and Coconnas were to be tried on another charge. What other charge, Margot could not imagine; but she was very quickly to discover, for the whole court was soon ringing with the news. La Mole and Coconnas were accused of conspiring against the life of the King.

They were tried and condemned to death. They had, it was declared, made a waxen image of him which they had pierced to the heart with a red-hot pin; and all knew that this meant that they had employed the Devil's aid to bring about Charles' death. This was treason of the worst kind.

It had been impossible to keep the maker of the image out of the case, and Cosmo Ruggieri, primed by Catherine, when arrested admitted that he had made the image for La Mole and Coconnas. He said that it was an image of the King.

'They came to me,' he said, 'and begged me to make an image of a royal person.'

'And you guessed who this royal person was intended to be?'

Cosmo bowed assent.

'Did you ask for what purpose the image was made?' asked his judges.

Cosmo said that he had not asked.

'You must have guessed that it was for some evil purpose since you supplied also the pins with which to pierce the heart.'

La Mole and Coconnas swore that the image did not represent the King, but a lady of whom the former had become enamoured.

'A lady in royal cloak and crown! Come, sir, you must think that we are a little foolish. It is clearly an effigy of His Majesty.'

'It is the image of the lady whom I love, and whom I wished to win,' insisted La Mole.

'The name of the lady?'

Catherine had been right when she had guessed it would be safe for such a question to be asked. La Mole, with his ideas of chivalry and gallantry, would never allow scandal to touch his mistress.

He sighed and said it was a lady whom he had met when he was travelling in another country.

'What country? And the name of the lady ... this royal lady?'

But he would not mention her name. He was stubborn and, said his judges — as Catherine had known they would — his inability to answer betrayed his guilt. He was, therefore, with his accomplice Coconnas, sentenced to be taken from his prison to the Place de Grève, there to die the traitor's death of decapitation; while for his part in the affair Cosmo Ruggieri was condemned to the galleys for life.

Margot appealed to the King. She flung herself on her knees before him.

'Sire, I beg of you to listen to me. The Comte de la Mole is being wrongly accused. I can tell you all you wish to know about that image. Oh, Sire, dearest brother, it was not meant to be of you, but of myself.'

The King was in the throes of that hysteria which always resulted from fear of assassination. He did not trust his sister. He knew that La Mole had been her lover; and he knew that previously she had worked for Henry of Guise against himself. Now he believed that her only thought was to save her lover, and that she cared not how many lies she told in order to do so.

He demanded that she leave him before he put her under arrest. He shouted that he did not trust her.

In desperation, Margot went to her mother. 'You know the truth of this. You must. You must help me.'

Catherine smiled sadly. 'If I could help you, my daughter, I would do so. But you know how deeply enamoured you become of certain men. You do not see in them any villainy while you desire their persons. It was thus with Monsieur de Guise. Do you remember?' Catherine laughed. 'Well, so it is with Monsieur de la Mole. You do not consider the important fact that these men are traitors, for all that matters to you is that their beauty pleases you.'

'La Mole is not a traitor.'

'What! Is not a man a traitor who conspires against the life of his King?'

'He did not. The waxen image was of me. I swear it. Cosmo Ruggieri knew it was of me. Why did he lie?' Margot looked at her mother with terrible suspicion. She said softly: 'He is a great favourite of yours, this Ruggieri. It was a stupid pretence, that trial. You allowed Ruggieri to be sentenced, yet you assured him that he would never see the galleys as a slave. You have had him pardoned; you have sent him back to his brother to work for you. You could save those two men as you saved the liar Ruggieri.'

'If I could be convinced of their innocence . . .'

'Do not pretend to me! You *know* they are innocent! Involved in a plot with my husband and brother they may have been. But they are my brother's men. How could they help being involved if they were chosen to obey certain orders? But you know that they are innocent of this other charge of conspiring against the life of the King.'

'They did not seem so at their trial, alas! La Mole said the image was of a lady, and he would not give her name. That was a little stupid of him.'

'He is a chivalrous fool! As if I cared whether he mentioned my name! What is my reputation compared with his life!'

'You shock me, daughter. Your reputation as Daughter of France and Queen of Navarre is of the utmost importance. Moreover, you should choose less chivalrous lovers.'

'It is true then that you know the image was of myself?'

Catherine lifted her shoulders. 'We must abide by the judges' verdict, my dear.'

When Margot had gone, Catherine summoned Madalenna.

'See that the Queen of Navarre is closely watched,' she told Madalenna. 'See that all her letters are brought to me . . . without fail . . . let nothing pass. See that all her actions are reported the instant they occur.'

＊

Margot took Henriette to her *ruelle* and there they wept together.

'But it is no use weeping, Henriette,' cried Margot. 'We must *do* something. I will not stand by and let this terrible thing happen to our darlings.'

'But, Margot, what can we do?'

'I have thought of something we might try.'

'Margot! What is this?'

'You know how we ride about unchallenged. The guards never look into my coach when they recognize the royal arms it bears. Henriette, I believe we *could* do this. We will dress ourselves in two gowns and two cloaks apiece; and masked, we will ride in my coach to Vincennes.'

'Yes?' cried Henriette. 'Yes?'

'I will first of all make sure that I can bribe the jailers.' Margot's eyes began to sparkle in spite of her tears. This was an adventure such as she loved. 'That should not be difficult. I think I can do it. And then we shall visit our lovers. You shall go to the dungeon of Annibale and I to that of Boniface. When we are there we will, with all speed, take off our top cloaks and one of our dresses. La Mole shall get into mine and Coconnas into yours.'

Henriette said: 'They will not fit very well.'

'We will find the most voluminous in our wardrobes. We have something suitable, I am sure. They shall put the cloaks right over their heads; and they shall wear the masks which we shall take for them. And then quickly, and with the utmost assurance, we shall simply walk out of the dungeons, out of the castle, to the coach. It should be easy because it will be thought that the men are women we have taken with us. We will all ride away ... out of Paris ... and we shall be gone before they know what has happened. We must make sure of our jailers. The rest will be easy, providing we are calm.'

'I am eager to begin,' said Henriette nervously. 'I cannot wait.'

'You must curb your impatience. There must be no carelessness. First we have to talk to the jailers. We shall have to offer a large bribe, as it will be necessary for *them* to escape afterwards.'

'A bribe?' said Henriette. 'How can we come by as much money as will be necessary?'

'We have our jewels. What are a few diamonds and emeralds compared with the lives of our beloved!'

'You are right,' said Henriette.

'Perhaps tomorrow,' said Margot. 'Yes, we will do it tomorrow; and this afternoon I will ride to Vincennes in my coach and you will come with me. You will warn Coconnas of our plan while I whisper it to La Mole. It will be a rehearsal for our great adventure. But first I will see the jailers, and if they are the men I think they may be, it will be easy. Henriette, we must succeed tomorrow.'

'If we do not,' said Henriette, 'I shall die of a broken heart.'

*

Inside the coach which rumbled along the road to Vincennes sat the two young women, tense and nervous. Henriette pulled her cloaks about her and shivered; she felt in the bag she was carrying for the mask which would hide the features of her lover.

Margot also trembled with excitement.

'If only we succeed!' murmured Henriette for the sixth time through her chattering teeth.

'Don't say "If", Henriette. We shall. We *must*. You must look *distrait* or it will be known as soon as we enter the castle that we are planning something of this sort. All is arranged. The horses stand ready saddled for the jailers. You have your jewels; I have mine. It is quite simple. I do not think this will be the first time men have walked out of their prisons in the dress of women. In less than an hour we shall be on our way.' Margot talked continually, for she found it stemmed her own nervousness to talk. 'Now, Henriette, there must be no delay in the dungeon. Immediately the door has closed on you, you must remove your cloak and top dress. It must not take more than a few minutes for you and Coconnas to be ready. We will meet outside the dungeons and walk quickly out of the castle. Oh, do not be foolish! Of course we shall do it. It is so simple.'

The coach had drawn up.

'Now, Henriette, pull yourself together. Look sad. Remember you are going to see your lover for the last time . . . so they think . . . for tomorrow he is to be executed. Think how you would be feeling if it were not for our plan . . . and look like that. Look at me. Like this . . . you see? I declare I want to laugh aloud when I think how we are going to fool them all. Come, Henriette. Ready? All we need is courage and calm.'

The coachman held open the door for them. His face was grave. He had his orders: two ladies were leaving the coach; four would return, and no sooner were they inside than he was to gallop with all speed to a certain inn where fresh horses were waiting.

It was all carefully planned; and in the service of the Queen of Navarre one was called upon to do strange things.

It seemed very cold within the thick stone walls of the castle. The guards saluted the Queen and her friend with sombre gallantry. They knew of their relationship with the prisoners in the dungeons below, and in their romantic chivalry they shed a tear for the sorrowing ladies. There were many of them who would have been ready to risk punishment in order to allow the beautiful Queen and Duchess to say a last farewell to their condemned lovers. Gallic sympathy for all lovers showed itself in their eyes as they watched the heartbroken and charming ladies.

The door of the cell was opened by a silent jailer, who looked sadly at Margot. How frightened they all are! she thought. All except myself.

And as she stepped into the cell she felt nothing but the joy of the adventure and the sure hope of success; she felt that the suspense and misery of the last weeks were almost worthwhile, since through them she could enjoy this supreme moment, this intense pleasure of offering his life to her lover.

The door shut behind her.

'My darling,' whispered Margot. 'My Hyacinth ...'

Her eyes had grown accustomed to the dim light, and she could see what looked like a bundle on the floor.

'Where are you? Where are you?' she cried in alarm.

The bundle seemed to stir slightly. She went to it and knelt down.

'My love ... my darling ...' she muttered; and she drew back the rough blanket. There he lay, his face deathlike, his black curls damp on his forehead.

Margot cried in anguish: 'What ails you? What has happened?'

In silence he gazed at her.

'Oh, God!' she whispered. 'Blood ... blood on the floor ..., on the blanket ... blood everywhere ... *his* blood ...'

With the utmost gentleness she lifted the blanket further; she cried out as she saw those broken bleeding legs and feet.

She understood. They had applied the Torture of the Boot; they had broken his beautiful limbs and he would never walk again. Her magnificent plan to save him had been foiled.

'Oh, my darling,' she cried, 'what can I do? What can I do to help you!'

He was now aware of her, for she saw the faint smile on his lips.

He was murmuring something and she had to bend over him to catch his words. 'You came ...' he said. 'Dearest ... that will suffice. It is all I ask ... You did not forget ...'

She put her face against his and he tried to raise a hand to touch her, but the effort brought an agonized groan to his lips and the sweat to his forehead.

'You must not move,' she said. 'Oh, my darling, what can I do? Why did I come too late?'

Again he spoke. 'You came ... That ... is enough.'

The jailer came silently into the cell.

'Madame, you must go. Oh, Madame, most deeply I regret. The order came, Madame, and there was nothing I could do to prevent its being carried out. There was nothing I could do ... nothing ...'

She nodded. 'The order came,' she repeated; and she seemed to see her mother's smiling face. 'I understand,' she said. 'I understand.'

Henriette was waiting in the corridor; she was holding a kerchief to her eyes.

'Annibale also?' murmured Margot.

Henriette nodded.

And together they walked out to the coach. There was no need to act the part of two broken-hearted women who had said a last farewell to their lovers.

*

Before the Hôtel de Ville in the Place de Grève the crowd had assembled to see the execution of the two men who had conspired against the life of the King. This execution had attracted a good deal of attention because it was said that the two men who were to die had been great lovers – one the lover of no less a person than the Queen of Navarre, the other of another lady of quality, the Duchess of Nevers.

The crowd grumbled. It was the wicked Queen Mother who was responsible. All the ills and sorrows of France came through her. There had been books written about her. Some said she was jealous of her daughter, and that was why she had cruelly tortured Margot's lover and had decided to destroy him. Nothing too bad could be said about the Queen Mother. At all public ceremonies other emotions gave way to hatred of her.

'He made a waxen image of the King . . .'

'Ah! It is time he was dead, that madman.'

'Hush! You know not who listens. And what if he dies? Who follows? Our elegant gentleman from Poland? Little Alençon? They are a swarm of vipers.'

The sounds of tumbril wheels were heard and for a while silence descended upon the crowd.

Then someone whispered: 'They say he has been cruelly tortured. It was the Boot. Both have been tortured . . . La Mole and Coconnas. They cannot walk to their execution.'

'Poor gentlemen. Poor handsome gentlemen.'

'How long shall we allow that woman to rule this land?'

But the tumbrils had stopped, and the two men were being carried to the scaffold.

The packed crowd watched; many among it wept openly. It seemed so cruel that these men should die for making a waxen image of one who was all but dead himself. Tortured as they had been, they still bore signs of handsome elegance.

The executioner signed to the men who carried La Mole to set him down on the scaffold.

'Your time has come, Monsieur,' he murmured.

'I am ready,' said La Mole. 'Adieu, my darling,' he whispered.

The executioner placed him where he wished him to be.

'Have you anything more to say, Monsieur?'

'Nothing, but that I ask you to commend me to the Queen of Navarre. Tell her, I beg of you, that her name was the last that passed my lips. Oh, Marguerite, my queen . . . my love . . .'

He laid his head on the block and waited for the deft blow of the executioner's sword.

A deep sigh broke from the watching crowd.

It was the turn of Coconnas. First the brief and terrible silence, then the muttered words, the flash of the sword, and the head of Coconnas lay with that of his friend on the blood-stained straw.

*

Catherine was triumphant. There was now no doubt that the King was dying. He was no longer strong enough even to be carried about in a litter. He could not leave his bedchamber.

It was May month and the apartment was full of sunshine. Close to the King's bed, the little Queen sat, pretending she had a cold that she might now and then furtively wipe away the tears which she could not suppress. Madeleine's face was distorted with grief. Marie Touchet watched, pale and full of sorrow. These women who had guarded him knew that the end could not be far away.

Margot also watched, but Catherine guessed that her thoughts were not on the King. She was still, as Catherine put it to herself, 'temporarily heartbroken' over the La Mole affair. What a complex creature Margot was! The document she had recently drawn up in defence of her husband had astonished Catherine. She realized that her daughter was one of the cleverest people at the court. She had the brain of a lawyer, and Monsieur Paré said that had she wished she could have been the best of all his pupils. Her mind was lively, shrewd and cunning; she had the Medici mind; yet she had inherited many traits from her grandfather, Francis the First, and her sensuality was so dominant that it overshadowed other more noble characteristics. She spent many hours at her writing desk; she was a dreamer and her imagination was so vivid that she must continually concoct adventures, when they did not occur in fact; and herself, whether in fact or fiction, must always play

215

the heroine. She wrote her memoirs regularly, and these, Catherine knew, were highly coloured versions of what actually happened at the court, with Margot always portrayed as the central figure of romance and intrigue.

Watching her daughter now, she thought of how, after the execution of those young men, Margot had given orders that their heads were to be brought to her; and now she and that frivolous Henriette de Nevers had had the heads embalmed with sweet spices and fitted into extravagantly jewelled caskets, so that they could spend a good deal of time lavishing caresses on them, recalling past pleasures, curling the hair on those dead heads and weeping with bitter enjoyment. No, Margot was certainly not to be unduly feared while her sentimental nature was allowed to override her intelligence.

There was little to fear from Charles now. His son was dead, and his other child, being a girl, was no obstacle to Henry's coming to the throne. Charles could not last many more hours. Alençon and Navarre were in semi-captivity; Montgomery and Cossé were to be removed at the first opportunity. Why should she delay? She slipped out of the death chamber to her own and sent for six of her most trusted men.

When they stood before her, she said to them: 'Ride as fast as you can to Poland. The King is dead . . . or so near to death that one may call him so. Long live King Henry the Third!'

She smiled contentedly after they had gone. The great moment for which she had waited so long had arrived. Her darling Henry was about to be King.

But in the royal bedchamber the King was clinging to his life.

He cried weakly in the arms of Madeleine. 'Oh, God,' he murmured, 'what blood! What murders! Oh, God . . . forgive me. Oh, God, have mercy on my soul. I know not where I am. Marie, Madeleine . . . do not leave me. Do not leave me for an instant. Tell me where I am.'

'In my arms, my dearest,' said Madeleine. 'Safe in my arms.'

Marie stood on the other side of the bed, and Charles took her hand.

'What will become of this country?' he said; his voice rose to a shriek and died away pitiably. 'And what will become of me? It was in my hands that God placed the fate of this great country. There is nothing you can say to alter that.'

'There, my darling, my Charlot,' soothed Madeleine. 'May the murders and the bloodshed be upon the heads of those who compelled you to them . . . on your evil counsellors, Sire.'

Madeleine, looking up, met the cold eyes of Catherine fixed upon her; Catherine's cold mouth smiled slightly. Charles was aware of his mother's presence and held out his hand as though to ward her off.

'Madame,' he said, 'I must trust you to look after my wife and daughter.'

'Rest assured, my son, that they will be well cared for.'

'And Marie . . . and her son . . .'

'You have provided for them, Charles. I promise you that no harm shall come to them.'

Catherine smiled on Marie, poor meek Marie. She had caused little trouble except in those last weeks when she, with Madeleine, had stubbornly refused to leave the King's side. But that was forgotten now, for the King was dying and that was what Catherine was waiting for. It mattered very little whether he had died a few weeks ago or now; his death was all that mattered. Let Marie live in peace, then; she was not of sufficient importance to be considered. Charles had created her son Duke of Angoulême, so Marie – the provincial judge's daughter – had nothing of which to complain.

'I will look after your Queen and her little daughter. I will see that Marie and her son are cared for. Have no fear. These matters shall be attended to.'

He looked at her suspiciously and then asked that Navarre should be sent for.

Navarre was brought by guards, who waited for him outside the King's bedchamber.

'You plotted against me,' said the King. 'That was unkind. Yet I trust you . . . as I cannot trust my brothers. It is because of something plain about you . . . something that smacks of honesty. I am glad you came to say goodbye to me. I sent for you for a reason, but I cannot think what it was. There are enemies all about you. I know. You should be warned. There is one here whom you must not trust. *I* was warned, but I think the warning came too late for me. Mayhap it will not be too late for you. Do not trust . . .' He turned his eyes on his mother, and stared at her as though unable to take them away. 'Do not trust . . .' he began again. His lips were trembling and Marie had to bend over him to wipe the foam from his mouth.

'You tire yourself, my son,' said Catherine.

'No, I will say it. I will. It is the truth, and because it is the truth I must say it. Brother . . . Navarre . . . look after my Queen and my daughter. Look after Marie and her child. To you I leave the care of Madeleine. For you are the only one I dare trust. Promise me. Promise me.'

Navarre, whose tears came easily, wept without restraint. He kissed the King's hand. 'Sire, I swear. I will defend them with my life.'

'I thank thee, brother. It is strange that you should be the one I trust . . . you, who have plotted against the crown. But trust you I do. Pray to God for me. Farewell, brother. Farewell.' He looked at his mother and said: 'I rejoice that I have no son to leave behind me who would have to wear the crown of France after me.'

He lay back in his bed after that speech; he was overcome by exhaustion.

He has spoken his last, thought Catherine. And now . . . that for which I have longed over so many dangerous and bitter years . . . that for which I have worked, schemed and *killed* . . . has now come to pass. My mad King Charles is dead, and my adored darling must now prepare to mount the throne.

Four

The King of Poland was exhausted. He lay back on his cushions while two of his favourite young men fanned him . . . du Guast, the best loved of them all, and that amusing fellow Villequier. Others sat close to his bed; one picking out the best of the sweetmeats; another admiring the set of his jacket in the Venetian mirror which the King had brought with him from France. The King smiled at them all. He was not really dissatisfied with his little kingdom. It was gratifying to be loved as his subjects loved him. He had only to appear in the streets to be surrounded by admirers who deemed it a privilege to look at him, for they had never seen anyone so magnificent as this painted, perfumed King. Sometimes he wore women's clothes, and in these he looked more fantastic, more like a person apart from other men — which was what, his Polish subjects felt, a King should look like.

He had deteriorated a great deal since he had left France. He had lost even the slight energy he had possessed in his teens; he had become more selfish, more dependent on luxury. Now he feigned exhaustion because there were state duties which should be attended to. He loathed the meetings of his ministers; their councils bored him. He continually assured them that they could hold their gatherings without him. They must understand, he pointed out, that he was of gentle breeding and came from the fair and civilized land of France, from the most intellectual court in the world. He was no barbarian. He must have music to soothe him, not council meetings to plague him; he must listen to the reading of poetry which delighted him, not the harangues of politicians which tired him.

Count Tenczynski, his chief minister, was bowing before him, overcome with delight by the sweet perfumes and the sensuous *décor* of the King's apartments, admiring, as all his fellow countrymen did, this air of luxury and civilization which French Henry had brought into their land.

'And so, my dear Tenczynski,' said the King, 'I am weary. You must conduct your politics without me.' He turned towards the gentleman who was eating sweetmeats. 'One for me, dear fellow,' he said. 'You greedy creature, would you eat them all yourself?'

'I but tested them, dearest Majesty, to find which was worthy of your palate.'

The sweet was popped into the royal mouth by the gentleman, whose hand was patted affectionately by his master.

Tenczynski murmured: 'We would not tire your Majesty. If it is Your Majesty's wish that we should proceed without you . . .'

Henry waved his beautiful white hand. 'That is my wish, my dear Tenczynski. Go to your council and when it is over come back and we will tell you of the wonderful ball we are giving tomorrow night.'

Tenczynski lifted his shoulders and laughed. 'A ball . . . tomorrow night?' he said.

'A ball, my dear Tenczynski, such as you have never before seen. Now leave me, and when you return for my *coucher* I shall tell you all about it and what I shall wear.'

'Your Majesty deserves the grateful appreciation of your subjects,' said Tenczynski, bowing low.

When he had gone, Henry yawned. He decided to tease his young men by talking of the Princess of Condé.

'To think I have not set eyes on her fair face for six long months!'

The young men were sullen; but they knew that he was teasing. They were not really disturbed; nor was Henry really longing for the Princess. This was just a game they played between them.

'Don't sulk,' said Henry. 'And another sweetmeat. I am going to write to the Princess tonight.'

'You tire yourself with writing to the Princess,' said du Guast.

'You are mistaken, my friend. I am *stimulated* by writing to the Princess.'

Villequier pleaded: 'Leave it until tomorrow, dearest Sire, and talk about your toilette for the ball.'

The King was tempted irresistibly. 'I shall be in green silk, and I shall be dressed as a woman. My gown will be cut low and I shall wear emeralds and pearls. And now ... my writing materials, please. You may discuss together what *you* are going to wear, because I shall be rather cross if you do not surpass yourselves.'

They could see that he was determined to write to the Princess, so they brought the materials for which he asked. He sent for his jewelled stiletto and, when it was brought, he pricked his finger while the young men looked on in sorrow. Then he began to write to the Princess of Condé in his own blood, an affectation which delighted him.

'When you read this letter, my darling, you must remember that it is written in royal Valois blood, the blood of him who now sits on the throne of Poland. Ah, I would it were that of France! And why? Because of that greater honour? No, my love. Because, were I King of France, you would be beside me.'

While he was writing du Guast entered the chamber; he was excited, but Henry did not look up. He thought the favourite's jealousy had prompted him to interrupt the letter-writing on some small pretext.

'Sire,' said du Guast, 'there is a messenger without. He brings great news.'

'A messenger!' Henry laid aside his love letter. 'What news?'

'Great news, Sire. From France.'

'Bring him in. Bring him in.'

When the man was brought in, he went to the King and knelt before him with a great show of reverence. Then, having kissed the delicate hand, he cried aloud: 'Long live King Henry the Third of France.'

Henry lifted his hand and smiled. 'So,' he said, 'my brother is dead at last ... and you come from my mother. Welcome! You have other news for me?

'None, Sire, except that the Queen Mother urges your return to France without delay.'

The King patted the messenger's shoulder. 'My attendants will give you the refreshments you deserve for bringing such

221

news. Take him away. Give him food and drink. See that he is well looked after.'

When they were alone, Henry lay back, his arms behind his head, smiling at his young men.

'At last!' cried the impetuous Villequier. 'That for which we have long hoped and prayed has come to pass.

'I must return to France at once,' said the King.

'This very night!' cried Villequier.

'Sire,' said the more sober du Guast, 'that will not be necessary. The Poles know that they cannot detain you now. Summon the ministers and tell them what has happened. Make your plans to leave. You will be ready in a day or so. But to go tonight would appear as if you were escaping.'

Henry frowned on du Guast. He had already pictured himself and his companions slipping away, riding hard into France. He smiled on Villequier, for that gentleman's suggestion pleased him.

'They *will* try to detain me,' he said. 'You know how they love me. I have told them that there is to be a great ball tomorrow night, and they will not let me go until that is over.'

'Give them their ball,' advised du Guast. 'Let it be a farewell ceremony. Explain to them that, although you remain the King of Poland, it is necessary that you go immediately to France to show yourself to the people and to arrange matters of state for which you, as their King, are responsible.'

'But, my dear, you know I must *live* in France from now on. A King of France cannot live in Poland.'

'They will not know this, Sire. It can be broken to them later on.'

'He is wrong,' said Villequier, who was impatient to feel the soil of France under his feet. 'We must leave for France at once . . . tonight. Does not the Queen Mother say so?'

'I believe you are right, dear Villequier,' said Henry. 'Yes. That is what I shall do. Now, my dears, let us make our plans. Have horses saddled ready for us. After the attendants have left for the night, I will rise, hastily dress, and we will not lose a moment. We will gallop off to our beloved France.'

Du Guast said wearily: 'Such dramatic action is not necessary, Sire.'

Henry was peevish. He had grown completely self-indulgent during his reign in Poland. He enjoyed acting strangely and in a completely unexpected manner. He did not care how foolish he was; he enjoyed astonishing himself as well as those about him. Du Guast, recognizing the mood, knew that it was useless to remonstrate.

'I long for the civilization of France!' cried Henry. 'The only things I shall regret leaving behind me are the crown jewels of Poland.'

'But they belong now to Your Majesty,' said Villequier. 'Whether you are in France or in Poland, you are still the King of Poland. Take the crown jewels with you, Sire.'

Henry languidly kissed Villequier on either cheek. 'You have made me very happy, dear friend,' he said. 'I could not have *borne* to part with those jewels.'

They dispersed to make their arrangements, and when the time came for the *coucher* they were ready for flight.

Tenczynski presided over the ceremony while the Polish nobles stood about smiling with pleasure, as they always did in the presence of the King. Henry lay back in his bed and talked desultorily, for a while.

He yawned. 'I declare I am tired tonight. I have been so busy all day with the preparations for tomorrow's ball.'

'Then,' said Tenczynski, 'we will leave Your Majesty to your slumbers.'

Henry closed his eyes, and the curtains about his bed were drawn. All left the bedchamber and there was quiet throughout the palace.

Half an hour later, as they had arranged, his young men, already dressed and booted, came quietly in. They all assisted in the dressing of the King, and, taking the Polish crown jewels with them, they left the palace, made their way to where the saddled horses were waiting, and rode secretly out of Cracow.

It was exciting to imagine themselves pursued. They rode on with great speed but without much sense of direction, and when they had ridden for some hours, they found themselves on the banks of the Vistula and had no idea how they had reached it, nor which way they should go.

They looked at each other in consternation. It was not part of the King's exciting plan that they should be lost. 'Let us ride into the forest,' said du Guast. 'We may find a guide.'

This they did, riding hard until they came to a woodcutter's hut, where Villequier, pointing his dagger at the man's throat, insisted that he leave his family and guide the party to the frontier. The trembling man had no alternative but to agree, but it was two days and nights before the party reached the frontier. There Tenczynski was waiting for them with three hundred Tartars.

Du Guast could not repress a smile of triumph, for he had at least proved his point that this piece of dramatic play-acting would be useless.

Tenczynski dropped on his knees before the King. 'I have followed you, Sire,' he said, 'to beg you to return to Cracow. Your subjects are plunged into sorrow because you have left them. Return, Sire, and you will find a great welcome waiting for you. Your subjects will be as obedient and loving as they have ever been.'

'My dear Count,' said Henry, 'you must know that I have been recalled to my native land. The French crown is my birthright. Do not think, because I must hasten to France, that I shall not return to Poland . . . the land which I have grown to love. Just let me settle my affairs in France and I will be back.'

'Sire, in France you will not find subjects as loving and faithful as Poland can offer you.'

'Dear Tenczynski, you move me deeply. But do not ask me to return with you now. Just a little grace . . . that is all I ask. Do you think I shall be able to stay away from our dear Poland? You must go back to Cracow and take care of matters for me until I see you again. Rest assured, dear Count, that will be sooner than you believe possible.'

With great deliberation, Tenczynski pricked his arm with his dagger and let the blood drop on to a bracelet. 'Here is my blood, Sire, on this ornament. Take it, I beg of you. It will be a constant reminder that my blood is yours should you need it.'

Henry pulled off one of his diamond rings and gave it to the Count in exchange for the bracelet. 'Take this in memory of me,' he said.

'And may I tell Your Majesty's subjects that you will soon be back with us, that this is just a short visit to France, Sire?'

'You may tell them that,' said Henry.

Tenczynski wept while the Tartars looked on in bewilderment. Henry and his followers rode on across the frontier.

'To our beloved France!' cried the King. 'Never again to set foot in that land of barbarians.'

But Henry found that, once he had left Poland behind him, he was in no great hurry to reach the land of his birth. Kingship brought many responsibilities which he was not eager to shoulder, and governing France was not going to be such a pleasant matter as pretending to govern Poland had been. He thought irritably of those tiresome Huguenots and fanatical Catholics who were always making trouble; he thought of the domination of his mother, the perversity of his brother, and the slyness of his sister. It was pleasant therefore to linger on the way.

In Vienna there was a great reception for the new King of France. He could not leave in a hurry after such a reception; it would seem so churlish. And beautiful Venice gave him a welcome which made that he had received in Vienna seem quite cool by comparison.

What joy it was to recline in a golden gondola rowed by eight gondoliers in Turkish turbans, while the Venetians looked on at the glittering figure adorned by French and Polish jewels!

He could not tear himself away from Venice. He was deeply susceptible to beauty; and to glide along the Grand Canal, to see the Venetian beauties wave to him from their lighted windows, to be with writers and artists once more, gave him an exquisite pleasure. How had he endured those months in a savage land? He allowed artists to paint his portrait; he wandered in the Rialto disguised as an ordinary citizen; he bought perfumes such as he had not been able to buy since what he called in tragic tones 'his exile'. He bought numerous jewels.

'My dears,' he said to his young men as he perfumed them

with his new purchases and hung recently acquired jewels about their necks, 'is it not wonderful to be once more in a civilized land?'

Urgent dispatches from the Queen Mother began to arrive. She had set out with her entourage and was waiting for him at the frontier. His people were eager, she wrote, to welcome their King.

He grimaced. He was not sure of the welcome he would receive in France. He could not forget those scowling French men and women who had lined the streets in the Flemish towns to shout insults at him and to bespatter him with mud and foul things.

But Catherine's appeals could not be continuously flouted, and Henry knew that he must say goodbye to the dear people of Venice and push on to the frontier.

When at last Catherine met him she embraced him fervently.

'My darling, at last!'

'Mother! I have been unable to sleep these last days and nights in my longing to see you. The exile has been terrible dear Mother, terrible and tragic.'

'It is over now, my darling. You are home. You are King of France. I do not need to tell you how I have longed for this day.'

She was studying him anxiously. He seemed to have aged six years in a little more than six months. It was so with these sons of hers. Their lives seemed to burn out quickly. They were mature in their teens and old men in their twenties. She was afraid that he would grow sickly as Francis and Charles had done.

She explained to him that she was admiring his healthy looks, for she knew that he could not endure criticism, particularly of his appearance. 'You look younger than you did when you went away, my darling. You must tell me all about that terrible exile later.'

She had, she said, brought Alençon and Navarre with her. 'They are kept under close supervision,' she added. 'I make them ride with me in my coach, and they always share my lodging. We must watch those two.'

226

She rode beside him during the state entry into Lyons. This is how it shall be from now on, she decided. I shall always be beside him, and together we shall rule France.

Lyons brought bitter memories to Catherine. She recalled another entry into this city – oh, long ago! – when she, the Queen of France, had been deeply humiliated by the honour which had been done to the King's mistress, Diane de Poitiers.

How different was this entry! She was happy now. Her son Henry would never treat her as her husband Henry had done. This was the happiest relationship of her life.

News was brought to Catherine, while the royal party rested at Lyons, that the Princess of Condé had died; Catherine was surprised to find how genuinely grieved she was at the thought of the sorrow this would cause Henry. She kept the news from him for as long as she could.

His way of showing his grief was typical of the King; he used it to increase the jealousy of his favourites. His heart was broken, he declared. Oh, what a cruel fate was this! He had been living only in the hope of reunion with his love. And after all those months of exile, he had lost her!

He shut himself in his rooms; he wore deep mourning – black velvet ornamented with diamonds; and diamonds, he said were *not* his favourite stones. He needed colour to set off his skin and eyes. 'You see how I loved her, when I will wear nothing but these sombre garments because of her. Oh, my heart is truly broken.'

Catherine remonstrated. 'My darling, you must not stay here. You have been away from Paris too long. There is your coronation to be considered. The sooner you are crowned King the better. I insist.'

He was playful. 'You insist, dear mother. Ah, but I am the master now, am I not?'

And two months were frittered away before she could induce him to proceed, and then he would go no farther than Avignon.

*

Catherine quickly realized that those happy plans of sharing the throne with her beloved son had little hope of fulfilment. He consulted her less than he used to. She had always known that he was wildly extravagant, but never had he been so extravagant as he was now. He had always enjoyed doing what was unexpected; but previously his tricks had held a grain of humour in them; they seemed now to be all stupidity. She blamed his young men; she would have to break that influence as quickly as she could.

He had formed an attachment to a young woman whom that sly old man, the Cardinal of Lorraine, had called to his notice. The Cardinal was trying to win the confidence of the King, Catherine assumed, so that he might dominate him as he had once dominated poor sickly little Francis. Louise de Vaudemont was a fair-haired young woman who belonged to the Lorraine family.

Henry took a half-hearted interest in the girl at first, for he was, he declared, still broken-hearted by the loss of the Princess of Condé; but after a while it occurred to him that he should have a mistress, and Louise de Vaudemont was as suitable as any. She was already the mistress of Francis of Luxembourg; thus she would not make too many demands on the King; she was therefore very worthy to step into the shoes of Madame de Condé. The Princess had had a husband; Louise had a lover; that was very convenient when love-making wearied a man.

He was not eager to leave Avignon. He wished to postpone his arrival in Paris, for he did not like his capital; he never rode through its streets without being aware of the antagonism of the people. They did not appreciate his beauty, nor that of his gentlemen. He had acquired Louise because he felt that it would please the people of Paris to know that he was sufficiently natural to love a woman. But he did not wish to think of Paris; be became petulant when anyone mentioned the city. 'Avignon is a charming town,' he would say. 'Let us stay here awhile. We shall have plenty of time for Paris.'

He joined the new brotherhood of the *Battus*. 'I wish my people to know,' he said, 'that I am a serious man, a deeply religious man.' The *Battus* was a sect whose members dressed themselves in sacks, and, wearing masks, paraded the streets thrashing each other as they went; their feet and shoulders were bare and they carried lighted tapers and crucifixes as though they were doing a penance. Henry was enthusiastic about the *Battus*. All his young men must join. It gave one such a sense of spirituality, said the King; and it was *heavenly* to feel the lash on one's shoulders. He had death's heads worked in jewels all over his clothes; he had them worked in silk, even on his shoestrings.

Navarre joined the order. He enjoyed thrashing the King and his favourites, but managed to avoid being beaten himself. '*Chacun à son goût!*' said the incorrigible Navarre.

The Cardinal of Lorraine also joined the order, for he wished above all things to enjoy the favour and confidence of the King.

Catherine watched their antics in dismay.

It is nothing, she assured herself. He has waited so long. Now his triumph has gone to his head. He will tire of this folly soon, and then he and I will rule together.

*

Catherine was sitting at dinner when, suddenly and without warning, the knowledge came to her that the Cardinal of Lorraine was dead.

She paused in the act of carrying a goblet to her lips and said calmly: 'Now we may have some peace, for the Cardinal of Lorraine is dead, and folks say that he was the one who prevented it.'

One of her women said: 'Madame, I saw the Cardinal but two days ago. It was in a procession of the *Battus*. He was walking barefoot and his shoulders were uncovered. He was well enough then.'

'He is dead,' Catherine persisted. 'He was a great prelate.' She smiled slyly. 'We have suffered a grievous loss.' She saw Madalenna's eyes upon her and and she drew the woman closer to her, whispering: 'Today has died the wickedest of men, the saints be praised!'

At that she dropped her goblet and stared before her. 'Jesus!' she cried. 'There he is. There is the Cardinal!'

229

Madalenna's teeth were chattering. 'Madame,' she whispered, 'we see him not.'

Catherine sat back in her chair. She was calm as she said: 'It was a vision. I have had such now and then in my life. I doubt not that this day we shall hear of the death of that old man.'

Her women could not forget the incident. They talked together of it in awed whispers. They remembered the occasion on which she had told them of the death of the Prince of Condé at Jarnac and the victory of her son on that field, when, though miles away, she had seemed to see it all pass before her eyes while it was happening.

'The Queen Mother is not quite human,' they said. 'That is what terrifies us all.'

Later that day, when news was brought to Catherine of the Cardinal's death, she said: 'You bring no news to me. I saw him as he left this Earth on his way to Paradise.' And to herself she added: 'To Hell more likely, if such a place there be.'

That night a heavy storm arose and, as Catherine lay sleepless in her bed, she could not shut out of her mind the memory of that man who had dominated her son, King Francis the Second, and made that boy's life miserable to him. She remembered so many incidents from the past, the sly, deadly remarks of the man, his lecherous eyes, his shrewd determination to advance his house, the cowardice which had made him wear a suit of mail under his Cardinal's robes. She remembered how, of all the men in France, he had been her greatest enemy; a wicked man, a man of contrasts, a man of the Church who was ready to pay great rewards to any man or woman who could think of some new method of interesting his erotic tastes, who could cap any quotation from the classics, who excelled at repartee, and the more *risqué* it was, the more it was to his liking. She thought of how, during the last years, when he must have known that he was approaching death, he had looked at her with a new affection, seeing in her one whom he considered so wicked that beside her he felt innocent. She imagined him, standing before God and saying in that sly clever way of his: 'Yes, I did that, and I am guilty of that . . . but my Lord God, consider that greater sinner Queen Catherine, and

230

you will see that I am a novice in sin.' This imaginary scene made her laugh aloud.

But as the storm buffeted the walls of the château, and it was impossible to shut out the sound of the wind and the incessant beating of the rain, a terrible fear gripped her and she thought that the Cardinal stood in her bedchamber. She touched her bracelet and repeated the words of a protective charm which René had taught her; but even when she shut her eyes she could see the long, sly face of the Cardinal with those finely chiselled features which, before depravity had set their mark on them, had been so beautiful; she saw the eyes with the dark bags beneath them; she saw the thin lips moving. And she thought: he wants to take me with him. He wants me to stand before the Judgement Seat beside him. He wants to say, 'Compare us. Here is the wickedest woman who ever lived. You cannot see her, scarlet with her sins, and think so badly of me!'

It was a ridiculous fantasy; she did not believe in that Judgement. But she could not forget the Cardinal, and it seemed to her that he was there in the shadow of the hangings at the foot of her bed.

At length she could bear the strain no longer and called to her women. They came, surprised.

'Light candles,' she said. 'The Cardinal is here. The lights and your company will drive him back to Hades.'

They stayed with her for the remainder of the night.

At last the King agreed to leave Avignon for Rheims.

'You must be crowned King of France as soon as possible,' said Catherine.

One of the greatest days of her life was approaching, she assured herself: the day her darling was to be crowned King of France. She had not time for whimsical fears and she had ceased to think about the Cardinal of Lorraine, although for a few nights after his death she had kept her women about her bed until dawn. That man who had been called *Le tigre de la France*, the leech, the bloodsucker, the enemy of God, was soon forgotten; although immediately after his death, tales had been whispered about his passing. The Huguenots declared that the great storm which had burst over them on the night of his death had been stirred up by witches at their Sabbat, so that they might carry his soul away to eternal torment. They said also that he was greatly perturbed while he was dying, and aware of the evil spirits about his bed who were waiting for his soul to be released. The Catholics had a different story to tell. To them the storm represented God's anger with a country that did not appreciate a good Catholic such as the Cardinal had always been; God had taken him, since his country did not appreciate him. They said that when he had died he had spoken with the tongues of angels, two of whom had stood at the head of his bed and two at the foot to take charge of his soul.

'It would be interesting to know who finally won the man's black soul,' said Catherine cynically, 'the witches or the angels. But I have no doubt that he will cause a bloody conflict in Heaven or Hell as he has throughout France. Enough of him! Let us leave him to his rest or his torment, for he is gone, and it is with those who remain that we must concern ourselves.'

And so to Rheims, where Henry startled his mother by declaring his intention to marry without delay.

Catherine was horrified. 'If you wish to marry, my son, we will find a bride worthy of you. But negotiations must take place. First there is your coronation to be taken care of.'

'I intend to marry two days after my coronation.'

'That . . . that is impossible.'

'With me,' said Henry in his new arrogance, 'very little is impossible. Certainly not marriage.'

'Henry, my love, I do not think you understand the dignity of your position. As King of France . . .'

'As King of France, I, and I alone, will decide whom and when I will marry. Louise is eager to become my Queen and I see no reason for delay.'

'Louise!' cried Catherine in horror.

'We are in love,' said Henry, patting his curls.

She looked at him in astonishment. What had happened to him during those months he had spent in Poland? She was wondering with dismay whether he was tainted with that madness which had tormented poor Charles.

'You are the King,' she protested. 'You must have a marriage worthy of you.'

'I must marry and have children, Mother. Why, if I were to die tomorrow, Alençon would mount the throne. Such a calamity must never be allowed to fall upon France.'

'You must have children, yes . . . but you must also marry in accordance with your rank.'

He took her hand and lightly kissed it. 'My rank is such,' he said, 'that any raised up by me appear exalted. The marriage will take place immediately after the coronation. The people will be pleased.'

Catherine saw the petulant droop of his lips; she knew that he was defying her to attempt to frustrate him. She was unable to arouse fear in him, as she had been able to to do so effortlessly in her other children. She must not despair; she must try to rule by cunning. Why should she not? She had done so successfully before. But how alarming it was to discover this irresponsibility in him, for, in a person of his position, it amounted almost to madness.

The coronation did not go smoothly. He showed his annoyance at the way in which the crown was placed on his head. It hurt him, he said aloud; and he shook his head pettishly so that it almost fell off. He must learn to control his temper in public, thought Catherine. What had those Poles done to him? They had changed him. He must not behave before his French subjects as he obviously had before those barbarians. To the Poles he had been a glittering oddity; to the French he was a ridiculous pervert. Catherine's fears grew with every manifestation of the strangeness of her son. The people were saying now that the incident regarding the crown was an evil omen. 'Did you see the way it all but fell off his frivolous head? He'll not reign long. That was a sign. A sign that need not cause us much concern.' This was bad; a King should be popular, at least during his coronation. Henry was angered by the sullen attitude of the people. The Poles had been so proud of him; what was wrong with the French that they could not also be?

And immediately after the coronation the startled population was informed that he was to marry without delay.

233

His behaviour now became preposterous and it was obvious that he had become so arrogant, so conceited that he did not care what his people thought of him. He insisted that the Church should waive its customs, and that the wedding should be celebrated at night. 'For,' he explained, 'we need to dress in daylight, and it will take the whole of the day to arrange our jewels and dresses.'

The Church was angry; the people were shocked. He had not only made this sudden decision but he had chosen as a wife a woman who was known to be the mistress of Francis of Luxembourg. The French were already beginning to despise this painted, perfumed King who did not seem to be able to make up his mind whether he was a man or a woman.

He committed a further indiscretion by summoning Francis of Luxembourg to his presence.

'My cousin,' he said to this young man, and he said it before so many that the story was carried through Rheims to Paris and circulated throughout France, 'I am about to marry your mistress. In exchange I give you Mademoiselle de Châteauneauf, who was mine. You shall marry my mistress and I shall marry yours, for that is a very piquant situation, I think, which amuses me and will amuse my people.'

Francis of Luxembourg, completely taken aback by the proposal, bowed low and said: 'Sire, I am indeed glad that my mistress is destined for such honour and glory. I beg you, however, to dispense with my marrying Mademoiselle de Châteauneuf.'

Henry frowned, 'Why so? Mademoiselle de Châteauneuf was good enough for me. She is, therefore, good enough for you.'

'That is so, Sire,' said the discomfited gentleman, 'but I would beg time to consider a step which, Your Majesty will agree, is an important one.'

'I cannot give you time,'said the arrogant King, 'I insist that your marriage to Mademoiselle de Châteauneuf takes place at once. I wish there to be two speedy marriages. It is a romantic and saucy situation which pleases me, and will make my people understand the man who is their King.'

Henry was married with great pomp to Louise de Vaudemont, but Francis of Luxembourg was missing from his apartments a few hours after his interview with the King; and later it was discovered that he had fled with all speed to Luxembourg.

Henry shrugged his elegant shoulders; he was too busy with his new clothes and the entertainments he was planning to think very much about his kinsman's flight. But the people were shaking their heads in disgust and asking themselves what lay ahead for a country with such a King on its throne. 'Have we finished with one madman, only to set another in his place? They are vipers, these Valois. What can you expect? Remember who their mother is!'

And from coronation and marriage in Rheims came Henry to his capital city, there to indulge in more orgies, more processions of the *Battus* through the streets.

The Parisians watched the antics of their King with sullen eyes. It seemed to them that nothing but evil could come from the domination of such a man as Henry the Third, who would rule them with the Italian Jezebel at his side.

*

The King continued his frivolous existence unaware of the storms which were rising all about him. Catherine watched him with apprehension and offered advice which he pretended to act upon and then allowed himself to forget. He had his special young men always about him; the people of Paris had begun to call them his *mignons*. There were four whom he seemed to favour more than any others: du Guast, Caylus and the Dukes of Joyeuse and Epernon. They scarcely ever left the King's side; they enjoyed his confidence and shared his pleasures. Catherine often heard them laughing together as they planned some ludicrous amusement or discussed the new styles in clothes and jewels or told each other of the antics of their lap-dogs.

All over Paris the people were becoming restive. Two cold summers in succession had caused a famine in wheat. The Huguenots, as ready with their assurances that God was on their side as the Catholics were that He was on theirs, declared this to be a result of the massacre. One ill which could, without

235

doubt, be attributed to the massacre was the plague of wolves which harassed the countryside; they had been attracted by so much carnage and looked for more. The Huguenots had been clever and industrious merchants and France was missing the prosperity they had created. Epidemics were raging through the land; lepers roamed the countryside, spreading their terrible afflictions; and still there was perpetual strife between the remaining Huguenots and the Catholics.

Moreover, the King needed money, and declared he must have it. He and his favourites had planned many amusing entertainments, but these would be expensive. The people were heavily taxed now; and in particular, the people of Paris murmured against the King; they were on the spot and they saw the extravagant processions; they glimpsed the expensively dressed guests, the lavish banquets that took place in the palace of the Louvre.

They had never hated any as they hated this King and his mother; but it was Catherine whom they blamed for the King's misdeeds, as they would continue to blame her for all the ills which befell France. The King they despised; his mother they feared and loathed.

The people of Paris were hungry, and when they were hungry they were reckless. Lampoons were scrawled on walls; coarse jokes about the King and his mother, Alençon and Queen Margot, were circulated. France was simmering on the point of revolt, and this showed itself in small eruptions. Once the carriage in which Catherine and Margot were travelling was stopped by students, who ordered the two women to alight; realizing that it would have been dangerous not to obey, they did so, when obscene remarks were shouted at the Queen Mother, and some students thrust their hands into the bodice of Margot's gown. Only the haughty demeanour of the two Queens prevented more rough handling; and displaying a dignity which eventually overawed the young rioters, they stepped calmly into their carriage, which was driven speedily away. On another occasion the King stopped to see the fair at Saint-Germain, and he found the place full of students burlesquing the *mignons* in long chemises with grotesque frills made of white paper. They minced through the town, calling each other

236

'*mignon*', stroking and petting each other. Those *mignons* who were with the King wept with anger, and the only way of pacifying them was to place the students under arrest. Catherine arranged that they should be quickly released; but she was alarmed by Henry's irresponsibility.

The citizens shouted after the King when he appeared in the streets, and even when he rode in a procession. 'Keeper of Four Beggars!' was the favourite gibe, and this was used particularly when he was in the company of his four especial favourites.

The people jeered: 'He dresses his wife's hair. He chooses her clothes. Who is this Henry the Third? Is he a man or a woman?'

'*Concierge du Palais!*' yelled the children, imitating their elders.

The wits amused themselves by inventing stories of the King's ridiculous behaviour; others talked continually of the Queen Mother's villainy. The city was realizing that it hated the House of Valois, and no member was spared vilification. Alençon and Margot, it was said, were guilty of incest. Margot took new lovers as frequently as she took her meals. She had a hundred different dresses in her wardrobe, all costing a fortune; and she kept special flaxen-haired footmen simply that she might use their hair for making wigs.

'How long shall we allow these vipers to rule us?' grumbled the people. 'How long shall we allow them to make us poor with their extravagances?'

And so the rumble of coming disaster rose and died away to rise again. There was perpetual strife between Huguenots and Catholics, who hated each other almost as much as they hated the royal family.

August came, hot and stifling. The filth in the streets of the towns and the stench from the gutters kept people behind doors. Beggars grew in numbers; they lay sprawled on the cobbles, diseased and dying; and the pickpockets did good business in the market-places. Outside the town robbers abounded, and murders were committed for the sake of a few francs.

In August came the anniversary of a day which would never be forgotten.

Every year – for years to come – Huguenots would lie awake on the night of the 23rd and listen for the sound of the tocsin, remembering those lost ones, trembling at the thought that they might be called upon to share the fate of those martyrs.

In Paris some Catholic joker had spread panic among the Huguenot population by chalking crosses on the doors of several well-known Huguenots' houses. Men sharpened their swords and saw that their guns were in readiness. It was an unhealthy time of the year.

The Eve and the Day of St Bartholomew passed in uneasy quiet; but a few days later a few Huguenots who had held a *prêche* in one of their houses came out to find a group of Catholics about the door. One bold spirit had dared to put a white cross in his hat. They had only come to jeer, but the terrified Huguenots held their heads high while their lips moved in prayer as they passed along the street. Had they not prayed, all would have been well. Neither Catholics nor Huguenots could bear to see the other side appeal to God. God was *their* ally; they grew angry that any other sect should dare claim Him. Someone threw a stone and a riot started, which ended in tragedy for some of those concerned before it was quelled.

A deputation of Huguenots went to the palace to demand audience of the King. He kept them waiting, for he was playing at tilting with some of his young men; not the rough tilting at which his grandfather, Francis the First, had excelled, and at which his father, Henry the Second, had lost his life, but gentle tilting in the costumes of ladies. And when he had finished the game, he declared he was too tired to see the deputation.

The Huguenots murmured against him. 'This is the city of Babylon!' they cried. 'Of Sodom and Gomorrah. The Lord will not rest content until he has destroyed this city.'

The poor huddled on the street corners, but when lights sprang up in the palace they would stand as close as they could and try to see what was going on inside. They saw something of the fantastic balls at which the King danced in a low-necked gown with pearls about his throat; they saw him at the banquet where all the men were attired as women, and the women were in men's clothes. They knew that the silk for these garments had been especially acquired and that it had cost a hundred thousand francs. To pay for this Paris must be taxed.

There were many about the King who remonstrated with him: Catherine herself, the Guises, the Marshal Tavannes.

'Only fools spend money on folly,' said Tavannes daringly.

'One cannot treat the people of Paris thus!' said Guise.

'My son, take care!' begged Catherine. 'If you must have these pleasures, take them in secret. Do not let the people see how you frolic while they starve. It is not possible to go on in this way.'

'I am the King,' said Henry. 'With me all things are possible.'

Meanwhile a sullen, starving city watched the reckless extravagance of a King it hated.

*

Louis Bérenger du Guast was curling his master's hair. He kept up a light chatter as he did so, but he was not really thinking of his master's appearance. Du Guast was different from the other *mignons* in as much as he was a politically ambitious man; he wanted official position, and if it meant posing as an effeminate young man who doted on fine clothes, perfumes, lap-dogs and his master, he was ready to do what was required of him.

He had already succeeded in bringing about strife between the King and his sister Margot, for he recognized Margot as the ally of Alençon, who was the deadliest of all his foes. Du Guast had accused Margot, before the King and court, of the impropriety of visiting the bedchamber of one of the gentlemen in Alençon's *entourage*. Margot had hotly denied this, but the King was more ready to believe his favourite than his sister; as Margot's reputation was such that she might very well have committed the indiscretion, others believed du Guast to have been right. Since then Margot had allied herself more closely with Alençon, which meant that her friendship with her husband had grown.

The King was suffering from an affliction of the ear rather similar to that which had resulted in the death of his brother

Francis, and it had occurred to du Guast that there might be some in the palace who were trying to bring the King's life to an end. When poison was suspected, the thoughts of all immediately flew to the Queen Mother, but no one would suspect Catherine of trying to remove her favourite son, who was, as everybody knew, her 'All' as she herself called him. Whom else then? Obviously Alençon would take the throne.

There was another fact which disturbed du Guast. He was deeply attracted to Madame de Sauves; nor was he, she had obligingly demonstrated, repulsive to her. She had continued to retain other lovers, among them Guise, Navarre and Alençon; and this angered du Guast, who liked to stand first, both with his mistress and his master. But of his rivals he most feared Alençon, for if the King died and Alençon took his place, then he, du Guast, would fall very low.

'How is the ear today, dearest Sire?' whispered du Guast.

'Very painful,' whimpered the King. 'Is it swollen? Dress my hair over it to hide it.'

'Dearest Sire, I wish to speak to you alone.'

Caylus and Epernon frowned.

'It is of the utmost importance, Sire,' urged du Guast.

Henry nodded. He was sometimes not so foolish as he appeared to be; and his neglect of his duties was in some measure due to physical weakness. Most of the virility which he had possessed in his teens had by now disappeared and physical exercise really did exhaust him. He had the frailty of body and the weakness of constitution which had shortened the lives of his two elder brothers; but his mind was more alert than theirs had been. Like all the Medici-Valois brood, he was possessed of a complex nature, and the traits inherited from his mother mingled uneasily with those of his Valois progenitors. He could be a foolish and extravagant pervert, yet, like his paternal grandfather, a lover of all that was artistic; he could, like his slow-minded yet statesmanlike father, try to grapple with matters of importance.

So he now dismissed his attendants and listened to what du Guast had to say.

'Dearest Sire, I am afraid. Your ear . . . it perturbs me.'

'What do you mean?'

240

'Your brother Francis died of an affliction of the ear, Sire, and some say that he was hastened to his end.'

'My God!' cried Henry. 'You mean that someone is trying to get rid of me!'

'It may well be so.'

'But . . . my mother loves me.'

'I did not think of your mother, Sire.'

'Alençon?' muttered the King.

'Who else, Sire? He is your enemy.'

'What can we do? We must act quickly. I shall call in my mother. She will know.'

But du Guast was not going to let him call in Catherine. She would never agree to the murder of Alençon – the only remaining Valois heir.

'We can arrange it without her, Sire. We can commission another to do the work. As you know, anything that concerns your dear Majesty concerns me. I lie awake at night thinking how best to serve you.'

'Louis, my beloved!'

'My adored sovereign. This is what I have been thinking: there is another who hates Alençon.'

'Who is that, dear fellow?'

'Navarre.'

'Navarre! They are allies!'

'They were. But now they quarrel. It is over a woman. They were at each other's throats the other day. Navarre plays his crude jokes. He fixed some heavy object over the lady's door when he last visited her, and arranged that when Alençon called the object should fall on his head. *Ma foi!* You should have seen the mess it made of our Alençon's countenance . . . never one to be greatly admired, as Your Majesty knows.'

'I rejoice to hear it. A pity it did not break his ugly neck as well as bruise his ugly face.'

'There was trouble over that. There might have been a fight to the death. But you know Navarre, Sire; he twists and turns and, before Alençon knew where he was, Navarre had made the whole affair something too ridiculous to duel over. But it rankles, Sire, it rankles. They are both in love with the same woman . . . whom they share.'

'This Madame de Sauves seems a very accomplished lady,' said the King, looking slyly at du Guast, for he had heard the rumours.

'One amuses oneself,' said the favourite. 'Your Majesty also enjoys his little *chasse de palais*. Although, Sire, you know how the ladies tire you, and being in love with one of them, even for a few minutes, means you must rest for a few days afterwards.'

'Let us not speak of our peccadilloes, dear Louis. We are both a little guilty of them.'

'My dear lord, my association with Madame de Sauves is conducted solely that I may discover from her what she learns from your enemies.'

'You are a good friend, my dearest fellow. Tell me more of Alençon and Navarre.'

'They quarrel. There is perpetual strife between them. Alençon is a fool, but not so Navarre; he merely pretends to be one. My lord, my plan is this: call Navarre to your presence and explain to him how tiresome your brother has become. Tell him he has your permission to deal with him as he pleases. Not only would he remove a rival for his mistress' favours, but he would be next in direct succession to the throne, should Your Majesty leave no issue.'

'I shall leave issue,' said the King. 'I am going to Notre Dame with the Queen to ask God's help in this matter. Moreover, to talk to Navarre of his being next in succession could be dangerous, do you not think?'

'He would be next in succession — if Alençon were removed — only until Your Majesty produces issue. You would only be reminding him of what he knows already; and, Sire, what a good thing it would be if we were rid of Alençon. He is your greatest enemy. I should like to see all your enemies removed, but it is advisable to start with the greatest of them. I believe that was your mother's procedure; and you will admit that she is an adept at the art of removal.'

'You are right. As usual, my darling, you are right. Send at once for Navarre.'

Navarre was brought before the King, and Henry said to him: 'Brother, come sit beside me and tell me about the bruises

242

you inflicted on Alençon. Du Guast here has just been re-counting something of the incident to me, and it amused me much.'

Navarre talked with a lack of ceremony. If he was a little insolent in the presence of his superiors and he was re-primanded, he would always say: 'Oh, but I am but a provincial, an uncouth Béarnais.' And they had to excuse him. 'He is just a provincial, an uncouth Béarnais,' they would say, while he smiled at them with his slow, lazy smile.

When he had told the story, the King said: 'Madame de Sauves has come between your friendship with Alençon, which I believe was, at one time, great.'

'A little rivalry in love, Sire,' said Navarre lightly. 'That is no real barrier to friendship if the friendship be strong enough.'

'Alençon is no friend to you. He never had a true friend in his life.'

Navarre shrugged his shoulders and smiled at the King.

'My dear Navarre, why do you not revenge yourself on this rival in love? Think! If he were out of the way, you would be next in succession to the throne. You would not have to fix traps over the door of your mistress' apartments. The lover and the heir to the throne would be triumphant.'

Navarre's eyes narrowed. 'What means this, Sire? Is it a command?'

'It is not a command,' said the King. 'But you may call it a suggestion.'

Navarre pretended to breathe freely. 'Ah, Sire,' he said, his eyes mocking the King, 'I have always been very successful in my affairs. I have never needed to use dire methods to get what I want. As for my being heir to the throne, Your Majesty will forgive me if I say that I do not see how that can be. All know that Your Majesty and the Queen pray for an heir. How can it be possible that God would deny the request of two as devout as you and the Queen? Moreover, I am not tempted by a throne so exalted. My own is good enough for me. Your Majesty will, I know, forgive me if I say that the greater the honour the greater the disquiet that accompanies it. Such honour seems hardly worth committing murder to obtain.'

'You are a great fool, Navarre,' said the King.

'That may well be. But there is often some wisdom in great folly. I will not protest when Your Majesty calls me "fool". It may be that I am a fool who does not wish to burden his conscience with murder.'

The King and du Guast exchanged uneasy glances. They had exposed their design. They guessed that Navarre might very well carry an account of this interview to Alençon. How could anyone know what was in the mind of that crude provincial, that uncouth Béarnais?

❋

Catherine realized that the court was divided into two camps; one contained the King and his *mignons*, the other, Alençon and his followers. Margot hovered on the periphery of her younger brother's circle and had now taken one of his men as a lover – the dashing, dangerous Louis de Clermont d'Amboise, Lord of Bussy, who was known as Bussy d'Amboise, and on account of his dashing exploits simply 'The brave Bussy'. This man was the male counterpart of Margot herself; he was continually on the look-out for adventure, amorous or otherwise; and being Alençon's man was opposed to the King's *mignons*.

Navarre was aloof, but he was ready – Catherine knew through Charlotte – to ally himself with Alençon if it would prove advantageous to him, although their perpetual bickering over Charlotte made them more often enemies than friends. Margot had made several efforts to patch up the quarrel between her husband and Alençon, and through the influence of Bussy she was now a strong adherent to the Alençon-Navarre alliance. Margot was dangerous, as Catherine well knew; clever and shrewd, she was yet unaccountable, being always governed by her emotions rather than her common-sense, always ready to apply her sharp wits to the cause followed by her lover of the moment.

At the present time, it seemed that events were against Catherine. She had just heard of the death of her eldest daughter, Claude. She had not greatly loved Claude; but it seemed to her that her children were dropping one by one, like rotten fruit, from the great family tree. Of her large brood there were only three left now – her beloved King, mischievous Alençon and dangerous Margot. The King was ageing; it was unnatural for a man who was not yet twenty-five to tire so easily, to show signs of age so soon. Alençon suffered now and then from an affliction of the chest. Were her children unable to live to a normal span, to produce healthy children of their own? She told herself that she must not be unduly depressed by the death of Claude; she must not be unduly depressed by her son's absorption in his *mignons*. She must exert all her powers to remove him from the influence of these gentlemen; and the one who perturbed her most was du Guast. She must find some means of removing that young man as soon as possible. She dared not administer one of her *morceaux*, for Henry would suspect her at once if she did, and he would never forgive her if his favourite died from poison. She must stir up trouble for du Guast in that other camp by seizing on some apparently trivial happening which could, as on other occasions, serve her purpose. It might be that Margot's lover could provide it. She remembered that Monsieur de la Mole had once proved useful. She must forget her grief at her son's neglect; she must work her way back to his affection and trust.

She was deeply shocked when she discovered that Henry had ordered state documents to be diverted from her and to be brought direct to him. Du Guast had suggested that should be done, she was sure; and this was the most alarming thing that could have happened, because it could eventually cut her off from all state secrets. When she had discovered this treachery she had been more hurt than angry, so great was her love for her son and her desire for his affection.

She had written to Henry at once. 'You *must* let me be told of your affairs. I do not ask because I wish to control them, but because, if they go well, my heart will be at ease, and if they go ill, it might be that I can help you in your trouble. You are my "All", but even if you love me, you do not trust me as you ought. Forgive me if I speak frankly to you, but if you no longer trust me I have no wish to live longer. I have never greatly cared for life since your father died and I only cared to live that I might serve you and God.'

But when she had written that, she had had to smile. There

was only the smallest grain of truth in those words. He had wounded her deeply by his lack of trust, but she wanted fervently to live, even if she had to work against him to keep her power.

Well, here were the rival camps – Henry and his darlings in one, Alençon, Margot, Bussy and Navarre in the other. It was like the old fight between the Bourbons and the Guises. That reminded her that she must not lose sight of Monsieur de Guise, for he was only temporarily in eclipse.

The old stimulation was working within her. Discord between the two camps was to be the order of the day.

'And as for you, Monsieur de Guast,' she muttered, 'make the most of your stay on Earth, for I do not think, little *mignon*, that you will enjoy it much longer!'

*

Du Guast was quick to realize that the person most to be feared in the opposite camp was Margot. He therefore planned to have her discredited so that it would be necessary to banish her from the court.

An opportunity came when he knew her to be visiting the house, not far from the Louvre, in which she was accustomed to meet Bussy. Du Guast decided that if he could catch her and the young man there it would be possible to have them both banished.

He had arranged that he and the King, together with Navarre and an attendant of du Guast, should be in that quarter of the town during Margot's rendezvous with her lover. It was perfectly timed; the King's coach drove slowly past the house, and du Guast's man, primed by his master, said to Navarre: 'There is a house which is owned by the brave Bussy. I'd wager you, my lord, that if you were to break in there now, you would find your wife with him.'

Even the lazy provincial must make some show of indignation at such a suggestion; and the outcome was that the man who had made the remark so damaging to Margot must be challenged, which resulted in the whole party's breaking into the house. There they discovered a disordered bedchamber; on the bed were black satin sheets such as Margot was known to favour; there was a heavy perfume in the air; but there was no sign of the lovers.

'They have been here!' cried the King. 'We took too long in getting in. They have been warned and have flown.'

Navarre, aware of the mocking eyes of the King and du Guast, took du Guast's man by the throat and shook him. 'You shall not,' he said, 'make accusations against my wife.'

The King said languidly: 'No violence, I beg of you. This is the perfume Margot favours. I do not like it. Do you, dear Louis? It contains too much musk. I should know it anywhere for Margot's. There is not a doubt that she has been here; she was warned in time to get away.'

Navarre shrugged his shoulders. It seemed absurd for him to protect Margot's name and reputation when she herself took no pains to do so. Everyone knew that she was Bussy's mistress; why make a fuss about discovering that they had met on a particular occasion?

But the King, with du Guast at his elbow, was not going to let the matter pass. He now feigned fury at his sister's conduct. He would, he said, severely reprimand her; and on his return to the Louvre he went straight to his mother.

'I want your help,' he said.

Catherine smiled warmly, despite a conjecture that it could not be a matter of importance, since he came to her instead of going to du Guast.

'It concerns your daughter.'

'And what has Margot done?'

'She behaves like a courtesan.'

'That is not such a clever discovery, my son. Had you come to me, I could have told you all you wished to know of her conduct. I will speak to her, warn her to be more careful.'

'I want you to be really angry with her.'

'I will, if you command it.'

'I do command it. I will have her sent to you at once.'

'Tell me all that has happened. I must know all.'

'We were riding through the streets when we passed the house where she was misconducting herself so shamefully.'

'Who was with you?'

247

'It was a party which Louis had arranged. We were going to call on Caylus.'

Louis! thought Catherine. Monsieur Louis Bérenger du Guast! So this is your work!

'Very well, my son,' she said. 'I will do as you say.' And she thought: it might be that this will offer an opportunity. Who knows? It will be as well to look for it!

*

Margot, breathless from her hurried return to the palace, had hardly time to compose herself before she was told that her mother wished to see her at once.

As she hurried to Catherine's apartments, she came face to face with Henry of Guise. She became immediately excited, as she always did when she met him; she looked at him disdainfully, thinking: he has grown older since I loved him; he has become the father of several children. He is no longer young Monsieur de Guise even if he is still handsome.

He smiled at her. She wished that he would not smile in that way. She remembered those smiles too well.

'I was looking for you,' he said.

She was silent, her eyebrows raised, her eyes haughty, her expression cold.

'I wanted to warn you,' he went on. 'Come in here.'

He took her by the arm and drew her into a small chamber close by. She felt angry because she could not stop herself recalling other occasions when he and she had been together in other small rooms.

He closed the door quietly and said: 'The King is angry with you. Your mother is furious with you. Do not go to her yet. Let her anger cool for a while.'

'It is good of you, Monsieur de Guise,' she said, 'to concern yourself with my affairs.'

'I would always do that,' he answered. 'I shall always hope that you will allow me to help you when your affairs go not well.'

She laughed. 'How could that be? You have no place in my affairs.'

'Alas! That is a matter of deep regret to me. Nevertheless, I

248

can warn you when I see that you are in danger. That is a privilege I may still enjoy, though others are denied me. I ask you not to go to your mother now. You remember that occasion when your mother and Charles between them almost killed you?'

'That is an occasion, Monsieur, which I have taught myself to forget, being deeply ashamed of it.'

'But you should remember it – even if you forget your partner in that adventure. You should profit by it. And you should profit by it now.'

She wished he would not speak to her in that tender voice. She knew that she had only to fling herself into his arms to join together the broken strands of that wild and passionate affair. What is the use of pretending, said his eyes, that any man can please you as I do, that any woman could please me as you do? Have done with this folly. Come back to me. Even now it may not be too late for that divorce. We will marry and rule France together.

Now she saw his meaning clearly. Ambition first, love second, with Monsieur de Guise. What had she that Charlotte de Sauves had not? The answer was simple: royalty. She was a Princess of France.

Bussy was a fine man, a very fine man, she assured herself, He was amusing, virile, passionate – a good lover; if he was not so completely devoted as Monsieur de la Mole had been, he was more amusing than the melancholy gentleman whose head she had forgotten even to look at for many months. She was happy with Bussy. She would never again love as she had loved Henry of Guise perhaps, neither would she suffer again as she had suffered through him.

She laughed. 'Oh, come, Monsieur de Guise, why do you pretend to be sorry? My brother is angry with me. My mother wishes to punish me. My younger brother hates my elder brother. We are a family working against itself. We are not like the family of Guise, are we? We have our passions, our jealousies, our loves, our hates. We lack the overpowering ambition of the House of Guise and Lorraine. Do you think I have not noticed you during these terrible weeks? Do not look so delighted with yourself. It was not your beauty that I admired;

it was your cunning. You strut through Paris – the King of Paris. The people almost kiss the hem of your robes. I have seen them. You are restrained. When they cry, "*Vive le bon Duc de Guise!*" you urge them to cry, "*Vive le Roi!*" But I know you well. I know what goes on in your mind. I know why you are so anxious for these poor people. I know why you offer them sympathy and alms. I have seen you shake a dirty hand with tears in your eyes. It is said that the great Duke of Guise never fails to take a man by the hand, be he Prince or beggar. He is familiar with all – a friend of the poor, yet the greatest aristocrat in France. I have heard them. "Ah," they say, "there is a true gentleman, before whom these Valois striplings are like strolling players!" And they weep for the great gentleman. They more than weep. They look up to him . . . hopefully, and they wonder when he is going to make himself the King in very truth.'

'Margot!' he cried in horror. 'What do you mean? This is madness!'

'Madness? You are right. Curb your madness, Monsieur, before it is too late. You aim too high, my lord Duke . . . in politics and in matrimony. Now, pray let me pass.'

She went out smiling. She had alarmed him. She had left him wondering whether he had been too rash. Had others noticed his little game?

Then she wanted to weep, and she whispered to herself: 'No, others have not noticed. You have been very clever, my darling; and it is only Margot who notices, Margot who understands you so well that she is aware of everything you do while she pretends to ignore you.'

She went to her mother's apartment. Catherine dismissed her attendants and began to attack her daughter – not physically this time, but with words, which could not hurt; and in any case Margot was not listening; she could think only of Henry of Guise.

*

Du Guast was not satisfied with Catherine's single reprimand. He wished Margot to be completely discredited, and to be recognized at the court as a loose woman who could bring only dishonour to any party she favoured. He wished everyone to

250

know – and in particular the Queen Mother – that when he asked a favour of the King it must always be granted.

There must therefore, du Guast assured the King, be more open reprimands.

Henry went to his mother.

'I cannot allow my sister to behave as she does. The whole of Paris talks of her wantonness. She should be banished from court.'

'Paris has always talked,' said Catherine. 'They talk of you in Paris, my son, and they talk in the same treacherous way as they do of your sister. Why, they even talk of a poor weak woman such as myself.'

'You must speak to her again.'

But Catherine was not going to do that even to please Henry. Margot was no longer merely an impetuous girl. Margot was involved in the plots of her younger brother and her husband; she was shrewd and clever and must be treated with the respect such shrewdness and cleverness demanded.

'Firebrands have inflamed your mind, my son,' she said. 'I do not understand people today. When I was young we talked freely with all the world, and all the well-bred men who followed your father and your uncles were seen in my rooms every day. Bussy sees my daughter in your presence and in her husband's. What harm is there in this? You are unwise in this matter, my son. You have already offered her an insult which she will not readily forget.'

Henry was astonished that she could appear to work for Margot against him. 'I only say what others tell me,' he said.

'Who are these others?' she asked. 'People who wish to set you and your family by the ears!'

That was said while there were attendants present; when Catherine was alone with her son, she had more to say on the subject.

'It is not your sister's morals that worry you. It is that swaggering lover of hers. He goads Alençon and feeds your brother's ambition. It would be wiser to dismiss Bussy from court than your sister.'

'I will do it. He shall go.'

Catherine caught his arm and brought her face closer to his.

251

'Use my subtlety, my son. There are more ways of banishment than one. It would be easy for an assassin to pick Bussy out from a group. You know that because of a recent wound he wears his arm in a sling, and the sling is of beautiful silk, the colour of the columbine flower. That sling would make of him an easy target.'

'You are right,' said the King. 'When there is a question of removing a nuisance, you always have the right ideas.'

'Always remember that I work for you, my darling.'

She thought: once I have rid myself of that odious du Guast he will be all mine once more.

Catherine waited for news. What would follow the death of Bussy? It must be the death of du Guast, for all would believe that man to be behind the assassination, and Bussy had too many friends to allow his murderer to escape. No one would guess that the Queen Mother had anything to do with the affair, and she would enjoy comforting her beloved son when he mourned the death of his favourite.

But matters did not go quite according to her plan.

That night du Guast sent three hundred men of his Sardinian regiment to wait along the route which Bussy must take from his lodgings to the palace; these men were divided into groups so that it would be impossible for Bussy to escape detection by some of them. Bussy was with a few friends when a group of the soldiers attacked him; but Bussy was one of the finest swordsmen in Paris, and even through his arm was in a sling, he gave a good account of himself and left many of the soldiers dead. The scene was lighted only by flambeaux and, as one of Bussy's followers had also hurt his arm and was wearing a sling of the same columbine shade, though not so elaborately embroidered as his master's, it was an easy matter for the soldiers to mistake the one for the other; and when Bussy's man had been run through and lay dead on the cobbles, they thought their work was done, and retired.

Meanwhile the Louvre had been aroused by the return of one of Bussy's men who had escaped at the beginning of the battle. Alençon was furious, and was preparing to go to the support of Bussy, when Bussy himself, wounded but by no means fatally, came running into the palace.

Margot was there with Catherine and her brother, and, impetuously, before them all, Margot embraced her lover.

'It was nothing,' said Bussy. 'Little more than a joust. They have killed some of us, but we have pinked twice as many.'

This affair brought matters into the open. The King ordered the arrest of Bussy, and Alençon himself was put under closer restraint.

Catherine now began to play her game very carefully. She offered sympathy and advice to Alençon. 'The King is ruled by his favourite,' she said, 'and it is this favourite who is responsible for the trouble. You can guess that he is no more my friend than yours, for while he seeks to plague you, he leads the King away from me.'

It seemed reasonable to Alençon and Margot that their mother might wish to help them, as she must hate du Guast as much as they did.

To the King, Catherine said: 'It was unfortunate that Monsieur du Guast's men were not more careful. But at least you have Bussy and your brother under control. It would be better to banish Bussy. I will persuade Alençon to let him go, so that there shall be no more trouble between you and your brother.'

She conveyed this to Alençon and he, guessing that if his friend remained in Paris some means of murdering him would be found, agreed to Bussy's temporary banishment, although the loss of such a friend weakened his position considerably. As for Margot, she was furious to be robbed of her lover, and she blamed du Guast; she was determined that he should suffer for what he had done to her.

Catherine offered sympathy to Margot as well as to Alençon. 'Bussy is a fine man,' she said. 'A most amusing gentleman. He is the best swordsman in Paris.' To Alençon she said: 'He would have been a good friend to you, my son, if you could have kept him with you. You know whom you have to blame for his banishment.'

'Du Guast!' said Alençon and Margot simultaneously.

'He grows too important,' said Catherine. 'He has cast a spell over the King. There will be no releasing His Majesty from the spell while that man lives.'

'It would be well,' said Margot, 'if someone shot him as he tried to shoot poor Bussy.'

'Yes,' agreed Catherine. 'But such affrays often fail. Remember Monsieur de Coligny. And there is this affair of Bussy himself. There are better methods. Let us hope that one day this man will be strangled in his bed. There would be no mistake then. An assassin . . . secreted in his bedchamber, and while he sleeps . . . Why, it would not be known who had done the deed, and that is important when a man is such a favourite of a King.'

Margot and Alençon were silent. They both understood. Catherine wanted du Guast out of the way, but, in view of the King's devotion to the man and Catherine's desire not to offend her beloved, she wished it to seem that she had had no hand in this murder.

'It would assuredly be a pleasure to hear that he had been strangled in his bed,' said Margot.

Catherine left them together, to talk over, as she thought, this idea she had given them. She did not know that her son and daughter were busy with another plan.

Alençon was not going to endure being kept in semi-captivity. He was impatient. Margot called in Navarre, and the three of them talked together.

'It is very necessary,' said Margot, 'that you two sink your differences. Madame de Sauves is very beautiful, I grant you; but she is far more fond of Messieurs de Guise and du Guast than of either of you. Moreover, do you not see that du Guast has become her intimate so that he can discover all that he wishes to know about you? You are fools, both of you. You let that woman lead you by the nose.'

'Love, I fancy, has led you by the nose more than once,' retorted Navarre.

'In my youthful folly that may have been so. But I grow up, Monsieur. I profit from experience. But . . . to this matter which is of such great importance: you must bestir yourselves. You must escape. While you stay here the King will continue to insult you both; he will kill your men, as he nearly killed Bussy. This is my plan: you, my brother, are not kept in such restraint that you cannot visit your mistress; so we will use that woman

254

as she has been using you. You will go to visit her in your coach. When you arrive at her house she will be engaged with my husband, and' – Margot shot a glance at Navarre – 'she will not have time to tell anybody that she is spending the evening with him. He will detain her while you, my brother, make your way to the back of the house, where horses will be waiting with a few of your trusted friends. It will be simple if only you two will do your best to make it so.'

Navarre gave her a heavy slap on the back. 'What a wise woman I have married!' he said. 'I admire in particular the way in which she arranges my assignation with your mistress, Alençon.'

Alençon scowled at his rival in love; but they both realized the wisdom of Margot's plan and determined to carry it out.

*

When he heard of his brother's escape, the King flew into a passion of rage, and the first person he sent for was his sister.

'Do not think you shall thus flout me!' he cried. 'Where is Alençon?'

'I do not know, Sire,' answered Margot calmly.

'You shall tell me. I will have you whipped. Do not think that I will endure your insolence. When did you last see him?'

'I have not seen him this day.'

'After him!' cried the King to his men. 'Bring him back. By God, I'll teach him what it means to flout me.'

Catherine was beside him. 'Calm yourself, my dear. You can do no good by flying into such rages. He shall be found, never fear.'

'My sister shall tell me what she knows. She has aided him in this. They have been great friends ... more than friends, if I can believe reports ... and I *do* believe reports. There is nothing too immoral for those two to indulge in.'

'Now, my son! There are always evil reports about us. I recollect similar reports about you and your sister. Do you remember the time when you and she were so fond of each other?'

'I was foolish ever to be fond of her. She is a sly, deceitful wanton.'

'We learn by our mistakes,' said Catherine. 'Sometimes we turn our backs on our real friends and trust our enemies ...'

'Mother, what shall I do? I must find him.'

She smiled tenderly. 'Have no fear. This is not such a calamity as some of your friends ask you to believe it to be. I will see that nothing ill comes of it. As for your sister ...' She smiled at Margot as though to say: 'We must soothe him, for I declare his passions resemble those of our poor mad Charles.' 'As for your sister,' she went on, 'I have no doubt that she knows nothing of this. Why, had she helped anyone to escape, surely it would have been her husband.'

'Keep Navarre under control.'

'That shall be done. My daughter, you may go now. Your brother is sorry that he misjudged you.'

Margot was glad to escape. She felt gleeful. Alençon was gone. Next it would be the turn of Navarre.

Catherine went to her daughter's apartment. Navarre was with her.

'It is that favourite of the King's who works him up into these rages,' said Catherine. 'It surprises me that du Guast is allowed to live. There must be many who would like to see him out of the way. There is much crime in our country. Innocent men are murdered for a few francs, they tell me; and yet Monsieur du Guast is allowed to live! The ways of God are strange indeed.'

'Perhaps,' said Navarre, 'the gentleman will not live much longer, for although the good God works in a mysterious manner, the ways of men – and women – are more transparent.'

Catherine felt uncomfortable under that shrewd scrutiny.

She went to the apartment which her son had recently vacated. There she found some of his most intimate friends. She looked sadly about her and wiped her eyes.

'You must forgive me, my friends,' she said, 'for you are my friends, since you love my son. It is a worried mother whom you see before you. I pray the saints will preserve Monsieur d'Alençon.'

'Is is true, Madame,' asked one, 'that the King has threatened his life?'

'Nay. That is the kind of tale that is bruited abroad. My son is surrounded by evil advisers, I fear. I would God would free him from all evil men. Perhaps He may, for the *mignons* have their enemies. It surprises me that he – and you know, my friends, that I refer to the greatest and most destructive of them all – it amazes me that he has not been murdered in his bed, for such murder would be easy, and who would be able to name the murderer? I am sure Monsieur d'Alençon would be safer than he is now if that deed were committed; I am sure he would be ready to reward with his favours the one who should rid him of such a menace. But I talk too much. I know, my friends, that you will pray with me this night for my younger son's safety.'

She left them, wiping her eyes as she went.

*

Du Guast lay in his bed. It was ten o'clock and he was tired. He could hear the first of the October gales stripping the leaves off the trees and rustling the hangings at the windows of his bed-chamber.

He was well content with life, for he considered that the King was ready to be swayed whither he, du Guast, intended. The King adored his favourite and du Guast was growing richer every day. His latest acquisitions had been some rich bishop-rics, which he had been able to sell for vast sums. He could, he believed, call himself the uncrowned King of France. It amused him to think of all the arrogant princes – men like Guise and Navarre – who were of little account when compared with Louis Bérenger du Guast. But it was more gratifying to con-template the Queen Mother than any of those others in this connexion.

He was tired and preferred sleep even to such contented contemplation.

He dozed, but was almost immediately awakened by the sound of groans close to his bed. He opened his eyes, startled, and peered into the darkness. He thought that he must have been dreaming.

He had closed his eyes again, but the sound of his bed-curtains being pulled apart made him open them quickly. He

257

could make out the shadowy shapes of several men who stood about his bed. One of them clapped a hand over his mouth as he opened it to scream.

He did not have time to think with regret of the great wealth he had amassed, to ask himself whether the Princes of Navarre and Guise were not better off than he was; nor was there time to wonder whether, after all, the power of the Queen Mother was as great as it had ever been.

There was no time to do anything but to die.

*

Catherine had quietly assumed control of the King, who, stricken with grief, declared nothing could compensate him for the death of his favourite. Epernon, Joyeuse and Caylus tried to arouse his interest in clothes and jewels, while they vied with each other in trying to win the place of first favourite which had become vacant by du Guast's death. The King's lap-dogs seemed to comfort him more than anything, and he and his wife the Queen, rode together round Paris looking for new ones which they might add to their collection; but everywhere he went, the King complained, he was reminded of his lost darling; and the people called out unkind and obscene remarks after his carriage as he drove about.

He blamed Margot for the murder of du Guast, and his hatred of his sister was intense. Catherine, fearing that he might have her murdered, suggested that she be kept a prisoner, a hostage for Alençon. 'If we keep her under lock and key,' she said, 'we shall know that she is not helping Alençon; besides, he is fond of her, and he will not be too rash if he knows that she may have to answer for his misdeeds.'

Henry nodded. 'You are right. Let us lock her up.'

It was like old times, thought Catherine; she had only had to rid herself of du Guast, and she and Henry resumed their old relationship. How foolish she had been – and how unlike herself – to lose heart as she had done! She could always gain control over her sons by careful action.

Henry grew a little brighter; he was grieving less, and he was beginning to bestow a great deal of attention on Epernon. She must watch that young man and be certain that he did not become too influential; it would not be so easy to remove another favourite.

But what a mischievous family was hers! Alençon was determined on revenge, determined on power; he was now mustering an army and was in touch with the two Montmorencys, Thoré and Méru; he was calling together the subjects of Navarre. He had written several letters to various people of the court – and unfortunately they had not fallen into Catherine's hands – and the object of these letters was to discredit the King and his mother.

'It was very necessary for me to escape,' he wrote, 'not only for the sake of my liberty, but because news was brought to me that His Majesty was about to take some advice concerning me which was moulded on the counsels of Cesare Borgia.'

That was a direct stab at his mother, for her knowledge of those *morceaux Italianizés* was alleged to have been acquired from the Borgias.

Alençon also wrote that he had heard the news which was circulating about Montgomery and Cossé, who had been in prison ever since they had been arrested at the time of the affair of La Mole and Coconnas. There had been orders to strangle these two men in their dungeons, but their jailers had refused to carry out such sentences. Nor would they administer the *morceaux*, no matter whence came the instructions.

'*I* have narrowly escaped,' wrote Alençon. 'There are spies in my camp. Last evening when we were at dinner, wine was offered to me. It was very well mixed, sweet and delicious, but when I gave it to Thoré and he tasted it, he commented on its extreme sweetness, and it struck me that there was too much sweetness in that wine. So I would drink no more, nor allow my friends to do so; and although shortly afterwards we were very sick, we were saved through the grace of God and the good remedies which were at hand. My friend, you see why it was necessary for me to leave my brother's court.'

The King raged against his brother; the restraint in which he had declared Margot and Navarre must be kept was increased. He appealed to his mother to end this intolerable situation.

She said that she would ask Alençon to see her, and as a sign of her good faith would take Margot with her. She would urge her younger son to come to peace with his brother, explaining to him what an evil thing it was when members of a family fell out.

'Go, Mother,' said the King. 'You alone are clever enough to deal with this.'

She kissed him fondly. 'You realize now, my son, how close your good is to my heart?'

'I do,' he answered.

Catherine felt all her energy return; and very soon, with Margot and their trains, she set out for Blois, where it was decided that the meeting should take place.

Alençon was truculent.

Catherine watched him with a certain sadness; she was a little ashamed of this son of hers. He was conceited in the extreme and he had few qualities which recommended him to her. Her mind turned to Henry of Guise, and she thought, fleetingly, how different she would have felt if that young man had been her son.

Alençon had assumed the air of a conqueror and explained his demands to her as though she were a vassal of a defeated state.

She laughed outright at him.

'Do you realize, my son, that you are a rebel against the King, and that it is only because you are my son that I come to talk to you thus?'

'A rebel with an army behind him, Madame.'

'If you were not my son and the King's brother, you would not dare to talk thus. You would have lost your head ere this.'

'That was a good attempt which was made to poison me through my wine, Madame.'

'That was but fancy on your part – fancy bred by a guilty conscience.'

'Then Monsieur Thoré, as well as myself and everyone present who tasted that wine, was very fanciful, Madame.'

She refused to show her impatience. 'Now, my son, I have come here to reason with you. Your sister is here and you will be glad to see her, I know. Will you not return to Paris and try to live in reasonable peace with your brother?'

'Madame,' he answered, 'I know you sent men to capture me and take me back a prisoner. That failed, so you come to cajole me back; but I see that I should be a prisoner when I reached Paris.'

'You have behaved like a traitor to France. I know that you have written to Elizabeth of England and the Elector of Brandenburg for help.'

'There are many Frenchmen who would not call me a traitor to France.'

Her impatience got the better of her then. 'You ... a Huguenot? Why so?' She laughed loudly and ironically. 'Simply because your brother is a Catholic. Had he supported the Huguenots, depend upon it you would have thrown in your lot with the Catholics. You cannot deceive your mother. You want your brother's throne and you do not mind whether Huguenots or Catholics help you to it. Well, what are these suggestions you have to make?'

'I wish to be given this town of Blois. Here I will take up my residence.'

'A hostile Blois!' cried Catherine. 'Another La Rochelle.'

'Madame, there are many men willing to serve me. The Marshals Montgomery and Cossé, whom you have tried to murder – unsuccessfully, God be thanked! – must be released at once.'

'I will consider these matters,' said Catherine; and she retired to her apartments, wondering how she could best deal with this son whom she despised and who seemed to hate her, and yet, on account of his brother's unpopularity, was becoming a power in the land.

At length she decided that the marshals must be freed. It was impossible, after all the rumours, to murder them in prison. The King would have to placate them in some way.

While she was pondering her son's proposition concerning Blois, news came that Thoré and Méru had started fighting in the south. Guise was fortunately at hand to deal with them. He did this with the utmost success at Dormans, and the battle ended with such defeat for the Huguenots that Alençon was in no position to argue.

*

The streets of Paris were full. Beggars and vagabonds had come in from miles round to share in the occasion. The poor looked less dejected. This was a great day, it was said, in the history of France.

The King stood at the window of his apartment in the Louvre. He was sullen and angry. It was true that peace had been restored at an important moment with a victory for himself and the Catholics; but jealousy was in the King's heart and he kicked even his lap-dogs away when they approached. His *mignons* could do nothing to enchant him.

Out in the streets he could hear the shouting people. Thus they should shout for their King; but they never shouted like that for Henry the Third. There were no sly obscenities flung at the man who now rode among them.

He came through the Port St Antoine, a head taller than any of his men, riding with natural grace and dignity; and a great shout went up from the throats of merchants, from women who leaned from their windows to catch a glimpse of his handsome face, from the beggars, from the students, from the pickpockets.

'*Vive le bon Duc!*'

And so he came, fresh from Dormans; and when the people saw the wounds he had received in that battle they went wild with joy, for it seemed to them that here was a sign from Heaven. The cheek of Henry of Guise was slashed by a scar which many declared was exactly the same as that which had been so proudly carried through the last years of his life by Francis of Guise, *Le Balafré*.

The people cheered madly. '*Vive le Balafré!* Behold! Here is a miracle. *Le Balafré* has returned.'

They kissed the hem of his cloak; they scrambled and fought that they might get near him to press their rosaries against him. Many wept, and tears ran down the Duke's own cheeks. The eye above the scar watered when he was emotional, as his father's had done, while the other eye seemed to smile at the people who pressed about him.

'It is the great Duke Francis come down from Heaven to save us!' cried the superstitious. 'This is a sign. This is an omen.'

'The evil days are coming to an end. *Le Balafré* has looked down from Heaven and seen our sufferings. He is giving us his son to lead us away from our misery ... away from the Valois vipers. Long live the scarred one! This is a sign from Heaven.'

In the Louvre the King listened in furious anger to the acclamations of the mob.

Meanwhile, the Duke rode on. He was asking himself if he had really heard someone in the crowd cry: 'To Rheims, Monseigneur! To Rheims with *Le Balafré*!'

*

There was consternation throughout the Louvre, for Henry of Navarre was missing and his gentlemen could give no account of him. He had not returned the previous night for his *coucher*. They had waited for some hours, they told the King and Catherine, but they had not been very seriously perturbed knowing their lord's amorous habits. The palace was searched, but discreetly, on Catherine's instructions. Navarre could not be found.

The King threatened to summon Margot from her bed, where she lay suffering from an illness which had rendered her very weak indeed. Catherine remonstrated. 'Do not show your concern. Do not let the people know that you attach such importance to this man.'

And after a time the King allowed himself to be soothed by his mother, and the secret search went on, but without success.

Henry, with his Queen and his mother, went as usual to Sainte-Chapelle to attend Mass, giving no sign of their anxiety. As they were leaving the church, Catherine was startled to feel a light touch on her arm, and turning, looked straight into the mocking eyes of Navarre himself.

'Madame,' he said, with a low bow, 'I present to you one whom you have so missed, and for whose sake you have been distressing yourself.'

Catherine laughed with relief. 'Oh, we were not unduly concerned, my son,' she said. 'We were well aware that you could take care of yourself.'

The King frowned at his brother-in-law, but he was too relieved to feel angry. Catherine thought: off on some romantic adventure, I suppose. We were foolish to worry about Navarre. He is too lazy to be over-concerned with matters of state. He likes the life here at the court among the ladies even though he is restricted. It might be that his disappearance was just to tease. That would be typical of him. He is a joker, nothing more.

Two days later Navarre suggested to Guise that they make up a party and hunt the stag in the forest of Bondy, close to Paris. They could, pointed out Navarre, visit the fair of Saint-Germain that morning and enjoy themselves there before going off to the hunt.

No one was perturbed at this suggestion. Navarre would be surrounded by Guise's men in addition to the two members of the King's Guard whose duty it was to accompany him everywhere he went.

Catherine watched them set off – Navarre and Guise riding together.

'I would,' Navarre was saying to Guise, 'that you might ride *incognito*, for I declare this adoration which the people of Paris have for you, can be embarrassing.'

'The scars of battle amuse them,' said Guise.

'*Le Balafré Fils!*' cried Navarre. '*Vive le Balafré!* The people have changed their cry. Once I heard nothing in Paris but that other one – Jezebel. And now it is always *Le Balafré*. These people must either abhor or adore. They never do things by halves, these ladies and gentlemen of Paris.'

'The hero of today is the enemy of tomorrow,' said Guise lightly. 'It does not do to attach too much importance to the cries of the mob.'

'Ah, but the Paris mob has always been faithful to you. I have heard it said that you are the King of Paris. That is a fine title. "The King of Paris!" It suits you, Monsieur.'

Guise was not displeased. He was human enough to enjoy flattery, and, moreover, he was beginning to wonder if this show of friendship meant that Navarre was considering throwing in his lot with him. Guise had not a very high opinion of Navarre's stability, but friendship was always welcome when a man was as full of projects as was the Duke of Guise.

They went through the fair arm in arm.

'See!' cried Navarre. 'The people even love me this morning. It is because they see that their hero is my friend, and any friend of Monsieur de Guise is a friend of theirs. I like my new popularity.'

He bowed; he smiled; he ogled the women; and he enjoyed himself thoroughly in his light-hearted way.

He had so successfully allayed Guise's suspicions that it was not until he had lured the Duke away from the fair that the latter realized that he had left his followers behind in the bustling crowd, while a dozen or so of Navarre's Béarnais surrounded him and the two guards.

'You will now come and hunt with me in the forest, Monsieur de Guise?' asked Navarre.

Guise hesitated.

'Oh come,' continued Navarre. 'Do not let us wait for those men of yours. The day will be done before we make a start if we do.' He turned to his followers and said with a laugh which contained a hint of mockery: 'Gentlemen, shall we take my dear friend, Monsieur de Guise, by force, if he will not come of his own accord?'

Guise looked down at the mocking face and wondered what lay behind Navarre's banter. He realized it would be folly to ride off into the forest with Navarre and his men, with only the two King's guards on whom he could rely in an emergency.

'I will assemble my men,' said Guise warily; 'and we will set off for the hunt as soon as possible.'

'In the meantime,' said Navarre, 'we will go on. Do not leave it too long before you join us.' He thereupon galloped off, followed by his men and the two guards, leaving the discomfited Duke looking after them.

Guise shrugged his shoulders. It was not his responsibility, but that of the King's guards, Monsieur de Martin and Lieutenant Spalungue, to look after Navarre.

Meanwhile Navarre himself was feeling delighted by the way he had managed to elude Guise and his men. He glanced at the two guards. Very charming gentlemen, he thought, but the Queen Mother would not be very happy if she knew I should hunt today without Monsieur de Guise and his attendants.

As the hunt began his thoughts were more on those two guards than the stag; as for his men, they watched him with alert eyes, waiting for the signal which would mean they were to throw off the guards and escape with their master.

One of the men came close to him as they pounded through the forest.

'We could rid ourselves of these two at once, sir.'

'Nay,' said Navarre. 'Do not harm them, for they are a charming pair and I have grown fond of them while I have been under their care. Let us forget the strength of our arms and allow our nimble wits to have full play.'

It was February, and Navarre knew that it would soon be dark; the sky was already overcast, and the bitterly cold night was almost upon them. They had started late and the time was fast slipping by. The guards did not seem to notice this; they took great pleasure in the hunt, and Navarre had lulled their suspicions by his exploit of a few days ago. It did not require, as Navarre had guessed, a great deal of cunning to allow them to go full speed ahead after the stag, to keep well behind and then gallop off in the opposite direction.

When Navarre and his followers reached the edge of the forest they did not stop to congratulate themselves on the first stage of their escape; they rode all night and by daybreak reached Poissy, where they crossed the Seine and continued towards the Loire.

Only when he felt himself to be too far from Paris for pursuit did Navarre pull up.

He burst into loud laughter in which his followers joined.

'Free at last!' he roared, 'My friends, it is well that we have left Paris behind us. My mother died there; the Admiral de Coligny died there; quite a number of our best servants died there too. I doubt that they had any desire to treat me any better. I will not return to Paris unless I am dragged there. There are two things which I have left behind me – the Mass and my wife.' He grimaced. 'I will *try* to do without the first. As for the second, I'll not have her back again.'

He laughed again for the joy of being free from Paris – free from the Mass and his wife.

'These which I have lost,' he said, 'I must do without. And, my friends, strictly between ourselves, I think I should receive your congratulations for these losses, rather than your condolences.'

*

Margot was kept in her own apartments; there were guards outside her door. She knew that the King wished to do her harm and that it was probably due to her mother that she was allowed to live. Although she suffered acute anxiety through her troublesome children, Catherine yet wished to preserve them; there were only three of them left and only through them could she retain her power. Margot was fully conscious of this. 'I owe my life to my usefulness to my mother,' she said to her friends. 'There is no need for you to fear that I shall be given the *morceau Italianizé*.'

Margot was more angry with her husband than with anyone else; he had not told her of his plan to escape. It was through her ingenuity that Alençon had got away; they had planned that together; so she was piqued that Navarre had gone off without a word. But then, she asked herself, what could one expect from such a boor?

She was spending her time between reading and writing. Every incident she could remember she wrote in her memoirs – a little highly coloured, a little flattering to Margot. But what a pleasure she found in her writing!

'I do not regret my illness,' she said. 'I do not regret my captivity, for I have found that in life which I shall never lose. While I can read and write I can regret nothing that sends me to these two occupations.'

There was one person now in whom she was interested beyond all others, and she ordered her spies to bring her all the news that was obtainable concerning this man. She thought of him – she assured herself and others – with cynicism; and it was only rarely that she admitted, even in her secret thoughts, that she would have delighted to share his intrigues.

In the streets they were singing a new song. It went something like this:

'The virtue, greatness, wisdom from on high,
Of yonder Duke, triumphant far and near,

267

Do make bad men to shrink with coward fear,
And God's own Catholic Church to fructify.
In armour clad, like maddened Mars he moves;
The trembling Huguenot cowers at his glance;
A prop for Holy Church is his good lance;
His eye is ever mild to those he loves . . .'

The Duke was on the alert; he was carefully nourishing his immense popularity. Great schemes were in the mind of the hero of Paris. He was now at the head of the Catholic League, that great federation, which contained in its ranks many members of the nobility and of the Jesuit brotherhood, whose object was to protect the Catholic faith against all who assailed it. The King, it was said, was a fop and a fool; the Queen Mother could not be trusted to work for the Catholics; therefore there must be a League – a Catholic League to protect Catholics all over France. But the League did not concern itself only with maintaining the Catholic faith; of late years there had been much unjust taxation, and the League declared its desire to regain for the people those rights which had been lost. The League looked to the most powerful country in Europe for support, and its members had no doubt that the gloomy Philip would give it aid if the need arose.

Margot knew that the King had not yet learned to fear the League; he was too concerned with his banquets, his lap-dogs and his darlings. But what of Catherine? Could it be that she did not understand, as fully as Margot did, the man who had placed himself at the head of the League? He was a Guise and therefore ambitious; but did Catherine realize how far his ambitions would carry him?

Margot thought not. Clever as her mother was, she believed so firmly in the divine right of Kings – and Queens – that it would not immediately occur to her that any, so far from the direct line of succession, would aspire to the throne. Catherine would not let herself think that Henry might die; and after Henry, there was still Alençon. But Alençon had already allied himself to the Huguenots; and after Alençon there was that other Huguenot, Navarre. One of the objects of the League, which so far had not intruded on state affairs to any great degree, was, Margot was sure, to prevent any possibility of a Huguenot King's mounting the throne.

Continually Margot thought of Guise; but she scarcely mentioned him in her memoirs, for she had no intention of recording in writing her deep preoccupation with the man. When she did mention him it was casually. 'Monsieur de Mayenne has grown very fat; as for Monsieur de Guise he is the father of many children, for he has a very fertile wife. His face is scarred and there is much grey in his hair. He has aged quickly.'

She was glad when a letter was smuggled to her and she found it to be from her husband. She smiled cynically as she read it. He did not pretend that it was out of love for her that he wrote. Remembering that they were supposed to be allies and that she was a clever spy, it had occurred to him that she could be very useful if she kept him informed of the happenings at court.

He knows full well, thought Margot, that if any letters I wrote to him were discovered – and my brother's and my mother's spies are everywhere – the result would doubtless be my death. But what does he care? He would, it is true, have lost a useful spy. Regrettable! But not a matter over which to shed too many tears. No, Monsieur de Navarre! You look elsewhere for your spies.

But eventually she became a little tired of reading and writing her memoirs and contemplating the strange behaviour of Monsieur de Guise; and she began to consider how she might smuggle letters to Navarre, which dangerous task would rescue her from boredom. It was not long before she was unable to resist an attempt to carry this out.

•

Catherine was in despair, for the King was once more in the hands of his favourites, and he had once more given orders that the official dispatches were not to pass through any hands but those of himself and his young men. This hurt Catherine more deeply than anything could have done, for it was fatal to her schemes that she should be kept in ignorance of what was going on. Charles had never flouted her quite so blatantly as Henry was now doing; and when she thought of all her plans for this son, how she had worked for him and removed his enemies, she could not help but weep.

Henry's young Queen Louise – a kindly creature as devoted to the King as his mother was – found Catherine in tears and, astonished by this strange spectacle, knelt to take her hands, to kiss them, while she tried to comfort her mother-in-law.

'There is nothing that I do which he does not seem to think is wrong,' said Catherine. 'Yet I have always worked for his good.'

'He knows that,' said Louise. 'It is just that, at this time, there are others to disagree with you . . .'

'He takes their advice and rejects mine!' cried Catherine.

'Madame, he is so firmly Catholic. He does not wish to show the leniency that you would show to these Huguenots.'

Catherine laughed contemptuously. 'Will his new friends help him to war, do you think? They are experts at curling his hair, I know, at helping to paint his face; and they know more than I do about the set of a jacket sleeve; but when it comes to war . . . what then? Will they help him to steer a safe course between Monsieur de Guise with his Catholics, and Navarre, Condé and their Huguenots?'

She grew calm immediately; she was astonished that she could so give way before the little Queen, who knew hardly anything beyond the care of lap-dogs. 'There, my daughter, you are a good, dear child, and I love you deeply.'

'I wish I could help you, Madame.'

'Get the King a son. That would please me more than anything.'

'Ah, Madame! If only that could be!'

Catherine dismissed her and tried to remove the havoc which that tempestuous outburst of grief had caused, by applying a light touch of powder to her face and fresh carmine to her lips.

What had happened to her, and was she showing her age, losing her faculties? She was getting so fat that she could scarcely move with ease. Every winter brought rheumatism. She looked into her mirror and shrugged her shoulders. Her eyes, however, still had the fire of determination, and she knew that would not be easily quenched. She would never loosen her hold on power, for if she did, what would life hold for her? It was not as though – like that arch-enemy of hers, Jeanne of Navarre – she believed there was anything waiting for her after death. She must face the truth. Her children, on whom she had, since the death of her husband, depended for her power, were a treacherous band. She must accept the fact that power – that most precious of all possessions which the world had to offer such as herself – was not easily achieved, and once achieved, not easily held.

Alençon, whom she had neglected in the past and dismissed as of little importance, was now making a nuisance of himself; he was treacherous, conceited and he longed to wear the crown. If he ever became King of France he would not be easy to control. There was Margot, equally treacherous, working with Alençon against her brother the King as well as her mother. She was now spying for her husband. Catherine dared not let the King know this, for if he knew he would demand the death of Margot. Catherine would agree with the King that her daughter was a menace to her mother's peace of mind and the provider of many anxious moments, but as there were only three children now to bring her power she could not agree to the elimination of any of them. And now Henry – the beloved one, her 'All' – had broken his allegiance to his mother and given it to a group of silly, simpering creatures.

She had married one of those creatures – Villequier, who had been with Henry in Poland – to a member of her *Escadron Volant*. She was surprised at the success of that venture. The woman had been ordered to keep her eyes on her husband and try to lure him from the King and those pleasures which had hitherto delighted him. Villequier was enchanted by his beautiful wife, and seemed to have become a normal husband. If only this treatment could be applied to more of that effeminate band!

She must not despair. There were always ways of setting matters right. She must fight this feeling of lassitude which was the inevitable accompaniment of old age.

Looking back, it seemed to her that there had been little else but wars for as long as she could remember – the dreary wars of religion, violent outbreaks, continual bloodshed, linked together by uneasy periods of peace.

But had the scene changed? Something was brewing in the streets of the capital. Had there ever been greater misery than there was among the poor at this moment? Had there ever been so many enemies of the throne? What was in the minds of Guise and his Catholics? What of that sly shrewd creature down in Béarn? Oh, what a pity that he was no longer under her eye! What fresh plots, too, were brewing in the fevered and ambitiously arrogant mind of Alençon?

The King came to her as she sat brooding. His face was white with rage and his lips trembled. She was filled with tenderness, for he had at least on this occasion brought his troubles to his mother.

'Mother,' he cried, 'I have planned such a procession! We were to go to Notre Dame to pray for a child. I had designed our dresses. They were to be of purple, with touches of green about them. They were delightful.'

'Yes, my darling. But why are you so angry?'

'The council has refused to grant me the money to pay for it. How dare they! Is it for them to prevent our getting a child? It is small wonder that we have no heir. How does God feel when He sees the meanness of my council? It is an insult to Him!'

'But how could the money be found, my son! The dresses would cost a great deal. Then there are all the trappings which must not be forgotten on such an occasion.'

'The people would enjoy the spectacle. They must therefore expect to pay for it.'

She drew him to the window. 'Come with me, my son. Look out on Paris. You do not have to look far. You see that bundle . . . lying against the wall there? I'd wager you the cost of your ceremony to a franc, that that is a man or woman dying of starvation.'

He stamped his foot. 'Those are the few. There are rich merchants in Paris. The Huguenots are such good businessmen, are they not? Why should they amass wealth to work against me?'

She looked at him sorrowfully. 'Oh, my son, do not listen to evil counsels. As you value your crown, take heed. You must not expose your desires to the world. Look at Monsieur de Guise and take a lesson from him. What is he doing? He goes

272

about Paris. He expresses sympathy for the people's sufferings. He distributes large sums in alms. The poor cry: "The good God keep the great Duke!" more often than they mutter their paternosters. To them he is already one of the saints.'

'So you would have me imitate Saint Henry of Guise, Madame?'

Catherine burst into laughter. '*Saint* Henry of Guise! There is little of the saint in that man. It is merely that he wears an imaginary halo with such charm, such assurance for the people of Paris, that he makes them believe that he works for the Catholic League and for them, when he is only concerned with the good of Monsieur de Guise. That is cleverness, my son.'

'Madame, since you admire Monsieur de Guise and despise your son, perhaps it would be better if you threw in your lot with him.'

She looked at him sadly. 'You mistake me, my darling,' she said patiently. 'I would kill him tomorrow if by so doing I could help you.'

'It would not seem so,' said the King sullenly. 'And if you are prepared to do so much for me, why not persuade them to let me have the money for my procession.'

'Because it would be unwise. You cannot parade through these streets in your fine clothes before people in rags. Do you not understand that?'

'I understand that you are on their side against me.'

He burst into tears; and she had already seen, by the traces on his face, that he had wept before the council.

What can I do? she asked herself. The King of France cries like a child for money to spend on his toys, while the people in the streets are starving and murmuring against him, while Paris scowls in sullen silence whenever either of us appears.

Is this how great cities behave when a kingdom is on the brink of revolution?

Five

Catherine continued, in the months that followed, to be troubled by her children.

Alençon, after escaping from Paris, had conducted a campaign in Flanders from which he had emerged triumphant; but Catherine knew that her son was too conceited, too self-seeking, to serve any cause well, although at this time the Huguenots might be deceived into believing that in the King's brother they had found a man they could follow. It had been necessary to make peace with Alençon and this Catherine had arranged. The *Paix de Monsieur* was signed that May and was so called in honour of Alençon, Monsieur, the King's brother. But what, Catherine must ask herself, did these spasmodic interludes of peace mean to France — merely lulls in the fighting, so that greater armies might be gathered together. The King hated his brother to receive honours, and even while he pretended to help Alençon — for Alençon was in turn fighting for the King and against him — he was secretly hampering him in every way he could. It was always so with these brothers — Charles had hated Henry in just the same way; their jealousy of each other was far greater than their love for France. Alençon had now been created Duke of Anjou, the King having bestowed on him that title as he himself no longer needed it now that he had the higher one of King of France.

If, thought Catherine, they would only work together, how strong we should be!

But these children of hers were half Medici; they could not go straight.

Margot had begged the King to let her join her husband, for, she said, that was a wife's place. They had, she pointed out, married her to Henry of Navarre against her will; and now, against her will, they kept her from him. It was a favourite fiction of Margot's that her husband pined for her company; though Catherine guessed that, since he had expressed a desire

274

for it, this must be because he felt it would be as well to keep such a natural trouble-maker under his eye.

Catherine and the King had decided that it would be folly to let Margot go back to her husband, but they allowed her to accompany the Princess de la Roche-sur-Yonne to Spa, whither that lady was going, to take the waters. Margot had been ill, suffering from erysipelas of the arm, so it was thought that the waters would do her good; and as all she desired was a change, a little excitement, the prospect of the journey through Flanders to Spa pleased her as much as a journey to Béarn would have done.

Margot was now back at court, but, according to her, she had had many an exciting adventure during her travels. She had renewed her tender friendship with Bussy d'Amboise, whose gallantry had proved a great delight to her; she was never tired of telling how he, the greatest swordsman in France, was continually becoming involved in duels and, when he had disarmed his adversaries would, like a hero in a fairy tale, tell them that their lives would be spared if they would seek the most beautiful Princess and lady in the world, cast themselves at her feet and thank her – for Bussy had granted them the gift of life only for her sake. It was evident that Margot had been delighted to renew her friendship with the dashing Bussy.

There had been other adventures; these included an exciting meeting with Don John of Austria, the hero of Lepanto and the illegitimate son of Emperor Charles of Spain, and Philip's half-brother. He had been charming to Margot and she had believed she had made a conquest, for Margot, who had so little difficulty in finding lovers, was apt to imagine that every man who looked her way and smiled on her was on the point of falling in love with her. She had been enchanted with Don John until her spies informed her that he was a spy of her brother, the King of France, and therefore could be no friend to herself and her other brother, the new Duke of Anjou; she learned too that while she dallied in Flanders, the deceitful Don John was making plans to take her prisoner.

This was a blow to her esteem, but she quickly forgot that in the excitement of making her way to France; and if Don John was not appreciative, there were plenty of others very ready to be.

Now another peace had been concluded – the Peace of Bergerac; and Anjou and Margot were back at court. Margot was once more demanding to be allowed to join her husband, and the King was again refusing her request. The old quarrels had broken out in the family; Catherine and the King were in one camp, Margot and Anjou in another. Catherine was the only one of these four who had the good sense to hide her feelings.

The King's *mignons* seemed, for the King's pleasure, to take a delight in insulting Anjou; and the climax came when the wedding of one of the court noblemen was being celebrated.

Anjou had honoured the bride by dancing with her, and he was feeling very gratified to note how delighted she was by the honour of being partnered by such an exalted person as himself. She talked with the proper amount of reticence and reverence for his state, and Anjou was happy, feeling himself to be of great importance, the hero of battles, the squire of ladies, the brother of the King, the man who might well one day sit upon the throne of France. But his pleasure was abruptly interrupted as he and his partner passed a group of the King's darlings.

Epernon said in a voice which was audible, not only to the little Duke of Anjou and his partner, but to many who happened to be in their vicinity: 'Poor bride! She is charming to look at, you know. It is merely because she dances with that ape that she appears to be ungainly.'

Anjou's pock-marked face went a deep shade of purple.

To cap the insult, Caylus called to Epernon: 'You would not think, would you, that he would wear that colour. With his ugly skin he should favour dove grey. Insignificant, I know, but suitable.'

'It is a pity he cannot put on a few inches,' drawled Joyeuse. 'He is like a child . . . playing at being a man.'

Anjou stopped in the dance, his hand on his sword; immediately he was aware of the menacing face of the King, who was ready to arrest anyone who attacked his favourites, and, realizing that if he offended in any way he might be put in prison,

276

there seemed nothing for him to do but to walk, with as much dignity as possible in such circumstances, out of the ballroom.

As he went, he heard the King say: 'Dance, my friends. Nothing of importance has happened. No one of importance has left.'

Anjou paced up and down his apartments, shaking with passion. He would not endure this. He would leave the court; he would show that brother of his that he was not so secure on the throne as he thought himself to be.

Next morning he arose early and sent a note to the King, asking permission to leave Paris for a few day's hunting.

The King did not answer the note, but he thought about his brother with fear and hatred for the rest of the day and, when the palace had retired, his anxiety so increased that he went along to his mother's bedchamber and sitting on her bed, awakened her to tell her that his fears were so great concerning his brother that he felt it was folly to delay acting against him any longer.

'He is up to mischief; I know it.'

'That, my darling, is hardly a matter to worry about at this hour. He is always up to mischief.'

'He wishes to leave Paris, to go hunting, he says. That is a ruse. You remember how Navarre went to hunt, and we have not seen him since – though we are much aware of him. I wish that we had the fellow under our guard still.'

'I wish that too.'

'I was wise, was I not, to refuse Monsieur permission to hunt?'

'Yes, indeed you were.'

'That, Madame, was the advice of my friends, those who, you think, counsel me ill.'

Catherine sighed. 'What is it you wish at this hour, my son?'

'To go to his chamber, to catch him unaware, and to look for fresh treachery.'

'I had hoped that relations between you and your brother were improving. But for that ugly scene at the ball last night I feel sure your brother would have been ready to be friends. It was unwise of those young men to taunt him because he is not so handsome as they are.'

277

'It was not for his ugliness that my friends taunted him; it was for his treachery. Will you come with me, Madame, or shall I take Epernon?'

'I will come.'

Catherine wrapped a robe about her and together they went to Anjou's apartments. The King peremptorily dismissed Anjou's attendants.

'What means this?' demanded the latter, rising startled from his bed.

'It means that we suspect you of further treachery,' said the King.

While he was speaking he began opening the coffer near the bed and scattering its contents about the room. Catherine looked from one to the other. Fools! she thought. Strength was in union.

There was nothing of importance in the coffer.

'Get up!' commanded the King. 'We will search the bed.'

Anjou quickly took a paper from under his bolster and screwed it up in his hand.

'Ah!' cried the King. 'This is it. Hand me that paper, Monsieur.'

'I will not!' cried his brother.

Anjou tried to reach for his sword, but Catherine cried out in alarm, and before either of them could touch the weapon, she had seized it.

'If you do not hand me that paper at once,' said the King, 'I'll have you taken to the Bastille. Madame, I beg of you, call the guards.'

Anjou threw the paper on to the floor. The King picked it up and read it while Anjou burst into loud derisive laughter. It was a love letter to Anjou from Charlotte de Sauves.

The King, scarlet with mortification, threw the paper at his brother. Catherine picked it up and read it. She smiled; she had read it before.

But the King was sure there was a plot, even if he had failed to discover it. 'He shall be kept under lock and key,' he said fiercely. 'In his own apartments . . . yes, but under lock and key.'

He strode out, followed by Catherine; he called the guard

and told them that the apartments of Monsieur were to be kept locked, for that gentleman was a prisoner.

The first thing Anjou did when his brother and mother had left him was to send one of his guards to his sister to beg her to come to him at once.

Margot came and she and her brother wept in each other's arms; but there was no sorrow in their tears. They were furiously angry and determined to be avenged on the tyrant.

The feud had started again in all its old fury.

This is not the way, Catherine told the King; but his *mignons* were delighted with the feud. They hated Margot; they feared Anjou; and they enjoyed a quarrel.

Catherine however decided that there must be a reconciliation, and at length she prevailed on both sides to bring this about. She accordingly staged one of those farces — at a ball, or a banquet — where enemies met, kissed and pretended to be friends, swearing eternal friendship with hatred in their hearts, while the gullible looked on and said 'All is well' and the cynics set the smiles of pleasure on their faces and sneered inwardly.

*

It was not long before Margot had planned her brother's escape. The plan was dramatic, since it was Margot's; and as soon as she had conceived it, she was all impatience to put it into action.

'We must be very careful this time,' Margot whispered to two of her women. 'Such plans have a way of reaching my mother's ears. If she discovered what we have in mind, it would make everything very difficult; but if she discovered the means I intend to employ, it would make the plan impossible of achievement.'

Catherine did discover something of the plan, but, fortunately for Margot, neither her method nor the date when she intended to carry it out.

There were guards posted at all exits from the palace; all staircases were watched.

Catherine sent for her daughter and questioned her closely.

'You know, my daughter, that I have given my word to the King that Monsieur shall not go away, that there shall be no attempt at escape?'

'Yes, Madame.'

'I am a little perplexed. There seems a certain coming and going between your brother's apartments and yours.'

'We love each other, Madame.'

'In a seemly fashion, I hope.'

Margot looked innocent. 'Madame, how could love between a brother and sister be unseemly?'

'You know full well how that could be. You know that there are some who say that your love for Anjou is such a love.'

'Madame,' said Margot maliciously, 'you have been listening to His Majesty's *mignons*.'

'I am rejoiced to hear that it is just wicked gossip, my dear. What plans are being made for Monsieur to leave court?'

'Plans, Madame? Dare I say a second time that you have been listening to gossip?'

Catherine gripped her daughter's arm, and Margot flinched with the pain; she now looked like a younger Margot who had been very much in awe of her mother. She has not changed so very much, thought Catherine. She can still be afraid of me.

'You may say that if you will, my daughter; but I think there is often some truth in gossip.'

'Madame, do you not think that if my brother had made a plan for escape he would have confided it to me? I am his greatest friend. He would never do anything without consulting me. Why, if he escaped, I would be ready to answer for it with my life.'

'Consider what you are saying!' retorted Catherine. 'You may well answer for it with your life.'

'I should be ready to,' said Margot with dignity.

That conversation might have been alarming to some, but not to Margot. She felt that, as her mother suspected a plot, the only safe thing to do was to carry it out as soon as possible. She decided on that very night. As for answering for her part in it with her life; that might be the wish of the King, but Catherine would never allow it to happen. And all because I am the

280

wife of that erring husband of mine! thought Margot with a chuckle. All because I may one day be Queen of France! So, husband, you have some uses!

She went quietly to her room and her *coucher* proceeded. Anjou, with two of his friends, was in her *ruelle*. He was not under strict personal surveillance, as the palace was so well guarded, and was allowed to go from his own to his sister's apartments, or those of his mistress. It would be supposed that he was with the latter this night, instead of reclining, fully dressed and booted, on the satin-covered couch in Margot's *ruelle*.

Margot lay in bed excitedly waiting for the sounds in the palace to end, and for that silence which would mean that all had retired for the night.

At length, when all was quiet, she sprang out of her bed, and, whispering instructions to her women, with their help took a long rope from a cupboard. This rope had been smuggled into the palace by a young boy whose duty it was to bring her clean clothes from the washerwoman, and who was ready to die if necessary in order to serve the beautiful and romantic Queen of Navarre. To this rope, Margot had already attached a weighty stick, and this was let down from the window.

Anjou slid down the rope and his two friends followed him. Then Margot and her women drew up the rope.

Margot was almost choking with the laughter she dared not allow to be heard. Such adventures were the delight of her life. But she reminded her women that they must immediately rid themselves of the rope, for as soon as Anjou's departure was discovered, her apartments would surely be searched and such a rope would betray not only them but the method of Anjou's escape.

'Who knows when we may need such a rope again?' said Margot. 'But I doubt not that, if I should need one, I should find an adoring young boy to bring me another. Now . . . let us set about destroying the evidence, my friends.'

To burn the rope was more difficult than Margot had antici-pated. It was so thick that it was impossible to cut it, and it was necessary to put it on to the fire by degrees. This was slow work, and in a burst of impatience, Margot ordered the women to put the entire rope on the fire. 'The bigger the blaze, the quicker it will be over,' she said.

She was right when she said the blaze would be big. The flames roared up the chimney. The ladies tried damping down the fire, but that was of little use; and they stood round watching with apprehension.

Suddenly there was a loud banging on the door. It was one of the outer guards who had seen smoke and flames coming from the chimney.

There was temporary panic in the ladies' apartment; but Margot quickly recovered. 'Go to the door,' she commanded, 'but do not let him in. On no account let him in.'

'Madame, he will awaken the whole palace.'

'Tell him that you made too big a fire. Tell him I am sleeping and that you dare not waken me. Ask him to go away quietly for your sake, and tell him that you have the fire under control.'

Margot stood listening to the whispering at the door. The man went away and her frightened women returned to her. But Margot sat down, rocking to and fro in an effort to smother her laughter. Nothing was quite so enjoyable as danger.

They stood round the blazing fire, watching it roar up the chimney.

'Let us pray that that guard does not point out the blaze to others. Let us hope none notices the smoke. If any does and the palace is aroused, depend upon it I shall be a prisoner tomorrow, and my brother will be captured.'

But luck was with them. The rope had become a charred mass before the chimney was thoroughly alight; and after a few moments of real anxiety, the conspirators knew that they were safe from discovery through a burning chimney.

'He will be far away by now,' said Margot. 'Let us retire to our beds. Remember! We have to pretend this is a normal night.'

Margot was not, however, left long in peace. Before daylight there was a banging on her door and when, in terror, one of her women opened it, she faced two members of the King's Guard.

282

'What do you want?' she demanded. 'What do you mean by knocking on the Queen's door at this hour?'

'The King's orders,' was the answer. 'The Queen of Navarre is to come to His Majesty's apartments without delay.'

Margot rose. She noticed that there was just the faintest streak of light in the sky. If all had gone well, Anjou would by now have found the spot where Bussy was waiting for him with horses ready, and they would be miles away. She was not afraid. She was beginning more and more to rely on her resourceful mind, her quickness of thought in an emergency.

Her mother was in her brother's bedchamber, and they both looked at her malevolently as she entered. The King's face was livid; he looked old at this hour in the morning when his toilette had been neglected.

'So,' said Catherine coldly, 'here is the breaker of promises, the one who aided her brother's flight.'

'Traitress!' cried the King, completely lacking his mother's restraint, and yet not terrifying Margot as Catherine did. 'I'll have you imprisoned. You shall not be allowed to go free . . . to flout me . . . to aid my enemies. You shall be whipped. You shall be . . .'

Catherine laid a hand on his arm, restraining him; she came close to Margot.

'Your brother has escaped,' she said. 'And you, I dare say, have not forgotten our conversation of yesterday?'

'No, Madame,' said Margot, her eyes innocent. 'I am as astonished as you are.'

'Do not lie to me!' cried the King.

'God forbid that I should lie to my King. But I do not think Your Majesty should be unduly disturbed.'

'Not disturbed! He has escaped once more. He has gone to gather an army which he plans to lead against me.'

'Nay, Sire; I was to some extent in my brother's confidence, and this much I know: his one desire was to carry out his plan for the Netherlands. If he has escaped it is to do this. And that, as Your Majesty must agree, would further your own greatness.'

Margot cast down her eyes while Catherine studied her daughter. 'Clever Margot!' thought Catherine. Of course she had helped her brother to escape. Of course she was guilty. But

she certainly knew how to be calm in the face of danger; she
knew how to think quickly and how to say the right thing. It
was a fact that she had, to a certain extent, succeeded in molli-
fying her brother by reminding him of that dream which had
been Coligny's and enchanted them all, the dream of a French
Empire. If Anjou had escaped because he wished to fight for his
country against another, and not to plunge his own land into
civil war, then his flight was no real calamity.

'Let your sister retire to her apartments,' said Catherine.
'We shall soon discover whether she has spoken the truth; if
she has, all will be well. If not, we shall know how to act.'

*

Margot had been right when she had said that Anjou had
wished to escape from the court that he might carry his war
into Flanders. News came of certain successes which he had
gained there. The Protestants had readily made him their
leader; gleefully he had accepted the role and, in his gran-
diloquent manner, had promised them his devotion, declaring
that he would do all in his power to help them regain their
liberty. The Flemings rallied to him, declaring their belief in
him. Catherine waited – not without scepticism – for results.
The Flemings had suffered great cruelty at the hands of the
Spaniards and had been without a leader. Could her weak,
conceited son bring them the victory to which greater men had
been unable to lead them? Catherine had not such a high
opinion of Anjou's abilities as he himself and the Flemings
seemed to have. There was nothing to do but await news; and
meanwhile there was a good deal to worry her at home, the
chief cause for anxiety being the *mignons*.

They strutted about the court; they were everywhere; they
held all the important posts; there were always a few of them
at the side of the King to advise him, to turn him against his
mother.

In the past, when Catherine wished to humiliate the Bourbons, she had called in the aid of the Guises, and when she had
desired to act against the Guises, she had turned to the Bourbons; and, in the present crisis, as the most natural enemies of

the *mignons* were the Guises, she sent for Henry of Guise.

While she waited for him she thought a good deal about him. He had not been so much in her thoughts of late as there had been so much to occupy her; but now she was struck by the thought that these Guises had been very quiet lately. It was not like those troublesome people to stand aside. What was it that demanded so much of their attention? The Catholic League? Catherine wanted to laugh at the thought. Henry of Guise was like all the rest – a fanatic. While they strove to keep their place on Earth, they were thinking of another in Heaven. That was where they failed. All the skill of which one single person was capable was required to achieve power and to keep it. Catherine could think of a long list of people who had failed for the simple reason that they had thought too much of Heaven and not enough of Earth; and at the head of that list would be the name of Gaspard de Coligny. So, Monsieur de Guise was occupied with his Catholic League, through which he hoped to preserve the Catholic faith in France – so much so that he was content to stand aside while others ruled the country.

But what of that? Her concern now was the elimination of the *mignons*.

Guise knelt and kissed her hand.

'We have seen little of you lately,' said Catherine. 'That does not please me. My dear Duke, perhaps it is because I grow old that I grow sentimental, but I was about to say that I look upon you as one of my children.'

'Your Majesty is kind.'

'Well, were you not brought up with them? Many are the times when I have watched a quarrel between you and my sons . . . a little friendship between you and my daughter. Ah, but the days of childhood are past. You and I, you know, are of the same mind about many things. Perhaps that is why I feel tender towards you; for it is a fact that we feel tender towards those who think as we do.'

'To what things does Your Majesty refer?'

'Chiefly religion. I am as good a Catholic as you are.'

'I rejoice to hear that,' said the Duke not without a trace of sarcasm.

'It would be a matter for rejoicing if we could say the same for the whole nation, eh, Monsieur?'

'Ah, yes.'

'But there is this war in Flanders . . .' Catherine lifted her shoulders expressively.

The Duke's eyes flashed. 'It would seem, Madame, that there are some in high places who give their support to the enemies of Catholicism; and the enemies of Catholicism, I have always maintained, are the enemies of France.'

'Monsieur, speak low. There was a time when I had some say in the affairs of this realm. That is so no longer. There are certain gentlemen who rule the King, and those who rule the King rule France.'

Guise nodded his assent and went on: 'Madame, I can say this to you in confidence, and you will understand that no treason is meant: the friends of the King are turning the people against him.'

Catherine took a dainty kerchief from the pocket of her gown, and flicked her eyes. 'Monsieur de Guise, you are right. Would I could get some patriot to remove these gentlemen! Is there not some way?'

'Madame, I feel sure that if there was, Your Majesty would be more likely to know of it than I.'

Catherine gave no sign of having understood this insult.

'Were I a man,' she said, 'I should know what to do.'

'Madame,' persisted that most arrogant of young men, '*your* skill is known to be greater than that of any man.'

She smiled. 'You are too kind. I am a mother who has watched over her children — perhaps a little too jealously, a little too anxiously. I was left a widow, Monsieur, with young children to care for. What can I do? Can I challenge these . . . I must say it . . . these traitors to France?'

'Not with the sword, Madame,' admitted Guise.

'Assuredly I cannot. But others could. You realize that these men are working against France . . . and the League?'

'I do,' said Guise.

'Monsieur, forgive me, but I am astonished that you have allowed them to live so long.'

'Madame, what would be the reaction of the King to the death of his . . . darlings?'

'Grief, of course; but it is necessary to take a dangerous toy from a child, Monsieur, even though for a time the child weeps bitterly. It is for his good in the end.'

'Let us consider this matter carefully,' said Guise.

Catherine smiled. She guessed that she had won her point. She had seen his expression when she had mentioned the League. He was wondering whether this meant that Catherine had realized the importance of the League. If she had, and she considered that it was likely to become as great as he intended it should, she would doubtless have decided to throw in her lot with it, for it was ever her desire to be on the side of the most powerful.

He found it difficult to hide his emotion. That scar of his was like his father's in more ways than one. The eye above it watered when he was under the stress of any emotion. Ah, *Monsieur le Balafré*, thought Catherine, that scar has done you much service in the streets of Paris, but it is apt to betray you to those who would read your thoughts.

*

She sat at her window, looking out on the spring evening, and wondered how long a time would elapse before Guise took action.

She did not have to wait long.

Early on that morning which followed the day she had spoken to Guise, she heard shouts below her window while she lay in bed. Her woman came to tell her that there was a crowd making its way towards the palace. It appeared that someone was being carried.

'A duel, I suppose,' said Catherine, smiling to herself. 'Jesus, why do they not choose a more reasonable time to settle their quarrels!'

'It must be some important gentleman, Madame, to judge by the crowds.'

Catherine did not rise with any haste; and it was during her *lever* that the King rushed into her apartment as though he were demented. He had carelessly thrown on his clothes, and his tear-stained face was pallid.

He flung himself at her knees and, leaning his head against her, wept bitterly.

'My darling, my darling, what has happened?'

'Madame, terrible tragedy! Scoundrels have set upon my friends. It is too terrible to speak of. I shall *die* of grief. Quick! Dress quickly, I beg of you. You must come to my poor Caylus. I fear for him. I fear he will not live. Paré is with him but ... I tremble. Maugiron is dead. Oh, I thank God those wicked murderers have not escaped.'

'My dearest,' said Catherine, 'go back to poor Caylus. I will come to you as quickly as I can. He will wish you to be at his side.'

The King nodded and hurried back to Caylus.

Catherine heard the story from the women whom she had sent out to discover it.

Three gentlemen of Guise's suite – Messieurs d'Entragues, Riberac and Schomberg – had been loitering near Les Tournelles at dawn, when three of the *mignons* – Caylus, Maugiron and Livarot – had strolled by.

'Only those three?' questioned Catherine.

'Yes, Madame.'

She was irritated. It should have been Epernon and Joyeuse, of course.

Riberac had shouted an insulting remark at the *mignons*, who, thinking it came from some members of the Paris mob, and having grown accustomed to such insults from that quarter, were inclined to ignore it; but when more remarks followed and it was realized that they came from noblemen, it was impossible to disregard them. Moreover, one of the gentlemen, d'Entragues, was approaching with a drawn sword.

'Are you too lady-like to fight, then?' he asked mockingly. At this, Livarot – the best swordsman of the three *mignons* – had his sword out of the sheath and the fight started. The duel was a desperate one, for, realizing that they were fighting for their lives, the *mignons* lost their languid ways and proved themselves to be fair fighters. Maugiron had been killed outside Les Tournelles; Schomberg also lost his life. Riberac had received such wounds that it was hardly likely he would recover; Caylus, as the Queen Mother knew, was in a very bad state.

Catherine hurried along to her son's apartments, where he had installed the wounded Caylus. Catherine felt reassured when she looked at the man. Surely those wounds must be fatal.

'This is terrible,' she said. 'Oh, my poor son, my heart bleeds for you as freely as this poor gentleman's wounds, for I know how you love him.'

The King took her hand and she was happy, since in his trouble he had turned to her. It was pleasant too to reflect that he was not the least suspicious of her. Once I have rid him of these accursed men, she thought, he is mine.

Caylus lingered on for a few days, during which the King rarely left his bedside; Henry wept continually, imploring his darling not to die, begging his surgeons to save the life of one whose welfare was dearer to him – so he declared – than his own. But nothing could be done to save Caylus.

There was a good deal of satisfaction for the King in the fact that the Guisards, Riberac and Schomberg, had both lost their lives. Two Guisards for two *mignons* was a fair enough exchange. This proved a lesson to all that a *mignon*, when roused, could put up as good a fight as most men.

While he wept for his dying friend, the King swore revenge on the man he knew to be behind the affray. His mother begged him to keep such threats to himself.

'Are you a supporter of Guise then, Madame?' demanded the King.

'I support one man and one man only, as you should know; and it is in my fear for him that I beg him to be silent. Take your revenge on the remaining Guisard, this d'Entragues, if you must; but as you value your life, do not suggest for one moment that Henry of Guise was behind this affair. Do not talk recklessly of what you will do to that man.'

'So then I must stand aside and let him plot to kill my friends?'

'My dear son, have you not yet learned, in spite of all that I have told you, that when you plot against the great you must do it in secret?'

QJ–13   289

'Madame, I swear to you that I will never forgive the man responsible for this.'

'I understand, my son; but remember, I beg of you, who that man is. Remember the position he holds in this country – particularly in Paris – and keep your thoughts to yourself. We are one, my darling. Your good is my good, your wishes mine.'

Believing her to speak the truth, he embraced her warmly.

'Mother,' he said, 'I could not reign without you.'

Then there were real tears in Catherine's eyes, for this was one of the rare, happy moments of her life.

Caylus died and the King tenderly took from his darling's ears those earrings which he himself had given him; he had the hair cut from his dead friend's head and put with that of Maugiron in a jewelled case, that he might, he said, look at it in the years to come when he mourned the friends he would never forget.

A month or so later another of the *mignons*, Saint-Mesgrin, was assassinated by masked men as he left the Louvre one night.

The fury of the King was intense. He wept in his mother's arms. Guise was suspected of arranging this murder, but at length Catherine persuaded the King to give no sign of his suspicions that this was so.

About this time yet another assassination took place. This happened during a ball and in full view of the guests. The murderer on this occasion was Villequier, a man who had once been a great favourite of the King's – one of the *mignons* who had accompanied him to Poland. Catherine herself had removed Villequier from the King by marrying him to a member of her *Escadron Volant*, who had received orders to lure her husband from the King's side. This the lady had done so successfully that – as it was necessary for her as a member of Catherine's band to continue the duties such membership demanded – her husband had become jealous; and there, before the whole court, he plunged his dagger into her breast.

There was hardly a day when a duel was not fought in the streets of Paris. Travellers were more unsafe on the roads than they had been a few years previously. Life had become cheaper as food became dearer. Catherine became faintly disturbed that others should hold life as cheaply as she had always done.

*

Anjou's promises to the Flemings had come to nothing. Philip of Spain had countered those fine promises of the arrogant little Duke by sending into Flanders Alexander Farnese, the great Duke of Parma, with an avenging army. Since Anjou had been looking for easy victory, he had no desire to face Parma; he therefore decided to let the Flemings look after themselves, and, assuring himself that he had won the laurels of a great general already and could be content with that, he returned to France.

Catherine now had the King's confidence once more. The *mignons* who remained seemed once again more interested in clothes, jewels, cosmetics and lap-dogs than in politics. The Guisards had done their work well.

There had been one or two risings in different parts of the country; Margot was once more agitating for permission to return to her husband; Navarre had said he would receive her and her mother; and it seemed desirable that Catherine should travel to Nérac, ostensibly to return her daughter to her husband, but in reality to quell any rebellion in the provinces through which she would seize the opportunity to travel; at the same time she could interrogate Navarre himself and ascertain, in the King's name, how matters stood in Béarn.

Margot, delighted at the prospect of a journey which should prove exciting, made her preparations with zest; Catherine made hers with less enthusiasm, but with equal care. She decided that she would take Charlotte de Sauves with her in case it was necessary to revive that old passion; but since she must have a spy in close contact with Navarre, and it might well be that he would not wish to renew that old liaison, she also took among her women a charming girl known as La Belle Dayelle. This girl was a Greek who, with her brother, had managed to escape from Cyprus eight or nine years before, when Cyprus had been taken from the Venetians by the Turks. Catherine had been struck by the girl's charm and had arranged for her brother to be taken into the service of the Duke of Anjou —

Alençon, as he had been at that time – while she took Dayelle into hers. With her beautiful almond-shaped eyes, this girl was enchanting, and her exotic beauty set her apart from the French women. A good reserve, thought Catherine, for Navarre – just in case he was tired of his old love.

Margot lay back in the litter which she had designed herself. Such a litter had never been seen before; but Margot was determined to impress her subjects who had never before seen her. The pillars were covered with scarlet velvet, and the lining decorated with gold embroidery. Devices in Italian and Spanish had been cut on the glass and worked on the lining; these dealt with the sun and its powers, for Margot had not forgotten that one of the court poets, who had been enamoured of her, had likened her, in her beauty, her wit and her charm, to the sun of the court of France.

But Margot was not merely content to lie in her litter and think of the effect her beauty and magnificence would have on her subjects. She must amuse herself during the journey. She considered the men who were accompanying her and her mother: the Cardinal of Bourbon and the Duke of Montpensier, both kinsmen of her husband's; the one was too old, the other too fanatically Catholic to make a good lover. There was Gui de Faur and the Sieur de Pybrac. She stopped there, for although Pybrac was a serious young man, he was quite handsome. He was perhaps *too* serious to contemplate becoming Margot's lover, but why should she not enthral him, lure him from his seriousness? It was absurd for such a young man – when he was tolerably handsome – to think that nothing existed beyond his work as her Chancellor.

It was always a delight to have a pen in her hand, so she wrote to him immediately, purely on state matters, for she realized that she must go slowly with Monsieur de Pybrac.

Catherine in her litter was a little sad. The rigours of such a journey brought home to her the fact that she was growing too old for such an undertaking. Completely unsympathetic with the sufferings of others, she determined to master her own. Previously she had been able to ignore her minor ailments; but it was not so easy now. Her rheumatism came regularly with the winter, and she could not laugh at it as she had once done.

'Oh, that,' she had said. 'That is my *rente*. It comes regularly with the first cold winds.' But now it compelled her attention, and it was often too painful to allow her to walk, so that sometimes she must ride on a mule. This made her laugh, for she knew that, being far too fat and heavy for the creature, she made a comic figure; but she was always ready to laugh at herself. 'I look like fat old Maréchal de Cossé now,' she declared. 'I wish my son, the King, could see me, for there is nothing in the world I should like to hear so much as his laughter.'

She worried about Henry. What was he doing now? She longed to see him. Had she been wise to leave him? What was Henry of Guise planning? Was that League of his becoming too powerful? She did not trust her son-in-law. She had with her a goodly band of men, all of whom would work for her son, she was sure. She had several members of her *Escadron* with her, whom she could use to good purpose. If only she could trust her daughter to work for her! But how could one trust Margot? She seemed to have little desire but to intrigue with her lovers. She was doubtless planning a campaign of love at this moment.

And that indeed was the case. Margot had received a fulsome note from Pybrac in which he declared that his one desire was to serve his mistress.

That letter was a delight to Margot. She wrote back telling him how she admired him. She hinted that he might become something more personal to her than her Chancellor if he cared to do so.

When Pybrac received this letter that modest young man was terrified. He had heard many tales of his wayward mistress, but he had not believed that such a brilliant creature could look his way. That letter which he had written to the Queen, he had written as a servant, not as a lover. He remembered what had happened to another lover of Margot's, the Comte de la Mole. It was not for such as himself to venture so far into that dangerous orbit.

He therefore did not answer that warm, inviting letter of hers, and when she demanded to know why, he wrote that he had not intended his letter to be taken as a love letter; he had

293

written in an exaggerated manner, it was true, but he explained that the fashion in letter-writing was exaggerated, and he merely followed the style of the day. When he had said he loved her, it was as his Queen; when he said he had wished to serve her, it was purely in the role of Chancellor. He craved her pardon for not replying at once to her letter, but he had been ill and unable to do so.

When Margot received this letter she was furious. She could not believe that anyone, whom she had selected for a lover, could refuse her. Impetuously, without waiting to consider the justice due to Pybrac, she wrote to him:

'There is no use to excuse yourself on the score of illness for not answering my letter. I suspect that this illness and the responsibility of handling my seals, have damaged your health. I, my dear Pybrac, am as concerned for your health as you for mine, so I am asking you to return my seals.'

After that rebuff Margot was a little subdued; she wondered whether she was going to enjoy her new life; she was already thinking regretfully of the Paris court where men's manners were as elegant as their clothes; she thought of her boorish husband and she thought of Henry of Guise.

Then she wept a little and looked through her tears at the magnificence of her litter.

'If they had let me marry the man I loved,' she muttered, 'what a different life mine would have been! As it is, I am the most unfortunate Princess that ever lived!

*

Navarre was exhilarated by the prospect of seeing Margot again. Trouble-maker she certainly was, but she never failed to amuse him. He was fully aware that the object of this visit was to spy upon him, and so he was not unprepared for that.

Margot herself was not so eager for the meeting. She had agitated for it when she was in Paris because she was always driven by a desire to make things happen, and a journey through France had seemed an exciting project. But now that it was all but completed, she was wondering again and again how she was going to adjust herself to the humbler court of her husband when she was already beginning to feel homesick for

294

the French court. She was still suffering from the slight which her ex-Chancellor had given her, and she was realizing that she had been foolish to demand his resignation from office, because it was generally known for what reason the efficient young man had been dismissed.

She was feeling indisposed, she said when they were nearing Toulouse, and not well enough to accompany her mother to the meeting-place; she would, therefore, take a short rest, and, with her attendants, come along afterwards.

Navarre looked for her in vain, while Catherine embraced him and congratulated him on his healthy looks. In his blunt Béarnais way he told her that she was not looking as well as when he had last seen her, and he trusted that the journey had not been too strenuous for her. He looked at her with that shrewd twinkle in his eyes and added that he greatly appreciated the honour of her coming, but he feared the journey might have taxed her strength and he hoped that she would not undertake too much during her stay in his dominions.

'Ah,' responded Catherine, 'I have come merely to chaperone my daughter and to admire your scenery, which is superb.'

He then asked for his wife and was told of Margot's indisposition.

'Then, Madame,' he said, 'you will forgive me if I ride to her. I long to see her.'

Catherine gave her permission, for she guessed that if she did not he would ride off without it.

He came unceremoniously to Margot's lodgings and found her with her women, trying on a new gown.

He picked her up and gave her two noisy kisses. Margot wrinkled her nose; he smelt none too sweet, and she saw at once that a certain deterioration had taken place in his appearance and manners since he had left the French court.

'I was not expecting you,' she said coldly. 'Did you not hear that I was indisposed?'

'Your indisposition would be blooming health to most, my dear wife. I doubted not that the indisposition was some new-fashioned Paris custom.'

She was aware of the old resentment; yet with it was

mingled a faint attraction; his bluntness was piquant after the meaningless compliments of court gallants.

'More beautiful than ever!' he cried. 'I have thought a good deal of you, Margot.'

'And of others. We at court hear of the doings at Béarn, you know.'

'Wherever I go there is news! Thus it is to be a King.'

'Wherever you go there is scandal.'

'Not a quarrel already! Come, I will ride with you to Toulouse.'

She was not really displeased; it flattered her to think that he had ridden to meet her.

'You must have behaved in a most ungallant manner to my mother,' she said.

'It was you I came to meet, not your mother.'

But later she was not so pleased with him. To see him in his native setting was to discover that while he had been at the court of France, he had been behaving, according to his lights, in a most elegant fashion. Now that he was in his own country he felt that he could be natural and proceeded tó be so, to the horror of Margot and her mother and those accustomed to the Paris court. In some ways he had become like a Béarnais peasant; he mingled with the humble people of his towns and villages; he used coarse oaths; and it seemed that he had nothing to recommend him to a fastidious Princess but his wit and his shrewdness.

When she reached the court of Nérac, Margot soon learned that her husband's favourite mistress was a certain Fleurette, the daughter of one of his gardeners. This girl was brought into the palace when he required her; he could be heard coarsely whistling to her from a window, or seen indulging in horseplay in the gardens. Such conduct was extremely shocking to both Catherine and her daughter. He knew this, and it amused him to think of fresh ways of shocking them. He developed a passion – or pretended to – for Margot's chambermaid; and he would stroll to the bakery in the town for a tender *tête-à-tête* with the *boulangère,* Pictone Pancoussaire.

Margot was so angry that she wanted to return to Paris at once. Indeed, this behaviour on the part of Navarre seemed as good an excuse as any. She knew that she would continue to feel out of place in this little court, which seemed barbaric when compared with the ceremonious state observed at the Louvre, Blois or Chenonceaux. But Catherine calmed her, refraining with an effort from reminding her daughter that this journey had not been made solely for Margot's pleasure.

Catherine surveyed her band of ladies; they would very soon do their work. In the meantime let the boor of Béarn show them that he cared nothing for Paris manners and Paris ways. Let him frolic awhile with his little Fleurette and Picotine. It would not be for long. Dayelle had already lifted in admiration those beautiful almond-shaped eyes to the King of Navarre; and although he had pretended to be completely absorbed in his humble mistresses, he cast an occasional glance at the beautiful Greek. He was, Catherine reasoned, the son of Antoine de Bourbon and Jeanne of Navarre, so there must be some good taste in him. Catherine was confident that Dayelle – or, failing Dayelle, Madame de Sauves or one of her women – would lure the King away from his humble playmates in due course.

Catherine directed Margot's attention to a man whom the latter had favoured a year or so before, when they were in Paris together. This was a handsome nobleman named du Luc. Margot was pleased to be entertained by this gentleman; and this, thought Catherine, would keep her satisfied at Nérac for a little while.

And Margot did become absorbed. She amazed her subjects, and it was only a few of the most puritanical who looked upon her as a wicked, brazen woman. Her delight in living captivated most of them, and now that she had a lover who satisfied her temporarily, this love of living was apparent to all. What did she care for the puritans? She cared only for those who admired her. She appeared in public dressed in gowns designed by herself – gowns which would have startled even the court of France. She appeared in red wigs, blonde wigs, and sometimes without a wig, showing her abundant dark hair, which was more beautiful than any wig. She danced in white satin, in purple velvet, in cloth of gold and silver; she favoured Spanish velvet the colour of carnations and had one gown of this material and colour which was weighed down with sequins. She adorned herself with jewels and plumes. She was the magnificent, the fantastic Queen of Navarre. Once she appeared at a function in a robe which had needed fifteen ells of fine gold material, while about her neck hung a rope of four hundred pearls. Diamonds sparkled in her hair, which was decorated with white feathers. She would put on a different personality with each dress. In the gold-thread gown she was all regal dignity; in carnation velvet she would dance madly and recklessly, sometimes with amorous glances at du Luc, sometimes with speculative ones at the handsome Henri de la Tour, the Vicomte de Turenne, who was beginning to interest her. She sang romantic ballads composed by herself; she showed the people of Nérac how to dance those dances which were fashionable in Paris – the Spanish *pavana* and the Italian *corrente*.

Her mother looked on, watching her daughter as well as Dayelle and Navarre.

Navarre himself was reluctantly fascinated by his wife. She could have used her influence with her husband had she wished. Ah, thought Catherine, if only she would obey me. If only she were a member of my Squadron! But Margot's weakness in her mother's eyes was her lack of any motive beyond the gratification of her sexual desires.

It was when Margot was in her apartments after that ball at which she had enchanted many in her carnation-coloured Spanish velvet, that Navarre came to her. She now seemed to him more attractive than any woman at his court. He was amused by Dayelle, who was obviously at the Queen Mother's command, just waiting for him to notice her; but this wife of his, with her elegance, her arrogance and her sharp wit, he had to admit – while the most infuriating – was the most fascinating person he had ever met.

He decided to spend the night with her.

She raised her eyes slowly and looked at him with that haughty disdain to which he had become accustomed, and his desire for her faded and the impulse came to him to strike her. He was the King of Navarre, he would like to remind her; and though she was its Queen, her title came through him.

He sat on a stool, his knees apart, a hand on each knee.

She shuddered at this most inelegant attitude, and she noticed that his jacket was torn, and splashed with wine. No amount of jewels or ornaments could cover his slovenliness; and having other plans, Margot had no wish to entertain him tonight.

He dismissed her attendants and, when they had gone, he came over to her and laid his hands on her shoulders. She stiffened, wrinkled her nose, wondering when he had last washed. She could see the dirt under his nails; it seemed more noticeable than all the sapphires and rubies on his hands.

'How delightful it is when Paris deigns to come to Nérac!' he said.

'I am glad that Your Majesty is pleased.'

He put his hand under her chin and, jerking it up, kissed her fiercely on the mouth. She was unresponsive. She had seen him make the same gesture that morning to Xaintes, her chambermaid.

'You do not seem to like my kisses, Madame.'

'Monsieur, I am not a chambermaid.'

'Ah,' he said, squeezing her shoulder, 'you must not be jealous. What was that? A little frolic. Nothing more.'

'Such frolics,' she said, 'might be conducted with a little secrecy, I suggest.'

'In Paris perhaps, for in Paris everything is sham. Here in Nérac . . . if a King wishes to kiss a chambermaid, that is very pleasant . . . both for the King and the chambermaid.'

'It is not so pleasant for the Queen.'

'What! Can a Queen be jealous of a chambermaid?'

'No, Monsieur, she cannot; but she can be sensitive of her dignity, of her honour.'

'You think too much of dignity and honour. Come, do not sit there brooding. I would like to see you gay, as you were in the ballroom. You should not brood over a few kisses. You should not wonder whether I love too much these little friends of mine.'

'I was not wondering that,' she said.

'What then? What did you wonder?'

'When you last bathed.'

He let out a bellow of laughter. 'Bathed!' he shouted. 'Bathed! We do not bath in Nérac.'

'Nérac's King certainly does not.'

She rose and walked away from him, looking superb, with her train of velvet sweeping behind her, and the flash of her eyes matching that of the diamonds in her hair.

'We should get ourselves children,' said Navarre. 'Here we are . . . a King and a Queen . . . and no heir to offer Navarre. It cannot go on. I have many sons, many daughters; and not one heir to the throne of Navarre.'

She shrugged her shoulders. 'I agree,' she said, 'that that is a necessity.'

She was silent for a while. She did not believe that she could bear children. She thought of all the lovers she had known . . . and never a sign of a child from any of them. Henry of Guise was the father of a large family; and as Henry of Navarre had just said, he too had many children; but by Margot, who had had a thousand opportunities, not one had been conceived. Still she was young, and they needed an heir. She sighed, but made no attempt to hide her distaste.

'Yes,' she repeated at length, 'it is a necessary duty. But first I must ask you to grant me a favour.'

'Anything!' he said. 'Anything you ask. What is it?'

'You will see. You need not look dismayed. I shall not ask you to change your faith again. No. But this is the smallest favour.'

She went to the door and called to one of her women. Navarre watched them, whispering together. Margot's great attraction lay in her impetuous actions. The woman went away and Margot returned.

'Come,' he said. 'I am impatient. What is this favour?'

'Simply this. It is that before you come nearer to me you will allow my woman to wash . . . at least your feet.'

He stared at her. 'You call that a favour!'

'I should not have asked any such favour of you, had I not been afraid that the odour of your feet would make me faint.'

He was angry. He thought of the ready surrender of the little Fleurette, who was so like her name; the thought of the eagerness of the *boulangère*. And this woman dared to tell him that he should wash his feet before he approached her!

300

'Madame,' he said, biting back his fury, 'must I once more remind you that this is not the Louvre?'

'Alas,' she said, '*you* need not remind me. There is too much to remind me already.'

The woman had come in. She set the gold basin on the floor and stood waiting.

'If,' said Margot, 'you would rather the duty was performed by one of your gentlemen, please say so.'

For a few seconds Navarre was speechless. Then he turned to the woman. 'Get out of here,' he said.

She did not wait. She fled instantly.

Margot stood, drawn up to her full height, the velvet gown like a sheath of scarlet flame that enveloped her, her eyes flashing scorn, her lips mocking. You are dirty! said those eyes. You offend me.

He was half inclined to tear the scarlet velvet from her, to force himself upon her; but his anger was short-lived, like all his emotions, and it was already failing.

He stooped, picked up the bowl, and threw it at the hangings. Then he began to laugh.

'Madame,' he said, 'shall I perfume myself? Shall I repose on black satin sheets? Shall I bathe in asses' milk? Shall I become as one of the *mignons* of the King of France?' He began to mince about the room. 'Oh, smell my feet! Are they not enchanting? This new perfume comes from René, the Queen Mother's poisoner.'

His anger had not entirely left him and he turned on Margot. 'Madame, I would have you know that I am the King in this realm. If I do not wish to wash my feet, then unwashed feet shall be the order of the day. You will *like* my unwashed feet, as you like your brother's scented ones. Madame, here in Béarn, we are men, not popinjays! Do I ask you to give up your baths ... your milk baths that make your skin so white? No, I do not! Then I beg of you, do not ask me to follow a decadent fashion of your brother's crazy court.'

'I only ask it,' said Margot, 'if you wish to come near *me*. The dirt and sweat of your body is so precious to you, I do not ask you to part with it ... so long as you do not bring it near me.'

301

'Madame,' he said, 'the price you ask is too big a one for something which I do not greatly care whether I possess or not.'

And with that he left her and went to Dayelle. Margot was pleased. She retired to her private apartments and sent one of her women with a message to du Luc, who had had the gallantry, the chivalry, to bring the manners and customs of the Louvre to Nérac.

*

During her stay in the dominions of her son-in-law, Catherine felt a return of her old strength. Her rheumatism worried her, but her spirits were better. She had come in order to discover what Navarre was doing in his realm so far from the court of France; to see what resources he had at his disposal; to set her *Escadron* loose among his ministers that they might worm out their secrets; she had come ostensibly to make peace between the King of Navarre and the King of France, to call at Nérac a council of Huguenots and Catholics, and to make one more attempt to settle their differences. She fancied she had had some success. Like a chameleon, she changed colour according to her immediate background. Here, in the Huguenot stronghold, her sympathies were for the Huguenots. She even learned to speak in the simple phraseology which these people favoured, suppressing the extravagant, flowery language which was the fashion at the court of France. There were times when this would become too much for her sense of the ridiculous, and she would shut herself in her apartments with her women, where they would amuse themselves by talking what she called '*le langage de Canaan*', exaggerating the puritan speech, introducing into it a touch of ribaldry which would set Catherine laughing until the tears ran down her cheeks. But the next day she would greet the Huguenots calmly and, without a twitch of her lips, address them in their simplified form of language as though it came as naturally to her as to them.

Were these people beginning to forget the rumours they had heard of her? Were they beginning to trust her? The massacre of St Bartholomew was like a black shadow behind her. Could they ever forget it?

302

Margot was now deeply involved with Turenne. Ah, if Margot could be induced to pay more attention to politics than love, what an ally she would have been! Turenne was – next to Navarre – the most important man at the court of Navarre. He was the nephew of Montmorency and Navarre's kinsman and chief counsellor. He was an amorous man and, but for his preoccupation with Margot, Catherine could have set one of her *Escadron* to seduce him. Never, thought Catherine, did a Queen possess such a perverse daughter.

The months went by, and during them Catherine thought continually of the King of France; there were times when her longing to be with him was intense and her only solace was to express her feelings in her correspondence. To her trusted friend, Madame d'Uzès, whom she had left at the court as her spy, to keep her informed of the King's actions, she wrote: 'Give me news of the King and Queen. I envy you the joy of seeing them. I have never been so long without that happiness since he was born; for when he was in Poland, it was only for eight months, and now already seven and a half have gone and it will be full two months before this boon is granted me.'

The meetings of Huguenots and Catholics continued and some agreement was reached. She had Navarre's assurance that he wished to keep his wife with him; and Margot had said that she would stay in her husband's kingdom. So now Catherine was ready to return to Paris.

Navarre was satisfied by the agreement he had made with the King of France through the Queen Mother. Huguenots and Catholics were now more or less of equal standing in France; nineteen towns had been made over to the Huguenots. Catherine was leaving, and that delighted him, for he neither liked nor trusted his mother-in-law; she was taking Dayelle with her, and Dayelle had been a charming mistress, but he had for some weeks had his eye on a frail and delicate creature – a Mademoiselle de Rebours, who seemed different from any woman he had loved before, as he usually chose them for healthy looks which matched his own. No, he had few regrets when he contemplated the departure of the Queen Mother.

As for Margot she was so deeply absorbed in her love affair with the handsome Turenne that she had forgotten her longing for Paris. And so, unregretted, Catherine began her journey northwards.

But her troubles were not over. There had been an attempted rising against the crown in Saluces, a town of some importance because of its position on the borders of France and Italy. A certain Bellegarde, who was the Governor of the dominion of Saluces, had descended on the capital town and fortified it against the French.

Catherine was travelling through Dauphiné when she heard this news, and she summoned Bellegarde to her there; but he ignored the summons; she then ordered the Duke of Savoy to bring the man to her; and after an irritating delay of weeks, during which her desire to see the King made her both uneasy and depressed, the man was brought to her.

With the Cardinal of Bourbon at her side, she received Bellegarde and the Duke of Savoy.

She talked sadly to them of the virtues of the King, of all he had done for his subjects; she spoke of the shock it was to her to discover that there were those who did not appreciate his goodness. She wept a little. She brought out her favourite fiction: 'Who am I but a weak woman? What can I say to you? How can I deal with traitors?'

Bellegarde was so overcome by her tears and her eloquence that he wept with her; but when she asked him what he intended to do about the dominion of Saluces, he talked at length of the religious differences between the people of that town and the court of France, and he stressed his opinion that the will of the people must be taken into account. He could not be held responsible for what had happened, he told Catherine; the people had simply chosen him as their mouthpiece because he was their Governor.

'Monsieur,' said Catherine, no longer the weak widow, 'I have come to settle this matter and nothing more. I shall not leave this town – nor shall you – until you have sworn an oath of allegiance to the King. If you will not do so . . .' She shrugged her shoulders and gave him the full force of one of those quiet smiles which had never failed to terrify all those on whom they were bestowed.

The outcome of his interviews with the Queen Mother was

that Bellegarde, in the presence of the council, vowed his allegiance to the King. But Catherine was not satisfied with this man's conduct. She kept him surrounded by spies, and nothing he said or did was allowed to go unnoticed.

'I do not trust a man who has betrayed his King,' she said to the Cardinal of Bourbon. 'It is never wise to do so.'

She certainly did not trust Bellegarde. He died quite suddenly one night. There had seemed nothing wrong with him on the previous day and he had eaten a hearty supper and drunk his share of wine.

Catherine was now free to go back to her son.

She shed real tears of joy when once more she held his scented body in her arms.

*

It did not take Catherine long to realize that while she had been away time had not stood still at the court of France; and she began to wonder whether she could not have been better employed by staying at court than effecting a peace between Huguenots and Catholics and patching up a marriage, the parties of which were two such feckless and immoral people that they had no more hope of achieving happiness together than had the Huguenots and Catholics.

She was greatly disturbed by the activities of one man about whom she feared she had not thought sufficiently during the months she had been absent. It was never wise to forget the existence of the Duke of Guise.

The Catholic League, she discovered, had grown enormously since she had left Paris. It was spreading its roots all over the country, and offshoots were springing up in most towns. It was supported by Spain and Rome. What was the object of this League? Not quite what it professed, she was sure. It was reputed to be endeavouring to bring comfort to the multitude, but Catherine suspected that its real object was to bring power to one man.

She had found that the extravagances of the King were as great as ever. Joyeuse and Epernon were now his chief darlings. Joyeuse was but a simpering fool; but she was not sure of Epernon. Henry had made gifts to his friends of hundreds of his abbeys, and these places were now mainly in the hands of people who should have had no connexion with them at all. The *Battus* paraded the streets with their fantastic processions; and the King's banquets had become more preposterously extravagant.

Catherine was terrified, too, of what her younger son, Anjou, would do next; and when Queen Elizabeth declared to Simiers, who was now in England trying to persuade the Queen to a French marriage, that she would not marry a man whom she had not seen, Catherine felt it was a Heaven-sent opportunity to rid France of the mischievous youth; and, if Elizabeth would be so benevolent as to keep him, she should have the sincere gratitude of his mother.

Anjou, looking for fresh adventures, was not averse to making the journey, and so, one day in June, he crossed the Channel and landed in England.

Catherine, with the aid of her spies, followed that most farcical of all courtships. She knew that Elizabeth was as shrewd as she was herself, but that the Englishwoman was possesed of many feminine qualities with which Catherine was not burdened. Catherine laughed to contemplate that other Queen, whose vanity she believed was her most powerful characteristic. She knew of the coquetting with Leicester, who, in despair of ever marrying the Queen and becoming King of England, had recently married the Countess of Essex in secret. Simiers and his spies had, on Catherine's orders, brought this about by assuring Leicester that the French match was further advanced than he knew, and that he had no prospect of marrying the Queen, since she had decided on the Duke of Anjou.

As for her son's method of courting the woman who was forty-six while he was only twenty-five, she left that to him; he was, after all, very experienced in the ways of making love.

So Anjou went in disguise to Greenwich Palace, asked permission to see the Queen, and when it was granted – for she was well aware who her visitor was – threw himself at her feet, murmuring that his admiration rendered him speechless.

Elizabeth found this method of approach romantic and enchanting, although it set her countrymen jeering at French habits and customs. She confided to her ladies – and this was brought back to Catherine – that he was far less ugly than she had been led to believe. His nose was big, admitted the Queen of England, but all the Valois had big noses, and she had not expected his to differ very much from those belonging to other members of his family; if his skin was pitted by the smallpox, she was prepared for that; he was small, it was true, but that merely made her feel tender towards him. She liked his fancy manners; he was bold, but she liked his boldness; and he could dance more daintily than any English courtier.

Catherine knew that the red-headed Queen was making secret fun of her suitor, just as her subjects did. In the streets young gallants and even apprentices would affect mincing manners as they walked, deliberately provoking the onlookers to laughter; these young men had taken to exaggerated fashions, copied, they said, from 'Mounseer' – as they called Anjou – and his pretty entourage. Catherine knew that once Anjou realized that he was being made fun of, he would be furious; but apparently the dry-humoured English had managed to keep this from him.

The Queen petted him as she might have petted a monkey; she made him appear with her in public; she called him her 'little frog'.

She knew, of course, that her actions were being watched. She was coquettish and vain enough to wish to be courted by the quaint 'Mounseer', but at the same time she had an eye for the advantages and the disadvantages of such a match. A Protestant Queen of forty-six to marry a Catholic Prince of twenty-five! It was not the most satisfactory match she could have made, but as long as her ministers dissuaded her, she was ready to view it with favour, simply because she wished to keep the young man gallantly dancing attendance on her as long as possible.

Catherine had seen a copy of the letter the great Sir Philip Sydney had written to the Queen concerning this marriage. It was daring, and as she read it, Catherine wished she could have asked Sir Philip to dine with her. He would not long have survived that meal.

'Most beloved, feared, most sweet and gracious Sovereign.

How the hearts of your people will be galled – if not alienated –
when they shall see you take a husband, a Frenchman and a
Papist, in whom the very common people know this, that he is
the son of that Jezebel of our age – that his brother made
oblation of his own sister's marriage, the easier to make massacre of our brethren in religion. As long as he is Monsieur in
might and a Papist in profession, he neither can nor will greatly
shield you; and if he grow to be a King, his defences will be like
Ajax' sword, which rather weighed down than defended those
that bare it.'

This letter the Queen of England received, and Catherine
understood that she seemed to consider it with the utmost
seriousness. But a man of Lincoln's Inn, a certain Stubbs, who
had dared to make a written protest, who had insulted the
young suitor by calling him 'unmanlike and unprincelike', was
very severely punished by having his right hand cut off; and this
fate also befell the man who had published what Stubbs had
written.

Catherine studied the printed matter which had cost these
men their hands. 'This man is a son of Henry the Second,' it
ran, 'whose family, ever since he married Catherine of Italy, is
fatal as it were to resist the gospel and have been one after the
other as a Domitian after a Nero. Here is therefore an imp of
the crown of France to marry with the crowned nymph of England.'

It was typical of the Queen of England that she should have
these men punished while she seriously considered the words
of Sir Philip Sydney. Perhaps her real reason for pretending to
be so enchanted by the prospect of the match was because she
wondered what the reactions of France, Spain and Rome would
be if she refused it.

So she kept her young suitor at her side, first behaving like
an affianced bride, then drawing back in an assumption of
maidenly modesty which was ridiculous in a woman of her
age whose reputation, in spite of her unmarried state, was not
without tarnish; she had made for her a jewelled ornament in
the shape of a frog on which she bestowed much tenderness;
she lowered her sandy lashes over her too-shrewd eyes, now
eager, now reluctant, while she waited for the moment when it

would be opportune to send her suitor back where he belonged.

At length, sighing deeply and assuring the Duke of Anjou that a Queen's heart was not her own to give away, she told him that since the Protestants of England and the Catholic Guisards of France did not wish for the marriage – and as her aim was to keep peace between quarrelsome people – reluctantly, oh, most reluctantly, she must let her dear little frog go. She made him a loan of money for his campaign in Flanders, bade him a fond farewell, and sent him across the Channel in the company of Leicester.

Those two Queens, Catherine and Elizabeth – the two most forceful personalities of their age – knew then that the French-English marriage would never take place. Catherine was angry. The English woman had fooled her. But the two Queens continued to exchange friendly letters, with distrust and hatred for each other in their hearts.

*

Trouble came, and it blew with the winds from Béarn. For what else could one hope, Catherine asked herself, from that storm-centre – Queen Margot?

Margot was in fact reconciled to life in her new kingdom. This was partly due to that most satisfactory of lovers, the Count of Turenne. As he was the chief minister of the kingdom, and the King's first counsellor, there were political schemes in plenty in which Margot might share. She had had many a skirmish with Navarre's mistress, Mademoiselle de Rebours, a most unattractive creature, according to Margot. The thin, sickly woman was not of the kind to retain the position of King's mistress for long, and since she had made it her pleasure to proclaim herself an enemy of the Queen, Margot did not intend that she should. During brief lulls in her love-making with Turenne, they discussed together the deposition of this frail girl who had the King's ear at the moment.

Turenne brought to Margot's notice a young girl who was not yet fifteen – a delightful, simple creature – Françoise, the daughter of Pierre de Montmorency, the Marquis of Thury and Baron de Fosseux. She lived with her father at Nérac, and Turenne had noticed her during her childhood. He felt that such a girl would be irresistible to the King – young, fresh, charming and *healthy*. She would provide such a change from Mademoiselle de Rebours, and surely the King must be growing tired of that one's vapours!

'When we go to Nérac,' said Margot, 'we must bring the little Fosseuse to his notice.'

Opportunity favoured them. When the court left Pau for Nérac, Mademoiselle de Rebours was too ill to accompany it. Navarre left her with tears and protestations of fidelity, but at Nérac the little Fosseuse was waiting for him, and, face to face with such charm and youthful innocence, it was not difficult for Henry of Navarre to forget those vows of fidelity which he had made so many times before and to so many different women. Within a few days he declared himself the slave of his new playmate.

Margot and Turenne sighed with relief. Fosseuse was a sweet child who knew that she owed her advancement to the Queen and the Queen's lover. She was wise enough to suspect that if she wished to keep her high place it would be as well to keep also in the good graces of those two; and this she did to the complete satisfaction of all concerned.

At this time, Margot wrote in her memoirs: 'Our court is so fine and pleasant that we do not envy that of France. My husband is attended by as fine a troupe of lords and gentlemen, folks as seemly and gallant as I ever met at court; and there is nothing to regret in them expect that they are Huguenots. But of that diversity of religion one hears no one speak. The King and his sister go on one side to the preaching, and my retinue to Mass in a chapel which is in the park; after which we all meet and walk together in the very fine gardens with their long paths, edged with laurels and cypresses, or in the park which I have caused to be laid out, along paths stretching for three thousand paces beside the river; and the rest of the day we spend in all sorts of seemly pastimes, the ball usually taking place in the afternoon and evening.'

Some of the Huguenots were not so content. Their Queen, they murmured, had brought vices to their court. She had grafted on to the pure tree the fruit of Babylon.

Margot shrugged elegant shoulders. She was happy; she was

on moderately good terms with her husband; she had found a means of having her own way with him through La Fosseuse; her mild sister-in-law, Catherine, gave her little trouble; Mademoiselle de Rebours had completely lost her power; and Monsieur de Turenne continued to please.

This paradise was invaded by couriers from Paris. Her brother's hatred had followed Margot to Nérac.

Neither side was very pleased with the peace which the Queen Mother had taken such pains to bring about. The King of France suspected his sister of being an evil influence at the court of Nérac; he was now wishing that he had never allowed her to join her husband, and was seeking means of having her brought back. His couriers, therefore, brought letters to Navarre telling him that evil stories were circulating in France concerning the Queen of Navarre; in these were related the scandalous behaviour of that lady, who was, it was said, now deep in amorous intrigue with the Count of Turenne; it was hinted that these two not only made immoral love, but dangerous plots.

When Navarre read these documents, he laughed. He was less satisfied than the King of France with the peace which had been made. He was ready, therefore, to allow hostilities to break out once more in the hope that a new peace might be made.

He called Margot and Turenne to him and, assuming an air of mock-horror, he showed them the slander which the King of France had written of them.

The two lovers were prepared to defend themselves, but they soon realized that there was no need to do that. Navarre, showing quite clearly that he believed all the French King had said, asked mockingly: 'How can a man allow such things to be said of his virtuous wife? This is an insult which can only be answered with the sword.'

Turenne agreed with the King that the terms of peace were not satisfactory; and Margot agreed with her lover. In a very short time there was again war between Huguenots and Catholics – a war which the people of France, who had few illusions as to its real cause, ironically named *La Guerre des Amoureux*.

In Paris, Catherine watched events with increasing gloom, for during that war Navarre proved himself to be a fighter who would have to be reckoned with in the future. One by one towns fell before him; it soon became apparent that he could win this Lovers' War. It was doubly gratifying, in view of this, to note that he had not left his follies behind him. He was so enamoured of that silly child, the little Fosseuse — barely in her mid-teens — that on the brink of victory he would leave the field because the desire to be with her was urgent and immediate, and of greater importance to him than victory over the armies of the King of France. Again and again he lost his chances, merely by throwing them away. For one thing, he declared Nérac neutral; and to this the Catholic party had agreed, providing Navarre should not return to it while the war was in progress; but Fosseuse was at the Château of Nérac, and when Navarre desired his mistress, nothing else was of any importance at all. On one occasion when it was discovered that Navarre had broken his word and was actually in the castle, cannon shots were fired into it. Margot was furious at her husband's folly, but Navarre only laughed. This was fair play, he insisted, and he was ready to take the consequences. He was with his beloved Fosseuse; he was ready to risk his castle for that satisfaction. Only the great skill of his soldiers under his leadership saved the castle on that occasion.

From this it was easy to see that Navarre, although a brave man and a commander of genius, was yet completely the thrall of his own sensuality. Catherine fervently hoped that he would continue to be so bound; the weaknesses of others added greatly to her own strength, and it was gratifying to contemplate that, but for this foible of the King of Navarre, the war might have had disastrous effects on the King of France. As it was, hostilities dragged on for nearly a year and might have gone on longer had not Anjou suggested that through his friendship for his brother-in-law of Navarre he might be able to make the peace. Anjou was still obsessed by his dream of a French Empire, which he planned to bring about through a war in Flanders. It seemed to him absurd that Frenchmen should fight Frenchmen when they might fight foreigners to the glory of France. He set out for Nérac, where he was received with much affection by Margot and friendship by Navarre.

The *Paix de Fleix* was duly signed, but no one had much faith in these peace treaties now. There had been too many of them. They were flimsy, creaking bridges that linked one war with another.

Having arrived at Nérac, Anjou did not seem in any hurry to leave it. He declared himself to be enchanted with the place, but it soon became apparent that it was not the place which enchanted him so much as one of the ladies living there. Anjou seemed as determined to pursue trouble as Margot was; the lady he chose to honour with his devotion was none other than La Fosseuse, the King's mistress.

This naturally proved very enlivening for the court. There was a return of that rivalry, that horseplay which the brothers-in-law had enjoyed in connexion with Madame de Sauves some years before. They both indulged in practical jokes on each other, and as before, these grew so wild that they bordered on the dangerous.

It was Margot who put a stop to this. She called her brother to her one day and talked to him with great earnestness.

'Dearest brother,' she said, 'I know you love me.'

Anjou kissed her tenderly. He was very susceptible to flattery and admiration, and Margot had seen to it that he received these in great measure from her.

'I would,' she continued, 'that your love for me was of such magnitude that it transcended that which you bear for all others.'

'Dearest and most beautiful sister, why should you wish for what is already yours? There is no one whom I adore and admire as I do my own beautiful sister.'

'La Fosseuse?' she asked.

He laughed. 'Dear Margot, that is indeed love . . . but a passing love. But for you, my love is eternal.'

She embraced him, lavishing caresses upon him. 'That delights me. Now I know that you will listen to my advice. You are wasting your time here, dearest brother. You are a great general. In your hands lies the glory of France. You should seek an Empire, not a woman.'

Margot enjoyed playing on his susceptibilities; she made him see himself as the empire-builder, the future King of France, the greatest King that France had ever had. And so well did she do this that, not long after that conversation, he was taking a regretful leave of Fosseuse; duty called him, he explained; he was a man with a mission.

He left Nérac and eventually arrived in Flanders, where he collected an army and entered Cambrai; but as usual he had planned without caution, and Philip of Spain had not been idle. In a few months Anjou found himself in a precarious position, faced by the might of Spain and without money to continue the campaign. Defeated, he went to England, begged Elizabeth for a loan which she granted, and returned to make war in Flanders.

But his departure from Nérac meant only temporary peace for those of that court.

La Fosseuse had become *enceinte*. This irritated Margot for two reasons; first that the King's mistress could produce a child while his wife could not; secondly, the meek little girl changed with pregnancy and did not remain meek; she was no longer content to take orders from the Queen. Moreover, Mademoiselle de Rebours, disgruntled at having lost the King's favour and blaming Margot for this, seized upon every opportunity for spreading scandal about both the Queen and La Fosseuse.

If it became known throughout the country that a daughter of the great House of Montmorency was about to bear the King's bastard, there would be – particularly in certain Huguenot quarters – a great deal of shocked dissatisfaction. In view of this, Margot decided to take matters into her own hands, as she said, for the good of all concerned.

She commanded Fosseuse to come to her, and when the girl stood before her, she looked at her with kindness and said: 'My dear Fosseuse, this thing has come about and it is no use blaming anyone for it. We must do our best to keep it quiet. As you know, it would do the King's cause much harm throughout the land if it were known that you were to bear this bastard. The Huguenots are puritans and they do not like what they call immorality among their leaders. For the King's sake and your own, since it is not suitable for a daughter of your house to bear a child while still unmarried, I offer you this solution: I propose to take you with me to our very secluded estate of Mas d'Agenais, which, perhaps you do not know, lies on the Garonne between Marmande and Tonneins. There you shall have the child in great quietness and no one will be any the wiser. I suggest that when the King and the court leave for a hunting party, we accompany them part of the way; then you and I with our ladies and attendants, will leave the King's party for Mas d'Agenais.'

La Fosseuse listened to this suggestion and lifted suspicious eyes to the face of the daughter of Catherine de' Medici.

'Madame,' said Fosseuse, 'nothing would induce me to accompany you and your friends to a quiet spot.'

And with that she curtsied, and, leaving the Queen, went straight to her lover. When he saw how distraught she was, he demanded to know what had happened.

'It is the Queen,' said Fosseuse. 'She plans to murder me.'

'How so?' demanded Navarre angrily. It seemed to him, as it did to his mistress, possible that the daughter of Catherine de' Medici would plan to eliminate those she wished out of the way.

'She proposes a hunting party on which we shall all set out; then she and her women will take me to a secluded château where I shall stay with them until my child is born. I *will* not go. I know that she intends to murder me.'

'*Ventre-saint-gris!*' cried the King. 'I believe she would try it too. Don't fret, my love. You shall not go with her.'

He strode to Margot's apartments. She was reclining on a couch, and she turned and looked at him with haughty dignity, moving her head elegantly to one side in a mute plea that he should not come too near her; since she had asked him to wash his feet, he had taken a great delight in them. He would sit smiling at them – and she believed he had not yet washed them.

'So,' he said, ignoring one or two of her attendants, 'you follow your mother.'

She raised her eyebrows interrogatively.

'See here, Madame,' he cried, 'enough of those haughty

315

looks! What is this about taking Fosseuse off to a lonely spot to murder her?'

'I do not understand why my offer of help should be construed as intent to murder,' said Margot.

'You . . . *help* her?'

'Why not? Your Huguenots will not be pleased when they hear about the bastard. I remember your father's plight when his mistress bore him a child. We Catholics are more broadminded, you know. A little confession . . . and we are forgiven. But you chose the more rigorously righteous religion. I merely wished to help you and Fosseuse.'

'By murdering her?'

Margot shrugged her shoulders. 'Very well. I withdraw my offer. If you insist on leading an immoral life you cannot hope to do so in secret. You must be exposed to your righteous followers.'

'*You* dare to talk to me of leading an immoral life!'

'At least there are not these sordid complications in mine.'

'Do not boast of your barrenness.'

'I have no cause to be ashamed of unpleasant consequences. I am sorry I offered to help. I merely thought that, as the reputation of this court is as dear to me as to you, I might help in this matter. That is all.'

'How would you help?' he demanded. 'Did your mother leave you a selection of her *morceaux* when she was here?'

Margot reached for a book and began to read. Her husband stood staring at her in angry silence for a few seconds; then he strode out.

He was worried. He was anxious that his Huguenot friends should not be too scandalized, and it was a fact that these self-righteous people did not so much object to secret immorality in itself; it was when it was exposed that they held up their hands in horror; but he was still enamoured of his little Fosseuse and he did not want her to be neglected.

The weeks went by; it was now impossible to ignore the condition of the King's mistress. Navarre began to feel that he might have been rash to neglect Margot's offer of help.

He came to her when she lay in bed, and, drawing aside her curtains, assumed a humble air.

316

'I need your help,' he said. 'I wish you to look after Fosseuse.'

'I can do nothing in that matter,' she said with pleasure. 'There was a time when I offered my assistance, but it was most churlishly refused. I will have nothing to do with the matter now.'

He caught her wrist and looked at her menacingly. 'You will obey my commands,' he said.

Margot was not displeased. She and Turenne greatly desired to have charge of Fosseuse, and she made up her mind there and then that she would carry out her original plan; but she must exploit the situation; she must have a little fun with Navarre to punish him for his recent rejection of the help she had offered. She wished to refuse, and be persuaded. So now she tossed her head.

'Monsieur, you ask me, a Princess of France, your Queen, to act as midwife to your slut of a mistress!'

'Why have you become so dignified? A few weeks ago, my dear Princess of France, my Queen of Navarre, you were asking for the privilege of acting as midwife to my mistress.'

'My kind heart got the better of my good sense,' she said.

'Your kind heart will have to repeat its action, my dear.'

'You insult me.'

'Then it is no more than you deserve. You will take care of Fosseuse.'

'I will do nothing of the sort.'

He caught her by the shoulder, but something in her expression set him laughing. She had great difficulty in steadying her own expression.

'You are the most maddening woman in France,' he said.

'And you, Monsieur, are the crudest, coarsest, most hateful . . .'

He shook her and kissed her; and they were both laughing together.

'No one amuses me as you do,' he said. 'It is a pleasant thing to be amused. If you were less immoral, I could easily love you.'

'Alas!' sighed Margot. 'If you were a little cleaner in your personal habits I could love you.'

'If you took fewer lovers . . .'

'And you took an occasional bath . . .'

They laughed again and she said: 'Enough of this folly. You need have no fear. I will look after the girl.'

'My sweet Margot!'

He would have embraced her, but she drew back. He looked down at his feet and let out a great roar of laughter.

'So much do I admire you,' he said, 'that I shall now leave you. Tell Turenne that he takes so many baths of late that he reminds me of one of the dandies of the Louvre, and nothing . . . nothing on this Earth . . . would induce me to follow his example.'

Later Margot discussed the situation with Turenne.

'This will be the end of Fosseuse, my dear. She will regret showing her insolence to me.'

'What do you plan?' asked her lover.

'Ah, my dear! You too? Can you be thinking as those others thought? I see it in your eyes. You say to yourself: "This is the daughter of Catherine de' Medici." But I would not murder. In this case it would be folly. Now that the King has suffered so much anxiety over Mademoiselle de Fosseuse, he is already half out of love with her. He does not like to feel anxiety. After all, it is the duty of a King's mistress to lure him from troubles, not to cause them. Fosseuse will come with me. I will take her away, and she will not see the King for some weeks . . . and during that time, you will make sure that he sees others. I think it may well be that our pretty little Fosseuse will find that someone else has taken her place when she returns to court. If this thing were bruited abroad, the King would be less pleased than ever. Why should it not be? It is ridiculous to try to keep such a matter secret. My darling, we cannot allow this girl, who has shown us how arrogant she can be, to work against us.'

Turenne agreed. The King must be provided with a new mistress, for it was obvious that La Fosseuse had reigned too long.

Margot managed the affair very satisfactorily, but Fate helped by allowing the child to be still-born. The King's little affair was over, and so was the brief glory of the little Fosseuse, who, to her great chagrin, when she returned to the court,

318

found that the King was amusing himself with several light love affairs; but as these proved to be nothing very serious, La Fosseuse tried to regain her position, and she might have done so but for the fact that Diane d'Andousins, the Countess of Gramont, whom Navarre had loved at the time of the Countess' marriage when he was a boy of fourteen, had reappeared in his life. She was the Corisanda of his youth, and he was enchanted to find her more beautiful than he remembered her.

But the story of the King's love affair with Mademoiselle de Fosseuse continued to live after that affair was over. It was discussed throughout the country, and the scenes which had taken place between the King and Queen of Navarre were exaggerated until it seemed that the court of France talked of nothing but the shameful lives lived by those two sovereigns.

The people in the streets talked of it. The Parisians shivered and starved while they grumbled and compared the misery of their lives with the wanton extravagance of those of the royal family.

*

Catherine had suffered a crushing blow through her old enemy Spain, and, as always at such times, she felt the need to act quickly and to neutralize those enemies nearer home, since there was little she could do to lessen the power of the great and perennial enemy.

It had been a tragic miscalculation on her part, and the King did not hesitate to remind her of this. He was falling so completely under the spell of Joyeuse and Epernon that all they suggested seemed right, and if it should happen to fail it immediately became, in his eyes, of no importance. But when the mother, who had sheltered him from babyhood, who had schemed to put him on the throne and keep him there, made an error of judgement, he was the first one to blame her.

The King of Portugal had died suddenly and there had been two men who laid claim to that throne; both of these claimants were the nephews of Philip of Spain – one named after his mighty uncle and the other Antonio. Then Catherine surprised everyone by declaring herself a claimant to this throne. The late King's family, she announced, was illegitimate; and by

319

delving into the past she found an ancestor of her own who had been connected with the Portuguese throne. Philip of Spain treated this with scorn, and Catherine, in high indignation and at a crippling expense to France, mustered a fleet to support her claim. The French were not good sailors; whereas the Spaniards were the greatest sailors in the world, with the exception of the English, and Catherine should have known that her men would have no chance against them. Her fleet was routed at Terceira, and those ships which did return home presented a miserable sight to all who saw them. Philip of Spain took the throne of Portugal for his namesake, and the people of France had yet another grievance against the King and his mother.

'We have been taxed to starvation to pay for her follies. She murders the courtiers with poison and the people with starvation. How long shall we tolerate the Italian woman and her vile nest of vipers?'

Catherine would stand at the windows of the Louvre and look out; she would see the people huddled together, gesticulating; now and then one would turn towards the palace and shake a fist. She heard what they said as she mingled with them in the markets. 'Jezebel . . . Queen Jezebel! Only you'd not find a dog to eat *her* flesh!'

They sang:

> 'L'une ruyne d'Israel,
> L'autre, ruyne de la France.'

But they sang it sullenly, not gaily; and it was that brooding sullenness which Catherine feared more than anything. It was like a smouldering fire, she knew, ready to break into flames.

She must watch all her enemies. And what of those two at Nérac? What did they plot and plan?

She spoke to the King while he fondled his lap-dogs.

'My son, we should have your sister back at court.'

The King looked at her in dismay. 'It is much pleasanter without her.'

'That may be, my darling. But how do we know what she is about while she is away from us?'

320

'It is Navarre who is more to be feared than Margot.'

'I am not sure. They are both dangerous. Ask them to pay us a visit. I should feel happier if they were here on the spot. I can find a woman for him, and you know that I have means of hearing most things that go on around me. It is not easy when they are so far away. Unfortunately, my listening tubes do not extend to Nérac.'

'They would not come, even though I commanded them.'

'She would; and it might be possible to get her help in luring him here.'

'Would you keep them prisoners here?'

'I would see that he did not find it easy to escape again.'

'But do you think she would come? Do you remember how importunate she was when she wished to get away?'

'My dear son, Margot is never happy in one place for long at a time. She writes now that she has no news worthy of report, for Gascony grows news only like itself. By that she means that she longs for the court of France. She wants to hear about Paris. She only has to think of the Seine and her eyes fill with tears! Do you think any place but the court of France could please Margot long? Depend upon it, she now wishes to return as once she wished to go. We should have no difficulty in persuading *her* to return.'

'But what of Navarre? Would he agree to her coming?'

'If it were put to him as Margot would put it, he would agree. She would doubtless offer to act as his spy here at court. We should see all that she wrote to him. It would be our task to get her to lure him here. I will suggest that she comes. I am sure that she must be tired of Monsieur de Turenne; I am astonished that she was faithful to him for so long. What does the air of Béarn do to these two? Navarre was faithful to La Fosseuse until she wearied him with her troubles; and now they say he is showing the same fidelity to Corisanda. Oh, certainly Margot will have grown tired of Turenne ere this. That must be why she says Gascony grows only news like itself!'

'Very well,' said the King. 'Ask them both to come. I should feel happier to have Navarre here as my prisoner.'

'Send her a gift of money. Tell her that you would like to see her. Be warm and loving. I doubt not that then she will come.'

Catherine was right. Although Navarre refused his invitation bluntly, Margot was delighted with hers. Navarre reminded Margot that his mother had died in Paris, very suddenly, very mysteriously. 'Remember Monsieur de Coligny,' he said. 'Remember hundreds of my friends who once went to Paris for a wedding.'

Margot lifted her shoulders. 'It may be better for me to go alone. I will keep you informed of all that happens at court. It is well that you should know something of what they are planning.'

He agreed with this, and Margot made her preparations for the journey. There was a reason, other than boredom with her husband's court and her distaste of staying too long in one place, why she wished to leave for Paris. When Anjou had stayed at Nérac there had been a very charming gentleman in his suite, a certain Jacques de Harlay, who was the Lord of Champvallon. Margot and he had been mutually attracted; there had been one or two tender meetings between them; unfortunately, they were surprised during one of these, in somewhat compromising attitudes, by Margot's greatest enemy at the court – a sly and very virtuous Huguenot, Agrippa d'Aubigné. D'Aubigné, a gentleman of Navarre's chamber, was as fond of writing as Margot was and, like her, took a great delight in chronicling the events of his day as they occurred. He knew his Scriptures well; he believed that he who was without sin should cast the first stone; and as he was certain that he himself was without sin, he had always a very big stone ready to cast. To such a man a beautiful, fascinating and vivacious Queen such as Margot seemed the embodiment of all evil; his hatred of her coloured all his writings; nor was it his pen alone which he employed against her.

Margot at that time, deeply involved with Turenne, had no great wish to give him up for the handsome Champvallon, who would leave the court of Nérac with Anjou; but she wrote to him frequently and in a more hyberbolic style than she usually employed, even in her love letters. 'Farewell, my beautiful sun,' she wrote, 'you beautiful miracle of nature. I kiss you a million times on that loving, beautiful mouth.' Such letters did not always find their way direct to the one for whom they were intended, and Margot's passion for Champvallon was known to others besides themselves.

Now, having tired a little of Monsieur de Turenne, Margot looked forward to reunion with Champvallon in Paris.

Arriving at the capital, Margot was warmly welcomed by Champvallon, but less warmly by the King and her mother. She saw now that they had asked her to come so that they might keep her under surveillance, and that they had no intention of altering their attitude towards her.

Margot was unperturbed. She was in her beloved Paris; she was at the court of France where she belonged; she took an immense delight in her surroundings and many of the courtiers were declaring that the sun had come back to shine once more upon them. She was the centre of all balls, masques, and entertainments; she was the leader of fashion; and as she was by this time passionately in love with Champvallon, she was enjoying life.

Sometimes she encountered Henry of Guise, and these meetings never failed to excite her. He was still the lover of Madame de Sauves, but Margot knew that his dreams of his future greatness occupied him far more than any mistress ever could. The League, under his guidance, was spreading across the land. There were occasions when she longed to ask him to tell her of the League's activities, of his plans which, had they all gone as she had once so ardently desired, would have been *her* plans, *her* dreams, *her* hopes.

But there was Champvallon to remind her that she had done with the old passion for Henry of Guise. Why fret about it when there was a new one, and when there had been many in between, and would be many more to follow.

Catherine was urging Margot to persuade her husband to come to Paris, but Navarre sent continuous refusals. Catherine knew that as soon as Margot had arrived at court she had begun to act as her husband's spy, but that had been expected and provided little occasion for anxiety, for Catherine believed she intercepted all their correspondence.

Margot had been some months at court when an incident occurred which aroused the King's wrath to such an extent that he determined on revenge.

His beloved *mignon*, Joyeuse, had desired to become the Archbishop of Narbonne and envoy to the Holy See, and although this young man was not yet twenty-one years of age and was completely lacking in the necessary qualifications, he had so charmingly begged for the honour that the King had been unable to resist throwing it to him as though it were a sugared plum – even though it meant that the darling must absent himself from court for a while to visit Rome. While Joyeuse was in Rome, Henry sent dispatches to him, but the royal courier had been waylaid and shot, and these dispatches were stolen.

The King was furious, half suspecting his mother, for this smacked of her methods, yet he decided he would blame his sister, for he was looking for a charge to trump up against her.

He wished to take his revenge in a manner which would bring her the greatest shame, and, acting without consulting his mother, but taking instead the advice of his darlings, he chose the state ball as the occasion.

Margot looked as striking as ever that night; she wore her hair loose about her shoulders and adorned with diamonds; her dress was of scarlet velvet.

She was dancing when the King gave a sign to the musicians to stop. The dancers stood silent, wondering what was wrong. The King then strode to that spot where his sister stood.

'Behold!' he cried, addressing the assembly. 'Behold this wanton! My friends, I am ashamed to own her as my sister. I could not begin to enumerate her crimes to you. There are too many, and I, mercifully, am unaware of them all. I might name forty men who have been her lovers . . . but, my friends, that would by no means complete the list. There is one Champvallon. Do you know that she bore his son recently here in Paris? This is so. With wicked secrecy she endeavoured to keep this from us, but we are not foolish, nor so blind as she thinks.'

Margot's eyes blazed. 'You . . .' she cried. 'You . . . with your painted *mignons* . . . to call me immoral . . .'

The King's eyes narrowed, and Margot was aware that two of his *mignons* had taken their stand on either side of her.

Beware! mocked their eyes. No one speaks to the King of France as you have . . . and lives!

Margot's fear was greater than her fury. Never before had she realized the depth of her brother's hatred. She had been foolish to plague his *mignons*, to show her enmity towards them. She saw now how right her husband had been when he had refused to walk into the trap by coming to Paris. She was sure this was a prelude to her arrest.

She looked appealingly at her mother.

Catherine stood silently watching. She was sick at heart. These children of hers, with their folly, were wrecking all that she had worked for. This story would be told all over the streets of Paris, distorted, enlarged; and the sum of the iniquities of the house of Valois would be totted up afresh, with the result that there would be a bigger total for the discontented to grumble over.

'Brother,' said Margot, 'you have been listening to lies. I have no child.'

Her mother whispered to her: 'Say nothing. Depart at once. Go to your apartments. It is your only chance if you would escape your brother's anger.'

Margot bowed and, holding her head high, walked out while the assembly, in silence, made way for her.

Her women gathered round her in her apartments. What now? they asked each other.

Margot lay on her bed, apprehensive, yet enjoying, as usual, a dangerous situation; and, although the King had accused her of having an illegitimate child, and that news would soon be all over Paris, all over France, she was not entirely displeased. Her sterility – the result of the sins of her grandfathers – was deeply regretted by her; so, if she could not bear children, it was a little gratifying to be suspected of having done so.

Nothing more happened that night, but when she awakened it was to find sixty archers in her bedchamber. This was a meaningless indignity put on her by the King, for they had not come to arrest her, but merely to bring a message from him commanding her to 'deliver the city of her presence without delay'.

As Champvallon, when informed of the scene in the ballroom during which his name had been mentioned, had fled to Germany fearing the vengeance of the King, Margot decided to obey her brother without delay, and accordingly set out that very day for Gascony.

The King came delightedly to his mother. 'There, you see! I have rid our court of that spy, and done it promptly. As Epernon said from the first, it was a mistake to bring her here.'

Catherine shook her head. 'My son, how I wish that you would take my advice before you act rashly. It is far better to have such a dangerous person under our eyes than far away. And I greatly fear that your manner of dismissing her was most unwise.'

'I am a man,' said the King, 'who, once he has made up his mind, acts promptly.'

'Sometimes it is wiser to ponder awhile,' said Catherine. 'We shall see whether you were right or whether you should have taken my advice and acted more cautiously.'

Henry soon did see. Navarre, having heard of the King's attack on Margot, sent dispatches to the King telling him that he could not be expected to take back a wife whom the King of France – her own brother – had so publicly slandered.

The fact was that Corisanda was pregnant and, being very eager to possess a son and heir to his dominions, the King of Navarre contemplated marrying her. He said in his dispatches that he thought he should receive reparation for the royal family's having married him to such a woman. He wanted a divorce. What would Christendom say, he demanded, if he received a woman on whom the great King of France had inflicted such public scandal before banishing her from his court!

Catherine raised expressionless eyes to her son's face; but the King ignored her and refused to admit that he had been wrong.

'A curse on Navarre!' he cried. 'A curse on his harlot wife! There will be no peace for this realm while either of them live.'

'She must go back to her husband,' said Catherine. 'What is done cannot be altered. My dearest son, those friends of yours advised you to behave as you did, not for the good of France, but on account of their own petty jealousy. You must not allow personal feelings to enter into the government of a country.'

He frowned. That was the most she dared say against his *mignons*. Meanwhile, she wondered how she could rid herself of those two, Epernon and Joyeuse, the most dangerous of them all. But so many of his *mignons* had died that she feared he would be suspicious of her if any further accidents overtook them; and she could not bear to lose that little affection, that little respect which he still had for her.

But she should rejoice. Such matters as this should prove to him that his *mignons* only led him into folly. It proved something else; it showed up clearly the growing shrewdness of Navarre.

Envoys were being sent back and forth between the courts of Paris and Nérac. The King of France was placating the King of Navarre. He was now weakly declaring that he had not meant what he had said regarding his sister, and that he had been misinformed; it was a fact, he realized, that very often virtuous Princesses were not exempt from slander.

Secure in his little kingdom, Navarre laughed with glee. Although he adored – for the time being – his beautiful Corisanda, and although she carried his child, he was not altogether sure that he wanted to lose Margot, that most amusing and amazing of women; and he might, if the King of France offered him big enough concessions, consider taking her back.

And at length he did agree to take her back, since, as the main concession, the King of France had withdrawn his garrisons from several towns close to Navarre's domain.

Navarre laughed, well pleased. Margot's trip to the court of France had been advantageous as well as highly diverting.

*

There was consternation throughout the Louvre and throughout Paris. In the court of Nérac there was such excitement as had rarely been known there before. Even the King of Navarre was silent, contemplating the future.

The Duke of Anjou had fallen seriously ill, and there was little hope of his recovery.

Margot was weeping for her brother; she had loved him,

some said, more than a sister should love a brother. Yet, in spite of her grief, Margot was as alert as was her husband and his ministers. If her brother should die there was nowhere in the world where that event could be considered of more importance than at Nérac.

In the streets of Paris people were whispering against the Italian woman. 'They say that Jezebel has poisoned him.'

'But can that be so? Her own son?'

'Her own son! What of poor little Francis the Second? What of poor mad Charles? They'll tell you that she sent those two to the grave before they need have gone. Many have received her Italian poisons – son, daughter, cousin . . . what matters it to her? She is evil . . . this Queen Jezebel of France.'

But Catherine sincerely regretted the sickness of her son and was, in fact, frantic with anxiety. Anjou dying! What would happen if Henry were to die? These children of hers did not seem to be able to grow to maturity. Henry himself had aged far beyond his years. If Henry died, Navarre would be next in succession. It was true that Margot would be Queen of France, but could she trust Margot? Could she trust Navarre?

The people in the streets were fools to think she would poison this son. They did not understand her. They did not know that her murders were not real murders; they were merely eliminations of tiresome people who stood in the way of the power of the house of Valois – nothing more! There was no personal feeling in the killing of those who must be removed. Had she murdered that woman who had caused her years of humiliation and torture during the lifetime of her husband? No! Diane de Poitiers had gone free simply because, when Catherine would have been able to murder her, Diane had ceased to be of any importance.

Catherine felt herself to be a sorely misunderstood woman. But the slander of the streets had never hurt her. Why should she bother herself with it now? Could she be feeling this faint resentment because she was growing old, because she sometimes felt weary of the continual struggle to hold the power she had won?

Her thoughts went at once to her old enemy, Philip of Spain. How would he react to the death of Anjou? What would he do to prevent the Huguenot King of Navarre's becoming the King of Catholic France? She was sure he would do something. The Netherlands were not causing him so much anxiety now as previously. Parma had done good work for his master; and a few months ago the Prince of Orange, that bulwark of all Protestants, had been assassinated. Thus Coligny's daughter Louise, who had married the Prince after the death of Téligny, had lost both her husbands in violent circumstances. Coligny's wife, Jacqueline, was still in prison, where she had been since the murder of her husband. Catherine must watch those Huguenots. She must watch Philip of Spain. Poor Anjou had been ineffectual in life, but his death was going to make him the important figure he had always longed to be.

The news came that Anjou was dead. His poor Valois constitution had not been able to throw off the inflammation of the lungs. Anjou dead . . . and Henry of Navarre was heir to the throne of France. The whole of Europe was alert. A Protestant King of France was going to alter the balance of power. England prepared to send help to the Netherlands under Leicester; and in spite of the loss of the beloved Prince of Orange, the Netherlanders were filled with new hope. Philip of Spain had turned an anxious eye towards Paris and was calling his council meetings. He was looking to the one man in France who, he knew, would never allow a Protestant to rule; and Henry of Guise, the leader of the Catholic League, was fast becoming the most important man in France.

Catherine waited apprehensively. She held long and secret councils with the King; but the King was in no mood for business, for he had recently had a new collection of monkeys and parrots sent to him and was deciding which friends should share them with him. There were his dogs to claim his attention; there were his *mignons* to amuse him and charm his time away. Epernon and Joyeuse were rivals in his affections now, and if he gave Joyeuse a present, he must cap it with a more extravagant gift to Epernon; and that only resulted in increasing jealousy on the part of Joyeuse. Epernon had been given the Colonel-Generalship of France; Joyeuse had therefore to be made Admiral of France; then Epernon must have the government of Metz, Verdun, and Toul. And so it went on. The richest men in France were Epernon and Joyeuse; and if Joyeuse were the richer one day, on the next Epernon must be.

Joyeuse, back from Rome, wanted to be married. He asked for a rich wife, a woman who could bring him honour. 'You have a wife, dearest Sire; and you know it is my aim to be as like you as possible.'

The King was amused. His darling should have a wife; and his bride should be the Queen's own sister, who could bring him a very large dowry.

Joyeuse clapped his hands with glee and, with the King and the other *mignons*, began planning the wedding festivities. These were to last for two weeks and they were going to cost a fabulous sum. That was unimportant. The people of Paris loved festivities, and it was well known that people must pay for what they liked.

So the people looked on at the wedding of Joyeuse; and after Joyeuse was married, Epernon must be married too.

The King was at his wit's end to provide an equally rich wife for darling Epernon; as for his wedding festivities, coming so close to those of that dear wretch Joyeuse, he really did not know how he was going to provide such a show and so prevent Epernon's being hideously jealous. He managed it partly by rifling the Municipal Treasury; and he thought of a very good way of adding to the proceeds of that robbery; he put up the price of judgeships. He and his darlings laughed together. For a King there were always ways and means of finding money.

The *Battus* loomed into prominence once more. The King and his *mignons* organized processions through the streets. It was such fun, after the ceremonies in their gorgeous jewelled garments, to parade in sacks. They had white sacks which were so much more charming to look at than the sacks previously worn; and these white sacks looked delightful with skulls embroidered on them.

The King was enthusiastic. It did show the people – after those really extravagant weddings of the two darlings – that the King and his friends were a very religious band of young men at heart.

Catherine tried remonstrating as she watched uneasily. She

330

knew that all eyes were on Paris now. Elizabeth of England watched; William of Nassau watched from Holland and Zeeland; Henry of Navarre waited slyly, as one who could afford to wait; Philip of Spain was on the alert; and Henry of Guise was at hand. Had the two latter exchanged secret communications which had not come into the Queen Mother's hands? she wondered.

The ridiculous ceremonies went on; there were bursts of extravagant feasting; the shivering Parisians looked through the windows of the Louvre and saw the King in a woman's gown of green silk; they saw his *mignons* dressed as court ladies.

Paris looked on, silent and sullen, while revolution quivered in the air of that city.

Six

Catherine, throwing off the rigours of her increasing years, trying to ignore the nagging pain of her rheumatic limbs, for the first time being careful of what she ate – for too many years she had shown little restraint where those foods which she loved were concerned – bestirred herself to fresh energies. Disaster was near. Her power might at any moment be snatched from her. She realized that during the last few years she had followed will-o'-the-wisps; she had travelled about the country making peace, removing her enemies, keeping the crown safe – so she had thought; and because one man had seemed to lose his ambition, to have been content with his place in life, she had ignored him; and thus he had been free to continue with his secret work and, like some underground creature, he had tunnelled beneath the very foundations of her power, so that instead of its being on firm ground, it was ready to totter. She should have known that the most ambitious man in France would never lose his ambition. She should never have allowed her attention to be diverted from Henry, Duke of Guise.

What did he plan? His League was now the most powerful force in France. Insidiously it had grown, and in silence, while the attention of those who should have watched it had been cunningly directed to minor dangers. And the League was working against the King.

Catherine looked back on the years of her son's reign. The clever though effeminate young man he had been in his teens had changed. The better side of his nature had been suppressed, so that now, apart from those moments when he displayed his wit and an unexpected grasp of affairs, he seemed nothing but a decadent fop. His health was poor, his constitution weak; and there was a strain of cynicism in him which seemed to indicate his belief that his life could not be a long one and that he intended to use it exactly as he pleased for that reason. He had disappointed his mother, and she had allowed herself to be hurt. There had been times when she had let her love for an ungrateful son override her love of power. She should have been wiser and remembered a bitter lesson which another beloved Henry had taught her years ago; and she thought now of those years of misery and humiliation, of the wasted torture of watching her husband and his mistress through a hole in the floor; so much unhappiness had been the result of self-inflicted wounds. She was surprised that she had not learned how futile that line of conduct could be, for evidently she had not learned this lesson, since, with this Henry as with the other, she had allowed her emotions to intrude into her plan for living. Emotion should have had no part whatsoever in the life of Catherine de' Medici.

But that was over now; yet it had taken the threat of disaster to show her the folly of her ways. She loved her son, but it was more important to keep her power than his affection. If necessary, she might have to work against him.

Events had been moving out of her knowledge. Where were her spies? They had doubtless done their best, but the Guises' spies were better. Hers had helped her to discover one thing, however – that Henry of Guise had dared to communicate with Spain as though he were already the ruler of France.

That old fool, the Cardinal of Bourbon – brother of that greater fool, Antoine de Bourbon, who had made such a laughing-stock of himself at her court years ago – was to take the throne on the death of Henry. Henry was a young man still and the Bourbon was an old one, so what was in the minds of the Guises? What other secret documents had passed between the Duke of Guise and Philip of Sapin? Did Philip really think that Guise intended to stand by and let the Cardinal take the crown? Perhaps Guise wished to rule through the Cardinal. There was a great advantage, as she could have told him, in being the power behind the throne.

The Cardinal was sixty-four. How could he be expected to outlive Henry, unless ... But she would not let herself believe that it was possible for them to be planning to destroy her son; she must forget that she was a sick and ailing woman, for she had much to do.

The Bourbon, an ardent follower of the Guises, such a good

333

Catholic, had agreed to ignore the prior right of his nephew, Henry of Navarre, and to take the throne himself; he had sworn that when he was King he would forbid heretical worship.

Catherine summoned Guise to her and demanded to know why he had communicated with the King of Spain without the knowledge and consent of his King.

Guise was arrogant – more arrogant than ever, she thought. It was evident that he knew more of what was happening than she did. His manner, but for his aristocratic bearing, would have bordered on the insolent.

'Madame,' said Guise, 'France would never tolerate a Huguenot King, and should the King die without heirs – which God forbid – the Huguenot King of Navarre would feel he had a right to the throne unless the people of France had already chosen their new King.'

She gazed at him in thoughtful silence. The sunlight which came through the embrasured window, shone on his hair, turning it to gold and silver. He was taller than any man at court and that spareness of his gave him a look of added strength; the scar on his cheek but augmented the warlike look. She was not surprised that a man of such presence should have the people of Paris at his feet. The King of Paris! they called him; and one would have been a fool not to realize that, when he talked of the future King of France, he was not thinking so much of an old Cardinal in his sixties as of a handsome Duke in his thirties.

Then she said: 'You presume to negotiate with a foreign power without consulting the wishes of your King, Monsieur!'

'The King occupies himself with other matters, Madame. There was the wedding of Joyeuse, which was followed by the wedding of Epernon. I did approach the King, but he was discussing the garments he would wear at the weddings and he told me he was too busy to talk of anything else.'

What insolence! What arrogance! she thought; but she was aware of a slight feeling of pleasure. Had *he* been her son, how different everything would have been! She made up her mind then; she was going to walk in step with the arrogant Duke . . .

for a little way at least. It was, after all, the only wise thing to do. Matters had gone too far from her control for her to be able to ignore him; and if she could not show herself to be his enemy, she must appear to be his friend.

'Ah well, Monsieur,' she said, 'you are right when you say that the people of France would never tolerate a Huguenot King.'

'Madame, it delights me that you approve my action.'

He bent and kissed her hand.

'My son,' she said, looking at him tenderly. 'Yes! I call you son. Were you not brought up with my children? My son, these are bad days for France. The King delights in his pleasure, surrounded by frivolous young men. But France has no place for frivolous young men at this hour. You and I must work together . . . for the good of France.'

'You are right, Madame,' said Guise.

For the good of France! she thought, as she watched him retire. He is clever enough to know that I shall work for the good of the Queen Mother, while he works for the good of Monsieur de Guise.

'Holy Mother of God!' she muttered. 'Nothing that man does in future must escape my notice.'

*

Margot was not happy in Béarn. Life had become very dull. Her husband had taken her back, but he had let her see that he had been in two minds about it.

He was still devoted to La Corisanda, who was by no means the stupid little creature La Fosseuse had been; and he had decided that Margot, though still the Queen of Navarre, should realize that it was the King who ruled.

'You have changed,' she told him, 'since you have taken a step nearer the throne of France.'

'Nay!' he answered. 'I am the same man. I still do not wash my feet.'

'That is no concern of mine,' she retorted.

'I am glad that you have learned some sense,' was his answer, 'for I do not intend that it shall be any concern of yours.'

She was furious.

He made it quite clear that there would be no resumption of their intermittent conjugal relationship; he told her carelessly that he had taken her back solely because the concessions her brother had offered, if he would do so, were very necessary to him. She was bored as well as furious; she was restive, looking for new adventures, and none of the men of her husband's court pleased her.

News had come that the Pope had excommunicated Navarre as a heretic, and that release was offered to any of his subjects from their oath of fidelity; moreover, Navarre was, by edict of Rome, denied the succession to the French crown.

Navarre's eyes blazed with wrath. He cursed the Pope; he cursed the Duke of Guise; and he cursed the Queen Mother. He was seriously perturbed, as he knew that the Pope's edict would carry great weight in France. He raged against his uncle, the Cardinal of Bourbon, who had, he declared, betrayed him.

Margot listened, not without sympathy.

'I am my father's son!' he cried. 'I am heir to the throne of France. My uncle deceives himself if he allows the Pope and the Guises to convince him he is right. *Ventre Saint Gris!* If I had the old man here I'd lop off his head and throw it over the battlements. It is a conspiracy. The Guises have done this, and your mother is behind them.'

'I do not believe that my mother agrees with this,' said Margot.

'She is continually with Guise in council. That is the news we get from Paris.'

'Even now you do not know my mother. She may seem to agree with the Guises; she may applaud all that is said by Philip of Spain and the Pope of Rome; but you may depend on it, she has made her own plans, and while there remains one of her children to sit on the throne, she will never willingly stand by and see any other take it.'

'Ah,' he said, smiling at her, 'I see you have your eyes on the throne, Madame.'

She returned the smile. They were allies. They must be, for their interests ran together.

Navarre became more energetic than he had ever been

before. Not only did he publish his protests throughout France, but he had them posted in Rome and on the very doors of the Vatican.

This forthright action astonished all, and even the Pope secretly expressed admiration for the young man. This boldness of his, said the Pope, made it all the more necessary for him to be most closely watched.

Margot was not content merely to play the part of consort to the young man who seemed to be growing in importance now that the might of Spain, Rome, and France was directed against him. She must have excitement; she could not endure being bored. She took to the pen and wrote long letters to her friends at the French court; her mother wrote to her kindly and affectionately, and Margot replied. It was easy for Margot to forget the past and all that she had suffered at those maternal hands. She began to send accounts of all events of importance at her husband's court.

Any correspondence with Catherine de' Medici seemed, to the friends of the King of Navarre, a dangerous procedure, and one of his gentlemen decided to tell him that his wife was acting as the Queen Mother's spy in Béarn.

The enraged Henry of Navarre determined, now that so much was at stake, to be increasingly watchful, and had one of Margot's couriers arrested just as he was leaving Nérac for Paris. This man, a certain Ferrand, was brought into the King's presence and, greatly daring, even as he stood before him, managed to throw quantities of paper on to the fire. These roared into such a blaze that they were burned before they could be recovered. The remaining letters were taken from him, but these proved to be only love letters from Margot and her women to lovers they had known in Paris.

After he had laughed at these revealing epistles, Navarre had Ferrand arrested, and during painful cross-examination, Ferrand told the King that the Queen was planning to poison him because of the insulting way in which he treated her.

In horror, Navarre confronted Margot.

'You are exposed, Madame,' he said.

'How so?'

'Your evil plans concerning me are known.'

'I know of no evil plans.' She was genuinely surprised, being quite innocent of the charge. She was no crafty poisoner; all her sins were committed impetuously. Moreover she was always most furious when she was falsely accused, and when she heard from her husband of what Ferrand had said against her, her rage broke forth.

'How dare he suggest such a thing! It is cruel; it is folly.'

'You are in communication with your mother, are you not?'

'Why should I not be?'

'She has declared herself in favour of the Cardinal's succession.'

'What a fool you are! She is in favour of *my* succession, and that must be yours. And you are foolish enough to think I would poison you!'

'You are your mother's daughter.'

'I am my father's daughter also. I do not love you; that would be impossible. But I realize my position rests with yours. Do not be such a fool as to believe the confession of a man, made under torture. You will have to be shrewder than that if you are ever going to win what is yours by right.'

'Your mother is in constant council with Guise. To my mind, he is the one who, backed by the League, is going to make a bid for the throne.'

Margot smiled faintly. Yes, she thought; and if all had gone as I once wished it to, I should be with him now.

She thought of him – tall, spare and handsome still; more noble now, more distinguished, some said, than he had been even in the fresh beauty of his youth. There was a yearning within her, a longing for Paris, for a different life, to go back and act differently. Marriage with the man who now stood before her had been inevitable; but there had been an occasion later when she had had a chance to break away from him. She had refused it in her blind and stupid pride.

'You,' she said at length, 'have suspected me of trying to bring about your death, and I find that hard to forgive. I am tired of your court. I am tired of your people. I do not like your mistress, who is the real Queen of Navarre; and that is something I cannot happily endure. I would like to leave Nérac for a while.'

338

'You shall not go to Paris,' he said.

'I was not thinking of Paris. During the Lenten season a great Jesuit father is to preach at the cathedral at Agen. May I have your permission to make the journey there?'

He hesitated. It would be a relief to be rid of her. How did he know what secrets had been in those documents which she sent to Paris? How could he be sure that, however closely she was watched, she would not smuggle out important information? If she went, he could see that she was well guarded.

'Very well,' he said. 'Go to Agen for the Lenten season. I will give my consent.'

She was happy now. She thought: once I have left him, I will never return to him. Why should I tolerate a husband who scorns me – me, the daughter of France, the sun of the court of Paris, the most beautiful of Princesses ... when he is nothing but a provincial oaf!

But why concern herself with a man who meant little to her? Her thoughts were of another – that man whom she firmly believed would be King of France, for he was surely destined for greatness; the gods had fashioned him for it.

Margot was now deep in intrigue such as she loved. She would hold the town of Agen for the Catholic League. She would show France and Henry of Guise whose side she was on.

*

Catherine saw clearly for what Henry of Guise had been working all these years. He had decided not to depend entirely on his popularity. Rumour was circulated throughout the country that the Guises had been proved to have a stronger claim to the throne than had the Valois; and although these rumours did not appear to spring from Henry of Guise, Catherine knew that he was behind them.

It was said that 'The line of Capets had succeeded to the temporal administration of the kingdom of Charlemagne but it had not succeeded to the apostolic benediction which appertained to none other but the posterity of Charlemagne. The House of Lorraine sprang from the issue of Charlemagne, and as certain members of the line of Capet were possessed of a spirit of giddiness and stupidity while others were heretic and excommunicated, it was now time to restore the crown to its new heirs . . .'

This was ominous. So he would be King, not by popular acclaim only, but by right. That was typical of Guise, she was beginning to understand. He must be King not only because the people wished it, but because he was heir to the throne. As an aristocrat of aristocrats, he worshipped law and order; and mob rule nauseated him.

Catherine was disturbed to realize that this was not only being said throughout France, but that Cardinal Pellevé, a firm supporter of the League, had given his approval of it, and that it was being submitted to Rome and Spain. She knew that she had not been wrong when she had guessed that Guise and his supporters had no intention of allowing the Cardinal of Bourbon to rule.

She sought out Guise at once.

'There is much in this account of the House of Lorraine's being descended from Charlemagne,' she said. 'You know of what I speak, of course?'

The Duke admitted that he had heard the rumours.

'My lord Duke, it seems to me that there is one course we must take. If it is true that the Capets have forfeited their right to the throne, then the Cardinal of Bourbon has no right.'

'That is so,' admitted Guise; but apart from the brightness of his eye above the scar he showed no sign of emotion.

'The House of Lorraine,' she said slowly, 'according to this new authority should be the rulers of France. There will be some to agree with that, and some to dispute it.'

'There are always some who are for us and some who are against us, Madame.'

'And it is wise in some cases to placate both sides. Do you agree?'

He indicated his agreement, wondering what suggestion she was going to offer. He was certain that it concerned Margot. Divorce for him; divorce for Margot; and that marriage, which had been proposed before, could take place.

Catherine understood his line of thought and let him pursue it. Then she spoke. 'I was thinking of the son of my dear daughter Claude, a boy whose parents were a Duke of Lorraine and a daughter of Valois. What could be more suitable? The supporters of my House would be pleased; the supporters of yours should be pleased.'

In his astonishment, he was silent for a second or two before he regained his composure. 'Madame,' he said, 'that is a most excellent proposition.'

They smiled at each other; but she knew that he intended that no man should mount the throne of France after the death of Henry the Third but Henry of Guise; and he knew that she knew it.

❁

Events were moving fast in the lives of the three Henrys of France – Henry the Third, Henry of Guise, and Henry, King of Navarre.

Guise was growing daily more powerful. The Treaty of Joinville, which Guise and the leading Catholics of France had made with Philip of Spain, was followed by Philip's promise of troops and money for the cause to which Guise had pledged himself – the defence of the faith, the wiping out of heretics, and the disinheriting of Henry of Navarre. The League was everywhere; all over France it had sprung up in small groups to work not only against the Huguenots, but against the throne. Guise was now in control of a great army, one section of which was commanded by himself, the other by his brother, the Duke of Mayenne. The Pope, however, was now suspecting that the League had not been formed so much for the sake of Catholicism as for the elevation and advancement of the House of Guise and Lorraine. He foresaw that the arrogant man who was making a bid to rule France would be no humble vassal of Rome and Spain, for he had already announced that high offices of the Church should be appointed by the League and not as hitherto by Rome. The Pope was watchful; it might be that the pleasure-loving King would be easier to handle than the warlike Guise.

Catherine, eagerly watching, had, as she had planned, walked step by step with Guise. The League was now putting forward demands which the King must either concede or refuse; and if he refused, he would have to face the mighty army of the League. The King was angry at being bothered, for he was in the midst of a delightful carnival. He wanted peace in which to enjoy himself. So he allowed Catherine to treat with Guise. The King was to force all his subjects to accept the Catholic Faith, and those towns which had been given to the Huguenots were to be taken from them and given to the League.

Catherine toyed with the idea of playing Navarre off against Guise, in accordance with her well-tried policy, but she decided that Guise was her man. The Catholics were in the ascendant, and if Philip of Spain sent the help he had promised Guise, Navarre's case was hopeless.

She flattered the Duke and tried to convince him that she was his ally, while between them they kept up the fiction that her grandson should be King of France if the present King should die.

'I am old,' she told Guise. 'I am weary. I have worked hard in my long life and I now have need of peace. You, my dear Duke, are as a son to me; you are my helper, my counsellor.'

She was seen walking with him, arm in arm; and when she referred to him it was affectionately as *'le baton de ma vieillesse'*.

Navarre watched from afar, gathering his followers, waiting for the moment when he would ask them to prove their allegiance. Meanwhile, the familiar clouds of civil war were gathering over the land.

Margot, her husband was relieved to contemplate, had been separated from him for some time. She had acted with her usual careless impetuosity at Agen. She had settled in at the château there and declared that she had come to hold the town for the League. The townsfolk had been sympathetic at first; they had been enchanted by her vivacity and her dark beauty; they had seen in her a romantic Princess fleeing from the husband to whom she had been married against her will, the husband who had a faith different from her own. But very soon scandalous stories of the happenings inside the castle seeped out. It was said that there were scenes of unparalleled immorality between Margot and certain gentlemen of the

342

castle; and that her women were no better than she was. The people of Agen did not wish to be 'protected', as Margot called it, by such an immoral woman; they now began to believe the stories which for so long had been circulating about her. They became threatening, and in the end Margot had been forced to leave Agen, fleeing as her brother had fled from Poland – in a manner more dramatic than was necessary. She had ridden pillion with her lover of the moment, the Lord of Lignerac; and her women had followed in the same manner on the horses of the officers of her court. Lignerac had taken her to his castle in the mountains of Auvergne and kept her there as his prisoner, so enamoured of her was he, so distrustful of her fidelity. There the troublesome prisoner was forced to stay, although it was said that she was making attempts to evade the old lover with the help of several new ones.

Navarre could smile at the exploits of Margot; but his own life was too exciting just now for him to think very much about her. He knew that in the civil war which seemed inevitable, Guise and the King of France would be uneasy allies; and that he would be the opponent of both of them. He knew that he would be faced by a formidable force, so he asked that, rather than plunge the country into another war, Guise should meet him in single combat, or, if it was preferred, with ten men aside, or twenty – the number could be decided on.

'It would give me great happiness,' he wrote, 'to deliver at the price of my blood, the King our sovereign lord from the travails and trials a-brewing for him, and his kingdom from trouble and confusion, his noblesse from ruin, and all his people from misery.'

The Duke of Guise replied that he must decline the honour while appreciating it; had this been a private quarrel between them, then gladly would he have accepted Navarre's proposal; but it was no private quarrel; theirs was the cause of the true religion against the false. It could not be settled by two men's fighting together, or even by ten or twenty on each side.

Navarre now knew that war was inevitable; and within a very short time after he had made his offer and Guise had replied to it, the War of the Three Henrys had begun.

*

It was called The War of the Three Henrys, although one of these Henrys, the King of France, wished to have nothing to do with it. He was more furious when he heard of Guise's successes than when he heard of those of Navarre; he was piqued and jealous on account of Guise's. He was a strange creature, this King of France; in his early years he had been by no means stupid, but his love of his *mignons* and all those young men stood for had blighted that intellect which had undoubtedly been his. It emerged occasionally when he addressed the council meetings; there he could show by a sharpness of wit that he was a man who had profited from his reading of the greatest books of his age; but the determination to pursue pleasure at all costs, his great vanity concerning his personal appearance, the dominance of those worthless young men whose elegance, beauty and charm had won him — together these things had almost succeeded in suppressing the intellectual side of his character. But he still had enough sense to realize that in this war of the Henrys, it was his ally, Henry of Guise, of whom he must be wary — far more wary than of his enemy, Henry of Navarre.

Guise was fighting in the north against the Germans and the Swiss who had come in to help the Huguenots, and news came of the tremendous victory he had scored over these foreign troops. He had surprised the Germans while they were sleeping and so demoralized them that before they were able to collect themselves together, there was no German army. At this the Swiss took fright and were bribed to withdraw. News of this great victory was brought to the King. But it was a Guise victory; it was not even called a King's victory.

In the south events did not turn out so happily for the King's forces. Against the advice of Guise and his mother, the King had given the command of the southern army to Joyeuse, who, having been a successful *mignon* and bridegroom, now wished to make his name as a soldier. He had cajoled and wept when asking for the command of the army; and he had looked so charming a suppliant that the King had been unable to refuse him. And so, with six thousand foot, two thousand horse and six pieces of cannon, Joyeuse marched into the Gironde country to meet the little army at the head of which was the King of Navarre.

There were members of that tiny Huguenot force who trembled at the thought of the mighty army which had come to attack them; but when Henry of Navarre heard who was at their head he laughed aloud.

Before his men went into battle, he addressed them in his coarse Béarnais fashion, which, though it might offend the ears of elegant ladies, put great heart into soldiers about to go into battle.

'My friends, here is a quarry different from your past prizes. It is a brand-new bridegroom with his marriage-money still in his coffers. Will you let yourselves go down before this handsome dancing-master and his minions? No! They are ours. I see it by your eagerness to fight.'

He looked about him at the glowing faces of the men touched by the faint dawn-light. His shrewd eyes twinkled. They would beat the dancing-master no matter how many cannon he had against their two, no matter if he had five hundred men to twenty of themselves.

Now for that little touch of spirituality which, he was aware, was so necessary to men such as these before they went into battle.

'My friends,' he resumed, 'all events are in the hands of God. Let us sing the twenty-fourth verse of the one hundred and fifteenth psalm.'

Their voices rose on the morning air: 'This is the day which the Lord hath made; we will rejoice and be glad in it.'

The sun now appeared above the horizon and, before it was high in the sky, Navarre, at the cost of twenty-five men had inflicted a loss of three thousand on the enemy.

Joyeuse, bewildered, found himself surrounded by Huguenots, and saw that they recognized him. Fresh from the court, he believed his beauty must appeal to these men as it had to others; but these warriors saw no handsome *mignon*; they saw their enemy, a sinner from the cities of the plain who had led the King into extravagance and folly.

Joyeuse in horror cried out: 'Gentlemen, you must not kill

me! You could take me and demand a reward of a hundred thousand crowns. The King would pay it. I assure you that he would.'

There was a second's pause, and then the shot rang out. Joyeuse opened his beautiful eyes in astonishment before he fell bleeding to the ground.

This was the greatest victory that the Huguenots had ever won, and all knew that they owed it to that quality in their leader which almost amounted to genius. The King's army had been a mighty one, and even though it had been under the command of Joyeuse, would, but for Navarre, have gained the victory. The careless philanderer could throw off his laziness after all; he was a great soldier; the careless joker was, after all, a great King.

It was a fact that the character of the King of Navarre had been gradually undergoing a change for some time. There were occasions when he was a great leader, but almost immediately afterwards he would revert to the man they all knew so well. He was a man of contrasts, of a strange and complex nature. The rough Béarnais with his coarse, crude manners hated to see suffering; it affected him more deeply than it did most people of his time; and yet the emotion of horror and pity which it aroused in him were so fleeting that they would pass if he did not act at once. Now these feelings came to him as he surveyed the carnage of that battlefield, and it robbed him of his feeling of triumph. His men rejoiced while he mourned for the slain. He was a great soldier who hated war; he was a coarse and careless man, fond of horseplay and discomfiting his enemies, who in a moment could change to one far in advance of his time to whom cruelty and suffering could be utterly distasteful. He had little relish now for the conqueror's feast which was prepared for him; he commanded that the fallen men should be treated with respect, and that everything possible should be done for the relief of the wounded.

He knew that he had won not only a great battle but a moral victory. He could push on while his men were drunk with success, for they were now ready to face anyone – even Henry of Guise.

But this new King of Navarre had suddenly reverted to the

old one, and he was filled with one desire and one only. He longed for his Corisanda. Loving was so much more satisfying that killing; dallying with a beautiful mistress more to his taste than contemplating carnage. He was a great soldier, but he was an even greater lover; for while the former calling gave him brief triumph, the latter, he knew, would not lose its charm for him as long as there was life in his body.

And so, neglecting the great opportunity that he had won, he prepared to forget military matters and return to Corisanda.

*

The war dragged on; in some parts of France there were local truces; in others the battles still blazed. The King of France, overcome with grief, must have fresh entertainments to stifle his sorrow in the loss of Joyeuse. The country was in revolt – Catholics and Huguenots together – against the fantastic extravagances of the King. The yearly cost of keeping his birds and dogs, with the great retinue of attendants he must employ solely to look after them, was enough to feed a town for that period. He paid great sums for miniatures which were bought by him from the greatest artists, but when they were his he cut them up that he might paste them on his walls. He wallowed in all the luxuries and comforts which went with his position and lightly discarded every responsibility.

The Sorbonne voted in secret that the crown should be taken from a King unworthy to wear it. Guise had made a trip to Rome to confer with the Cardinal Pellevé, who had supported his claim. As a result of these two moves, a third followed – the League presented the King with an ultimatum. He must establish the Inquisition in France while he took every measure to suppress the Huguenots.

The King was filled with rage at the arrogance of the Leaguers. Catherine begged him to ask for time to consider this proposal. Meanwhile, she secretly let Guise know that she was working for the League and him, and meant to do everything in her power to persuade the King to do as Guise and his Leaguers demanded.

She was beset by fainting fits and nausea at this time, and her rheumatism was so bad that she could scarcely walk; the

347

gout was attacking her; and it seemed to the worst of bad fortune that, now when she needed all her faculties, she should be denied that good health which had been hers throughout her life. She was nearly sixty-nine, which was a great age; but her mind was as good as it had ever been, and she cursed her failing body. Her spies seemed less alert than they had once been; that was because she herself was failing. She was no longer the energetic Queen Mother, gliding about the palace, opening doors with her secret keys and coming upon people unawares. Now she must walk with the aid of a stick whose tapping betrayed her; or she must be carried in a litter; the pain in her joints had become so great that even such a stoic as herself could not ignore it. Those fainting fits betrayed her. All the people whom she had successfully governed in their youth had now grown up. The three Henrys were the most important figures, and the Queen Mother – who had once held their destinies in her hands – was being forced into the background; and not because her mind had weakened, not because her purpose had failed, but because of the disgusting decay of a body which was becoming senile while her mind retained its full vigour.

She had never given in; and she would not do so now. She would go on with what she had begun; the throne should be kept for Henry, even though he, in his folly, had left his mother's side and tried to hold his power on ground undermined by the folly of his favourites, by the impudence of Navarre and the secret aspirations of the Duke of Guise.

The House of Valois had never been in such a dangerous position as it was now; and this, to Catherine, was like a nightmare. That which she had dreaded above all things was about to come to pass, unless she could find some means of preventing it.

Philip of Spain had offered Guise three hundred thousand crowns, six thousand *lanzknechts* and twelve hundred lances, to be sent to his aid as soon as he broke with the King and established the Inquisition and the Catholic faith in France as it was in Spain.

Epernon, cleverer than Joyeuse, had not met with disaster in the field. He had bribed the Swiss mercenaries, who had been fighting for the Huguenots, to join the King's army and link up with the King's Swiss Guard in Paris. He was now just outside Paris with the guards, waiting for the King to summon him to the city. Guise had announced his intention of coming to Paris. He declared he had heard that there was a plot among the Huguenots to rise and murder Catholics in retaliation for the St Bartholomew massacre. The King's answer was to forbid Guise to come to Paris.

Catherine, in that magnificent palace, the Hôtel de Soissons, which she had built for herself, lay in bed too weak to rise, her mind tortured with the knowledge of impending catastrophe.

The King was at the Louvre, which was well fortified with his Swiss Guard; the people of Paris were tense, waiting. If ever a city had been on the edge of revolt, Paris was at that moment.

As Catherine's thoughts meandered through those gloomy avenues, one of her dwarfs, who was standing by the window, turned to her in great excitement.

'Madame,' he cried, 'the Duke of Guise comes this way.'

Catherine painfully lifted herself. 'Nonsense! The King has forbidden the Duke to come to Paris. He would not dare.' She thought: this cannot be. This cannot be. This must not be. He would not dare to come. The King is protected by his Swiss Guard, but the people of Paris would give their allegiance to Guise if he came among them now.

The excited dwarf jumped up and down, clapping his hands, pulling at the tassels on his red coat. 'But, Madame, I swear it is the Duke of Guise.'

'Take him away!' cried Catherine. 'Whip him. I will teach him not to tell lies to me!'

The dwarf began to whimper and to point to the window; and others had joined him there now.

'Madame,' said Madalenna, 'he does not lie.'

Catherine could hear the shouting in the streets. So Henry of Guise had ignored the King's command.

*

Henry of Guise was determined to see the King, for in commanding Guise not to enter Paris the King had shown he was not aware of current events. The last place which must be forbidden to the man who saw himself as the future ruler of France was its capital.

Guise knew that he was walking into danger. The King was sure to be well guarded, and if Guise entered the Louvre he would be in the midst of enemies. He had therefore decided to enter the city in disguise and present himself to Catherine – who had declared herself to be his friend – in order to explain his desires to her and insist that she accompany him to the Louvre. She still had some influence over her foolish son and she might be able to maintain the peace between them, while Guise laid before the King the demands of the League. But even though he was enveloped in a long cloak and a big slouched hat covered his face, he was very soon recognized, for there were few men in France of the stature of Guise. He had scarcely entered the city when a young man ran along beside him crying: 'Monseigneur, show yourself to the people. There is no sight they would rather see.'

Guise wrapped his cloak more tightly about him and pulled the brim of his hat down over his face. But it was no use; too many recognized him, and a crowd quickly gathered about him.

'It is *Le Balafré* himself. Praise the saints he has come to rescue us.'

The people came running into the streets. The news spread quickly that their hero was among them.

'*Vive Guise!*' they cried. '*Le Balafré* is here.'

They kissed his cloak; they brought out their rosaries and rubbed them against his garments.

'*Vive le pilier de l'église!*'

Flowers were strewn before him; a garland was placed about his neck. Men brought out their knives to show him. 'Let any traitor lay hands on our great Prince, and we shall know how to deal with him.'

Guise pushed his way through the hysterical crowd.

'*À Rheims!*' someone shouted; and the crowd took up the cry.

And so at length he came to the Hôtel de Soissons.

As soon as Catherine was sure that he was on his way, she

350

dispatched a messenger to the King to tell him that Guise was in Paris. Then she prepared herself to receive the Duke.

As he knelt by her bed, she saw at once that he was not quite so calm and self-assured as usual.

'Madame,' he said, 'I have come to you first, knowing that you are my friend.'

'That was wise of you,' she said. 'But why are you in Paris? Do you not know that this may cost you your life?'

The roar of the crowd outside seemed to grow louder in the silence which followed those words. It might cost Guise his life, but what other lives would that mob demand as a reprisal for the man they adored?

'I know it,' he answered, 'and for that reason I come to you first. You have agreed with me that the King dare not stand against the League. He must agree to its demands. Delay is dangerous to him ... and to France. I must see him at once; and therefore I have come here to ask you to accompany me to the Louvre.'

She must accompany him, she knew. Ill as she was, she dared not let him go alone. Who knew what her son might do if he imagined that for a moment he had the upper hand? And what dreadful consequences might follow! If ever her son had had need of her, he had need of her now.

She called her attendants to help her dress, and when she was ready was helped into her litter. Through the streets her litter was carried, while the Duke of Guise walked beside it.

Even Catherine, in all her years of danger, had never experienced anything quite like that walk from the Hôtel de Soissons to the Louvre. She laughed cynically to herself. Here was the woman the Parisians hated most, side by side with the man they loved and admired more than any other. Madame Serpent, the Italian Woman, Queen Jezebel! And with her as her friend and ally, Henry of Guise, *Le Balafré*, the most aristocratic and adored Prince in France.

She listened to the mingling jeers and cheers.

'There she is. She dare not show her face. Murderess! Italian! Remember the Queen of Navarre! Remember the Dauphin Francis! That was a long time ago. That was the beginning. It went ill with us when we let Italians into France.'

351

But for *Le Balafré* they would have broken up her litter; they would have dragged her from it and torn her flesh from her body; they would have kicked her corpse through the streets. That was their mood. Before this they had hated sullenly; now they hated vociferously; before they had uttered insults; now they were ready to hurl stones and use knives. The mood of Paris had changed and the storm was rumbling louder.

But beside her, to protect her, was their hero. The cheers were for him; the insults for her.

'How beautiful he is!' they cried. 'Ah, there he goes. A true King! Shall we tolerate these vipers . . . these Italians!'

They were illogical; they were fools. She wanted to shout: 'My mother was French, my father Italian. This Duke's father was French – or of Lorraine, if that is enough – but his mother was Italian!'

They would answer: 'Ah, but you are the daughter of merchants; he is a Prince. You were brought up in Italy; he was brought up in France. He fights with the sword; you with your *morceaux Italianizés*, which you learned in your vile country how to use.'

Catherine lay back in her litter. She was stimulated rather than frightened. She felt better, riding in a litter with a murderous populace about her, than she had in bed surrounded by her attendants. Now her ailments were forgotten.

Her expression did not change when she heard the ominous shout in the crowd: '*À Rheims!* Monseigneur, when do you go to Rheims?'

They reached the Louvre, and they were received in grim silence. The Swiss Guard filled the corridors and staircases. The Duke walked through them with apparent unconcern, but surely even he must tremble. Catherine noticed with some satisfaction that his face had lost its healthy colour. It was like a man's might be if he knew he was walking into a lion's den. King Henry was waiting to receive them, his hands trembling, his eyes betraying his fear. One of his courtiers had, when he had heard that the Duke was on the way, offered to kill him as he came into the room. The King had hesitated. He wanted Guise out of the way, but he was not sure whether he dare give the order for the deed to be done.

He was in a state of terrible uncertainty when the Duke with Catherine came into the audience chamber, where he stood, surrounded by counsellors and guards, waiting to receive them. As soon as his eyes fell on the Duke his fury burst forth.

'Why do you come here thus?' he demanded. 'You received my orders?'

The Duke did not say that he took orders from no one, but his haughty looks implied it. Catherine sent a warning glance at the Duke; and from him she turned to her son; her eyes pleaded with him to be calm, for she knew that he was so angry that he could be capable of any folly.

'Did I command you not to come, or did I not?' cried the King. 'Did I command you to wait?'

Guise said coldly: 'Sir, I was not given to understand that my coming would be disagreeable to you.'

'Then it is!' cried the King. 'It is.'

'Sir, there are matters of which we must speak.'

'I shall be judge of that.' The King looked about him for the man who had offered to kill Guise, but Catherine had intercepted that look and understood its meaning.

'My lord,' she said quickly, 'I must speak with you. Come with me.' She did not lead him from the room, but to the window. About the Louvre the crowd had gathered. They carried sticks and knives. They were crying: '*Vive Guise!* Hurrah for our great Prince!'

Catherine murmured: 'My son, you dare not. This is not the time. This is not the way. You have your guards, but he has Paris.'

The King was shaken. Like his brother Charles, he was terrified of the people. He remembered that whenever he went into the streets, he was greeted by silence; or if any spoke it was not to wish him long life, but to fling at him some insulting epithet: '*Concierge* of the palace! His wife's hairdresser! Keeper of beggars!' Remarks which were thrown quickly and sullenly at him; and those who delivered them made off before they could be recognized, while the mob made way for the traitor and laughed behind their hands at their King.

How he hated that man, with his tall spare figure and that masculine beauty which appealed to the people! How dared

353

they treat Guise as their King while they insulted their true ruler!

'Mother,' he said, 'you are right. Not yet . . . this is not the time.'

He returned to the Duke and after a brief discussion the meeting broke up.

'I shall call again on you, sir,' said the Duke, 'when I shall hope to receive a satisfactory answer.'

When he had left, the King roared aloud in his fury. 'Who is the King of this realm?' he demanded. 'The King of France or the King of Paris?'

Catherine looked on uneasily, asking herself what would happen next.

*

Guise had set up his headquarters in his hôtel in the Faubourg Saint-Antoine. He was not quite certain how to act. A great part of the army was with the King; and it was largely the mob on whom Guise must rely to support him: and when he stood at his window and looked at those people, cheering him madly, tears streaming down their grimy faces, it occurred to him that that hysterical adoration could quickly be turned to hatred. He was not of the people; he was an aristocrat of aristocrats; and he did not trust the people. He was almost at the summit of his ambition, but he was wise enough to know that the road grew more slippery towards the top.

He waited.

The next day he presented himself at the King's Levee, but he did not go alone this time; he took four hundred armed men with him. The meeting was fruitless.

The King, in great terror, refused to take his mother's advice to stay in the Louvre and ignore the state of the city while giving no sign of his fear; she had begged him to give no special instructions for his protection, and certainly to make no attempt to double his guard. But the King would not listen, and he sent for Epernon and the Swiss Guard whom the favourite had with him outside Paris.

The people watched the soldiers march in. They knew how to act then. By sending for the foreign soldiers, the King, they declared, was making war on them. Merchants ran into the streets with their apprentices; students, *restaurateurs*, fathers, mothers and their children came hurrying into the streets, to be joined by beggars and the homeless. The King had called in foreign soldiers against Paris, and Paris was ready. Arms were brought out from secret places; chains were placed across streets; the barricades went up all over the city. All churches and public places were boarded up. And the battle began.

The people killed fifty of the Swiss Guard before the rest surrendered, declaring to the enraged mob that they were good Catholics. The French guards gave up their arms, and the King was barricaded in the Louvre.

The streets were filled with shouting people.

Guise stood at his window watching the demonstration with feigned astonishment, as though it had nothing to do with him. Catherine, ill as she was, went bravely through the streets from the Hôtel de Soissons to the Hôtel de Guise. The people allowed her to pass in silence, as they knew whither she was bound.

Guise received her coolly. He was the master now. The King, he told her, should immediately appoint him Lieutenant-General of the country and carry out the demands of the League.

Catherine was desperate. 'I am a weak woman,' she said, 'and a sick one. What can I do? I do not rule this realm. My dear Duke, where will this end? What are you urging these people to do? Assassinate their King and set up another in his place? You forget that death begets death. The people should not be taught that it is an easy matter to assassinate a King.'

After she had left, Guise thought of her words; indeed, he could not forget them. 'Death begets death.' She was right. Before he allowed himself to be set up as King he must make sure that he could hold the throne. It must be no brief triumph for him.

The people in the streets were growing impatient. The King was their prisoner; they were thirsty for his blood.

As the evening drew on Guise went into the streets; he was unarmed and he carried a white wand. The people clustered round him. '*Vive Guise! Vive le Balafré!*' They thought that he would lead them to the Louvre, that under his guidance they would drag the shrinking King from his apartments, that he would order them to kill Henry of Valois as he had ordered them to kill Gaspard de Coligny.

To them it was all so simple. They wished one King out of the way and another to be crowned. They thought that that would mean an end of their troubles. This was the most important hour in the life of Henry of Guise, but it found him unsure, uncertain how to act.

He wanted to be cautious. He wanted to make sure of what he had won.

'My friends,' he cried, 'do not shout, *Vive Guise!* I thank you for this expression of your love for me. But now . . . I ask you to shout *Vive le Roi!* No violence, my friends. Keep up your barricades. We must act with care, my friends. I would not see any of you lose his life for a little lack of caution. Will you wait for instructions from me?'

They roared their approval. He was their hero. His word was law. He had but to state his wishes.

He made them bring out their Swiss prisoners, who fell on their knees before him.

'I know you for good Catholics, my friends,' he said. 'You are at liberty.'

He then freed the French guards; and he knew immediately that he had acted wisely in this. He was now the soldiers' hero, for he had saved their lives; with tears streaming down their faces they promised that those lives should be dedicated to him.

The people fell on their knees, blessing him. Bloodshed was averted, they cried, by the wisest Prince in France. They loved him; they were his to command. They would follow him to death . . . or to Rheims.

For a short while danger had been averted. Guise wrote to the Governor of Lyons asking that men and arms be sent to Paris.

'I have defeated the Swiss,' he wrote, 'and cut in pieces a part of the King's Guard. I hold the Louvre invested so closely that I will render a good account of whatsoever is in it. This is so great a victory that it will be remembered for ever.'

*

356

Guise had taken over the Hôtel de Ville and the Arsenal. The tocsins were sounding in the streets. The spies of Spain were urging the immediate assassination of the King, the setting up of Guise in his place and the introduction of the Inquisition, which would result in an automatic suppression of Huguenots.

Guise's sister, the Duchesse de Montpensier, marched through the streets at the head of a procession, urging people to rally to her brother. This energetic lady was already known throughout Paris as the Fury of the League; there was no restraining her. She had distributed pamphlets throughout the city; she had had a picture painted to represent Elizabeth of England torturing Catholics. She was urging people to revolution, to the assassination of the King and the crowning of her brother.

But Henry of Guise could not bring himself to that climax which must mean the killing of the King. He could not share the emotional enthusiasm of his sister. He looked further ahead than she did. The title of King of France would not be so easily held as that of King of Paris, and in reaching for the first he might lose the second. Jesuits from the Sorbonne were congregating in the streets before the university declaring their determination to go to the Louvre and get Brother Henry. Guise knew that it would not be long before one of these fanatics – many of whom believed that the quickest way to achieve a martyr's crown was to plunge a knife into the heart of an enemy of Rome – found his way to the King and killed him.

He could not count on an army of sufficient size to back him up. He must not forget that it would be folly to put too much trust in Spain. The English, if he found himself in a weak position, would be ready to move in against him. In the Netherlands his enemies would be waiting; and he knew that Philip was more likely to squander his men and money in that country than to help to the throne of France a man who he was unsure would prove a good vassal. Nor must he forget the armies of Navarre, not yet subdued; the brilliant victory over Joyeuse could not easily be forgotten.

If the King was assassinated now, the King of Paris would

immediately become the King of France; and the King of Paris was not yet ready to assume that responsibility.

He had set a guard round the Louvre; he had declared that he would account for what was inside the palace; but he was careful to leave one exit unguarded. Let the King escape and, in escaping, postpone a situation with which the man who intended eventually to be King felt he could not yet adequately deal.

And so the gate to the Tuileries was left unguarded, and it did not take the King's friends long to discover this.

※

Catherine talked urgently to her son.

'It would be your greatest folly to leave Paris now. You must stay. I know it is very alarming, but if you went you would show your fear. You would leave Paris completely in the hands of Guise. You should not admit defeat.'

The King paced up and down his apartments, pretending to consider her words. He looked at her sharply. 'Mother,' he said with a nervous laugh, 'there have been times of late when I have wondered whether you have served me or . . . the *baton* of your old age.'

She laughed with something like her old abandon. 'Then you have been a fool. Whom should I ever serve but you? If I have seemed to be over-friendly with that man, it was that I might win his confidence.'

'It has been said that he fascinates you as he fascinates others.'

She blew with her lips as though to blow away in disgust that which was not worthy of consideration.

'You are my life,' she said. 'If aught happened to you, I should no longer wish to live. You have allowed evil counsels to lead you to this. You have not watched the growing discontent of the people, and the people of France are not a patient and long-suffering people. They love and they hate; and they do these things in good measure. Your young men, my dear son, have not pleased the people.'

'You are right, Mother. Ah, had I but listened to you! Go to Guise now, I beg of you. Plead with him. Tell him that I am inclined to accept his terms, and tell him he must control the people and take away those ridiculous barricades. Tell him he cannot keep his King a prisoner.'

She smiled. 'That is wise. You must pretend to agree with these Leaguers. You must lull their suspicions, and then, when all is peaceful again, we shall decide what we must do.'

'Ah,' he said, 'you are wise. You are subtle. You are the great dissembler. My mother, I know you have learned the art of saying one thing and meaning another. Go now to Guise. See what you can do. Mother, you gave me my kingdom; you must keep it for me.'

She embraced him warmly. 'Joyeuse is dead,' she said. 'Do not heed Epernon. Listen to your mother, who loves you, who has only your good at heart.'

'Mother, I shall listen.'

She told him what she planned to say to Guise. She felt almost young. The reins were in her hands once more. Never mind if she had to travel over the most treacherous country she had yet encountered.

She went in her litter to the Hôtel de Guise.

As soon as she had left, he strolled quietly out to the un-guarded gate, walking slowly as though deep in melancholy thought. A few friends were waiting for him with horses; he mounted and rode away; he did not stop until he had reached the top of Chaillot, then pulling up, he turned to his friends and smiled ruefully; but when he looked back at Paris there were tears in his eyes.

'Oh, ungrateful city!' he muttered. 'I have loved thee more than my own wife; I will not enter thy walls again but by the breach.'

Then he turned abruptly and rode on.

*

The crowned King had fled to Chartres, and Guise was the uncrowned King for a spell. The Château of Vincennes, with the Arsenal and the Bastille, were in his hands; he insisted on the election of a new town council and provost of traders; and all these were naturally composed of members of the League.

He was still uncertain. He shrank from violence and ardently desired a bloodless coup. He therefore allowed royalists to leave the city for Chartres if they so desired; his enemies, considering this action and the fact that the King had been allowed to escape, detected a weakness in him. He was now doing all in his power to restore calm, but the people's blood was up, and they would not be satisfied without violence. Atrocities were being committed and Guise knew himself powerless to stop them. All Huguenots were turned out of office; and there were Leaguers in control of all the churches. They shouted from the pulpits: 'France is sick and Paris has wealth enough to make war on four Kings. France needs a draught of French blood. Receive Henry of Valois back into your towns, and you will see your preachers massacred, your women violated, your friends hanging from the gibbets.'

The Guise family arrived in Paris. The Duke's wife, who was pregnant, was greeted as though she were the Queen of France, and all her children the heirs of a royal house. The Duke of Elboeuf came with her, as did their staunch ally, the Cardinal of Bourbon.

Catherine, closely watching events, had insidiously slid to the side of Guise. It was with her help that he formed a new government. She knew that her effort to have her grandson recognized as heir to the throne had failed; but while she feigned to work with Guise she was plotting secretly to depose him and put the King back in his place.

Epernon had escaped from Paris, but only with his life; he had tried to take his treasures with him on mules laden with those priceless gifts he had amassed during the years when he had enjoyed the King's favour; but the mules had been stopped and searched; so Epernon lost his treasure.

Never had Catherine worked harder than she did now; never had she displayed her craft to better advantage. She understood that Guise had deliberately made it possible for the King to escape, and although she deplored her son's action of running away, she construed Guise's conduct as weakness, for hesitation was the most fatal weakness a man could display at such a time. He was a great man, this Guise; she had always recognized that quality in him; he had ambition and courage; but he had failed to take an opportunity which could have put him immediately on the throne; he had hesitated at a crucial moment; he had been unsure. She, like the Parisians, had thought at one time that he was a god among men; but he was no god; he was human; he had a weakness, and his greatest folly was in showing that weakness to her. She knew her man now, and she would be equal to him.

How she longed for her youth! How she longed to throw off the nagging pains of her body!

She suggested to Guise that he should command the army, that he should be heir to the throne, and that Navarre's claim should be ignored, that the Duke of Mayenne should take charge of a wing of the army and go out to attack Navarre. She saw that, in order to avert revolution – which was very near – the King must join the League; and she would take it upon herself to persuade him to do so. Guise had to trust her; she was the only possible go-between. Her suggestion, if carried out, would be the only way of restoring temporary order in France.

She went to Chartres. The King had been badly frightened. Epernon had fled, so there was no one to advise him but his mother. On her advice, he signed documents which Guise had prepared for him. He could tell himself, if he liked, that he was now the head of the Catholic League, for the Catholic League had become royalist.

But when the Pope heard that Guise had allowed the King to escape from Paris he was filled with wrath.

'What poor creature of a Prince is this,' he cried, 'to have let such a chance escape him of getting rid of one who will destroy him at the first opportunity?'

Navarre in his stronghold roared with laughter when he heard the news. 'So all is well between the King of France and the King of Paris! What an uneasy friendship!' He spat. 'I would not give that for it! Wait, my friends. We shall soon see what happens. There could be little better news than that I might hear that she who was once Queen of Navarre – and is now so no longer, for I'll not have her back – has been strangled; that, and the death of the lady's mother, would make me sing the song of Simeon!'

Meanwhile, Catherine did all in her power to nourish that uneasy friendship between her son and Guise.

*

The King was in a fury, and all his fury was directed against one man. He would never be happy while Guise lived. If I do not kill him, he thought, he will kill me. The wiser of us two will be the one who strikes first.

Guise had become generalissimo of the armies, and was ready to make another bid for the throne. He was growing more and more powerful; he had the army with him, and the fastidious aristocrat need not now rely only on the mob.

When the States General had met at Blois, and the King had addressed it, the Duke of Guise, as steward of his household, had sat at his feet. Guise had not applauded the King's speech – and numbers of the men in the hall, all Guisards, followed their master's example – for the King had deliberately attacked them when he had said: 'Certain grandees of my kingdom have formed leagues and associations which in every well-ordered monarchy are crimes of high treason. But, showing my wonted indulgence, I am willing to let bygones be bygones in this respect.'

Guise had prevented the publication of those words.

The King had been more or less ordered to meet his committee, and there he had been respectfully but firmly informed that he must alter that pronouncement, for it was not his prerogative to forgive benignly; it was his duty to take orders.

Catherine had been there beside Guise, and it was she who had advised the King to comply, but it was obvious that no self-respecting King could bow to such tyranny.

It had come to the King's ears that the Cardinal of Guise had proposed the health of his brother – referring to him not as the Duke of Guise, but as the King of France.

Philip of Spain had been Guise's ally, but, a few months ago, that monarch had suffered a defeat so great that the whole of Europe was agape, for many believed that the greatest power in the world had been quenched for ever. There had been placards posted in the towns of France. Frenchmen had read them and tried to look perturbed while they laughed in their beards:

362

'Lost. Somewhere off the English coast, the great and magnificent Spanish Armada. Anyone bringing information of its whereabouts to the Spanish Embassy shall be rewarded.'

Spain was crushed, for there was nothing to be done which could minimize that disaster. Spain, which lived by her sea power, had lost her sea power; and a small island off the coast of Europe had risen high in significance during that fateful summer. In place of mighty Philip, Gomez, Parma and Alva, other great men had arisen: Sir Francis Drake, Sir John Hawkins, Lord Howard of Effingham. The little island had become a country of great importance. The red-headed Queen was smiling serenely on her throne; and she was a Protestant Queen ruling a Protestant people. The previous year, on the pretext of having discovered that her cousin was involved in a plot against the crown, Elizabeth had sent the Catholic Mary Queen of Scots to the block. She had snapped her fingers at Spain then; and this year her sailors had delivered what might well prove to be the final blow.

Guise's ally, Spain, was not going to be so useful to him as had seemed possible a few months ago.

When he had considered these matters, the King determined on action. Either he or his enemy must die, he was sure. It must be his enemy.

A plot fermented in the diseased mind of the King. He would not discuss it with his mother, as he knew she would not approve of it. She had taken to her bed once more; she was ageing fast; her skin was yellow and wrinkled, and those eyes which had once been alert now had a glassy look.

There was many a brawl, in the weeks that followed, between the supporters of Guise and those of the King. Men on guard in the courtyards picked quarrels, and often these would result in duels which were fatal.

The King hinted to one or two men whom he trusted that he did not intend to let traitors live. 'There is not room for two Kings in France,' he said. 'One has to go, and I am determined that I shall not be that one.'

He thought constantly of his mother and wished that she

363

would join him in this. She was a murderess of great experience; there was not a woman in the world who had removed so many enemies with such a deft touch. But she was old; she had lost her sharp wits; she was – for nothing she could say would convince her son to the contrary – fascinated by Guise. It might be the fascination of hatred; it might be the fascination of fear; but fascination there was. She had always wished to ally herself, at least outwardly, with the powerful party of the moment; and there was no doubt that she now looked on Guise as the most important man in France. No! The King could not take her into his confidence, but he could emulate her ways.

He arranged a public reconciliation with Guise; and at this meeting he declared he was going to hand over his authority to the Duke and his mother jointly; for, he said, he himself had had a call from God. He was going to spend the rest of his life in prayer and penance.

Catherine had left her bed in order to be present and hear this declaration. She smiled on her son. This was the way to lull suspicion. Her son was learning wisdom at last.

Guise was sceptical. The King had not deceived him, and he told Catherine so.

'You are wrong, my dear Duke,' she said. 'The King speaks truth. He is weary and he lacks the physical strength of a man like yourself. You cannot understand his abandoning his power, but I can. You see, I am getting old. My son also feels his age. He is a young man, but he lacks your physical perfections.'

She smiled at the ambitious man; she was telling him: 'you will not be bothered much, for I also am too old to care for power. All power can be yours. You are virtually King of France.

The King made plans and as usual abandoned them. He talked to his friends so frequently and with such lack of caution that his schemes inevitably leaked out.

One day Guise was sitting at table when a note was handed to him. On it was written: 'Take care. The King plots to kill you.' Guise read it and smiled. He asked for a pen, and when it was brought to him, he wrote on the note: 'He dare not.' Then, to show his contempt, he threw it under the table.

His brother, the Cardinal of Guise, remonstrated with him.

'You must leave Blois at once. You are not safe here another hour. Go at once to Paris.'

'My brother,' said the Duke, 'I have always been lucky. I will go when my time comes.'

'Why do you not leave at once?' demanded the Cardinal.

Guise lifted his shoulders, and his brother came closer to him. 'Could it be because of an appointment with the Marquise de Noirmoutiers?'

'That might be,' said Guise with a smile.

The Cardinal laughed bitterly. 'You would not be the first man who has been lured to his death by a woman. This Charlotte de Noirmoutiers was the Queen Mother's creature when she was Charlotte de Sauves. Her marriage with Noirmoutiers did not break the power of her mistress. Depend upon it, the King and his mother plot to kill you through that woman.'

Guise shook his head. 'The Queen Mother does not wish me dead. That fool the King does, I know. But he is weak and quite stupid. He has been plotting my death for months, but he is afraid to make the attempt.'

'Charlotte de Sauves is the tool of Catherine de' Medici.'

'Dear brother, the *Escadron* ceased to be effective when the Queen Mother lost her power.'

'You are wrong to trust Jezebel. She has always been a serpent and her fangs are poisonous.'

'She is a sick serpent who no longer has the power to lift her head and strike.'

'So you are determined to spend the night with Madame de Noirmoutiers?'

Guise nodded.

The Cardinal walked away in exasperation, but before he left the apartment a messenger arrived with a letter which he handed to the Duke.

'Leave Blois at once,' this said. 'Your life is in imminent danger. Do not spend another night there.'

Guise screwed up the paper in his hands. He was thinking a little of Charlotte and a good deal of death.

*

In his apartments Charlotte was waiting for him. She had never been so happy in the whole of her life. Guise was the only man she had ever loved. She was freed from the evil bondage in which Catherine had once held her, for she was no longer young, and in any case the *Escadron* was breaking up. How could the Queen Mother, so often sick and ailing, keep control over her women? How could she lead them in the hunt? There were some who, from time to time, were commanded to fascinate ministers of state, but age was robbing the Queen Mother of her vitality; and there was much that went on at court of which she knew nothing.

The Baron de Sauves had died two years ago and Charlotte had then married the Marquis de Noirmoutiers. She had not wished for this marriage, but it had been arranged for her by her family and approved by Catherine; she had found that her new husband was not so complaisant as the Baron de Sauves had been. He had threatened to kill Guise unless she ceased to be his mistress; but this she would not do. She sometimes wondered whether her husband would kill her as Villequier had killed his wife; she did not care. Her passion for Guise obsessed her; she was only happy when she was with him.

As he came in she noted that his stern expression changed when he saw her; he was as passionately in need of her as she of him. There were times when he thought of Margot, but he believed that the Margot of today was a different person from the Margot of his youth. He had loved Margot and she had disappointed him; she had allowed her pride to ruin the life they might have had together; he could forgive her most things, but not that which had seemed to him the height of folly. He had turned light-heartedly to Charlotte, and it was this woman – this loose woman of the *Escadron* – in whom he had found what he sought. It was many years since they had become lovers, but theirs was a devotion which had strengthened. Charlotte had her service to the Queen Mother; Guise had his service to France: these two facts had kept them apart for long periods; but they assured each other that they lived for those times when they were together, and there was truth in this.

Should I lose this, Guise asked himself, on account of plots and schemes to kill me?

But he could not help knowing – although he tried to disguise this fact even from himself – that it was not solely on Charlotte's account that he stayed.

She embraced him fervently, but she was aware all through the night that he was uneasy, that the sighing of the December winds in the hangings made him start up and sometimes reach for his sword.

As they lay in the darkness she said: 'Something has happened. You are listening for something … waiting … For what, my darling?'

'For an assassin, perhaps.'

She shivered. She knew well that he was constantly in danger, but this could only mean that that danger had moved nearer to him. She would not rest until he had told her of the warnings he had received.

'You must leave at once,' she urged him. 'Tomorrow … No … Now. Do not wait until the morning.'

'It seems as though you would wish to be rid of me.'

'I fear for your safety, my dearest.'

'Ah,' he said lightly. 'Are you sure you are not trying to get rid of me for the sake of another lover?' And he began to sing the popular ditty.

> 'My little rose, a little spell
> Of absence changed that heart of thine …'

But she had begun to weep silently. 'You must go,' she said. 'You *must*.'

To comfort her, he answered: 'Do not fret, my love. Never fear that I cannot defend myself. To please you, I will go tomorrow.'

But when the morning came he had changed his mind.

'How *can* I go?' he demanded. 'How do I know when I shall see you again?'

'Every hour you spend at Blois is a dangerous one. I know it. Go to Paris. You will be safe in Paris.'

'What!' he cried. 'I in Paris! You in Blois! What use is that?'

She was frightened. She realized that he was fully aware of his danger and that he contemplated it with a delight which was beyond bravery. She knew him well, but she had never known him like this before. She had a feeling that he was eager for death.

He met her eyes and a quizzical expression crept into his own. He was aware that he had betrayed his most secret thoughts to the woman who loved him. She knew that the greatest man in the country, as he had seemed to so many, was afraid – of life more than of death. That for which he had longed all his life was almost within his grasp, but he was afraid of the last few steps he must take to reach it. He was half egoist, half idealist; and the two were in conflict. The bravest man in France was afraid – afraid of the price he must pay for the greatness he desired. He could only take the crown when he had murdered the King, and the general who had organized the killing of thousands on the battlefield – like the fastidious aristocrat that he was – shrank from the cold-blooded murder of one useless man.

He had come so far, and he now stood face to face with this murder he must commit; he could not turn back. There was only one road to escape the result of ambition. That was the road to his own death.

Charlotte was looking at him through her tears. 'You will go?' she begged. 'You must leave Blois today.'

'Later,' he said. 'Later.'

And as the day wore on he told her: 'I will stay tonight and go tomorrow. Just one more night with you and then ... I promise I will go.'

All through her life Charlotte remembered that day. During the supper they ate together, five notes of warning were brought to him. His cousin, the Duke of Elboeuf, arrived and asked to see him.

'There is not a moment to lose,' said Elboeuf. 'Your horses are ready. Your men are waiting. If you value your life, go at once.'

Charlotte looked at him pleadingly, but he would not see the plea in her eyes.

He said: 'If I saw Death coming in at the window, I would not go out by the door to avoid it.'

'This is folly,' said Elboeuf.

'My love, he is right,' said Charlotte. 'Go ... go now. Lose not another moment, I beg of you.'

He kissed her hand. 'My dearest, how could you ask me to leave you? That is more cruel than any assassin's knife.'

She said angrily: 'This is no time for foolish gallantry.'

Guise looked from his mistress to his cousin, and answered with deep feeling: 'He who runs away loses the game. If it be necessary to give my life in order to reap what we have sown, then I shall not regret it.'

Charlotte cried out: 'You deceive yourself. It is not necessary to give your life. That is the pity of it!'

'If I had a hundred lives,' he went on as though she had not spoken, 'I would devote them to preserving the Catholic faith in France and to the relief of the poor people for whom my heart bleeds. Go to your bed, cousin. And leave us to ours.'

Elboeuf, shrugging his shoulders in exasperation, eventually retired.

'You are determined?' asked Charlotte.

He nodded. 'No more of death,' he said. 'Let it be life and love from now on.'

But when they were in bed, yet another messenger was brought to the bedchamber. He had a note for Guise which he had been ordered to hand to none other than the Duke himself, and that with all speed.

Guise read it and pushed it under the bolster.

'Another warning?' asked Charlotte fearfully.

He kissed her, but refused to answer.

*

The morning was dark and the rain beat against the windows of the Château of Blois. Catherine, racked with pain, lay in her bed. The King had risen early; he had urgent matters which demanded his attention. Guise did not awaken until eight o'clock. Then he raised himself and looked down on his sleeping mistress.

Today there would be more warnings; today he would be

asked to leave for Paris. All his friends would beg him to go, and Charlotte would join her appeals to theirs.

He shrugged his shoulders and got out of bed.

He put on a new grey satin suit in which he would attend the meeting of the council that morning. Charlotte, watching him, tried to chase away her fears. She found this easier by day, even on such a dark and gloomy day as this one was.

'You like it?' he asked, posing before her, speaking lightly, trying to cheer her.

'Charming! But it is a little light for such a dark day, you will agree?'

He kissed her. 'Charlotte, I am going to ask you to do something for me.'

'Anything I can do for you I will gladly do.'

'Then do not ask me today to leave Blois.'

'But you said you would leave today.'

'To ride through the rain, to spend the night at some gloomy château when I might spend it with you?'

She put her arms about him and laughed, because it was easy to laugh in the light of day; and when she looked at him, so much taller than all others, so much more distinguished than any man she had ever seen, she believed him to be invulnerable.

He was late for the meeting. As he walked through the corridors he seemed to sense the doom which lurked there. He felt a little cold, but he would not admit that was due to apprehension. It is a chilly morning, he thought.

He turned to one of the gentlemen who stood in the hall. 'Go to the staircase door,' he said, 'and there you will see one of my pages. Ask him to bring me a handkerchief.'

He could not help but be aware of the strangeness about him, of the fear in the faces of his friends. It seemed that a long time elapsed before one of his valets brought the handkerchief to him.

'How cold it is!' he said. 'Light the fire. I feel quite faint with the cold. Is there some trifle in the cupboard which might revive me?'

One of the men opened the King's cupboard and found in it four Brignolles plums.

Guise ate one of these. 'Would anyone care to eat some?' he asked.

One of the King's men appeared at the door of the chamber; the man looked pale and his hands were trembling.

'Monsieur,' he said, bowing to Guise, 'the King requests your presence; he is in his old cabinet.'

The man did not wait for a reply, but rushed away unceremoniously. Guise's friends looked at him; their glances warned him, but he would not see the warning.

He threw his cloak over his arm, and, picking up his gloves, walked to the door which led to the King's apartments.

*

The King was aroused early that morning. He had many preparations to make, and he had asked to be called at four o'clock.

The Queen, who was with him, looked at him in bewilderment for the candlelight showed how pale he was and yet how purposeful; he took no pains with his appearance that morning.

He went into his privy closet, where forty-five men were waiting for him, as he had instructed they should. Inspecting them all closely, he ordered them to show him their daggers. There was a long time to wait, for he had risen too early. There would have been enough time to make his preparations had he been called at six. Standing there, speaking now and then in whispers, he was reminded of the Eve of St Bartholomew. He thought of his priests and pastors who were already praying to Heaven for forgiveness for the crime which he had not yet committed.

He had had the corridors cleared so that none of the Duke's supporters might be near him, for he was terrified that his plan might miscarry, and of what might happen if it did. One of them had to die – the King of France or the King of Paris – and, as he saw it, the one who survived would be the one who struck first.

One of his men came hurrying in with great agitation. He told the King that the Duke was in the council chamber, but that he had sent one of his gentlemen for a handkerchief, and this gentleman would discover that the corridors and stair-cases, on the King's orders, had been cleared of the Duke's followers, and would guess the reason. If he carried this story to Guise, the latter would know at once that his assassination was to take place this morning.

The King gave hurried orders. 'When the valet approaches with the handkerchief, seize him, make him prisoner and bring the handkerchief to me.'

This was done. The King's hand trembled as he held it out to take the handkerchief. It was neatly folded and, inside it was a hastily scrawled note:

'*Sauvez-vous, ou vous êtes mort.*'

The King felt elated. His prompt action had been a wise one. He took the note and handed the handkerchief to one of his serving men — a humble man who would not be known to the Guisards in the chamber.

'Take this,' said the King. 'Knock on the door of the council chamber and hand it to the nearest gentleman. Keep yourself hidden as much as possible and murmur that it is the handker-chief for which the Duke asked; then hurry away.'

It was done as the King ordered, and the gentleman who received the handkerchief did not realize that he who had given it had been one of the King's men.

The time was at hand. The King looked at his men. Were they ready? he asked them; and their answer was to lay their hands on their daggers.

'Révol,' said the King to one of his secretaries, 'go to the council chamber, knock on the door and tell the Duke of Guise that I wish to see him in my old cabinet. What is the matter, man? Do not look like that. You are the colour of parchment and you shake like a leaf in the wind. Pull yourself together. You will betray us all.'

Révol departed.

The King retired to his bedchamber, and in the old cabinet, the assassins, their daggers unsheathed, awaited the coming of the Duke of Guise.

*

Guise walked through the little doorway into the King's apartments. One of King's guards shut the door behind him. As the Duke entered the old cabinet, a man who was standing by the door lurched forward suddenly and trod on Guise's foot. Guise looked into the man's face, immediately recognizing the look of warning there, and he knew that this was a last appeal to save himself. He was certain now that he was in acute danger, and with this knowledge came a great desire to preserve his life. Perhaps when he had contemplated death so light-heartedly he had not seriously thought that the King would dare attempt to take his life; but as he stood in the gloomy cabinet he realized that men like Henry the Third will suddenly and recklessly throw off their hesitancy and act rashly.

He heard a movement behind him and turned; but he was too late. They had already plunged their daggers into his back.

He said on a faint note of surprise: 'My friends ... my friends ...'

He felt for his sword, but it had become entangled in his cloak. He reeled, and one of the assassins struck him in the chest. His blood gushed forth, staining the new grey satin as he sank to the floor of the old cabinet.

He was not yet dead, and dying seemed to acquire the strength of two men. He had one of the assassins by the throat, and managed to crawl, dragging the man with him, across the floor of the cabinet.

'The King ... awaits me ...' he gasped. 'I ... will go to the King.'

And with an effort which astonished those who had stabbed him he dragged himself into the King's bedchamber, and it was not until he reached the state bed that he collapsed and lay stretched out while his blood stained the King's carpet.

'My God,' he muttered. 'My God ... have mercy on me.'

He lay still and the King came to look at him, while the murderers with their bloodstained daggers came to stand beside the King.

'Is he dead?' whispered the King.

One of the men knelt beside the Duke and opened the blood-stained coat.

'He is dead, Sire. The glorious King of Paris is no more.'

The King touched Guise lightly with his foot.

'There lies the man who wished to be King of France,' he said. 'You see, my friends, where his ambition has led him. My God, how tall he is! He seems even taller now that he is dead than he did when he was living.' Then he began to laugh. 'Ah, my friends,' he went on, 'you have only one King to rule you now, and I am he.'

◈

A little later the King went to his mother's apartments. She lay very still in her bed. The King was now gorgeously dressed, his face freshly painted, his hair exquisitely curled; he was smiling.

'How are you this morning, my dear mother?' he asked.

She smiled painfully. She hated to admit how ill she felt; always despising illness in others, she had no wish to complain of her own; she never gave sympathy and she expected none.

'I am improving, thank you,' she said. 'I expect to be about again very soon. I am tired of lying abed. And how is Your Majesty?'

'Ah, very well, Madame. Very well, indeed. There is a reason.'

'A reason?' She raised herself a little and tried not to wince from the pain in her limbs.

'Yes, Madame. I am truly the King of France this day, for there is no longer a King of Paris.'

She had grown pale. 'My son, what do you mean?'

'He died this morning.'

'Died! Died . . . of what?'

'Of loyal thrusts, Madame. The friends of the King removed his enemy.'

She lost control. She was weak from her pain and unaccustomed inaction. She said shrilly: 'You mean you have *killed* Guise?'

'You do not seem pleased, Madame. I had forgotten he was a favourite of yours.'

She cried out: 'Oh, my son, where will this end? What have you done? Do you not know what you have done?'

'I know that I am the true King of France now, and that is all I care.'

'Make sure,' she said grimly, 'that you are not soon the King of nothing at all.'

His eyes glinted. 'I understand, Madame. You grieve for your very dear friend!'

'I have no friends. I have only my devotion to you.'

'Yet that devotion sets you weeping for my enemies?'

'Enemy he was, my son; but there are some enemies who must be allowed to live. You have done murder.'

The King laughed aloud. 'You, Madame, to accuse *me* of murder! How often during your lifetime have you done murder?'

She sat up in bed; her eyes were tired and quite expressionless. 'Not foolish murder,' she said; 'never foolish murder. You have killed a man whom Paris loved. I pray that Paris will forgive you.'

The King was bordering on hysteria. 'You dare to talk thus to me! If I have learned to murder, from whom did I learn? Who is the most notorious murderess in France?'

'You do not learn your lessons well, my son,' she answered wearily. 'But what is done is done. God grant that no ill will come of it.' She was weeping from very weakness, but she quickly controlled her tears. 'You should not be here. You must take Orléans at once. You must not give them a chance to arm against you. Oh, my son, what will Paris do? You dare not show yourself in Paris. I beg of you, inform the Legate.' She lay back on her pillows. 'Holy Mother of God!' she murmured. 'Where will this end? I cannot say. I only know that what I have worked for all my life lies in ruins about me. Where are my children? Only two left to me! My daughter, a runaway, a wanton wife! My son, the King of France, but for how long? Oh, God, how long?'

The King stared at her. He sensed that she was in a prophetic mood and her words terrified him.

But she had thrown off her gloom. The lifelong habit, of never looking back, of accepting what it was impossible to reject, returned to her.

She began giving orders.

'Where is the Cardinal of Guise?'

'He has been arrested.'

'Let him go free.'

The King narrowed his eyes. He would follow his mother's lead. He would do as she used to do in the days of her prime. He must not forget that she was a sick old woman now, very weak, and probably wandering in her mind. He would humour her. The Cardinal of Guise should be let out of the dungeon in which he had been placed after the murder of the Duke, but only to face the daggers of the King's friends.

'My son,' pleaded Catherine, 'you must listen to me.'

'Mother,' he said gently, 'you have been ill. You do not know how matters go. Rest assured that I shall forget nothing that you have taught me. Have no fear – I will handle this affair as you yourself would handle it.'

*

She lay fretting in her bed. She had tried to rise, but nausea had overtaken her, and she fell back fainting. Her women were about her and she looked at them with distaste. Where was Madalenna? Where were the ladies of her *Escadron Volant*? What had they been doing? Why had she not been warned of these terrible plans of her son's?

They thought her old. They thought her finished; but she would never be finished while there was breath in her body.

She sent for Madalenna.

'What has happened to you?' she demanded. 'Why was I not informed? What news? What news?'

'Madame, the Cardinal of Bourbon has been arrested. The Duke's mother, the Prince of Joinville and the Duke of Elboeuf are all in prison. All those Guises on whom the King could lay his hands . . . all of them are in prison.'

She cried: 'I cannot lie here while such things are happening. Have my litter prepared. I will be carried to the Cardinal of Bourbon. I must talk to him.'

While her litter was being prepared, news was brought to her that the Cardinal of Guise had been murdered.

Does the King not see, she asked herself, that he brings the knife near to his own throat? Does he not see that when he pulls down the pillars of our state, like Samson, he destroys himself?

She was carried into the prison of the Cardinal of Bourbon.

'Monsieur,' she said, 'you are my friend, my wise old friend.'

But the old man lifted his head and laughed at her; there was hatred and contempt for her in his glance. 'Madame,' he said, 'these are *your* deeds. These are *your* tricks. Ever since you came into France you have played your tricks. And now . . . you are killing us all.'

'I had nothing to do with the murder of Guise . . . nor that of his brother,' she cried. 'This crime breaks my heart. May God damn me if I ever sought it.'

'Madame,' said the Cardinal, 'I can say now what I have not dared say to you before: I do not believe you.'

'You must believe me. Why should I commit such folly? Do you think I am ignorant of what this means?'

He turned away from her. He was too old to care what happened to him. He was worn out, as she was.

She felt the tears on her cheeks. She was faint and sick, and the journey, she knew, had used up most of her waning strength. 'There is nothing I can do,' she said. 'I see that now. No one will believe that I had no hand in this.'

'Madame,' said the Cardinal, 'why should they believe you when your hands are red with the blood of so many?'

'He was a great man . . . whom France needed.'

'There have been other great men, Madame, whom France needed.'

The close air of the dungeon was too much for her; she felt that she would faint if she stayed.

'This is too much for me to bear,' she muttered. 'I am too old now for such shocks. My sorrow will cause my death. I know it . . . as I know these things.'

She was taken back to her bed, and the news spread through the castle that she was very ill indeed.

*

When, in her exile, Margot heard that the Duke was dead, she wept bitter tears for the lover of her youth.

It seemed to her that the men she had loved best had all died violent deaths. Guise, La Mole and Bussy . . . all dead, for Bussy had been killed by the husband of one of his mistresses when, in the lady's bedchamber, disturbed by the husband, he had climbed through the window, and in doing so had caught his doublet on a nail, where he had hung until the husband had arrived to stab him to death.

She wept afresh for each of them in turn; but in particular she wept for Guise; and she shuddered to contemplate the future of her family, for, like her mother, she knew that her brother would pay for his crime.

She waited from day to day for news, desolate because she had been put outside the sphere of action, and there was only a lover left to her whom she must continually compare with the incomparable Guise.

*

The King of Navarre heard the news with gravity, for he knew that these events would affect him more than any man in France. In the weeks that followed the murder of Guise, while he waited for news, he seemed to age, to acquire new dignity; and it was as though that other Navarre, who had at times looked out of his shrewd eyes, took over the control from the irresponsible adventurer. The time would come when he must be ready to take on his responsibilities, eventually to show himself as one of the greatest Kings the French were ever to know.

*

There were times when Catherine was too ill to know what was said to her. News was brought to her, for when she was conscious, she demanded that it should be; but she was not always sure where she was. She thought she was a little girl in the Convent of the Murate, stitching at an altar cloth while the nuns told her the story of the Virgin's cloak; she thought she was riding through the streets of Florence while the Florentines called for Medici blood; then she was a bride with a sullen bridegroom; she was a queen with a husband who loved her not and did honour only to his mistress; she was a jealous wife peering through a hole in the floor of her apartment; she

378

was mixing a potion for someone whom she wished to remove; she was withholding Paré from her son, Francis; she was scorning Mary Queen of Scots; she was instructing mad Charles' tutors how to pervert him; she was waiting for the tocsin which would tell Paris that the St Bartholomew was about to begin. The shades of what she had been seemed to stand about her bed.

This was death; she knew it and she accepted it.

But when her strength rallied a little she must know what was happening about her; death receded then and she remembered the tragic state of affairs which she had been unable to avert. Then she would know that Paris was mad with fury, and that it called for the blood of the King; she knew that the man who had murdered the hero of Paris would never be allowed to evade the terrible retribution which Paris would demand.

The Duke's widow was *enceinte*, which made her a pathetic figure. She was known as the Sainted Widow. She went through the streets of the capital in deep mourning, while the people crowded about her, kissing her robes and calling for vengeance on the man who had murdered the Duke. The sister of Guise, Madame de Montpensier, the Fury of the League, led a procession which marched through the streets, torches held high, mourning the death of the idol, calling for the death of the royal murderer.

So Paris was in tumult, and Catherine, who knew her son so well, guessed that he waited in terrible apprehension, expecting at any hour to feel the cold steel in his heart. Did he realize now, she wondered, that he should have consulted his mother before ordering the murder of such a man as Guise; did he understand at last that she, the arch-murderess, had succeeded only because of the infinite pains she had taken to accomplish her evil deeds?

*

Henry, the King of France, had become like an old man. His limbs shook continually, and his thinning hair was quickly going grey. He moved restlessly from room to room, because he could never be happy in any apartment; he feared that an assassin waited for him, hidden in the hangings.

And in Paris, during those tumultuous weeks, a young Domi-
nican named James Clément sharpened his dagger every day,
because he believed that an angel had appeared to him and had
bidden him put to death great Guise's royal murderer, who was
the tyrant of France.

*

Catherine de' Medici was dying.

People talked of it in the streets. They recalled the day she
had come into France escorted by King Francis. Ah, little did he
know what he was bringing into France when he brought the
Italian woman!

'They say they will send her body to Paris . . . to be laid in
the magnificent tomb she has prepared for it.'

'Let them bring her here. Let them! We shall know what to
do with Jezebel's bones. Even the dogs would scorn to eat
them. There'll be nothing for it but to throw them into the
Seine. That's what we will do with Jezebel.'

And meanwhile Catherine lay watching the fading light in
her chamber. The end. She knew, as though she had lived to
see it, that her son would not long survive her. She had worked
to keep her sons on the throne and rule through them; and this
she had achieved. She had ruled as long as she had had the
strength to retain her power.

'She cannot last the night,' said one of her women. 'My God,
she looks dead already. Is she?'

'No; not yet.'

'I would not care to have her sins on my soul. What she will
have to answer for!'

Catherine heard them and smiled faintly. Fools! They did
not understand. She had worshipped no god; she had
worshipped power. She had no religion and no desire for eternal life. She had had one great wish – to rule France through
her children; and this had, in large measure, been granted
her.

She heard someone whisper: 'No one ever really loved her.
How terrible that is! To go through life unloved.'

Yes, thought Catherine. None loved me. But many feared
me.

And after a while she slipped away into darkness.

*

'Catherine de' Medici is dead!'

The news reached Paris.

'The Italian woman is no more. It is her turn to face her Maker.'

The people of Paris now hoped that her body would be brought to their city that they might have the pleasure of throwing it into the Seine.

Revolution threatened the whole of France; but in Paris, while some talked angrily of the retribution in store for the King, others found time to chant:

*L'une ruyne d'Israel,
L'autre, ruyne de la France.*

Acknowledgements

I wish to acknowledge the great help the undermentioned books have been to me in my research:

Paris. Bidou.

The Medici. Colonel G. F. Young, CB.

Foxe's Book of Martyrs. Edited by Dr A. Clarke.

National History of France. (*The Century of the Renaissance*.) Louis Batiffol. Translated by Elsie Finnimore Buckley.

France, the Nation and Its Development from Earliest Times to the Establishment of the Third Republic. William Henry Hudson.

History of France. Guizot.

Feudal Castles of France. Anonymous.

Dungeons of Old Paris. Tighe Hopkins.

Lives of the Queens of England. Strickland.

Catherine de' Medici and the French Reformation. Edith Sichel.

The Later Years of Catherine de' Medici. Edith Sichel.

The Favourites of Henry of Navarre. Le Petit Homme Rouge.

Mémoires de Marguerite de Valois. Marie Ludovic Chrétien Lalanne.

Les Mémoires et l'histoire en France. Charles Caboche.

Catherine de Médicis Presente à Charles IX Son Royaume. Pierre Champion.

J. P.

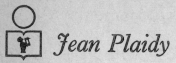

Jean Plaidy

Margaret Irwin

These and other PAN Books are obtainable from all booksellers and newsagents. If you have any difficulty please send purchase price plus 7p postage to PO Box 11, Falmouth Cornwall.

While every effort is made to keep prices low, it is sometimes necessary to increase prices at short notice. PAN Books reserve the right to show new retail prices on covers which may differ from those advertised in the text or elsewhere.